THE BLESSED

What Reviewers Say About Anne Shade's Work

Leather, Lace, and Locs

"*Leather, Lace, and Locs* is a wonderful book that works on so many different levels. It's a story of gender (female and nonbinary), race (Women of Color), relationships (families, friendships, and lovers), ambition (personal and professional), sexuality (lesbian and bisexual), and more. Anne Shade doesn't rush her story, but instead allows it to develop over a couple of years, dropping in and out of the characters' lives to show us how they've grown. ...As with any HEA romance, there's no real drama or suspense in wondering if the women of *Leather, Lace, and Locs* will find love, but the joy of discovering how they find love is exquisite. Just an altogether lovely read."
—*Sally Bend for Bending the Bookshelf*

Love and Lotus Blossoms

"Shade imbues this optimistic story of lifelong self-discovery with a refreshing amount of emotional complexity, delivering a queer romance that leans into affection as much as drama, and values friendship and familial love as deeply as romantic connection. ...Shade's well-drawn Black cast and sophistication in presenting a variety of relationship styles—including open relationships and connections that shift between romance and friendship—creates a rich, affirming, and love-filled setting...(Starred review)."
—*Publishers Weekly*

Masquerade

"Shade has some moments of genius in this novel where her use of language, descriptions and characters were magnificent."—*Lesbian Review*

"The atmosphere is brilliant. The way Anne Shade describes the places, the clothes, the vocabulary and turns of phrases she uses carried me easily to Harlem in the 1920s. Some scenes were so vivid in my mind that it was almost like watching a movie. ...*Masquerade* is an unexpectedly wild ride, in turns thrilling and chilling. There's nothing more exciting than a woman's quest for freedom and self-discovery."—*Jude in the Stars*

"Heartbreakingly beautiful. This story made me happy and at the same time broke my heart! It was filled with passion and drama that made for an exciting story, packed with emotions that take the reader on quite the ride. It was everything I had expected and so much more. The story was dramatic, and I just couldn't put it down. I had no idea how the story was going to go, and at times I was worried it would all end in a dramatic gangster ending, but that just added to the thrill."—*LezBiReviewed*

Femme Tales

"If you're a sucker for fairy tales, this trio of racy lesbian retellings is for you. Bringing a modern sensibility to classics like *Beauty and the Beast, Sleeping Beauty,* and *Cinderella,* Shade puts a sapphic spin on them that manages to feel realistic."—Rachel Kramer Bussel, *BuzzFeed: 20 Super Sexy Novels Full of Taboo, Kink, Toys, and More*

"Shade twines together three sensual novellas, each based on a classic fairy tale and centering black lesbian love. ...The fairy tale connections put a fun, creative spin on these quick outings. Readers looking for sweet and spicy lesbian romance will be pleased."
—*Publishers Weekly*

"All three novellas are quick and easy reads with lovely characters, beautiful settings and some very steamy romances. They are the perfect stories if you want to sit and escape from the real world for a while, and enjoy a bit of fairy tale magic with your romance. I thoroughly enjoyed all three stories."—*Rainbow Reflections*

"I sped through this queer book because the stories were so juicy and sweet, with contemporary storylines that place these characters in Chicago. Each story is packed with tension and smouldering desire with adorably sweet endings. If you're looking for some lesbian romance with B/F dynamic, then these stories are a cute contemporary take on the bedtime stories you loved as a kid, featuring stories exclusively about women of colour."—*Minka Guides*

"Who doesn't love the swagger of a butch or the strength and sass of a femme? All of these characters have depth and are not cardboard cut outs at all. The sense of family is strong through each story and it is probably one of the things I enjoyed most. *Femme Tales* is for every little girl who has grown up wishing for a happy ever after with the Princess not the Prince."—*Lesbian Review*

"If you're a sucker for fairy tales, this trio of racy lesbian retellings is for you. Bringing a modern sensibility to classics like *Beauty and the Beast*, *Sleeping Beauty*, and *Cinderella*, Shade puts a sapphic spin on them that manages to feel realistic."—Rachel Kramer Bussel, *BuzzFeed: 20 Super Sexy Novels Full of Taboo, Kink, Toys, and More*

"All of these characters have depth and are not cardboard cut outs at all. The sense of family is strong through each story and it is probably one of the things I enjoyed most."—*Les Rêveur*

Visit us at www.boldstrokesbooks.com

By the Author

Femme Tales

Masquerade

Her Heart's Desire

Love and Lotus Blossoms

My Secret Valentine

Securing Ava

Three Wishes

Leather, Lace, and Locs

The Blessed

THE BLESSED

by

Anne Shade

2024

THE BLESSED
© 2024 BY ANNE SHADE. ALL RIGHTS RESERVED.

ISBN 13: 978-1-63679-715-1

THIS TRADE PAPERBACK ORIGINAL IS PUBLISHED BY
BOLD STROKES BOOKS, INC.
P.O. BOX 249
VALLEY FALLS, NY 12185

FIRST EDITION: DECEMBER 2024

CREDITS
EDITOR: CINDY CRESAP
PRODUCTION DESIGN: SUSAN RAMUNDO
COVER DESIGN BY TAMMY SEIDICK

CHAPTER ONE

Louisiana, 1823

Layla stood by the well behind the plantation's stables filling a water bucket for her grandmother. As she pulled the rope to raise the bucket from the water, a set of hands appeared above her grasping it as well.

"Let me help you with that."

Layla gazed up to find Master Jonas, Master and Missus Crawford's youngest son, standing beside her.

"No need, Massa Jonas, I got it." Layla quickly averted her eyes.

Ignoring her, Jonas pulled down on the rope, forcing Layla to do the same. They worked together in silence until the bucket reached the top. Jonas grasped the handle, released it from the hook, and began walking away.

He gazed back at her over his shoulder with a smile. "I'll carry it for you, Layla."

Layla hurried after him trying to grab the bucket. "No, Massa Jonas, Missus Crawford likely to beat the color off my backside if she see you doing slave work."

Jonas halted. "Well, I wouldn't want that to happen." He handed the bucket back to her. "After all, you have such a nice backside." He gave her a wicked grin.

Layla took the bucket, feeling very uncomfortable with the way Jonas was looking at her.

"Thank you, Massa Jonas, I should go before Granmama come looking for me."

Jonas grabbed her wrist. "I've been gone a while and missed you something terrible." He pulled her back toward him. "You can't spare some time to talk to an old friend?" He pouted.

Layla looked nervously around her. It was getting dark, and everyone was more than likely in their cabins for supper. If anything happened there was no one around to witness it or help her. She dug her feet in to halt his pulling and put a smile on her face.

"Maybe we can talk in the morning, Massa Jonas, after Sunday service, while Granmama and I are getting things ready for your welcome home supper," she offered, but the dark look that came into his eyes told her he wouldn't let her go so easily.

Still tightly grasping the wrist of her free hand, Jonas took the bucket from her other and set it aside, then pulled her close.

"My my, how you've grown since I last saw you." He slid his hand over her behind.

Tears sprung to Layla's eyes. "Please, Massa Jonas, you don't want me. I ain't never been with a man before. I'm sure Cora Lee would be happy to keep you company tonight. I hear she take real good care of Massa Robert."

He grinned. "Cora Lee's skinny body doesn't hold a candle to your lusciousness, Layla. Besides, why would I want my brother's old used up goods when I can have you all fresh and young?" He grasped her behind fully with both hands while pressing his pelvis against hers.

Layla shook with fear as she felt the proof of his desire. Finding strength that she didn't even know she had, she shoved him away and slapped him hard across the face. Both were too shocked to react immediately. Too late Layla realized what she had done. Master Jonas wasn't a handsy field hand or one of the other young male slaves who tried feeling her up or stealing a kiss. He was one of her masters and she had committed a wrong that could see her whipped within an inch of her life. She watched in utter fear as the desire in his eyes turned to dark anger. She did the only thing she could think to do… run. Jonas was too quick for her. He grabbed her shirt and spun her around. Before she could steady herself, he swung back and brought the back of his open hand across her cheek. She fell to the ground, gazing up at him in terror.

Layla cowered at Jonas's feet. "I'm sorry, Massa Jonas, I truly am. I didn't mean to hit ya, I swear on my mama's grave I'm so sorry."

Jonas smiled cruelly. "You're gonna be sorry all right."

As he began unbuttoning his pants, Layla shook her head and with tears flowing down her face, she turned to crawl away. "No, Massa Jonas, please."

"I've seen you looking at me while you served our meals. Don't fight me. Just like Cora Lee, you might enjoy it."

Jonas caught her once again, but this time the hit that landed onto her jaw was from a closed fist. She fell to the ground once more, but he didn't give her time to recover. He straddled her hips and landed three more punches, rendering her immobile. He moved off her, threw her dress up over her midsection, spread her legs, and ripped her threadbare cotton undergarments off. Dazed and in pain, Layla could only whimper in protest as he spit into his hand, rubbed it up along his hardened appendage and forced himself inside of her. She closed her eyes and turned her face away as he roughly squeezed her breasts, grunting and groaning his way through the brutal rape.

Layla didn't know how long it lasted, but by the time he spilled his seed and rolled off her she opened her eyes to full night. She lay there, her face in too much pain to even cry, watching through swollen eyelids as Jonas stood readjusting his clothing.

"If you would've just cooperated it could've been so much easier." He had the nerve to sound regretful. "Next time will be better now that you're broken in and know what to expect."

"I'd rather die before I let you touch me again," Layla whispered bitterly.

Jonas gazed down at her as if he hadn't heard her correctly. "What did you say?"

Fortunately, the sound of her grandmother calling her name kept her from repeating herself and possibly getting beaten even worse. Jonas looked up in a panic, then ran around the other side of the stables. He was gone before her grandmother and her uncle Louis found her.

"Oh, my Lawd!" Layla's grandmother cried as she came upon her lying bruised and battered on the ground.

She was barely conscious as her uncle gently lifted her and cradled her in his arms. She whimpered and buried her swollen face against his chest before her world went dark.

❖

Layla felt as if she were floating in a warm pool of water. It felt so safe and comforting, but all too soon she was pushed forward and surfaced into a place of cold air and loud voices. She blinked open her eyes and saw Miss Mae, the plantation's midwife, and then her grandmother, gazing down at her curiously.

"I never seen a new baby look so watchful," Miss Mae said as she met Layla's steady gaze.

Smiling down at her, her grandmother picked her up and carried her away from Miss Mae. She didn't question how her petite grandmother could be carrying her. At fifteen years old, Layla was already a foot taller and outweighed her grandmother by thirty pounds. She was just glad she wasn't in pain anymore from Master Jonas's attack. Her grandmother laid her down, wrapping her in a warm, soft blanket, then carried her toward a familiar woman's voice.

"Is she all right, Mama? Why ain't she cried out yet?"

Layla's grandmother laid her down once again then placed a soft kiss on her nose. "She's fine, child, and as big and healthy as if you'd carried her for a full nine months. She's a good eight pounds, if not more."

Layla felt herself cuddled against a soft, warm body and gazed up into eyes the color of warm honey. Somehow, she knew the woman was her mother. As her mother held her, she began humming a tune Layla had heard in her dreams many times in her fifteen years. As their gazes locked, she saw her mother's love and strength in her eyes.

Her mother smiled lovingly down at her. "Layla," she said. "Her name is Layla."

She squirmed and cooed happily in her mother's arms. "You like that, don't you? He said you would. Said it meant Night." She placed a soft kiss on her forehead.

Layla stared into her mother's bright eyes, as she hummed that mysterious tune once again, never wanting to leave whatever dream had brought her here. Then the humming stopped, and her mother's eyes filled with fear.

Layla's mother held her tightly then whispered, "You be good, Layla. No matter what they try to do to you, remember that there's also goodness in you," she pleaded before the warmth of her gaze faded into a lifeless stare.

Layla felt her mother's warmth leave her body as she passed. Feeling suddenly bereft with loss, she began to cry, desperately wanting her mother's warmth back and the light of her eyes looking upon her once again. Her grandmother picked her up, tears of sadness shining in her own eyes. Layla continued to wail desperately until she felt the brush of a featherlight touch across her cheek and the sound of her mother's humming in her ear. She opened her eyes to find a blurred, sparkling image of her standing beside her grandmother.

"As long as you stay in the light I'll always be here," her mother whispered before fading away.

The next visions Layla experienced were moments in her life when her mother had appeared to guide her in times of trouble. The first was when she was five years old and had been picked on by a group of other slave children, led by Cora Lee. They had been calling her "little witch" and "demon's daughter" and throwing dirt at her for weeks until she finally tired of it and chased after them. They ran into the cane fields, and by the time Layla caught up to them they had stopped and were all gathered around staring wide-eyed at one little boy who lay crying in the dirt. Layla peeked through the group and saw a cottonmouth slithering off the boy toward Cora Lee who sat frozen next to him. They all knew any sudden movement could cause the snake to strike so they barely breathed as Cora Lee whimpered and gazed pleadingly up at them.

Layla felt a dark joy watching the fear on Cora Lee's face until her mother appeared beside her, whispering, "Remember the light in your heart." Then placing a featherlight touch to Layla's chest above her heart.

With a blink, the joy Layla had felt at Cora Lee's misery faded. She walked slowly through the group of children toward the snake.

Sensing movement, the snake turned its head toward Layla who slowly knelt in front of it and met its gaze with her own. The snake sat frozen in Layla's stare.

"Afternoon, Mr. Snake," she said, driven by some unknown force. "We're sure sorry to disturb you, but we'll be awful thankful if you let us leave with our friend without you making anyone else sick."

The snake turned its head back toward Cora Lee, who whimpered in response, then gazed back at Layla.

"I know, she's not the nicest person, but her mama would be really sad if anything happened to her."

The snake's tongue flicked out in response and Layla smiled. "Thank you." She reached out to pat the snake's head before it slithered back into the cane field.

When she looked up, the other children watched her with a combination of fear and awe. She reached out a hand to Cora Lee who hesitated for a moment before taking it to allow Layla to help her up.

Layla pointed to the boy who was still lying on the ground. "We need to get him to Miss Mae before the poison kill him."

His moaning seemed to snap the children out of their fear of her. The two biggest boys in the group helped carry him from the field. Layla moved to follow, but Cora Lee grabbed her arm.

"You really is a witch," she said in disbelief.

"If I am then you best be careful or I'll sic that cotton mouth back on you." Layla gave her a grin before walking away.

That memory faded into another when she was twelve years old. She had managed to sneak away from helping her grandmother in the plantation's hot kitchen to sit beside the pond behind the main house. As she was soaking her feet in the water and daydreaming, a shadow cast over her.

"Hot day, isn't it?"

Layla scrambled to stand. "I'm sorry, sir, I was just gettin' a little fresh air. Please don't tell Massa Crawford."

A white man, taller than anyone she had ever met before, with hair black as night and eyes to match, dressed in a white shirt, black pants, and black riding boots stood smiling brightly down at her.

"Don't worry, Layla, you're not in any trouble." He removed his boots and socks and sat down to put his feet in the water. "Won't you join me?"

Layla looked around nervously. "No, sir, I best be getting back." She turned back toward the main house.

"That's too bad. I've waited so long for the opportunity to talk to you." He sounded disappointed.

Layla looked back at the strange man then toward the house and panic set in.

"You lookin' to buy me from Massa Crawford, sir?" she asked worriedly.

The man laughed out loud. The sound brought chills down Layla's spine. He turned to look at her and Layla noticed a strange red tinge around the black of his eyes.

He smiled. "Ah, my dear, no, I am not here to purchase you. Just to get to know you."

"Why?" She was taught never to question a White man, but since this man wasn't her master, she didn't see any reason not to.

"I knew your mother." He stared sadly across the pond.

Layla looked at him a little more closely. She saw some of the same features that looked back at her in the mirrors at the main house. Eyes so black you could barely tell where the pupil was, hair just as black that lay down his back in thick waves and held back with a leather cord, eyebrows that arched slightly upward on the outside, and ears with the slightest point at the top.

He smiled. "You've figured it out, haven't you?"

Layla didn't want to say it aloud because every fiber in her being told her this man was not a man at all but something else. Something that frightened her enough to be wary but not enough to run away. She felt a kinship like she felt with her grandmother and uncle.

His smile broadened into something sinister as he offered Layla his hand. "Come, daughter, sit with me, let me show you who you truly are."

Layla's head told her to run, but her feet had a mind of their own and began moving toward the stranger until she felt a soft touch on her shoulder stopping her, followed by the sound of her mother humming that familiar tune.

ANNE SHADE

"You promised me you would not take her," Layla's mother said from behind her.

"Ruth, I've missed you, love. I only wanted to spend some time with our child." He gazed at her mother with a hurt expression. "I said I would not take her if she chose not to go. I'm allowing her to choose. I just wanted her to know where she came from."

"You're seducing her the way you seduced me all those years ago in this very spot."

"Mama, why can't I move?" Layla asked fearfully.

"Because you're torn between two worlds, my child," the stranger answered.

Layla's mother leaned over her shoulder and whispered in her ear, "Remember what I told you, Layla."

Even though she wasn't facing her, Layla thought of the warmth and light in her mother's eyes. Of her mother always there somehow to remind her to stay in the light when all Layla wanted to do sometimes was the opposite whenever she was hurt or wronged. Light was her grandmother and uncle. Light was her mother's memory. Light was knowing she was loved. She had a feeling the only thing that waited for her with the stranger was darkness and death. She gazed one final time at the dark-eyed man then turned toward the main house and ran. She got all the way there before she remembered she'd left her shoes. When she looked back there was no one there and she found it difficult to remember if anyone had been there at all. She ran, grabbed her shoes, and headed to the house without another look back.

❖

The memory faded, and when Layla opened her eyes again, she was in her and her grandmother's cabin on the plantation. Looking toward the window, she saw early morning light filtering through and smelled porridge brewing in a kettle on the fireplace. She sat up, wincing at a twinge of discomfort between her thighs. Memories of Master Jonas's rape hit her like a brick. She touched her face and, although it was tender, she could tell the swelling had gone down. She gazed around the cabin to find her grandmother asleep in her favorite chair with her bible in her lap. Layla saw a pitcher and tin cup on their lone table, then slowly made her way over to pour a cup of water. She drank thirstily and poured another.

"Slow down, child, you don't want to make yourself sick," her grandmother said from behind her.

Layla did as she was told and sipped at the second cup of water as she sat back down on her cot. "How long did I sleep?"

"You were in and out with a fever for two days. It broke last night. How you feeling? You want some food?" her grandmother asked.

Layla shook her head. "I want you to tell me about my mama and daddy."

Her grandmother looked down at the bible in her lap avoiding her gaze. Layla put the cup down then knelt before her.

"Granmama, please? There's somethin' dark growin' inside me that feels like it's gettin' stronger every day and I don't know if I can hold it back any longer." Tears gathered in her eyes.

Her grandmother sighed heavily as she pressed a calloused hand to Layla's cheek. "Your mama was about your age when she met your daddy, if that's what you want to call him," she said sadly.

"Like you, she used to sneak off to sit by the pond on hot days and soak her feet." Her grandmother smiled knowingly. "Then one day she came back different. Sad and quiet on some days, bright and happy on others. On those days I could smell him on her. It was like freshly turned dirt in the cemetery. She wouldn't talk to me about him, even though she knew I knew, until I noticed she was with child. When she could no longer hide it, she told me what happened."

Her grandmother ran one hand across the front of the bible and her other atop Layla's head, smoothing away hair that never seemed to be out of place. With a weary sigh, she continued.

"She had been sitting by the pond when he just appeared one day. She was afraid at first so in the beginning he would only stay long enough to talk to her, keeping his distance, then leave without even touching her. She wouldn't tell me what they talked about, but she said there were things he knew and places he'd been that we could only dream. He'd even let her see a few of these places. She didn't tell me how, but she said it was scary and exciting all the same. That's how he seduced her. He promised her he'd take her with him when the time came for him to leave, but she realized too late that she would have to give up more than just her family."

Layla looked down at the bible. "She'd have to give him her soul," she said quietly.

Her grandmother nodded. "Your mama's body may have been weak, but her faith was strong. When she realized what he really was she was already pregnant with you. She made him promise that he wouldn't take you unwillingly. The choice of which side of faith you walked on had to be yours."

"What did she give him in return for keeping his promise?"

Her grandmother smiled sadly. "Her heart. She promised that as long as she lived, she would never love another but him, and I guess evil must have a heart as well because he loved her enough to keep her promise, even after she died, before she really had a chance to live."

"That's why she told me before she died to stay in the light."

Her grandmother gazed at her in surprise. "How do remember that? You were just a few minutes old?"

"I remember everything, from the day I was born until Massa Jonas took away my innocence. I know who and what I am, Granmama, I just needed you to tell me if I was made from love or evil. What my daddy did, tricking Mama like that was wrong, but it's nothin' compared to the evil Massa Jonas done to me," Layla said.

"Layla, child, don't go doing nothing foolish. I couldn't bear it if Misses had you strung up and whipped."

When she stood, her grandmother's eyes widened in fear. "He has to pay, Granmama. My daddy may have tricked her, but in the end, he gave my mama a choice. Massa Jonas beat me and just took what he wanted."

Layla left the cabin. She knew exactly where Jonas would be. Getting ready for his morning ride. She headed for the stables feeling that darkness that she told her grandmother was growing inside her, slithering and coiling in her gut like a cotton mouth about to strike. As she reached the stables, she said one word to the workers, "Leave."

There was no hesitation. Everyone she passed dropped whatever they were doing and hurried out of her path. As she passed each stall, the noses of the horses within flared as they whinnied nervously at the scent of evil rolling off her. Some even tried frantically to get out.

"What the hell is going on out there?" Jonas stepped out of his horse's stall.

At the sight of him, the snake in her belly formed wings and grew and spread throughout her body, filling every limb and muscle, becoming a part of her very being. She smiled at the surprise on Jonas's face.

"Layla, what are you doing here? I heard you were feeling poorly." He sounded nervous.

Layla slowly sashayed up to him until she had backed him into the wall. Since they were near his stallion's stall, the horse began reacting the same way as the others, whinnying and pacing nervously.

Layla pressed her body along Jonas's. "You hurt me, Massa Jonas," she said softly. "You took away my choice and my innocence and you have to pay for that."

Layla placed her right hand on his chest, feeling the beat of his heart speed up under her palm. She closed her eyes and pictured her hand squeezing the life out of that beating organ and smiled as she heard Jonas's gasping breath. Then, suddenly, a soft touch was on her shoulder and familiar words were whispered in her ear. She opened her eyes and saw fear and death in Jonas's eyes and wanted so much to see the light go out of his as it did her mother's. Soft lips touched her cheek as she saw Jonas's light slipping away, then she released the death grip on his heart. He coughed and sputtered air back into his lungs, never taking his fear-filled eyes from hers.

"Death would be too easy for you." She slid her hand down the front of his body until she reached his manhood then grasped tightly.

Tears sprung to Jonas's eyes. He whimpered a plea for her to forgive him, but there was no longer forgiveness in her heart. The only reason he was still alive was because her mother reminded her not to give in to the darkness. Killing Jonas would be the act that would seal her fate to her father's. She would not diminish her mother's love and memory that way.

"You took my innocence, but I won't let you to take another's," Layla whispered in his ear. "This"—she squeezed him hard enough to make him cry out—"will be useless from this day on. Your line of evil ends here." She bore her gaze into his, making sure that what he saw there would haunt his dreams for the rest of his life.

Layla released him and watched as he slid, whimpering and crying, down to the floor, then turned her back on him. As she slowly headed toward the entrance of the stables, she closed her eyes then calmed the horses with whispered words she didn't even know she knew, then opened them to find her grandmother, uncle, and all the stable hands watching her cautiously. She stopped before her grandmother, regretting the fear she put in the eyes of the woman who raised her.

"You gonna have to leave."

"I know." She pulled her grandmother into her arms and they held each other tightly for a moment. Then she turned toward her uncle. "Take care of her for me." She stepped into his strong embrace.

"If I can, I'll try to send word to you that I'm all right," she promised, tears streaming down her face.

Her grandmother wiped them away with her thumb. "Just be safe and keep listening to your mama. She'll guide you in the right direction."

Layla nodded. As she waded through the group that had gathered at the entrance of the stable, they once again tripped over their own feet to get out of her way. She made her way around to the back of the building and took off running into the woods without looking back. She listened anxiously for the shout of warning that she was running, but there was nothing but the sounds of the woods.

She traveled on foot for days, eating what she could from the forest and streams she passed along the way that didn't require a fire. On the fourth day, she came upon a cabin that looked as if it had been abandoned some time ago. She sat outside in the woods until after dark watching to make sure no one came in or out. When no candle or firelight appeared, she knew it was abandoned. She quietly crept up to the porch, peered into the dusty window making sure she was right, then went to the door and found it unlocked.

"Anybody here?" she called out for extra measure.

When there was no response, she sighed in relief. She had only slept for moments at a time while she ran for fear of being found or stumbling upon slave patrols in the woods. If she slept too long, she would hear a whispered, "Run," that would jolt her awake and get her moving once again. She gazed around the one-room cabin, letting the moonlight shining through the windows be her light and saw a cot on one side, a table and chair in the middle in front of a fireplace, a few cupboards along the wall, and a small wood-burning stove on the other side of the room.

"Home," something whispered in her ear. Layla trudged over to the cot and lay down, not caring that there was no blanket to cover her. She just wanted to sleep so she curled into a ball and did just that.

❖

When she awoke, bright sunlight filtered through the grimy windows and the sound of a chair creaking had her quickly sitting up and scrambling off the cot. She looked frantically around the room until her gaze landed on the man that she had met by the pond all those years ago sitting casually in the lone chair in the cabin watching her with a smile.

"Good morning, daughter."

She gazed at him warily. "What do you want?"

"I only wanted to make sure you were safe. When I heard what happened I was worried."

"How did you hear about that?"

He shrugged. "I've had others keeping an eye on you for some time. You are my child, after all."

Layla laughed bitterly. "You want me to believe a demon can care?"

"You wound me." He looked genuinely hurt by her words. "Even demons were once God's children at some time. We are still capable of having a heart, some blacker than others."

"And your heart?"

"Before I met your mother, I wasn't even sure I had one, but then she gifted me with her love and I haven't been the same since. When I laid eyes on you for the first time the day your mother passed, I felt something even stronger. I knew that I could never let any harm come your way."

Although he sounded sincere, Layla looked at him doubtfully. "Where were you when Massa Jonas hurt me?" she said angrily.

Her father's face changed into a contorted mask that made her step back in fear. "I was called away and those that were supposed to be watching you saw an opportunity to play a cruel game. They have paid for their lapse of judgment."

Looking at him, Layla wondered if that was what she looked like to Jonas when she was hurting him.

"He deserved worse than what you gave," he said, as if he read her mind. She wouldn't be surprised if he had.

He smiled knowingly. "I can, and I can teach you to do the same, and so much more."

Layla shook her head. "I won't go with you."

"As I told you and your mother, I will not force you to go with me and I will not trick you into doing so either. As I promised, the choice is yours. I only want to teach you what you need to know to help you live a long life."

Layla studied him and felt the sincerity in his words. She knew then that she could *feel* others' emotions. She could tell if they were being deceitful or truthful.

"That is one of many gifts you have." He smiled proudly.

"Stop that," she said in annoyance.

He nodded. "For you, anything."

Layla thought quietly for a moment. "Teach me to be a witch."

He gazed at her curiously. "Why a witch?"

"Cuz witches are feared but they can also help people. At least that's what my granmama told me."

"Ah, I see, you want to be what is called a white witch."

She gazed at him in confusion. "No, I don't wanna be White."

Laughing, he walked over to Layla and grasped her hands, placing an affectionate kiss on her knuckles. "My dear Layla, it does not mean I will make you White, it means that you will practice the magical arts in a good way. I will teach you hoodoo, which is a magical practice that is traced back to your ancestors in Africa using root and spell work and the white magic of juju. Do not misunderstand me though. You will need to learn the good and dark left-handed magic of voodoo as well to discern the difference and practice wisely. Just as with the choice your mother spoke of, you will have to decide in what way you will use this knowledge."

He quickly gazed toward the window, cocking his head as if listening for something. "Your first lesson comes now. There are men approaching wishing to capture you and take you back." He scowled. "One is this Jonas who harmed you."

Layla's eyes widened in fear. She hurried to look out the window but didn't see anything.

"Close your eyes and listen," her father instructed her.

Layla closed her eyes, focusing her thoughts on the woods the way she had on Jonas's heart. She could feel it then, the anger and death rolling off an approaching group of mounted riders.

"I feel them."

"Good, now focus on this cabin and the land surrounding it."

She once again did as she was told.

"Now, picture a fence as far out around the property as you feel will keep you safe from unwanted visitors." He grasped her hand, which gave her a more defined feeling of strength.

"I'm adding my power to yours, not too much, just enough to strengthen the barrier."

She pictured a picket fence from the house all the way out to the surrounding tree lines.

"Excellent, you are a natural," he said proudly, giving her hand a quick squeeze.

"What will that do?" she asked fearfully as she heard men's voices and horses approaching.

"Unless you allow it, no person, will be able to pass through the barrier."

Layla watched out the window as the group came into view. They were led by a scruffy-looking man being pulled by a pack of dogs on leashes. The dogs stopped just at the tree line at the exact spot she had pictured the fence, baying and barking viscously toward the cabin.

"We know you're in there, nigga, so you betta come out for we have to come in afta ya," a man on one of the lead horses said, holding a rifle.

Layla gazed over fearfully at her father who simply watched them with a gleeful smile. "What now?"

"You go out to meet them. Only then will they know how powerful you are and not to bother you again."

She looked at him as if he were crazy. "They gon shoot me as soon as I step foot out that door."

"Layla, they cannot do anything you don't allow them to do. You are my child and I am a very powerful being where I come from. Belief in yourself and your mother's faith is all you need." He placed a kiss on her forehead then gave her a gentle nudge toward the door.

Once again, Layla could feel that he was truthful and that was all she needed to gather the strength to walk out and meet death head on. She took a deep breath then, just as she was about to turn the handle, a soft touch brushed her cheek.

"Remember who you are," her mother whispered.

Layla smiled. "I am good and evil, I am the light and darkness, I am my beginning and end, I am Layla." She opened the door and stepped out into the bright sunshine.

CHAPTER TWO

New York, 1995

Suri heard her name being called. She sleepily blinked her eyes open to find her grandmother sitting at the end of her bed.

"Gammy?" she said in confusion.

Her grandmother lived a whole plane ride away in Louisiana so how could she be sitting in Suri's room?

Her grandmother smiled. "You can see me?"

"Yes, ma'am." She wondered why she would ask such a silly question.

She sat up, wiping her eyes to clear the blurriness around her grandmother, but when she looked again, it was still there.

"Momma didn't tell me you were coming to visit."

"Because your momma doesn't know I'm here. I came all this way just to see you."

Suri smiled. The last time she saw her grandmother was two weeks ago when she had just come home from the hospital. Her mother told her that Gammy's heart was weak, but if she did what the doctor said she would be okay.

"Your heart is all better?"

"It is now, Lil' Bit." Gammy called her by the nickname she had given her as a baby. "Now, I need you to listen carefully. Do you remember why I always call you my Lil' Bit?"

She sat up proudly. "Because I'm a little bitty you?"

"That's right. God gifted you not only with your gammy's Georgia red clay hair but also my third eye."

"Third eye!" She frantically felt her face for the extra eye.

Gammy chuckled. "No, Lil' Bit, you can't see it because it's in here." She touched the center of her own forehead. "It helps you to see the truth among lies."

Suri wrinkled her nose in distaste. "Lying is bad."

"Yes, it is, and there are many bad people that will try to get you to believe their lies and tricks, but your special eye will always show you the truth."

"What do I do when I see the truth?"

Gammy's expression turned serious. "You run away, shut your inner eye, and don't let them know you saw them."

Suri was suddenly afraid. She pulled her blanket up under her chin. "Will they hurt me?"

Gammy gave her an encouraging smile. "Not if you do what Gammy says."

Despite the fear telling her she didn't want to know more, her child's curiosity got the better of her. "What do I have to do?"

"You're going to be coming to see me real soon and when you get to Gammy's house I want you to go to my room and get the special book from under my bed. It's very important that you keep the book a secret between you and me. Not even your momma can know about it. If she finds out she might take it away from you."

"What's the book for?" Suri whispered, wide-eyed and excited about having a secret.

"The book is magical and will teach you how to use your third eye and other secrets you will need to know, so study it well. Promise me you will do what I asked."

She nodded, attempting to imitate her grandmother's serious expression. "I promise, Gammy."

"That's my Lil' Bit." She gave Suri an affectionate pat on the cheek.

Suri's brow furrowed. Whenever her grandmother patted her cheek that way, she usually felt the soft calluses on her palm that she got from gardening and smelled the coconut oil she used on her hands to keep them soft. This time all she felt was a featherlight touch and no smell at all.

"Gammy needs to go, Lil' Bit. You be good and remember your promise. It's your turn to carry the blessing this family was given centuries ago." She stood to leave.

Suri felt an immense sadness. As if this was the last time that she would see her.

"Do you have to go, Gammy?" Tears gathered in her eyes.

"Don't worry, you'll see me again when the time is right. Until then, read the book as often as you can. It will seem like a lot at first with the big words, but you're a smart girl, I know you'll have it in no time." She gave her an encouraging smile.

When her grandmother's image started to shimmer and fade, Suri realized that Gammy hadn't traveled from New Orleans by plane to see her. She had visited her the same way others who had passed away did. As far back as Suri could remember in her young life, she was able to see people who really weren't there, but the only person who knew was her grandmother because she also saw them. The tears that had gathered in her eyes made their way down her cheek.

"I love you, Gammy," she whispered.

Gammy smiled one last time. "I love you too, Lil' Bit." Then she was gone and Suri's heart broke.

❖

Suri sat in the middle of her bedroom with tears in her eyes, staring down at the book in her lap. As she had guessed, her grandmother had passed away the very night she had come to visit. As soon as her grandmother's spirit had left, Suri had run to her parents' bedroom crying and repeating over and over, "Gammy's gone!"

Her mother had taken one look at Suri's face and called her brother, who lived with their mother in the family home. She had made him get up and check on her, waiting anxiously as he made his way to her bedroom while still holding the phone. Suri knew it was true when she heard the sadness in her uncle's voice over the phone and her mother began to cry.

"Suri, baby, how did you know?" her mother had asked.

Suri had wiped away tears that were just replaced by fresh ones. "Gammy woke me up. She was all fuzzy and sparkly so I knew something was wrong."

Her heart had been breaking as she remembered that she hadn't even hugged Gammy before she left. Can you hug a spirit? She wondered.

Suri's parents had exchanged a worried look before their gazes landed back on her. "What did she say?" her mother asked.

Suri tearfully repeated what her grandmother told her apart from information about the magical book. Seeing the panicked expression on her parents' faces made her wonder if maybe she shouldn't have told them any of it. Her mother had snatched her up into the bed with them, holding her so tight Suri almost couldn't breathe, and cried even harder.

"Lord, why my child?" her mother had said forlornly as she rocked back and forth with Suri in her arms.

After that night, everything had been a whirlwind of activity. Even the funeral had been overwhelming. She had been to a funeral before, Gampa Shields had died the year before, but there weren't half as many people at his funeral as had been at Gammy's. It was as if the whole city of New Orleans had shown up to say good-bye to Pearl Shields and they all seemed very fascinated by Suri.

"Well, aren't you the spitting image of your grandmother."

"She could be Pearl's twin."

"If I didn't know any better, I'd swear Pearl must've shaped the child out of clay in her image."

Were among just a few of the comments Suri had heard over the day of the funeral. The comment that seemed to make her mother grip her hand tighter was made by Suri's great-aunt Ruby, Gammy's sister.

She had knelt before Suri, stared into her eyes, and said, "She told you what you needed to do didn't she?"

Neither Suri nor her mother responded, they just stared at Aunt Ruby as if she had told them the sky was green. Aunt Ruby had nodded with a satisfied smile as if that was answer enough. Suri was so relieved when the week had come to an end and they headed back home to New York. She had run directly to her room and shoved the unicorn backpack with Gammy's book under her bed. That had been a week ago and she had finally gotten up enough nerve to look at it after she had a dream the other night of Gammy holding the book out to her and telling her to "get to studying." She laid the book in the middle of the floor and opened it. Taking up the entire inside cover and first page was a picture of a large tree labeled Tree of Blessings with names and dates written in gold on the branches. The first name and date at the very top of the tree was Athena, 1804. The last two names written were Gammy's—Pearl, 1903, and her name—Suri, 1988. Before Gammy's name, Suri counted ten other names, some with the same year, but after Gammy's name it appeared that she was the only one to have been "blessed" since Gammy was born.

She turned to the next page to find a letter written in her grandmother's neat, small writing. Suri had been reading since she was three years old, but her grandmother still made sure to write in a way Suri would have no problem reading.

My Sweet Suri,

If you are reading this then that means Gammy has left this world for the next. I know you're sad, but I don't want you to stay in that sadness for too long because where I'm going there is nothing but joy, love, and, of course, Gampa. I will be back to check on you from time to time so make sure you keep up with your studies at school, and with the book. Both are very important for your future. Say your prayers every night and every morning like I taught you because keeping your faith is also very important in making sure your inner eye stays strong. Remember what I told you to do about the ones that will try to trick you with their lies, stay as far away from them as possible. As you get older, and your gifts get stronger, you will be able to protect yourself when running doesn't work. I wish I could be there to guide you, but the Creator obviously had other plans for both of us.

Suri, don't let anyone make you believe that your gift is a burden. As you saw from the Blessing Tree, our family has been blessed for a long time with women like us, and you will not be the last. Hold on to your light and faith, Lil' Bit. They will guide you when I can't through the twisting road ahead of you. Remember that Gammy loves you and my heart is your heart, my eyes are your eyes, and my strength is your strength. You will understand that better when you're older.

With all my love, Gammy

Tears streamed down Suri's face as she ran her fingers over Gammy's signature and felt a featherlight stroke across her cheek.

Suri kept her promise to her grandmother. Through the years, she studied the Book of Blessings more than she did her schoolwork. In the beginning, she couldn't pronounce and didn't understand a lot of the words so she took a composition book her mother gave her to practice her writing and wrote those words and phrases down so that she could look them up the next time she went to the library. She had always been a curious child, so it wasn't unusual for her to spend hours at the library looking things up or reading about topics she found interesting. Both of her parents were college professors and encouraged her thirst for knowledge. She didn't think they would continue being so encouraging if they knew what she was spending so much time reading up on.

After the night her grandmother died, they never discussed what Suri had told them. On their last night in New Orleans after the funeral, Suri was supposed to be in bed, but she snuck down when she heard shouting. Her parents, Uncle Robert, and Aunt Ruby were arguing about her gift.

❖

"You need to find the child a guide," she heard Aunt Ruby say.

"She's only five years old. How do we know if she even has the gift? Because Mama came to her in a dream? I'm not subjecting my child to this family's ridiculous rituals based on that."

"Liv, I know this is scary, but you know what will happen if you just ignore it," Uncle Robert said.

"I won't let that happen to Suri."

"Do you think I wanted to let that happen to Aria? I thought I did everything I could to protect her…"

Everyone grew quiet. Then Uncle Robert continued.

"We lost her because of my stubbornness and lack of faith in our family's duty. Don't do the same to yourself or Suri."

Suri heard so much sadness in her uncle's voice that it made her heart ache for him. She didn't know who Aria was, but he must have loved her a lot.

"Didn't you all say that there's usually signs that a child in the family has the gift?" her father asked. "Suri hasn't shown any signs of talking to spirits, seeing things that aren't there, or making things happen with her thoughts. Maybe it skipped her."

"How would you know if you don't even talk to the child about it? My sister knew before she could talk that she had the gift, but she hid it until our daddy died because he was a nonbeliever just like you. If Pearl came to Suri, then she's got it, whether you like it or not," Aunt Ruby said.

"This conversation is over. We're leaving in the morning. *If* Suri has the gift, we'll deal with it," her mother had said followed by the click-clack of her heels on the wood floor heading toward the stairs.

Suri had scrambled back up, hurried to her room, quietly closed the door, then jumped under the covers. A few moments later, she'd heard the door open, then her mother laid down beside her, and pulled her into her arms. Suri had known she was crying by how her body trembled.

"Mommy, is everything okay?"

Her mother had kissed the top of her head. "Yes, baby. Mommy's just feeling sad about Gammy. You go back to sleep."

Suri had felt her mother's sadness the same way she had felt her uncle's. But there was something else there that caused a sharp pain in her belly. Fear. Her mother's fear of her being blessed overwhelmed her grief for Gammy and even her love for Suri.

That's when she knew that she could never tell her parents that she had been blessed. So, she hid it for years while self-guiding and strengthening her abilities through the Book of Blessings, library research, and eventually through the internet. Her grandmother also checked in, just as she said she would, guiding Suri as best she could from beyond.

Research was great when it came to learning more about the history and cultures associated with her family's gifts, but it wasn't enough to learn the spells and incantations within the book. For that, Suri needed someplace she could use as a laboratory of sorts. On the property of the two-family home that they shared with her other grandparents who lived on the first floor, was a shed that had been unused since they had an attached garage added to the house. Science had always been Suri's favorite subject so when her parents asked what she wanted for her tenth birthday she had requested to have the shed converted into a mini lab and study space. Her father and grandfather tore down the old shed to replace it with a roomier one that they could update with electricity, running water, and a small HVAC unit so that she wouldn't swelter in the summer or freeze in the winter. There was just enough room for her mother and grandmother to deck it out with a desk, a small lab table with stool, a full chemistry set, a bookshelf, and a plush armchair. It was perfect. The only thing she needed to figure out was how to get some of the ingredients she needed to practice making some of the potions and working the spells.

Suri did the only thing she could think of doing. She wrote to her uncle explaining that like her grandmother, she'd had her gift for as long as she could remember, that Gammy had left her the Book of Blessings, and included a list of herbs and plants that she would need help collecting without her parents finding out. Her uncle sent her a package in response that included a medium-sized wooden chest, a book about plants and herbs, several lab coats in the bright pink that Suri loved to wear and a letter signed *FOR MASTER SCIENTIST SURI'S EYES ONLY* with a smiley face. None of it gave away what Uncle Robert was really sending her. The letter explained everything.

Dear Suri,

Thank you for confiding in me, and although I don't think it's a good idea not to tell your parents, I will help you in whatever way I can. First, I think that it's important that I tell you something about the family's blessings that will hopefully keep you from making mistakes that could put you and the ones you love in danger.

You have a cousin that you've never met. Her name is Aria. She's my daughter, and I don't know where she is. Like your mother, I didn't want any of my children to have anything to do with the blessing and all the responsibility it entailed. Aria was what they call an en caul birth, meaning she was born with a veil over her head, which is a spiritual sign of a child born with good luck and strong gifts. Your grandmother knew as soon as she held Aria that she had the strongest gifts since her grandmother who had also been born en caul. She wanted to have Aria read and blessed by our family's spiritual leader, but I refused. I called it all superstition and didn't want to have anything to do with it.

By the time Aria started middle school, she became a dark, sullen child. Just before she started high school, we tried to get her counseling several times before we finally found someone to help her. I know you're wondering why I didn't just listen to Gammy, but as you can see from your mother's reaction, it's not easy as a parent to turn your child over to something you know could lead them down a path you will never understand.

It turned out that this woman wasn't who she said she was, but by the time I found out, the Aria we knew and loved was lost to us. She had begun to use her gifts but not for what they were meant for. The kids at school that bullied her were injured in mysterious accidents. Teachers that labeled her difficult were struck down with strange illnesses. By high school she would go to school and then we wouldn't see her again for one to two days. We couldn't take it anymore and confronted her. Aria told us that her therapist was a very powerful voodoo priestess, who had been helping her with her gifts, and that she was going to go live with her. Aria's mother threatened to call the police on the woman.

Aria was only fourteen, but the look on her face when she raised her hand and struck her mother without even touching her was not the face of my sweet young daughter until she realized what she had done when her mother didn't get back up. Aria left while I was trying to wake her mother and call for an ambulance. The doctors said that she had a heart attack due to advanced heart disease. If we hadn't gotten her to the hospital she would've died. Before that night, Aria's mother never had heart issues, and I knew then that Aria almost killed her to defend some woman she'd barely known for six months. That was three years ago. We haven't seen Aria since. Gammy had heard from her circle of friends that Aria was living in Mississippi and not using her gifts for anything good.

Suri, I'm telling you about Aria so that you'll understand why it's important for you to learn to use your gifts the right way. If Gammy's spirit is guiding you, then don't stray from that or what the Book of Blessings is teaching you. Our family was gifted with these blessings to protect, help, and heal our community. To use them to harm others will only lead to a path of pain and heartbreak. Aria's mother died just a few months after that night not just from the physical damage Aria had done to her, but also spiritually. She broke her mother's heart and will to live. She almost broke me as well as I spent a year searching for her and started having health complications. The only reason I stopped was because I received a letter from her asking me to do so or my health would only get worse. She didn't want to also be the cause of my death.

The chest has a secret drawer where I placed seedlings for the herbs and plants you asked for as well as packets of dried versions of those same plants for you to use right away. These were all taken from Gammy's supply. Let me know if you need anything else and I will get it for you. Do not try to find any of the ingredients in that book on your own until you have a better understanding of what you're practicing. You don't want to go to the wrong person who may take advantage of you or want to do you harm for having your gifts. And, Suri, whatever you do, stay safe and don't do anything that you think Gammy wouldn't want you to. Call me anytime. I love you.

Uncle Robert

Suri took the letter and chest out to the shed, closed the blinds, and locked the door before she set it down to find the secret drawer, which she did by pressing one of the metal studs along the top of the chest. A drawer popped open at the bottom crammed with seedling packets and small clear airtight bags with labels identifying the herbs inside. Suri's practice of spells and potions and tincture-making began, but out of fear of the unknown, she only created ones for simple things like healing small cuts and bruises, which she had a lot of as an active ten-year-old, and protection spells for her parents and grandparents. She assumed it worked because nothing bad happened to them.

Outside of her little lab, Suri made sure to practice as discreetly as possible. That was until the day Larry, the biology class lizard, got sick. Only Suri knew because she could feel the sickness of the creature whenever she came near the terrarium. She tried to tell the teacher but didn't know how without revealing her gift. When he began refusing to eat his favorite treat of meal worms, the teacher finally noticed. Because she couldn't bear to see anything sick or dying, especially since she could sense it happening, Suri decided to try a healing potion that was more powerful than the cream she created for her minor injuries. During recess, she snuck into the classroom, filled a dropper with the potion, and fed it to Larry. Then she chanted a protection spell just for extra measure. A warm light appeared around Larry then slowly faded. Suri collected a pinch of meal worms from the container beside the terrarium, placed them in her palm and offered them to Larry who eagerly ate them.

With a smile of satisfaction, she put a pinch more in his feeding dish, closed the top, then turned to leave only to be stopped by the sight of her classmate, Rachel Thompson, her wide blue eyes staring at her in surprise.

"What did you just do?"

Suri wanted to kick herself for not closing the door behind her. She had been so eager to see if her potion would work that she had forgotten. "Nothing. I was just checking on Larry."

"You made him glow and now he's eating. I've been trying to get him to eat for days now. I was just coming to check on him."

"Oh, well, he seems better. Maybe he just had a tummy ache." Suri hurried past Rachel and out of the room.

The next day at recess Rachel approached her again. "Do you know magic? I won't tell." she whispered. "It's just that my grandma used to know magic until she got Alzheimer's. Now she doesn't remember anything. Not even me."

Suri could feel Rachel's sadness. Her heart ached with it so badly she rubbed her chest to ease the discomfort. She didn't know Rachel well, she seemed nice enough. She had moved here over the summer and didn't appear to have made any friends. Suri listened to the sadness and knew that all Rachel wanted right now was to have a friend. To have one that was just like her grandma whom she loved more than anything, would be even better.

She smiled, leaned in close to Rachel, then whispered, "So was my grandma."

Rachel's eyes widened. "Did she pass it on to you? My grandma told me that sometimes it gets passed on, but I guess it skipped me and my dad."

Suri nodded, afraid of admitting her gift out loud.

Rachel grinned broadly. "So, you did help Larry?"

She nodded again. "I could feel him getting sick."

"That is so cool. What else can you do?"

That was the day she and Rachel became best friends. It was such a relief to have someone other than her uncle to confide in about what was going on. Especially since Rachel was her age and understood a little about the gift from her own grandmother. She would even assist Suri with making potions, but she never let Rachel read or even touch the Book of Blessings and Rachel was fine with that as she said the book gave her the creeps.

One afternoon as Rachel was helping Suri clean up after spending the morning making poultices and tinctures to store in her growing inventory that was kept locked in a cabinet, she broke a jar and sliced open her hand. As blood poured from the wound, instinct took over, Suri grasped Rachel's hand between hers and began chanting a healing spell she didn't even realize she knew. She was blinded by a white light, then warmth radiated from her entire body out through her hand toward Rachel who she heard gasp, then her vision slowly returned and she found Rachel looking at her as if she'd never seen her before.

"I'm sorry." Suri quickly released Rachel's hand.

Rachel gazed down, her eyes widened with amazement. She held her hand up for Suri to see. "It's gone."

Suri tentatively took Rachel's hand, staring at the spot where a moment ago a gash had stretched across her entire palm but was now just as smooth as it always had been.

"Suri, you can lay hands," Rachel said.

"What does that mean?"

"Your grandmother never told you about laying hands?"

"No." She released Rachel's hand and went back to her desk where the Book of Blessings was sitting.

"That's because there has only been two in our family that were blessed with that gift and your uncle told you about one of them."

Suri could feel her grandmother standing beside her gazing down at the book as well.

"Gammy is here." She liked to warn Rachel when Gammy showed up so that she wasn't surprised when Suri started talking to her.

"Hi, Gammy," Rachel said.

"Hello, Rachel."

"She said hi and that only two others in my family could heal. One was my cousin." Suri had told Rachel about Aria.

"You're not going to end up like her, are you?" Rachel asked.

Suri gazed up at Gammy who stood beside her as clearly as if she were in the room with them. "Will I? I've been trying to do everything right so that I won't, but new stuff seems to be happening now. Yesterday I was doing my homework at the dining room table and was thinking about the plate of cookies on the kitchen counter. Then the next thing I knew, the plate was sitting next to my book. Now I'm healing people with just a touch?"

"You didn't tell me about the cookies." Rachel hadn't moved from the spot where she'd been standing, trying to stay as far from the book as possible.

"It scared me so bad I wasn't sure I wanted to tell anyone."

Gammy looked thoughtful. "Did the plate float over to you or did it just appear?"

"It just appeared. At least I think it did. I saw something from the corner of my eye, looked up, and there it was. It's a good thing that nobody else was in the kitchen. Does it make a difference how it got there?"

Gammy nodded. "If it just appeared then you have teleportation abilities. If it floated over then you have telekinesis abilities, which means you can move things with your mind, a very rare gift in our family."

"And only two people had it, right?"

Gammy smiled. "No, Lil' Bit, only one. You."

She looked at Rachel. "Gammy says I'm the only one that has the gift to move things with my mind."

"That is so cool!"

Suri wasn't so sure how cool that was. Especially when she didn't do it on purpose. She felt a featherlight touch.

"There is nothing to worry about. You're just going to need the Book of Gifts. Ask your uncle to go into the library, grab the red leather journal from the top shelf, and send it to you. It looks like an empty book, but once you receive it, I'll give you the spell to break the illusion on it. It's a compendium of gifts that have been or may be blessed to members of our family that display gifts and how to control them. Until then, just do your best not to move anything else."

"Easy for you to say."

Gammy chuckled and placed a kiss on Suri's forehead before disappearing.

By the time Suri left for college, she had memorized the Book of Blessings from cover to cover, as well as all the information on her gifts from the Book of Gifts. Her gifts by then consisted of mediumship, empathy, healing, telekinesis, and chlorokinesis or the ability to control and manipulate plants. If she needed any other assistance, she used the hoodoo spells and potions from the Book of Blessings. She was determined to use her gifts to help people, never imagining that there would come a day that she would use them to harm anyone.

CHAPTER THREE

New Orleans, 2023

Layla sat meditating in the corner of her bedroom attempting to calm the anger that flowed heavily through her entire body like a churning lake before a storm. She took several deep, steadying breaths and focused on the bright light she still felt in her heart for her mother even after two centuries of life in this godforsaken world. The light grew and spread a sense of warmth and love, calming her, and pushing back the evil that threatened to breach the surface. When the darkness faded into a grayish tint around the white light, because it never truly went away, she took another calming breath and slowly opened her eyes to find Sebastian, her cat, watching her curiously.

"Hey, old man." She raised a hand to scratch behind his ear.

Sebastian purred happily and rubbed his entire head in her palm. When the black-and-white cat showed up on her doorstep two years ago and pranced into her house like he belonged there, Layla felt as if he had added something that had been missing from her life for a long time, family. True, he was a cat, but she knew he was not just any cat. Sebastian had been someone in his previous life, someone like her, and she felt a kinship with him that she hadn't felt in over one hundred years.

Layla had family, descendants of her uncle Louis, but even though she knew of them, they had no knowledge of her, and she kept it that way. They wouldn't understand or accept who and what she was. She had learned that the hard way when her uncle reached out to her after the Civil War ended and the slaves in the South were emancipated. When Union soldiers brought the news to the Crawford plantation, her uncle and most of the Crawford slaves dropped what they were doing, gathered what little belongings they had, and left the plantation right along with the soldiers. Unfortunately, her grandmother hadn't lived to see the day. She had died in a mysterious fire in the slave quarters that had only seemed to burn her cabin down without touching the cabins nearby.

Her uncle brought his family to her cabin, but they hadn't stayed longer than one night because his wife refused to stay in the home of a witch with her children. Her uncle tried to explain that Layla wasn't a bad person, but his wife wouldn't hear of it, so she said good-bye to her uncle and never tried to reach out to him or his family again. After that, her only visitors were those seeking tinctures, spells, and healing that ordinary doctors weren't able to provide.

Through the centuries, she mostly kept to herself. Layla's parentage made her almost immortal. She wouldn't live forever, but she began aging slower as she used her powers, having to use glamour to appear to age like a normal human over the years so that she wouldn't be found out. Then, when the elderly spinster in the woods passed on and her niece came to live there, people chose to believe what they needed because the truth would be too much to comprehend. She had been called a witch, voodoo priestess, demon spawn, and even the devil's mistress. People who heard rumors of her story both feared and revered her. A few had even tried to make a name for themselves by trying to kill her. But she and death were well acquainted, and she knew it wasn't her time yet. For two centuries, she had been mostly alone except when her father came for his visits. Other than that, she would take a lover here and there to appease the sadness that would overtake her at times.

Layla's longest relationships since the death of her grandmother had been with her father, the spirit of her long-dead mother, and a surprising companion that stayed with her for over sixty years. Her father's visits had become less frequent in the last century as she grew almost as strong as him in her powers. The only time he appeared now was when she was in danger by forces far beyond her control. It was at those times when she and death came face-to-face and her mother's light wasn't strong enough to help her. Only her father's darkness would keep them at bay. It was the only time her mother's spirit would not argue with her father about using his dark gift to interfere in her life. Her mother's visits were less frequent as well since Layla had obtained control over her powers and was less tempted to follow in her father's footsteps.

The last, her companion of over sixty years, had come to Layla not long after her uncle and his family had left. The ward Layla had put around her home aided her with sensing when someone was coming and whether they were a threat. The warning she received when Cora Lee came up to the property told her someone needed help. She stood in her open doorway and watched as her childhood nemesis stumbled up her walkway, beaten and barely hanging on to consciousness before she collapsed into Layla's arms. She had held no grudge against Cora Lee as her life had been more difficult than Layla's having to spend it as somebody's unwilling bedwarmer, then having to give up every child born from the acts. So, she cared for Cora Lee until she was healed well enough to take care of herself, never asking what happened, knowing Cora Lee would tell her in her own time.

When she did, Layla felt somewhat responsible. Master Jonas had taken to beating her whenever his manhood refused to respond when he tried to bed her. Cora Lee hadn't complained because it was never more than she could handle, but this time was different because he had come home drunk and angry about rumors growing that he would never be able to marry because he couldn't give any woman children, having been cursed by Layla. Cora Lee didn't blame her. Master Robert had told her that Jonas had been sent home from the fancy northern school he had been attending because he had raped and beaten several Colored maids while he was there so what he had done to Layla and to Cora Lee had always been in him. Not having anywhere else to go, Cora Lee had asked if she could stay with Layla for a while.

"I know what you are and I know you ain't evil or you woulda let that snake bite me back when we was children so I owe you my life anyway for sending it away," Cora Lee had told her, so Layla had let her stay.

Their relationship grew into friendship over several years before it became intimate. Over the decades, Cora Lee took care of and loved Layla, who returned the care and love while also teaching Cora Lee how to help her with the natural and herbal remedies she made for people. Cora Lee never said a word whenever Layla's father came to visit, but she kept her distance out of fear and awe of the power the two of them presented. Cora Lee didn't see spirits so she never knew when Layla's mother visited until Layla began talking to her.

The downside to Layla's slow aging was that she had to watch Cora Lee age before her eyes. When she offered her the opportunity to slow down the process, Cora Lee refused, telling Layla that she wanted to live and experience life as God intended. She lived to be ninety-five before she passed away peacefully in her sleep. Layla's heart broke as her mother's and grandmother's spirits came to guide Cora into the light. They promised to keep an eye on her for Layla and, although it didn't heal her broken heart, it eased the pain knowing that the only women who had loved her and who she had loved in return were together.

Since then, Layla had refused to open her heart to anyone. The pain of watching them age and wither away was too much to bear. Over the decades she acquired homes in difference cities and, with her father as her tour guide, traveled to places she hadn't even imagined existed outside of the plantation or her cabin filled with books that her father brought her through the years. She would stay in these places for a few months, maybe even a few years, at a time but she always came back to her little cabin in the woods. It had grown, but it was still just as secluded as it had been when she stumbled upon it all those years ago.

It seemed no one wanted to live near a witch. She was fine with that, buying up as much of the surrounding land as she could with money she not only made from her spells and medicines but also from mysterious fortunes she would find left behind after her father's visits. When she questioned him about it, he told her it was money owed to her, her mother, and grandmother for their years of labor. She accepted it as she knew no one would take her in as a domestic or any other kind of work that would require her coming into close contact with people. In later decades she learned about how to invest her money through businesses and the properties she bought. With her father's help, she hired a White attorney to help her with her business finances. Through him, she became an anonymous benefactor for many freed Colored men and women who were trying to start a life of their own.

With each generation of representatives, her father would be her face and voice working with the attorneys and the people benefiting from her investments. They never knew where the money came from nor did they question it. If they were successful, ran their businesses fairly, and gave back to their community in return they never heard from their wealthy benefactor. If they tried to take advantage of her kindness in any way or tried cheating their own community, then they were visited by her in their darkest dreams and left broken and destitute.

Layla's life for the past two hundred years had consisted of never staying in one location long enough to build roots and being looked upon as the strange loner who attracted even stranger visitors to whatever home, in whatever city, she decided to visit on a whim. Currently, she and her feline companion had been staying at her apartment in the French Quarter of New Orleans. They had been there for a month now and Layla was already growing restless. Something had pulled her here. Some unknown and seductive force had awoken her and drawn her out of seclusion to the city at one of the busiest times of the year. If she could help it, Layla never came to New Orleans this close to Halloween. Too many tourists, too much temptation, and too much sin sent her senses into overdrive.

Even now she could feel the wickedness creeping and crawling thick in the air like a river of molasses. If whatever brought her here didn't show itself soon, she was going to leave without finding out what, or who, it was before she was unable to hold her darkness back any longer. As if feeling her distress, Sebastian purred loudly and rubbed himself along her leg then climbed onto her lap. She felt calm once again, but it was short-lived when that pull tugged at her chest even stronger than it did when she first arrived. She gently picked Sebastian up and set him on a nearby chair then went out the set of French doors that led out to her patio overlooking Bourbon Street.

It was late morning, still early for the serious revelers to be out but late enough for the daytime tourists to fill the streets. Layla leaned on the balcony railing looking down upon the families and groups passing by. At the sight of a young woman with thick auburn curls tied back into a puffy ponytail standing across the way looking in confusion down at her phone, she felt a tug so strong it was as if someone had grabbed her heart right out of her chest. At the same moment, the woman folded into herself, grabbed her own chest, then turned her gaze up to meet Layla's. The woman stared at her curiously for a moment then her eyes widened and she quickly looked away as she hurried up the street.

Layla watched her go until she turned a corner out of sight and hadn't realized she had been holding her breath during the whole encounter until she felt Sebastian rub along her leg and heard the word "breathe." She turned to find her mother standing beside her, looking in the same direction the woman had gone.

"Who is she?" Layla asked.

Her mother gave her a sad smile. "Your salvation or downfall, it all depends on you."

"What's that supposed to mean?"

"It's all I can tell you, child. You know I'll help when I can, but I can't steer your fate for you."

Layla sighed, she knew her mother was right, but it didn't make trying to decide what her next move would be any easier. She gazed in the direction the woman had gone. One thing she'd learned in her long life was that putting off the inevitable did nothing but postpone whatever fate had in store for her, so she turned and went back into her apartment to get dressed and face her destiny.

Suri peeked around the corner of the building she had cowered behind to gaze toward the balcony where the dark-haired woman had been standing. She breathed a sigh of relief to find her gone. Ducking back behind the building, she closed her eyes, counting down from ten to try to slow her racing heart.

"Gammy, how did you live here for so long without losing your mind?" she asked aloud knowing she wouldn't get an answer.

She arrived in New Orleans just two days ago, and ever since, her third eye had been going into overdrive with the amount of energy and spirits permeating the city. She had managed to avoid the few dark energies she encountered, but that woman was something entirely different. Suri had been looking down at the GPS on her phone trying to get her bearings and felt a pull on her chest that couldn't be ignored. When she looked up, she met the dark gaze of the woman on the balcony. She felt a sense of familiarity and comfort that was quickly replaced by foreboding when her third eye picked up a darker energy surrounding the woman. The only time that happened was when she encountered an evil spirit or demon, but the woman was obviously a living person, not a spirit, and she didn't see a demon beneath her beautiful, angular face. Warning bells continued going off just the same, so she did what she had always done, ran the other way. Suri had lost too much already ignoring those warning bells and had come too close to death herself to continue to do so.

She looked back down at her phone and pulled her GPS back up. Her destination was just a block away. A few moments later, she stood outside the storefront of a spiritual shop. A bell above the door jingled lightly as she entered, and the scent of sage overwhelmed her.

"I'll be right there," a feminine voice called.

Suri strolled around looking over shelves filled with various crystals, oils, tonics, books, and every other homeopathic and spiritual remedy one could think of. She picked up a bottle of chamomile oil and inhaled deeply, sighing with pleasure. Chamomile helped to calm and clear Suri's mind when she was feeling overwhelmed, so she always tried to keep a small bottle of it with her.

"My apologies for keeping you waiting, how can I—"

Suri turned to find the shopkeeper, a beautiful, white-haired, petite woman with smooth deep brown skin dressed in a colorful kente caftan staring in wide-eyed shock at her.

Not sure why she garnered such a reaction Suri approached the counter slowly. "Hello, I was sent to this address to pick up a key to my grandmother's home."

The woman blinked several times then smiled broadly. "She told me you were coming and to have everything ready. I'm Phoebe. Your grandmother and I have been best friends since childhood. You were just a baby when we first met so I'm not surprised that you don't remember me. I was out of the country when she passed. It broke my heart that I couldn't be here for her funeral."

Suri smiled. "I remember my grandmother talking about you when I was little and all the trouble you two used to get into. It's nice to meet you, Miss Phoebe."

She waved dismissively then came from behind the counter. "What's this 'Miss' business. Call me Phoebe." She pulled Suri into a warm hug.

Tears came to Suri's eyes as she was enveloped in an embrace that was a lot stronger than she expected for such a small, fragile-looking woman. It had been months since she had allowed anyone to touch her in an affectionate way, other than to appease a sexual need, and she missed it. When she pulled away, she couldn't hide the tears in her eyes.

Phoebe grasped her face in her hands. "I know it's been hard, but it won't be for much longer." She wiped away Suri's tears with the pad of her thumbs. "Now, we have a lot to discuss so give me a minute to lock up and we'll go up and have some lunch and chat."

"I don't want to interrupt your business, I just thought I would pick up the key and go."

"Nonsense, I've been expecting you and I usually close up for lunch anyway."

Phoebe began bustling quickly around the shop straightening displays, locking the door and turning the OPEN sign to CLOSED with a little clock's hands pointed at a time an hour from now.

"Now." She looped her arm through Suri's leading her toward the back of the shop. "I hope you like chicken salad. It was Pearl's favorite, so I figured it's good enough for her Lil' Bit."

Suri smiled warmly. "Yes, it's my favorite as well."

"I knew it." Phoebe patted Suri's hand affectionately.

They walked through a large backroom that looked more like a chemist's lab than a retail shop, bringing back memories of her little lab in the backyard, then through another door that led to a set of stairs going to the second floor. Phoebe lived in a warm and beautifully decorated three-room apartment above the shop. Like the shop, it smelled of fresh sage as sunlight filtered in through lace curtains covering two large windows and a set of French doors leading out to a balcony.

"Your grandmother told me how sensitive you are, so I made sure to cleanse the space before you came so you wouldn't be bothered unnecessarily. Have a seat." Phoebe indicated the stools at the kitchen island.

Suri usually was not so trusting with people, especially within the past year, but she felt nothing but good energy from Phoebe. No warning bells sounded, and her third eye seemed quite content to close and rest for the moment. Phoebe busied herself with preparing two plates of chicken salad on a bed of lettuce with Ritz crackers just the way her grandmother used to make it for her. She set a plate with a glass of sweet tea in front of Suri then the other in front of the stool beside her.

"Eat, child." Phoebe settled into her seat watching her.

Suri scooped chicken salad onto a cracker, took a bite, then closed her eyes and practically hummed in delight.

"Put my foot in it, didn't I," Phoebe said proudly. "Took me years to get it just like Pearl's because she refused to tell me what her secret ingredient was, smoked paprika."

"Thank you for this."

Phoebe rubbed her arm. "I know you're missing her, especially since you've been struggling these past months."

Suri gazed at Phoebe suspiciously. "Excuse me?" She placed the cracker full of salad that she was about to eat back on her plate.

Phoebe smiled knowingly. "You think you and your grandmother are the only ones with the gift? There are many of us out there. The women in your family aren't the only ones to be blessed." Phoebe ate a forkful of the salad herself.

Suri knew there were others, but she rarely spoke to them because they avoided her just as quickly as she avoided the evil beings she encountered. They ate quietly for a few more moments before Phoebe pushed her plate away and gazed up at her.

"What happened to your best friend, your parents, and your girlfriend are not your fault. The darkness is trying to steal your light and if you keep heading in the direction you are, they will succeed."

Suri lost her appetite. "I don't know what you're talking about."

Phoebe took her hand, giving it a gentle squeeze. "Your grandmother and I have both been where you are, Suri. You can't let them win, and living the solitary life you're living now gives them room to move right in. They want you afraid and alone. That's the best way for them to turn you from the light."

Suri slid her hand from Phoebe's, stood, and walked over to the French doors that looked out onto the busy street below. She knew Phoebe was right. Since the death of Rachel, her parents, and then her girlfriend, she had stayed to herself. Her life consisted of work, sleep, TV, and meaningless sex with faceless women she met in clubs when the loneliness was too much to bear. After each encounter, her thoughts grew darker and it was becoming more difficult to pull herself out of them and find any joy in the solitary life she was leading. Work had become her only source of goodness. Being a delivery room nurse gave her the opportunity to witness the joy and miracle of life almost daily. It was what her grandmother did and it was what she had always wanted to do since she saw the joy it brought her, but that was even becoming a source of sadness lately. It seemed that more and more, premature and sickly babies were being born and barely surviving their first few weeks in the world. The last she had witnessed had been small enough to fit into the palm of her hand and only survived a few days in the NICU before its underdeveloped organs gave out.

It had been too much for Suri and she had gone home and not been back to work since, deciding to finally use the four weeks of vacation that she had allowed to collect over the past year. She had spent the time wallowing in self-pity until a certified letter arrived from an attorney who said that he represented her grandmother's estate. He claimed he had a final wish from her grandmother that was to be enacted before Suri's thirty-fifth birthday, which was a little over a week away. Suri had reached out to her uncle, who confirmed what the letter said and suggested she come to New Orleans to take care of it in person.

It turned out her grandmother had left her the family home with strict instructions that she was to live in it for at least one year. If, after that year, she wanted to return to New York, then she would still maintain ownership of the home until the family's next blessed child came along to take possession. Suri was told that she was not allowed to sell or rent the home out and that it must stay within the family whether a new child came along or not. Which was why she now stood gazing out at the city that might very well become her home.

"Holding your pain in won't help you, child," Phoebe said from behind her.

Suri turned back, making sure that her expression was pleasant. "Thank you for the lovely meal, Phoebe, may I have the key to the house now?"

Phoebe sighed. "Of course."

Feeling guilt over her rudeness, Suri assisted her with cleaning up. Phoebe smiled gratefully. When they finished, she opened a cat cookie jar, reached in, and pulled out a ring of keys.

Phoebe pointed out the small labels on the keys. "Your grandmother labeled each key to make it easier for you,"

Suri took the keys, gazing at them in confusion. She didn't remember there being that many rooms.

"Thank you."

Phoebe then pulled an envelope from the pocket of her dress. "This will explain what I can't."

To her surprise, her name was written in her grandmother's neat script as if it had been done just today and not decades ago.

"I've made sure to keep the house clean and in order, and your uncle has taken care of any repairs that were needed over the years since no one has lived in it since Pearl's passing. Since I knew you were coming, I had fresh groceries delivered yesterday and all the bedrooms have fresh linen in case you decide to have company." Phoebe smiled.

Suri grinned with amusement. "I've only been here a day so I can't imagine who I would have over, but that was very kind of you."

Phoebe grasped her hand and gave it a gentle squeeze. "I have a feeling you'll be meeting people in no time. Unlike up north, there are many of us here that embrace our gift and are happy to share it with others. Why don't you come by this evening, after you get settled in. I'm having a little gathering and I think it'll do you some good to socialize."

"Thank you, Phoebe, I'll think about it." Suri surprised herself by pulling her into a hug.

Phoebe hugged her in return and she felt as if her grandmother was right there sharing in the embrace. She eased out of Phoebe's arms, wiping away tears that threatened to fall.

"I'm sorry, I haven't been sleeping well lately and I think I'm just tired," Suri said with an embarrassed grin.

"Why don't I call your uncle to pick you up and take you to the house."

"No, I'm fine, really. I still need to stop by the hotel and pick up my things."

"All right. Be sure to call me if you need anything."

Phoebe led her back downstairs through the shop.

Suri smiled gratefully. "Thank you again."

"My pleasure, child." Phoebe gently patted her cheek.

The older woman watched the younger one until she turned a corner out of sight then her smile slid from her face as she closed the door. "I may not be able to see you, but I can feel you."

Layla stepped out of the shadows toward the same display of oils Suri had been looking at when she came into the shop. "I'm not here to hurt you. I just need to know who that woman was."

The woman turned toward her. "I can't give you the answers you need. It's your journey, not mine." She went to stand behind the counter.

Layla turned to watch her curiously. "How do you know what my journey is?"

"Both your paths lead in the same direction. What road you take is yours alone to decide, but I will not let you guide that child down the wrong path if that's your intention."

Layla sighed with frustration. She was tired of beings like herself and this woman assuming they knew who she truly was. "I am not my father."

"But you are his child."

"I am my mother's child as well." Layla walked to the counter, then set a bottle of chamomile oil down with a friendly grin.

The woman narrowed her gaze at Layla then nodded. "I can see her light around you is strong. You're gonna need it in the journey ahead." She took the money Layla offered and gave her change back.

Layla nodded. "Thank you." She turned to leave.

"Come back this evening around closing. Be sure to perform a cleanse before you do, or you will not be allowed to enter."

Layla gave her a broad smile. "Thank you, Priestess."

She acknowledged Layla with a nod.

Chapter Four

Suri arrived at her grandmother's home on St. Charles Avenue a few hours later. She stood at the wrought iron gate gazing tearfully into the neatly manicured courtyard and garden. Her uncle and Phoebe had taken such good care of the property it was as if Gammy were still there. She could almost hear her grandmother's melodic humming as she tended to her rose bushes. Since her uncle moved out after her grandmother died, Suri hadn't been to the house since the week after the funeral. It was difficult for her to imagine she would be living here for at least the next year at her grandmother's request. Just to show her commitment to following Gammy's instructions, she had called the hospital where she had been working to give notice. Her manager promised to write her a glowing letter of recommendation and she planned to apply for positions at pediatrician offices at the start of the week. She no longer had the heart for being a maternity ward nurse.

It didn't hurt that, to her surprise, her grandmother had left her a very generous trust fund, consisting of several well-made investments, that came along with the house if she followed through with her requests. With the house paid off and the amount of money in the trust fund that would continue to grow with the investments made, Suri really didn't need to work, but she couldn't imagine sitting around when she could be using her time productively by helping others.

She placed the key in the lock to open the door and felt a warm tingle run through her as she stepped across the threshold.

She recognized it as a protection spell, one that she had used for her apartment in New York and her hotel room here. Leaving her bags in the foyer by the stairs, she went straight to the den where the bar was. After opening and closing cabinets, Suri grabbed a glass and the whiskey that she remembered her grandmother kept stashed away, then poured herself a shot. She drank it down quickly, letting the liquid burn a trail of fire that spread throughout her chest and plopped into her stomach. It was a good thing she had eaten at Phoebe's.

She carried the bottle and glass into the kitchen with her, set them on the island, and opened the refrigerator to see what Phoebe had left her. It was fully stocked with all the fresh fruits and vegetables, cold salads, and almond milk products that she liked. The freezer was stocked with chicken, fish, and even her favorite frozen desserts. To the average person it would be creepy that Phoebe knew so much about her without even knowing her, but Suri's life had been filled with so many creepy things that someone supplying her with all her favorite things didn't even rank high on the creep factor list. She sat on one of the stools at the kitchen island, poured herself another shot, downed it, then took the letter Phoebe gave her and laid it open next to the bottle.

My Dearest Suri,

Happy birthday, my beloved granddaughter. I wish I could be there to celebrate this moment with you. I hope my gift to you hasn't uprooted you too much from the life you had in New York. By now you have met my spiritual sister Phoebe. I know how stubborn you can be about asking for help, but please let Phoebe assist you during this journey since I'm not able to be there for you. I know my requests may seem strange to you, but they are necessary for you to fully understand and accept your gifts as well as how to use them to save not only yourself but the future of the family.

In the living room is a hidden door behind the tapestry hanging next to the bar. The key labeled Entrance in Yoruba will lead you into a great hall below the house. I hope you kept up with your Yoruba lessons as all the keys are labeled that way. The orange labeled key leads to our ancestor altar; the seven green labeled keys on the ring will get you into the remaining rooms located in the hall which houses

Orisha altars. Your uncle and Phoebe are the only other people who know of these rooms. Until you have established yourself in the home, do not enter the basement without either of them with you.

Suri gazed up from the letter and turned to look skeptically in the direction of the living room. She knew there was a basement in the house but had never figured out how to get down there. She had asked her grandmother who offered to take her once, but as soon as she opened the door Suri had felt a fear like she had never known. She had run into the other room and never asked about the basement again. Now, here she was a grown woman, with a key, and being told she still needed a chaperone to go down there. She continued reading.

Since I'm sure you studied the Book of Blessings like you were supposed to, you should already know who the Orishas are, but you will need to be trained on how to call to them before you and Phoebe venture into their domain. The Orishas will guide you on this next part of your life's journey. Heed them well. You are one of the most powerful Blessed Ones in this family. Use your gifts and trust your instincts. They will never steer you wrong.

One last thing. You will not be taking this journey alone. I know I've told you to run away when the dark forces show you their true faces, but there is one whose face will always show you the truth, despite the darkness surrounding them. Trust her and know that even when it seems all is lost that she will be the one to guide you back into the light. I love you, Lil' Bit, and I will always be here whenever you need me.

With all my love,
Gammy

Suri frowned down at the last line of the letter. Her grandmother had told her before that she'd always be with her yet, at what seemed to be one of the darkest moments of her life, her grandmother's spirit was a no-show. In fact, she hadn't come to Suri since her parents' death. The past year had been a difficult one to say the least. First, Rachel's mysterious death just after the New Year while on her honeymoon. She and Anthony had been at a beach party at a resort in Antigua when she left her husband and another couple they were hanging out with to go to the bathroom and never returned. They found her naked mutilated body two days later in a wooded area behind the resort. She had scars and burns on her as if she had been tortured and her long blond hair that she took such pride in had been raggedly cut with a knife.

Anthony had told Suri that the scars weren't just injury scars, they were symbols of some kind. He had been too devastated to take pictures, but the police had and they were shown during the trial of the resort maintenance man in whose house they found Rachel's bloody clothes. The man had claimed that he hadn't done it and didn't know how those things got there, but it was an open-and-shut case when it was revealed that skin beneath Rachel's fingernails were a DNA match for his. His family and friends had pleaded that he didn't have a violent bone in his body and would never have done such a horrible thing. Reading his energy in the courtroom, Suri believed them. She had also felt another, darker energy graying the tinge of his. She deduced that he probably didn't remember doing it because something else had taken him over and used him as a vessel to commit the crime. Unfortunately, telling the police that the suspect was innocent because a demon had taken up temporary residence in his body wouldn't fly so Suri kept that information to herself.

Just two months later, her parents were killed while waiting for a parking attendant to bring their car after a dinner celebrating their fiftieth wedding anniversary. The attendant was pulling up with the car when he suddenly hit the gas heading straight for her parents. Her father managed to shove her mother out of the way before he was crushed between the car and the parking attendant office. Unfortunately, while her father had managed to save her mother from being crushed as well, her mother's head slammed into a cement pillar killing her instantly. Her father, on the other hand, had suffered until rescue workers freed him. He died before they made it to the hospital. The parking attendant said he had no memory of the incident. He remembered up until the moment that he pulled the car around the bend, then he blacked out and came to after he crashed. It was ruled an accident and Suri had no reason to doubt it until her grandmother came to her the day of her parents' funeral.

❖

As she stood alone between her parents' caskets letting heartbreak overwhelm her, Suri felt a familiar featherlight touch but it didn't give her the comfort she so badly needed.

"Why is this happening? I know this was not an accident. I can see and smell the evil surrounding this just as I did Rachel's murder."

"Because there are forces trying to deter you from using your gifts for what they are meant for."

Suri turned angrily toward Gammy's spirit, taking notice that her form wasn't as solid as it usually was. "What are they meant for, Gammy? To help people? That's what I've been doing for most of my life. Using my gifts to help others. What more does the Creator, the Orishas, or any other spiritual being want me to do?"

Suri's pain and anger seemed to burn hot within her. Her vision began to blur with a blinding light and her breathing became erratic.

"Lil' Bit, breathe. Don't let your anger control you. I don't have much time so I need you to listen to me and listen good, child."

Gammy's voice was gentle but commanding, reaching Suri through the rage threatening to overwhelm her. She closed her eyes and took several deep breaths to slow her heart rate, followed by a quick prayer to help ease her anger. When she opened her eyes again, Gammy's image was almost translucent. She felt a sense of panic.

"Gammy, what's happening?"

"Suri, I'm sorry I didn't have enough time here in this world to prepare you for what you'll need to do, but I hope what I have been able to do will be enough. Our family has held an important task for generations. Even before our Tree of Blessed Ones was recorded. The time is coming for you to take up the duty if you choose."

Suri looked at her grandmother in confusion. "Duty? You never mentioned any kind of family task or duty before."

"Because I thought I had more time." Gammy frowned then gazed back as if someone had come up behind her. When she turned back, for the first time in her life, Suri saw fear in her grandmother's eyes. "Lil' Bit, I can't stay here. Please don't allow the dark forces to lead you astray. Hold those you love close in your heart and we'll all keep you strong. I love you."

Gammy's image faded and Suri had a strange sense that she wouldn't see her again. She turned back to look at her parents. Both looked so peaceful, but she knew, like Rachel, their final hours weren't peaceful. She closed her eyes and did what Gammy had told her to do, she held Gammy, Rachel, and her parents close to her heart. A flicker of light and hope pierced the darkness that had begun to feed off her despair and she flamed it with her love.

Just a few weeks later, Suri met Tracey, a physical therapist at the hospital where she worked. Tracey had been funny, kind, gentle, and loving. She had been strong in faith but not with any one religion. She had also been a strong believer in the supernatural. She would sit for hours reading or watching shows about ghosts, angels, demons, and people with supernatural abilities. Despite that, it had taken Suri a few months just to tell her she practiced hoodoo. Because Tracey had been well-read in the subject of spiritual practices and religions, Suri didn't need to explain to her that hoodoo and voodoo were not the same. However, she never told Tracey of her gifts, hoping that would keep her from having the same fate as Rachel and her parents. She couldn't have been more wrong.

The day of Tracey's death, Suri had been working an overnight shift when she received a frantically whispered phone call from her at three in the morning saying that someone was in her apartment. When she had tried calling the police her phone would disconnect. The only call she'd been able to get through was to Suri. As Suri had hurriedly grabbed her purse and practically ran to get out of the hospital, Tracey began crying and chanting the Lord's Prayer, then she had screamed and the line went dead. Suri had kept trying to call her back, but it had gone straight to voice mail so she called the police as she frantically waved down a cab sitting in front of the building. The police and paramedics were at Tracey's when Suri arrived. She had taken the stairs, not wanting to chance waiting for the elevator, and burst into the hallway and a cluster of tenants trying to see what was going on.

Tracey's neighbor had recognized her and encouraged the others to let her through. She explained that she heard horrible screaming coming from Tracey's apartment and immediately called the police. They had burst the door open, then came out of the apartment throwing up. Right after that, the building was swarming with police. The policeman guarding the open door had refused to let Suri in and radioed for a detective to come out, but she didn't need to go in to know that Tracey was gone. Not only could she feel Tracey's lingering fear, but the taint of death had permeated the air along with that familiar evil that had been present around Rachel and her parents' deaths. Tracey's spirit appeared in the middle of her apartment looking around in confusion until her gaze met Suri's. Everything that Tracey had endured flashed through Suri's mind like a horror film. She had closed her eyes, said a prayer for Tracey to find peace despite the violent way she'd died, then opened them to find Tracey smiling. She had blown Suri a kiss then turned to enter into a tunnel of light where shadowy figures had taken her hand to guide her away.

Suri had vowed from that moment that she wouldn't let anyone get close to her. She even kept her uncle Robert at a distance. After learning about what happened to Tracey, he said he understood. Unlike Rachel's and her parents' murderers, Tracey's had never been found. It seemed that not only had the ones she loved been taken from her, but Gammy had stopped coming to her as well. Even when Suri called out to her, her grandmother's spirit was a no-show. Now, here she was in the home that had been handed down in her family since her ancestor Athena, who had been a free Black working for a wealthy spinster with no family, was gifted the house in 1830 upon her employer's death. She didn't feel an inkling of her grandmother's presence. She looked in the direction of the basement door.

"Fuck it. What could possibly be down there that I would need a chaperone for?"

Suri went to the door, lifted the tapestry aside, and reached for the doorknob. As soon as her hand wrapped around it, her head began to throb painfully. Like when she encountered something or someone with so much power it frightened her enough to run in the other direction. Not because it was evil but because it intimidated her. She snatched her hand away so quickly that she stumbled back, almost flipping over the back of the sofa.

"Suri, are you here?"

She gazed fearfully at the tapestry once more then got up and hurried out of the room. "Hey, Uncle Robert."

"Hey, how's my favorite niece doing?" He pulled her into a bear hug.

Robert was a big man. Six foot five inches and three hundred and thirty pounds of solid mass. He was a star football player through high school and college who everyone assumed was heading to the NFL but his dream was to become a veterinarian. The family's nickname for him was Dr. Dolittle because he had a special way of understanding animals. Any member of the family could be blessed with a gift, but it was the women that were blessed the most. The men in the family were blessed with gifts like her uncle's affinity for animals, or plants, empathy, a healing touch, but nothing compared to the ability that the women were gifted.

"I'm good. Just settling in."

Pulling away, he narrowed his gaze at her. "What's wrong? You look like something scared you."

Suri gazed back toward the living room. "I tried to go into the basement."

Robert laughed. "Mama said you wouldn't be able to resist."

Suri frowned at him. "You've seen her?"

"Not for months, but the last time I did she told me to make sure I was here when you arrived so that you wouldn't get into any trouble."

She sighed with frustration. "I'm not a child anymore. Y'all don't need to babysit me."

"Nobody is here to babysit you. Phoebe and I were charged with keeping you safe until you're ready to step into your duty, that's all."

"What duty? Gammy mentioned something about it, but no one is telling me what it is. How am I supposed to decide whether I even want it if nobody is telling me anything?"

Robert cupped her cheek with his big hand. "Patience, Suri."

Suri had a sneaky suspicion that her uncle also had other gifts because his gentle touch always seemed to bring a sense of calm and peace when she was feeling anxious as a child. She felt that same effect now.

"I was just going over Gammy's letter. Anything you'd like to add?"

"Just that if you need anything, I'm right down the street. I'm sure you felt the protection spell Mama placed on the house. It'll stay there as long as you or Phoebe don't take it down."

She nodded. "Phoebe invited me to some gathering tonight. I think I'm going to take a nap before I go. I didn't sleep well last night."

He smiled in understanding. "Yeah, it's probably going to take you a lot longer than usual to settle your empath gift with all the activity going on for Halloween. Phoebe also invited me. I'll come back later to pick you up so we can go together."

"Okay."

He turned to leave then stopped and turned back to her. "Do not open this door for anybody but me and Phoebe after I leave."

"Unc, like I said, I'm not—"

"Suri, promise me that you will NOT open this door for ANYONE."

She wasn't used to seeing her jovial uncle with such a stern look on his face. "I won't open the door for anyone but you and Phoebe."

He looked relieved. "The protection spell should keep anyone looking for trouble away, but it's better to be safe than sorry. Especially this time of year."

"Don't worry, I understand." Suri was tall but still had to stand on tiptoe to give her uncle a kiss on the cheek. "I'll see you later."

He smiled affectionately then left. Suri made sure to lock both the bolt and chain lock then grabbed her suitcase and headed upstairs to the room she always stayed in when she used to come to visit. She smiled as she noticed that it had been redecorated from the pretty pink princess room it had once been to a modern adult room with touches of pink. A queen size wood and wrought iron four-poster bed with cream and sage-green bedding had replaced the pink frilly canopy twin bed. Matching dressers and nightstands had replaced the white wicker ones she remembered. The walls were changed from bright pink-and-yellow floral wallpaper to a warm off-white paint, and in place of the pictures of unicorns and Black faeries and princesses that a friend of Gammy's had painted for her, hung a mirror and a few family portraits of Suri with her parents and Gammy. She had a feeling that Phoebe had something to do with the new décor. She would have to thank her later. All she wanted to do right now was shower and lie down for a few hours. She probably shouldn't have had the whiskey because she suddenly felt bone tired.

She wearily stripped then went to the bathroom naked since there was no one in the house with her. Well, unless you counted the ancestors that had a habit of popping up every now and then to check on things. Suri figured that as free as Gammy had been walking around the house sometimes sans clothes, it wouldn't be anything new for them to see. After a quick shower she didn't even bother putting on undergarments, just crawled under the covers and fell right to sleep.

❖

Layla finished up the last of the tinctures for a private client, cleaned up her supplies, then went to the kitchen to decide what to have for dinner. Sebastian sat on one of the stools waiting patiently for his own dinner.

"What shall it be tonight, old man, salmon or tuna?"

Sebastian cocked his head to the side as if in thought then meowed.

"Salmon it is."

Layla took out the leftover salmon from dinner last night, crumbled it onto a plate, then placed it on the island in front of Sebastian. He lowered his head to daintily eat his dinner as if he was still the human from his former life. Layla never thought that she'd be one of those stereotypical witches with a cat as her familiar, but Sebastian having been a former warlock rather than a normal human had a few of his abilities carried over into his feline form. He was able to read humans' thoughts, communicate telepathically, and use telekinesis. Even though Layla also had those same abilities, it still made for a helpful companion.

As Sebastian enjoyed his meal, Layla began to slice a piece of salmon off for herself to have with a salad when she suddenly felt extremely tired.

"Meow?"

"I don't know. I must've done too much today. Connecting with that woman was a little draining." She placed the salmon back in the refrigerator. "I'm going to lie down for a bit."

Sebastian watched her with concern. "I'm fine, really. Enjoy your dinner. Just don't forget to put your plate in the sink."

By the time Layla reached her bedroom she felt as if she were trudging through mud. She lay down and immediately fell asleep. When she opened her eyes again, she was standing in the courtyard of one of those grand old homes on St. Charles Avenue in the garden district. Nearby, water trickled in a fountain, the scent of honeysuckle filled the air, and a set of French doors that led out to the courtyard stood open. Layla knew this wasn't her dream. It had been a long time since she had purposely dream walked. It happened on rare occasions when she didn't have her guards up. Someone nearby unaware of their own supernatural abilities would unconsciously latch on to hers and she would involuntarily drop into their dreams, a gift she had inherited from her father. But that wasn't the case now. Her guards were up so she shouldn't be dream walking without having initiated it.

The sound of melodic humming drifted out, calling to her like a siren's song. She usually forced herself to wake up when she ended up in someone's dream like this, but she found such a wonderful sense of peace that she didn't want to leave. She entered into the house, following the sound of the humming. She entered a modern kitchen that blended in well with the historic home. There stood the woman she had seen earlier, hand-whipping a bowl of batter as she hummed a tune that Layla recognized but couldn't place. She leaned against the doorframe watching the woman whose curly auburn hair was piled high on her head and tied with a pink-and-purple headwrap. Her outfit, a fitted pink tank top and denim shorts, gave Layla the opportunity to admire her small waist, generously rounded hips, apple-shaped bottom and long sexy legs. Her feet were bare, but her toes were done in a soft pink French pedicure that matched her fingernails. Layla smiled. There was no need to guess what her favorite color was.

She had only briefly seen the woman's face earlier, but it was enough to notice that she was beautiful.

"Who are you and why are you just standing in my doorway watching me like some creepy stalker?"

Layla had been enjoying the sight of her behind again and gazed up in surprise. The woman hadn't turned around. She continued adding ingredients to another bowl without missing a beat.

"I'm Layla and I was hoping you'd tell me."

"Hi, Layla. I'm Suri. Were you hoping I could tell you why you're crashing my dream uninvited or why you're a creepy stalker?" Suri poured the batter into a square cake tin then sprinkled the crumbled mixture from the other bowl on top before bending over to place the pan in the oven giving Layla a delicious view that made her palms itch to grab a handful.

"I'll take crashing your dream for a hundred, Alex."

Suri turned with a friendly smile that didn't hide the suspicion in her gaze. "I guess we should talk." She offered Layla a chair at the island as she sat at one as well.

"You act as if you were expecting me."

"Yes and no. My grandmother told me I would be meeting someone to help me with a task. Since we saw each other earlier and now you're in my dream, I'm going to take a wild guess and say that you're that someone."

"What task? You don't seem to be thrilled about it."

"It's because I don't know who, or should I say, what you are."

"You could always ask me." Layla gave her a teasing grin.

"Okay. What are you, Layla? Your energy confuses me. I feel a strong power and energy within you that I recognize as a supernatural being, but there's also a darkness behind your light that I've spent most of my life trying to avoid."

"I'm a cambion."

Suri's eyes widened in surprise then she slid from the chair to back slowly away. Layla hated seeing the sudden fear in her bright hazel gaze. "You have nothing to fear with me. I've learned to subdue that side of me."

"You were born a cambion, how do you subdue what's in your nature?"

"By not letting my baser nature take over. If one of my parents was a serial killer, would that make me a serial killer by nature?"

Suri frowned. "Why, of all the comparisons, would you choose that one?"

Layla chuckled. "It was honestly the only one to pop into my head. Guess it's just in my nature."

Suri rolled her eyes in exasperation.

"So, I told you what I was. Now it's your turn. I haven't met any being as powerful as you in a very long time."

Not only could Layla feel Suri's power rolling off her like a wave of heat, but she could tell that she hadn't even tapped into the deep well of her abilities.

"That's probably because you're in a home that has housed generations of powerful women. I'm just one in a long line of many."

Layla didn't believe that for a minute. Although she could feel the power of Suri's ancestors in every nook and cranny of the house, Suri's abilities far surpassed many of them, but she wasn't going to be the one to tell her that.

The oven beeped, snapping them both out their perusal of the other. Suri grabbed oven mitts before opening the door and pulling out the most wonderful smelling cake. It brought a memory from her childhood when her grandmother used to bake a similar cake for the Crawfords and would sneak a small piece for Layla while it was still hot from the oven.

"Is that coffee cake?"

Suri smiled knowingly as she sliced a small piece, smoke rising from it as she placed it on a plate. "She said you would like this." She set it in front of Layla.

Layla closed her eyes and inhaled the warm cinnamon scent. "Who?"

"She said her name was Ruth."

A sudden ache rippled through Layla's heart. "She spoke to you?"

"She gave me the recipe and told me to be sure to serve it right out of the oven just the way you like it."

Layla narrowed her gaze at Suri trying to read any deception in her words. She could sense her genuineness. Obviously, her mother and Suri's grandmother were scheming somewhere in the afterlife to get them together. Layla didn't partner with anyone, not since Cora

Lee passed on, but she would play along until she found out what all of this was about. In the meantime, she took a bite of the soft pillowy cake, sighed happily over the warm rich cinnamon in the crumble that melted in her mouth, then asked, "You wouldn't happen to have a glass of cold milk?"

Suri chuckled. "She told me you'd want that too." She removed a frosty glass of milk from the refrigerator and set it before Layla.

"Thank you. You're not going to just stand there watching me eat, are you?"

Suri gazed at her for a moment then cut a slice of the cake, poured herself a glass of what looked like sweet tea, then sat back down beside Layla. "I have to say, this is the weirdest, while also the most normal, dream I've ever had."

Layla smiled. "You and me both."

They continued eating their cake in companionable silence.

CHAPTER FIVE

A beeping sound pulled Suri from her dream with a start. She gazed around the room confused by her surroundings before she remembered where she was. She turned off her phone alarm then flopped back with a tired sigh as she tried to recall her dream before it dissipated into a distant memory.

"Gammy, of all the beings in this world, why this one?"

There was no response, and she honestly hadn't expected one. She didn't know what was keeping her grandmother's spirit away, but it was serious enough that she didn't even feel safe coming to her own home. She wished that she could just lie in bed the rest of the night, but she didn't want her uncle or Phoebe to come looking for her. She would have to ask Phoebe about her dream. She knew deep down that Layla was the woman Gammy mentioned in her letter, but the fact that she was a cambion frightened her enough to hope that she was wrong.

Suri looked through her suitcase for something to wear. It was New Orleans in October, so layering was probably best just in case the weather took a turn. She decided on a dark pink lightweight sweater set with jeans and denim slip-on shoes, then fluffed her hair out, deciding to wear her mass of curls loose. Satisfied with her look, she went downstairs to wait for her uncle and stopped at the bottom when the smell of cinnamon drifted to her from the kitchen. She had never had any lingering scents or tastes from her dreams follow her into the real world before. She walked hesitantly into the kitchen and halted in the doorway at the sight of an untouched coffee cake cooling on the stove.

Already freaked out by the cake, the sound of keys in the front door had her jumping in fright. Her uncle entered and stopped when he saw her standing there.

"Are you okay? You didn't try to go in the basement again, did you?"

Suri tried to calm her racing heart. "No. I'm just not used to the weird stuff that happens in this house."

Robert chuckled. "Yeah, it took me a while to get used to it again when I came back home to take care of Mama."

Suri turned and went into the kitchen. She might as well bring it to Phoebe's gathering. No sense in coming empty-handed.

"You baked?"

"I guess so." She placed the cake into a cake carrier.

"Do I want to know?" he asked with amusement.

"I'm not sure if I even know."

"Well, it smells good. Are you ready?"

"Yep."

When they arrived at Phoebe's they went up the side stairs to her apartment. Phoebe was at the door waiting to let them in.

"You're the last to arrive. Oh, you didn't need to bring anything." Phoebe took the cake carrier from her.

"Apparently, somebody thought I needed to."

Phoebe gazed at her in confusion.

Suri waved dismissively. "I'll explain later."

"Okay. Well, c'mon in."

Suri followed Phoebe into the apartment. After the short walk from the entryway to the foyer, she turned to find five people smiling and looking expectantly at her. Suri smiled back until the sight of one of them made her pause, causing her uncle to bump into her. He caught her before she fell on her face.

"What are you doing here?"

Layla shrugged. "I was invited."

"I take it you two have already met," Phoebe said.

Suri gazed at her in confusion. "You know each other?"

"Not before she came into the shop this afternoon."

"And you just invited her into your home. Do you know what she is?"

Phoebe took the cake out of the carrier and set it on the kitchen island among other snacks and desserts. "Yes, I do. I also know that her presence is vital to what we need to discuss this evening. Since we're all here, why doesn't everyone introduce themselves to Suri and grab some food so we can get started."

"You brought the coffee cake," Layla said with a pleased smile.

"I guess I'm the only one that didn't know you'd be here."

Before Layla could respond, a beautiful woman with long golden blond hair, the bluest eyes Suri had ever seen, and who probably stood no taller than four feet, offered her hand in greeting.

"Hello, Suri, I'm Leandra. Your grandmother was a godsend and taken from us far too soon. If there is anything you need while you're here, please don't hesitate to ask. I own a boutique on O'Keefe Avenue in the Arts District."

Suri took her hand and felt immense light and love from her energy. "It's nice to meet you, Leandra."

Next was a man almost as big as her uncle, his smooth, bald ebony head glistened under the light, and his face was beautifully made-up with emphasis on his deep brown eyes. He was dressed in bright, colorful bohemian attire and bold red painted finger and toenails. She felt a wild but kind energy coming from him.

"Miss Suri, I'm Rory. I have a hair salon over on Magazine Street and I do drag performances at the Red Velvet. You are definitely Miss Pearl's grandchild with all that hair and those eyes. You absolutely must let me style it."

"It's nice to meet you as well, Rory, and I'll consider it."

Then came a young dark-haired woman with pale, almost translucent skin, dressed in dark baggy attire. She barely gazed up at Suri when she offered her hand.

"Hi, I'm Cassandra," was all she said before hurrying away, not even giving Suri a chance to read her.

"You'll have to excuse Cassandra. She's not good with living people. I'm Kenya."

Kenya looked as if she had just walked in off the set of *The Real Housewives of Atlanta*. Her hair, makeup, jewelry and attire were all sophisticated, fashionable, and expensive. When Suri took her hand, she felt an ancient and powerful energy. It wasn't anything she feared, but she also knew that she couldn't judge Kenya by her appearance.

"It's a pleasure to meet you."

"Same to you. If you ever need anything." She gave Suri an appraising look then offered her a business card. "Call me." The card was made of heavy cardstock and simply read, *Kenya Lane, Lane Realty,* with a phone number printed in gold foil.

Suri held back a grin. "I'll do that."

She watched Kenya walk away noticing the sexy sway of her hips.

"She'd eat you alive. Probably literally. It's how she stays looking so good and so rich."

Suri gave Layla an annoyed side-eye. The plate she held had a huge slice of the coffee cake she'd brought. "Did you save some for anyone else?"

"Of course, I'm not completely uncouth. I just figured since you made it for me, I was entitled to the largest slice."

Suri turned to face Layla. "Look, I don't know why my grandmother and Phoebe believe you're important to whatever this task is that everyone keeps mentioning, but unlike them, I'm not so easily trusting. If I get the smallest inkling that you're out to hurt any of my family I will end you." The vehemence in Suri's words surprised her. She was not someone who threatened people like that.

Layla's eyes widened. "Whoa, I'm just as clueless about what this is all about as you are. I'm just here for information," she held up her plate with a grin, "and coffee cake. You won't have any problems from me."

"Okay, folks, let's get started," Phoebe announced.

Suri shook her head in exasperation then hurried over to the island to grab something to eat since she hadn't had dinner. She skipped the coffee cake and opted for a small sandwich from a platter and a glass of sweet tea then joined the others. Her uncle made room for her on the sofa between him and Leandra. Phoebe and Kenya sat on the loveseat on the other side of the sofa, Rory lounged dramatically on a chaise beneath the window, Layla sat in a side chair, and Cassandra sat on the floor looking as if she were trying to make herself invisible. It was an eclectic group of people.

Suri gazed over at Layla who seemed to also be looking over the group that was gathered. Their eyes locked and a vision of them sitting quietly together enjoying the coffee cake she had made in her dream popped into her mind. Layla must have had the same thought because she gave Suri a soft smile and nodded before looking away to focus on Phoebe who Suri hadn't realized was speaking.

❖

"I know it's been some time since the entire group met in person because of busy schedules, so I truly appreciate you all coming out tonight to welcome Suri home." Phoebe directed a warm smile at Suri.

Layla gazed back at her as she blushed prettily. No, she was far more than pretty. Her fiery auburn hair haloed around her gently angular face, falling in thick curls and waves down her back making Layla want to just bury her face in the softness. Her bright hazel eyes drew her in like a beacon in the night, and her intense, powerful nature, made Suri breathtaking. The only problem was that Layla avoided getting involved with other supernatural beings. It always ended up in a power struggle that she had no desire or patience for.

"I'd like to thank Layla for joining us as well."

Everyone but Suri nodded in her direction.

"I appreciate the invitation. I'm curious to find out how I fit into whatever is going on."

Phoebe smiled. "Well then, let's get to it. First, Suri, I'm sure you're wondering why Pearl never mentioned any of this to you."

"I am."

"It's because we had to make sure you were ready to take on your duties before she did. Her plan was to teach and guide you until this moment, but it seems the Creator had other plans for her. So, she did what she could from beyond to get you here. Now it's up to us to assist you with the rest. To do that, I will have to step into Pearl's shoes to be your guide and reveal what she had hoped to be here to do herself."

Leandra clapped gleefully. "This is so exciting!"

"Leandra," Kenya reprimanded her like a mother hen.

Layla looked suspiciously at Kenya. She didn't trust her as far as she could throw her.

"The feeling is mutual, demon spawn," Kenya's voice said in her head.

Layla quirked a brow. *"Call me demon spawn again and we'll actually see how far I really can throw you."*

"Don't let these red bottoms fool you. I can get grimy with the best, and worst, of any of your kind."

"Promises, promises."

Kenya turned her head slightly to shoot daggers at Layla. *"I will no longer disrespect our priestess with this nonsense."*

Layla smirked. *"Another time then."* She brought her attention back to Phoebe.

"Suri, you already know some of your family tree, but what hasn't been recorded in the books she gave to guide you is your family's true legacy."

Phoebe looked to Robert who stood, held his hands out with his palm up, closed his eyes, then quietly spoke an incantation that made a scroll appear in his hands. Suri gasped and looked at him in surprise. It was obvious she didn't know of her uncle's abilities. He gave her a mischievous wink then unrolled the scroll.

"As you know, the men in our family aren't blessed with many of the gifts that the women are, but what you don't know is that what we are blessed with is used to take on the role of protector to the guardians of the gateways. Suri, you come from a long line of guardians that began centuries ago with our first known guardian ancestor, Ayomide, a descendant of Oduduwa."

"Wait, you're telling me that our family are descendants from an Orisha deity?" Suri said in disbelief.

Robert smiled. "Yes. Oduduwa was a mortal who possessed supernatural powers before he became deified. He had sixteen children, some of whom he made kings in different territories of the Motherland. We are descendants of his daughter Alaketu."

Layla found herself just as shocked as Suri. Her father knew of the Orisha Gods, had even told her of dealings he had with Elegua, known as the trickster, but he never once mentioned living descendants of an Orisha here in New Orleans.

"As I was saying," Robert continued, "Ayomide's parentage led to her being very powerful. Her supernatural abilities were perceived as gifts of blessings from the Gods themselves. The Gods that they worshipped, and that we still worship to this day—the Orishas. She grew to become a respected priestess who used her great powers for the good of the Yoruba people and honoring the Orishas. When the Yoruba empire fell and our people were taken to be sold as slaves across the sea, Yemaya, Orisha of the waters who heard their cries of despair, asked Ayomide to allow herself to be captured and sold into slavery so that she may be the goddess's physical embodiment to continue to protect and guide our people in this new world on the traditions and faiths of our Yoruba culture. That is how our family ended up here in Louisiana. Ayomide's sacrifice and devotion led to her not only becoming the first guardian to gateways between our world and the Orishas but being deified and given Orisha status when she passed. She is our family's personal Orisha and the one that we worship directly. She is our family's voice when speaking to the higher Orishas."

Layla gazed around at everyone listening to Robert with rapt attention while all she could think about was why hadn't her father told her any of this? He had to have known about Suri's family. How did she fit into all of this? Her mother's spirit, Suri's grandmother, and now this roomful of worshippers and hoodoo practitioners all believed she and Suri were tied somehow to whatever task was connected to the legacy Robert was repeating for Suri.

"Patience, daughter, all will be revealed. Once you are finished there, I'll be waiting to talk at your place."

"Oh, now you want to talk."

Layla heard a deep chuckle, then felt a mental door shut as her father closed her off from further communication. For two hundred years, she had managed to keep as low a profile as possible, and in one day she found herself entangled with a family descended from a deity who just so happened to be a part of a legacy of guardians to pathways between worlds. What more could she possibly be in store for?

Suri's mind was reeling from what her uncle was telling her. One of her ancestors was an Orisha. Not just any Orisha but the one that mythology said was the right hand to Obatala, the Great Creator,

Olodumare's, son. He was the god that is considered the creator of all humans who Olodumare breathed life into. How was that even possible? If that wasn't shocking enough, Robert was telling her that the women in her family had served as guardians between our world and the Orisha world for centuries. Was that why her grandmother had her come to New Orleans? She was suddenly overwhelmed with panic.

"Wait, are you saying Gammy had me brought here to be a guardian?" She didn't mean to shout, but this was all unbelievable.

Robert looked annoyed at being interrupted. "I would've gotten to that if you'd let me finish the telling of our history, but long story short, yes. You were brought here to DECIDE whether you wanted to pick up where Mama left off."

"So, I don't have to do this? I can say no?"

Robert looked confused now. "Yes, but why would you?"

Suri felt immense relief. "Why wouldn't I? You're asking me to pick up and leave my life behind to come here and basically be a bouncer for some doorways leading to gods. That may sound like a cool job for the average Jane, but it sounds dangerous to me. And where are these gateways anyway…" That's when her grandmother's warnings made sense. "The basement. There are freaking gateways to the heavens in Gammy's basement!"

She stood and began pacing. "You've got to be kidding me! How is that even possible?" She stopped, gazing wide-eyed at her uncle. "Did Mommy know this? You all were raised in that house, she had to have known, right? That's why she was so fearful of me being blessed."

"Suri, honey, sit down. Let me finish and you'll understand," Robert said in that tone he used to calm her, but it didn't work this time.

"You lied to me. All these years you made me believe that it was just me and Aria, but you also have more gifts than you let on. You're an empath, it's how you've been able to calm me down since I was a baby. You can also teleport." She pointed to the scroll in his hands. "What else can you do?"

"I didn't lie, I just didn't tell you everything. You weren't ready."

Suri threw her hands in the air. "Oh, I'm sorry, you lied by omission. That's so much better. What else can you do!"

"I have superhuman strength, but that's only during a supernatural fight."

He said it so matter-of-factly. "Do you get into fights like that often?"

He grinned sheepishly. "There have been a few."

Suri felt hysterical laughter bubbling up. "This is crazy," she said before letting it loose. She laughed so hard that her stomach hurt and tears were coming out of her eyes.

"I think we may have pushed her too quickly," Phoebe said.

"You didn't push her. This is nothing compared to what's coming." Kenya walked over, grabbed Suri by the shoulders, and gave her a slap across the face. "Snap out of it! We don't have time to coddle you through this!"

Before Suri could react, Layla was by her side and had Kenya by the throat with her feet dangling inches off the floor. One of her expensive shoes slid off her foot.

"Touch her again and you won't see another full moon," Layla growled, her eyes glowing blood red.

No one moved for a moment as Kenya struggled to breathe, clawing anxiously at Layla's fingers around her throat.

"Layla, please release Ms. Lane so that we may continue," Phoebe said with a grin.

Suri didn't find any of this amusing. Especially being slapped. Layla hesitantly lowered and released Kenya whose own eyes began to glow with an inhuman light, and a low animalistic growl rumbled from her as she stepped threateningly in Layla's face.

Layla grinned. "Try it."

"If you two are insistent on this battle of wills, please take it outside. I would prefer my home and shop not to be destroyed. It took too long to rebuild after Katrina."

Suri thought for sure that they would take it outside, but Layla seemed to back down first when her eyes returned to normal and she relaxed her stance. It took Kenya another moment. It wasn't until she turned to the love seat that Suri noticed her fingernails had elongated into claws and were retracting as she gave Phoebe a slight bow.

"Apologies, Priestess."

Phoebe nodded then brought her attention back to Layla who still stood beside Suri protectively. "Robert, it seems Pearl was right about this one."

"Have you ever known her to be wrong?"

"No, but there's always a first."

Suri looked from Phoebe to her uncle and back. "What was she right about?"

"That you would need a protector whose emotional attachment wouldn't endanger you when the time comes to perform your task."

Suri looked at Layla who frowned at Phoebe. "I'm not here to be somebody's bodyguard."

Phoebe shrugged. "As with Suri, the choice is yours. Might I suggest you take some time to think it over, but not too much. Time is of the essence."

This was all too much. Why would her grandmother not have told her any of this during the years she'd been guiding Suri? "What happens if we decide we don't want to do it?"

"Then our family, Ayomide's legacy, ends here. You are currently the only one in our family with the gifts to be a guardian. No other members, including distant cousins, have displayed signs of the abilities needed to take on the role," Robert said.

"The house would stay in the family, but there will be no one to be there to protect the gateways, leaving an opening for darker forces to use them for their own means," Phoebe said.

"What other forces?" Layla asked before Suri had a chance to.

Phoebe gazed over at Robert who looked as if he were about to be sick. "Aria, her vodun priestess, and whatever misguided demonic forces they've collected."

Suri felt his heartsickness as if it were her own. What would drive Aria to want to destroy her own family?

"Are you talking about Aria Dark, the consort to Priestess Sojourn?" Layla now looked as if she were about to be sick.

Robert's gaze narrowed on Layla. "Yes."

Layla shook her head with a heavy sigh. "Shit."

"I take it you know her," Suri said.

"Yeah, I'm the reason Priestess Sojourn was driven out of New Orleans."

"That was you?" Kenya said in amazement.

Suri gazed around the room and noticed everyone looking at Layla in awe. "Does anyone want to clue me in?"

Layla sat on the arm of the sofa. "Priestess Sojourn is a practitioner of dark magic. She's under the deluded impression that she is the reincarnation of Marie Laveau, which is laughable to say the least, especially since I knew Marie and Sojourn couldn't hold a candle to her. Many years ago, Priestess Sojourn, formerly known as Barbara French, was a PhD psychologist working as a therapist while practicing voodoo on the down low. As her followers grew, so did her greed for power. Rather than using her fancy degree and knowledge of voudon to help our community like the rest of us voodoo and hoodoo practitioners were doing, she chose to manipulate folks to become worshippers in her personal cult. The only problem was that she had no supernatural abilities. She made offering after offering to the voodoo loa and never received anything in return. Then she turned to the Orishas, but once again, nothing."

"If her offerings had been made with a pure and open heart then she probably would've been blessed, but they all knew what she did in the dark," Phoebe said.

Layla nodded. "All her sessions connected with the loa were smoke, mirrors, and mind games just to milk as much money out of folks as she could. When her followers started catching on to the ruse, they began leaving her. She made one final plea, but this time she turned to a darker more agreeable force who was willing to do anything to walk amongst humans again. An evil spirit who had been a dark arts practitioner herself centuries ago had heard Sojourn's plea. She came to her in the guise of a minor Orisha promising to appeal to the Gods on her behalf if she found a vessel for her to occupy for just twenty-four hours as a human to see her family once again. She agreed and offered her the perfect vessel. A young woman with powerful abilities of her own and obviously, from what I now know, a connection to a very powerful family."

Suri's heart ached with a grief that wasn't her own. She gazed up to see tears pouring from her uncle's eyes as he silently wept. "Aria."

He nodded and sat on the sofa. Leandra reached up to wipe a tear away, their love for each other obvious in their eyes. She was happy her uncle had found someone after all these years and almost smiled at the image they must have made walking down the street together.

"So, Sojourn got her powers, and this spirit has become a squatter in my cousin's body."

"Not just a squatter. Since your cousin was so young at the time, and it's now been about thirty years since this happened, they are intertwined in a way that could be dangerous for Aria's soul if you tried to expel the spirit," Layla explained.

"Are you saying that Aria could die?"

"Yes."

Suri found that she needed to sit down now. "What the hell did I get myself into coming here?" She looked back at Layla. "So how are you responsible for driving Sojourn and Aria out of town?"

"Sojourn became very powerful and began wreaking death and destruction within the community. It was well-known that Sojourn's consort had the ability to heal or harm. With an evil spirit's powers merged with hers, Aria's abilities strengthened, and Sojourn took full advantage of it. Powerful and respected priests, priestesses, and practitioners from every religion and magical practice including Wicca that spoke out against Sojourn began disappearing or were struck down by incurable illnesses and diseases. Their worshippers and covens were bullied and threatened to join Sojourn's followers. Because she had obtained her abilities through dark means, only someone more powerful could stop her."

"That someone was you."

Layla smiled sadly. "I wish that was the case. Not to say I'm not powerful, but her power grew with the more worshippers she obtained. I'm a hoodoo practitioner. I don't have worshippers pumping me up to make me powerful enough to take her out alone. All I could do was weaken and drive her out of town."

"Your demon daddy couldn't help you?" Kenya said sarcastically.

Layla gave her a bored look. "I'm sure he would have if I'd asked, but unlike some, I don't need Daddy to step in to fight my battles." That brought a low growl from Kenya, then Layla directed her attention back to Suri. "I also do my best not to take a life unless it's necessary."

THE BLESSED

Suri couldn't imagine what would make it necessary for Layla to take someone's life. "So now she's had decades to build her strength and is coming back for revenge."

Layla nodded. "Not against your family directly."

"She wants revenge on the Orisha, and my family is in the way." A thought occurred to Suri. She turned to her uncle. "I could be wrong since I was so young and didn't pay much attention, but if I do remember correctly, Gammy was as healthy and strong as a woman half her age. When did she develop heart issues?"

Robert gazed over at Phoebe, who nodded. He turned back to Suri. "For as long as I remember, Mama barely caught a cold, she was eating clean before it became a fad, and she walked at least five miles a day. Then one day she decided to confront Dr. French about Aria and a week later, she was having trouble breathing. I took her to the doctor, and they diagnosed her with congestive heart failure."

Suri's own heart ached for her grandmother being taken away from her while she was so young. She might not be able to see herself killing anyone, but she could hurt them for robbing her family of such a beautiful soul. "Did she know what was going to happen?"

"She did," Phoebe said. "But Pearl was obstinate. She was determined to get Aria back into the family fold and believed that whatever would happen was meant to happen."

Suri wasn't surprised to hear that her grandmother was willing to sacrifice her life to get Aria back. Family meant everything to her. Gazing around a roomful of people who, except for her uncle, she had never met until today, as they watched her expectantly waiting for her to step into her grandmother's role as if it were as easy as sliding on a pair of slippers was too much. She might look like her grandmother, but that's where the similarities ended. Suri wasn't cut out for a battle with voodoo priestesses and demons to protect Orishas that didn't seem to do a very good job at protecting the family they had chosen to be their guardian. Aria, her grandmother, her parents, all gone and these people expected her to happily put her life on the line as well.

Suri shook her head. "I'm not my grandmother." She stood to leave, catching Layla's sympathetic smile on the way out of Phoebe's apartment.

CHAPTER SIX

Layla kept to the shadows as she made sure Suri arrived home safely, then she transported to her apartment. She arrived to find her father, Isfet, lounging on the chaise end of her sofa eating a pint of vanilla ice cream while watching an episode of the television series *Lucifer*.

"I hope that isn't my last pint."

"Of course not. I made sure to bring several more just in case. I know how much you enjoy it."

Layla loved crumb cake, but her favorite treat was plain vanilla ice cream. The simplicity of it gave her a sense of calm and comfort in a life so full of complications. She should've brought a slice of Suri's cake home to have with a scoop. She sat beside him.

"Did you know that Morningstar often took sabbaticals like the one they humorously portray on this show?" Isfet never referred to his fellow fallen angel as Lucifer, Satan, or any of the common names Morningstar was known as. She also knew he was stalling.

"Interesting. Did you know about Suri's family?"

"Yes."

"For how long?"

He shrugged casually. "Since the birth of their first ancestor."

"Then I'm assuming that you knew where things would end up."

"Of course. So does your mother. Did you know that I brought her here once while she was pregnant with you? She worried that you would be tempted to follow in my footsteps, so I brought her here to the time just after the flood waters from Katrina receded and you were helping to organize shelters and food for the survivors." Her father smiled wistfully. "She was so proud of you. It was worth the torture I suffered when I returned to Hell."

Despite what Isfet was, Layla never liked hearing that he was punished for caring about his family. He may be a top-tier-level demon and incubus, but he still had the heart of the angel he once was.

"So, if what Suri's grandmother saw is destined to happen, then I guess I don't have much choice but to be a part of it." Layla slumped into the sofa. Why couldn't she just have a quiet boring life practicing hoodoo and doing as little as possible to attract attention to herself.

Isfet paused the television show and faced her. "You always have a choice, daughter. The options may not be to your liking but, like Suri, you won't be forced to choose one over the other."

Layla chuckled. "Some options. Walk away and watch the world fall into chaos or accept the role as protector to a future minor Orisha preparing for a supernatural battle."

Isfet grinned. "The choice just might be made for you if Suri decides that she doesn't want to accept her role in this."

Layla recalled the argument she heard Suri had going on with herself in her head as she made her way home from the meeting. "Oh, she may be hesitant right now, but she'll accept it."

Layla was surprised to see the look of relief on her father's face. "Is there something you're not telling me?"

"It's more like something I'm hesitant to tell you."

Layla gazed at him expectantly as he scraped and ate the last of the ice cream out of the container then set it on her coffee table. "There are even darker forces at work here than Sojourn and her lackies. Suri has barely tapped into her powers which rival those of her ancestor Ayomide. If she were to fall under darker influences, not even I could intervene to stop what could happen."

"What darker influences are you referring to?"

He glanced at the television screen. Layla looked to see the lead character Lucifer grinning charmingly, then she looked wide-eyed back to her father who frowned.

"Morningstar?"

"If only. I'd at least be able to talk some sense into him. Maybe offer to cover while he took another sabbatical, but it's someone far more cunning."

It only took a moment for Layla to realize who he was referring to. "Lilith."

Isfet nodded. "She's wanting her own sabbatical, and Suri would be the perfect vessel for her to take it in."

"Shit."

"Exactly."

They both sat quietly contemplating the hell that would literally come to earth if Lilith, Adam's first wife, the queen of the demons, came to earth and possessed a powerful supernatural like Suri.

"Can't Morningstar do something to stop her?"

Isfet laughed. "Has he been able to tell Lilith anything? You know as well as I do that if Father Himself couldn't force her stay with Adam that Morningstar has no control over her. She just likes to make him think he does, then she does whatever the hell she wants and what she wants is Suri. She's the reason for the darkness growing within her. I'm sure you felt it."

Layla had. That first time she saw Suri from her balcony. "How?"

"It's true that Sojourn and her consort were ultimately responsible for her grandmother's death, but the loss of her parents, best friend, and girlfriend were all Lilith. She couldn't get to Suri surrounded by the protection of loved ones so she took them away to make her vulnerable."

Layla knew what loss could do to a person. She'd experienced it the day Jonas took her virginity. The darkness that she had managed to keep at bay with the help of her mother's spirit had overwhelmed her and she'd almost killed him.

"Now that she's vulnerable, what's kept Lilith from taking her over."

"She's waiting for Suri to come into her full power."

"So, all she has to do is settle in without all the work."

"Precisely."

Layla had seen the havoc a supernatural human possessed by a minor demon could cause. She could only imagine what terror a high-level demon like Lilith possessing Suri would bring about.

Layla sighed heavily. "I guess I better up my training."

"You might also want to take a dip in Miss Suri's dreams tonight for a little discussion. Time is of the essence."

"No more dream walking for now. I won't gain her trust if I'm sneaking in and out of her head. Earlier this afternoon was not my doing. I'll drop by her place in the morning. Now, if you'll excuse me. I have work to do. Also, where's Sebastian? I haven't seen him since I came in."

"I'm in the bedroom. You know I'm not a fan of your father." Came Sebastian's voice in her head.

"You two really need to figure out how to get along," Layla said out loud for both to hear.

Isfet shrugged. "It's not my fault the little beast goes into heat whenever I'm near."

"He acts as if he has no control over his incubus nature, but that's not true. He does it on purpose," Sebastian whined in her head.

Layla ran her fingers over her braids in frustration. "Enough! I don't care what either of you do. I'll be in my workroom."

Her father chuckled as she left, then she heard the television come back on. She knew he was only staying to further annoy Sebastian. Isfet wasn't into bestiality, but he could sense Sebastian's human nature and took great pleasure in antagonizing it by using his incubus nature to drive Sebastian into heat despite him being neutered. It drove Layla just as crazy because he became pushy and demanding for attention, wanting to go out so much that she had to leave her window open so that he could come and go as he pleased, then there was the vocalizing in the middle of the night, when her father decided to drop in while she was sleeping to *check* on her. She threatened to cast Isfet from her apartment if he continued with the late-night torturing of her familiar. Now he just kept it to the rare occasions he dropped by like tonight. She could hear Sebastian's low mewling as he tried to resist it, so she went up to her bedroom, opened the window, and heard a nonverbal sigh of relief as he hurried out of the apartment. Then she entered her workroom from the adjoining door in her bedroom.

As Layla climbed a step ladder to grab the chest where she kept her mojo bags, her father stepped into the room.

"Party pooper."

"Since when do you enjoy torturing defenseless creatures?"

He sat on a stool next to her worktable. "Sebastian is far from defenseless. He wasn't so squeamish about me dropping in his dreams when he was human."

Layla gazed suspiciously over at him. "You knew each other?"

"He didn't tell you?"

"No."

"It was a couple of centuries ago. He was a warlock that ran in the same circles as a young witch I was seeing. We met at a gathering, he knew what I was, flirted and let me know that he'd always been curious about incubi. I visited him regularly at night until he became too demanding, so I stopped."

"In other words, you ghosted him."

Isfet chuckled. "I've come to like that phrase. Yes, I ghosted him."

"Did he know that you were my father when he ended up on my doorstep?"

"No, I think fate had a hand in that. He was just as surprised to see me that first time as I was to see him reincarnated as a cat. Kind of a cruel twist of fate for such a powerful being to end up a house pet."

"Not too surprising if he was being punished for past transgressions." Layla opened the chest and removed the mojo bags she had stored in it. She could feel the energy waning in some of them because she hadn't kept up with re-energizing them like she should have.

"Anything I could help with?" Isfet's question surprised her. His expression turned serious. "Morningstar as well as a few arches upstairs are just as desperate to keep Lilith from accomplishing her goal as we are. They can't interfere without possibly starting a war that could pretty much destroy humanity, but since I keep low under the radar, Lilith doesn't pay me any mind."

Layla placed a hand on her father's arm with a soft smile. "I appreciate any help you can provide."

As they worked together into the early hours of the morning, Layla was reminded of the years he spent teaching her everything she knew about hoodoo, voodoo, and dark magic and felt that familial bond that she hadn't felt in a very long time.

❖

Suri sat on the floor with her back against the sofa staring at the door to the basement. She could feel the immense power coming from whatever, or whomever, was down there. She'd barely practiced hoodoo, made offerings, or said a prayer since Tracey's death. All she felt was anger toward any Gods and Goddesses that would allow everyone she loved to be taken away from her when she had been so faithful since the day that she opened the Book of Blessings. Decades of her life dedicated to helping others, praying, and making offerings to the Orishas, and doing everything she could to live up to her grandmother's expectations. What did she have to show for that dedication? Heartbreak. Now they were asking her to literally put her own life on the line to protect those very beings that had not been there when she needed them the most.

The anger manifested itself in a dark ball in the center of her chest. Reaching its spindly tentacles toward her heart. Suri didn't try to stop it. She just reached down to stick her hand in the economy bag of miniature chocolate bars that she'd been eating for the past twenty minutes. She unwrapped one, not caring which flavor it was, shoved the candy into her mouth, then balled up and tossed the wrapper at the door. It landed on the floor among the dozens of others she had thrown there.

"You're not going to sleep well tonight. You never did if you had too much chocolate before bed."

Suri stopped chewing for a moment, allowing the chocolate to melt on her tongue as she decided whether to ignore her grandmother.

"Are you really going to give me the silent treatment?"

She swallowed the remnants of candy. "I'm thinking about it."

She closed her eyes, then took a deep cleansing breath to dispel the darkness. She felt it hesitantly retreating and had to pour more energy than usual to keep it at bay but she managed to reduce it back to the kernel-size irritation it had been for months now, then she turned toward her grandmother who sat on the floor beside her. Her spirit was still as transparent as it had been when she last came to her.

"You kept all of this from me for years. Why?" She didn't bother tempering her anger.

Gammy gave her a sad smile. "Because you weren't ready and I thought we had more time, but I hadn't foreseen all that was coming until it was too late."

"What does that mean? Phoebe and Uncle Robert said you foresaw all of this."

"Not all of it. Some things were set into motion out of my sight. It does have its limits. Especially when more powerful beings are involved."

Suri didn't like the worried look on her grandmother's face. "Gammy, please, no more secrets. What is going on? Why should I bother with any of this when I've gotten nothing but heartbreak for my efforts so far?"

Gammy placed her hand on Suri's cheek. The touch was like the edge of a feather brushing her skin. "My poor Lil' Bit. I know this is a lot and I'm about to pile more onto it, but this is no longer about what's behind that door or protecting our family's legacy. What's coming is coming for you directly and has been for some time now. You are going to need all your faith, strength, and power to save not just all who are here to support you but your very soul."

Suri saw the fear in her grandmother's eyes, mirrors to the eyes that she had inherited. "This isn't just about Sojourn and Aria, is it?"

"No. A being more powerful than any I've ever encountered has taken interest in you and I fear that you've already allowed her in without even realizing it."

Suri frowned. "Into where? As far as I'm aware, no one has been in the house except Uncle Robert since I arrived this afternoon. Well, at least not physically," she said, remembering Layla being in her dream.

"I'm not referring to Layla, although, it wouldn't be a bad idea for her to stay here with you for added protection." Suri started to argue, but her grandmother continued. "I'm referring to Lilith, mother of demons."

Suri snorted in derision. "What could such a formidable demon want from me?"

"You don't realize it yet because I wasn't able to help as I intended, but you've barely scratched the surface of your gifts, Suri. Your uncle has told you about our ancestor Ayomide, correct?"

"Yes. She was the most gifted of us all. So much so that they made her an Orisha."

"Yes, and you are equally as gifted. You hold a power that would tempt any supernatural being, good or evil."

"I just happened to attract one of the evilest demons around. Great."

Gammy chuckled. "Well, I've always told you that whatever you choose to do, make sure you do your best."

Suri didn't find it amusing enough to laugh, but it did make her smile. "If I have such great powers then why haven't I felt them? I figured I hit my peak around college. After that no new gifts popped up."

"Because Ayomide needs to deem you worthy of receiving them. She's been awaiting your arrival." Gammy directed her gaze toward the basement door.

Suri shook her head. "The last time I tried to open it I thought my head would explode."

"Because you weren't expected, now you are."

"You left instructions that I shouldn't go down there without Uncle Robert or Phoebe."

"As I said, she's expecting you. But only when you're ready. Neither I, nor anyone else, will push you to do anything you don't want."

"But if I don't, then a demon will take control of my soul and a voodoo priestess bent on revenge with the help of my possessed cousin will destroy our family legacy and the gateways between our world and the Orishas. But no one is forcing my hand," Suri said sarcastically.

"Well, technically we aren't," Gammy said humorously.

Suri stared at the door for another moment then sighed in resignation as she stood up.

"Would you like me to come with you?"

She turned to her grandmother and frowned. She had become even more transparent in the short time they had been talking. Something was dimming her grandmother's spirit connection. "No. I should be fine, but you don't look as if you are."

Gammy gazed down at herself then smiled. "Yes, well, hopefully this won't be an issue for much longer. Don't worry about me. Focus on what Ayomide needs to tell you. Her altar is the first door on the left at the bottom of the stairs. You'll need to bring an orange and a glass of rum for the offering. Also, a fresh glass of water for added protection. There's a shelf located across from the altar room where you can get fresh candles and matches if Robert has been keeping it up as instructed. Be sure to greet her properly or she will not pay you any mind even if she is expecting you."

"Yes, Gammy," Suri said as if she were that young girl still getting instruction from her.

"One last thing, I'm going to once again suggest you ask Layla to stay here. She'll be a great help in holding off anything Lilith might send your way as she is more familiar with demons than we are. I'm nearby if you need me." She leaned in and placed a ghostly kiss on Suri's cheek then faded away.

Suri felt the tug on her heart that she always felt when Gammy's spirit came and went. She cleaned up the mess she made with the candy wrappers, then went upstairs to prepare for her visit with her ancestor. First, she located the boxes that she had sent to her uncle prior to her arrival that held her hoodoo supplies such as tinctures, mojo bags, powders, and seedlings since she couldn't bring her plants with her. There was also a box filled with the proper attire for calling forth an Orisha to ask for their guidance and help. For calling her ancestor, she chose an orange caftan trimmed in gold thread, her family's colors.

Since Suri didn't have time for a cleansing bath, she chose to perform a smoke cleansing. From her supplies, she collected an herb burning bowl, a small bag of white sand, a chunk of charcoal, packets of dried lavender for creating a peaceful environment, white sage for clearing negative energy, and blue sage for a clear mind and for enhancing her intuition, then a white sheet from the linen closet. First, she filled the bowl halfway with the sand, placed the charcoal in the center, lit it, then placed the herbs on the burning charcoal. Once the herbs began to smoke, she undressed, knelt beside the bowl, and wrapped the sheet from her neck down, making sure to include the bowl to allow the smoke to swirl around her. Finally, she closed her eyes and recited a prayer to the Orisha in the Yoruba tongue.

May my ancestors continue to guide and protect me
May Elegua open the doors of opportunities and remove obstacles from my path
May Ogun give me courage to overcome my problems and defeat my enemies
May Oshosi bring Justice and Balance to my life
May Orunmila bestow his wisdom upon me
May Obatala bring peace, tranquility and harmony to my life
May Babalu Aye heal my body and soul
May Olokun grant stability to my being
May Yemaya renovate and refresh my life with the powers of her waters
May Shango give me the strength to fight and win my battles
May Oshun fulfil my dreams of love and riches
May Oya bring with her the winds of change and prosperity to my realm,
Ashé

Suri sat for a moment longer after completing her prayer to allow the ritual to soothe her mind and heart. She could almost see the darkness in her chest grow smaller until it was the size of a dust particle floating in the air. Her third eye sleepily blinked open and she saw what she had ignored while she had been wallowing in self-pity all these months. That darkness had been the opening Lilith needed to enter, and a little less than an hour ago she had almost let it take over. She had fallen off her daily rituals of keeping herself and her altars for her ancestors and Orisha cleansed as well as strengthening her gifts and her hoodoo with daily practice. She had let her Ashe, her belief and faith, dim. Ashe had been Olodumare's blessing to humankind, and she had set hers aside as if it were a nuisance rather than the gift it was. She would have to make an offering and say a prayer of forgiveness to Olodumare soon.

With one final cleansing breath, Suri opened her eyes to find her vision clearer and colors brighter. The herbs she'd cleansed in smelled even stronger than when she started despite the scent beginning to dissipate. She heard the grandfather clock in the foyer downstairs ticking just as loudly as if she were standing beside it. Her senses hadn't been this strong in a very long time. She unwrapped the sheet around her to let what was left of the cleansing herbs permeate the house and quickly dressed in the caftan before heading downstairs to gather her offerings for her ancestor. Choosing a silver tray from the China cabinet, she placed a shot glass of Gammy's best rum then went into the kitchen for an orange and a glass of water.

"I would also enjoy chocolate," a voice said.

Suri gazed around the room, but she was the only one there. She continued her task, placing the glass of water and a whole orange on the tray, then she opened the cabinet where she had placed the bag of miniature chocolate bars and grabbed three to place on the tray as well. Once she was satisfied, she carried it to the basement door, placed it on the bar next to it, took the keys out, then hesitantly unlocked the door. As she grasped the doorknob, she braced herself for a repeat of the headache she had earlier, but the only thing she felt was a subtle jolt of power up her arm.

Suri slowly opened the door and the fragrant scent of lilies drifted up to her. She picked up the tray, balancing it in her other hand while she located a light switch just inside the doorway. When she turned the lights on, her path was lit with the flickering glow of faux fire torches along the wall leading down a gleaming wood staircase with treads on the stairs to keep anyone from slipping and railings made from actual tree branches as thick as her thigh. The walls and ceiling were painted with a stunning mural depicting a clear bright blue sky scattered with a few fluffy clouds and soaring birds that subtly darkened, as if she were walking from day into night, in an ombre of blues as she descended the stairs to enter a long hallway. She gazed up and around feeling disoriented for a moment at the realism of the mural surrounding her. She could genuinely believe that she stood in a field of Nigeria grass, its pink to purple flowering branches swaying in a night breeze, beneath a star-filled sky unfiltered by light pollution which, to her further amazement, glimmered under the flickering torchlight.

When she finally managed to tear her eyes away from it all to take notice of the doors along the hallway, she counted eight of them. Just right of the staircase was the supply cabinet her grandmother had told her about. It seemed to be made with the same wood and gleamed with the same stain as the stairs. She set the tray on a step to collect the candles and matches that she needed for her ritual. She placed them on the tray then turned to the first door on her left decorated with a pictorial carving of a robed female figure, her arms spread with a look of pain and sadness on her face as she gazed down at a boat filled with people chained together, reaching toward her. Below that was the same woman, smiling proudly, her arms and robe extending out from her sides protectively embracing child-like figures. This was Ayomide's legacy, her family's history. The story she hadn't learned of until today. So much had been stolen from her with the loss of her grandmother, which made her heart ache, but it was nothing compared to what had been stolen from her ancestors with the loss of their freedom, their land, and their sense of self, so her pain was bearable.

Suri straightened her back, took a deep breath, picked up the tray, then opened the door. The room was about eight feet by eight feet painted in a warm creamy white with two large orange meditation cushions set before a two-tiered natural wood meditation altar. Placed on the top tier was a Yoruba maternity figure statue depicting an African woman kneeling and nursing a baby at her breasts, which she assumed was to represent Ayomide since they didn't have a photograph of her. On either side of the statue were black iron candle holders on the left and a vase of sunset orange calla lilies to the right that her uncle must have just brought since they looked so fresh. On the lower tier was a bowl made of selenite stone, which was used for clearing blocked energy as well as charging other crystals. Within the bowl was a thumb-size amethyst crystal, used to relax and focus, and arfvedsonite, used to increase connection to the spirit world. Next to the bowl was a small book of Yoruba prayers. It was a simple but beautiful ancestor altar.

Suri knelt on the pillow then set the tray beside it. She placed the glass of water beside the bowl of crystals hoping that the combination of the two would assist in a stronger connection with Ayomide. As her grandmother said, just because her ancestor was expecting her, it didn't mean she would come. Then she set the candles on the iron holders and lit them. Next were the offerings. She unwrapped the chocolate then picked up the orange and began peeling it.

"The wise and most blessed Ayomide, I ask you to join me here at our family's altar in your honor. I humbly offer you these gifts as a symbol of my love and respect." She placed the peeled orange, the glass of rum and the chocolates in front of the statue. "Please honor me with your presence and wisdom."

Suri closed her eyes, took a few deep breaths to clear her mind, and repeated her invitation to Ayomide two more times in Yoruba then took a moment to center herself to try again. Before she could begin her entreaty, she felt a presence in the room with her. Not wanting to get her hopes up, as the house was full of their ancestors' spirits so it could be any one of them, she opened her eyes to the tangy scent of the orange and the sound of chewing. As she gazed straight ahead, she noticed that the orange was missing from the altar. She slowly turned to look to her left where the chewing was coming from to find a regal mahogany-skinned woman as solid and real as her sitting cross-legged on the other cushion beside her peeling off sections of the orange, popping them into her mouth, and chewing happily. She wore a white caftan, like the one Suri wore with an orange scarf tied around her waist, and jewelry made of wood beads, small brass bells, and cowrie shells. Her hair was cornrowed toward the center of her scalp with cowrie shells woven through and the ends, threaded with orange strips of fabric and more cowrie shells. It was sculpted to resemble a cockscomb along the top of her head. She had almond shaped eyes edged with laugh lines, pronounced cheekbones and jawline, softly flared nose, and full lips currently shining from the juice of the orange she ate.

Suri chose to give her time to finish the orange out of respect but also to give herself time to get over the shock that her invitation had worked. She would've thought after years of seeing spirits that this wouldn't surprise her, but this wasn't just any spirit. This was Ayomide, their family's personal Orisha. The Orisha priestess who, at the behest of Yemaya, allowed herself to be enslaved and taken away from the land she loved to help her people to uphold their faith and traditions. The same faith and traditions she passed down to her own children.

"Yes, and it seems many of you have lost the way despite my efforts," she said in thickly accented English.

Suri shifted to her knees then turned fully toward Ayomide in a gesture respectful of greeting an elder. "Welcome, Ayomide, you honor me with your presence," she said in Yoruba.

Ayomide leaned over, dipped her fingers in the glass of water, then dabbed them dry on the scarf at her waist. "Thank you, daughter," Ayomide responded in Yoruba smiling appreciatively. "You know and speak the language of our people well." She switched back to English. "I worried for you when Pearl joined us in the afterlife before having time to properly prepare you, but it's good to know that you have not forgotten what she was able to teach you. Although," she picked up the shot glass with an amused grin, "I see she didn't show you how to pour a proper offering." Ayomide raised the glass to her lips, tilted her head back, and drank the rum in one shot.

Suri grinned. She could see that her ancestor must have been a force to be reckoned with. "Apologies. I will do better next time."

Ayomide set the glass down then faced Suri with a stern expression. "Now that the formalities are out of the way, we have much to discuss. There is no need for me to repeat what you already know. What I need to know is if you are ready to face what's coming or is my legacy ending with you?"

Suri hadn't expected her to be so blunt. "Uh…well…"

Ayomide's expression softened. She grasped Suri's hands within hers. Her palms were rough and calloused, more than likely from having to work the fields while she was enslaved. "Do you know why I called you daughter when I greeted you?"

"Because you're our ancestral mother?"

"No. It's because, of all my children, you are the one most like me. You are the one fate has chosen to bear my legacy and my powers. You are the one created in my womb, only to be lost and birthed by another to continue the task Obatala and Yemaya gifted me with. It is not just our family that is losing faith in Orisha. Minor Orisha like myself are being forgotten because their family, their worshippers have long since given up their faith or forgotten them. If they are not turning to Christianity or any of the other faith-based belief systems deemed more appropriate with little work to ask for a blessing or prayer, they're losing all belief entirely. They're turning to darker forces making promises with lies and deceit."

"How am I supposed to stop that alone? I'm one person who hasn't been practicing as faithfully and have used very little of my gifts because hoodoo is more useful in helping people than they are," Suri said in frustration.

"Daughter, you are not, nor have you ever been alone. Your ancestors have always been close. All you needed to do was call out to us. You also have your living relatives and the worshippers you met this evening. You've shut yourself out for so long that you don't even see the people right in front of you."

"I see them, I just don't want anyone else to get hurt because of me. I think the only reason Uncle Robert has stayed safe is because he's here. Now my presence here could put him in just as much danger as everyone I've already lost." Suri's chest tightened with grief.

Ayomide placed a hand along her cheek, wiping away a stray tear with the pad of her thumb. Suri's grief loosened its hold at her gentle touch. "I am deeply sorry for those losses, but they are not your fault. You hold no responsibility over what beings with ill intention bring forth in their greed for power. They attacked others with no power, out of fear of the power you hold within you, to weaken you. Don't give them the satisfaction of knowing they succeeded. It is what the Oyibo did to the Yoruba when they attacked and stole us from our land. Those of us that survived the crossing held strong to our faith and twisted the Oyibo's religion to hide our own. There would be no Santeria or Voudoun without the Orisha. Our grief made us stronger and that is what you shall do. You will take your grief and use it to strengthen you for the fight ahead."

Her uncle, Phoebe, and her group, and Ayomide all seemed so sure that she could handle what was coming, but Suri knew herself and her abilities better than anyone. There was no way she was ready to battle a voudon priestess and a high-ranking demon.

Ayomide smiled knowingly. "Shall I show you what you're truly capable of? Will that quiet your doubt and fear?"

Suri frowned worriedly. "How will you do that?"

"Look into my eyes, do not turn away no matter how much you wish to."

As Suri gazed into Ayomide's dark eyes, they glowed with an eerie light just before Suri was blinded by a blazing white light that didn't hurt or burn but felt intensely weird and almost made her turn away. Then she saw herself. Well, what she assumed was herself, but this woman was full of strength and power. Her hair flowed around her in a reddish orange halo, her eyes glowed a solid white, and balls of white fire shot from her hands toward shadowy figures coming at her. She moved with an agility and grace she could only imagine having as she fought off whatever was attacking her.

As she watched herself maneuvering around what looked to be a forest, someone else stepped into the fray. She looked like Layla dressed in black jeans, a black tank top, her long braids floating around her like serpents ready to strike, skin a deep reddish black, eyes glowing a bright yellow, ears pointed and lips spread in an evil grin showing frighteningly pointed teeth. Leathery, black, bat-like wings with talons sprouted from her back spreading an impressive six feet in length as she whipped them around to strike down an attacker. She was terrifying and awe-inspiring all at once. She and Layla worked in tandem, as if they'd always been fighting together. Their energies fed off each other, strengthening one another as who or whatever they were fighting began to retreat. They stood back-to-back as they turned in a circle to make sure their enemies were truly gone. They breathed a sigh of relief, chest rising and falling as one reached back to grasp each other's hands just as the vision began to fade into the white light.

Suri felt disappointment over the vision ending. She blinked her eyes repeatedly to clear it of the blur from the light as that began to fade as well.

"Do you see what you are capable of?" Ayomide asked as Suri focused her gaze back on her.

"Is that a premonition vision or just something to get your point across?"

Ayomide smiled. "Would it matter?"

Suri thought of the Layla she knew, compared to the fearsome creature she was in the vision and wasn't sure if that was something she wanted to see in real life, but seeing herself with such powers would make it worth it. Having taken for granted that she would always have her family then losing so many, including her found family of Rachel and Tracey, made her realize how important they were to her. She never thought she would be strong or powerful enough to protect anyone else she grew close to, but if she accepted what the vision showed her then she could not only protect her loved ones but anyone who was not able to defend themselves against forces they didn't even know were out there.

"Are you ready to accept your role?"

Suri nodded before she allowed herself to have second thoughts.

"Suri, descendent of the wise and powerful Oduduwa, daughter of my heart and soul, do you accept the role as guardian to the Orisha gateways and priestess of your tribe?"

"Yes. I do."

Ayomide gazed at her with pride. "Do you accept the gifts which your ancestors have bestowed on to you to perform your duty with all your faith in the Orisha?"

"Yes. I do."

"Then ask the seven for their blessings on your journey."

Suri gazed over to make sure the candle she had lit was still burning, then closed her eyes to clear her mind and heart of as much doubt as she could. She knew that her message would be delivered through Ayomide.

"Elegua, open the crossway to good and bad, but please always lead me to the correct pathway. Ogun, give me strength to do what is just and right. Obatala, open my heart to protect those in need. Yemaya, teach me to value my gifts as a woman of strength. Oshun, teach me to love myself as I love others. Shango, protect me from those who seek to harm me and my loved ones. Oya, give me the knowledge to see right from wrong and the wisdom to do what must be done. May your gifts protect and guide me on the pathway you have laid before me. Ashe."

Suri opened her eyes to find Ayomide's closed, her lips moving as she quietly murmured her own prayer. When she gazed at Suri again, her eyes lit with an unnatural glow and a power emanated from her like nothing Suri had ever felt before. Ayomide raised her hand to place her fingertips against Suri's forehead. She tried not to flinch as they were almost burning to the touch.

"We hear and accept your prayers, Daughter of Ayomide, and bless you with the fullness of the gifts that have been passed down from mother to child as Olodumare blessed his children. Use them with an open and pure heart to protect and guide the children of Yorubaland as your ancestors have done." Ayomide's voice reverberated throughout the small room not as one voice but a collective of voices.

Suri's vision went white again but this time her body felt as if she were on fire from an inferno that burned from within. She was sure she would spontaneously combust and her poor uncle would come to the house to find her charred remains splattered all over Ayomide's altar. Just as she didn't think she could take any more, everything went dark.

CHAPTER SEVEN

Layla stood outside the gate staring up at Suri's family home. There were many windows, and at each one a female spirit, all dressed in different periods of clothing throughout time, stood watching her as if they'd been waiting for her. She could tell by their facial characteristics that they were all ancestors of Suri, each one powerful in their own right. She almost changed her mind, but the look of expectation on their faces kept her from doing so. While her father helped her hone her supernatural abilities and taught her about the many forms of magic, her mother taught her the importance of her ancestors and respecting their role in guiding us through our lives. Suri's ancestors were obviously looking out for her, and the fact that they weren't warning Layla off told her that her presence was accepted by them.

Doing her best to put up her own spiritual guards, and not wanting to incur all these powerful women's wrath by bringing anything dark or uninvited into their home, Layla hesitantly walked up the pathway. When she reached the door, she felt traces of a magical ward. She wouldn't be able to cross the threshold without being invited in by Suri. If Suri had decided overnight that she didn't want to be involved with anything that had to do with what was coming their way, then there was nothing Layla could do but accept her decision. She rang the doorbell and waited. Minutes ticked by without a peep of sound coming from inside the house. Layla knew she hadn't gone out because she had been in the area since sunrise watching the house and had purposely waited until late morning to approach, not wanting to disturb Suri too early.

She closed her eyes and searched for Suri's energy. She was in the house, but her energy felt different. It was Suri, but more. Like her power had shifted and grown tremendously since last night. Layla felt intense fear. What if Lilith had already taken over? Could that be the immense power she was feeling from Suri? She rushed around the wraparound porch, looking for a way in, her anxiety growing by the second, but the entire house was warded, which meant that if she couldn't get in, neither could Lilith so she had no reason to panic. She breathed a heavy sigh of relief and made her way back around to the front door where she rang the doorbell several times then used the heavy knocker just in case.

"Whoever this is you better have a damn good reason to be waking me up at the crack of dawn," Suri said from the other side of the door.

A moment later, she yanked the door open with an angry glare. Power emanated off her in waves as she stood before Layla looking every bit like an avenging goddess about to strike down whomever disturbed her slumber. She wore a simple slightly wrinkled and disheveled orange caftan that was sliding off one smooth shoulder revealing part of a tattoo that covered her upper arm. Her bright auburn red hair haloed wildly around her head. Her skin and eyes glowed with a barely contained golden light, and she smelled of sunshine, citrus, and cinnamon…sharp, sweet, and warm. Layla became intoxicated by her scent. Her succubus nature, inherited from her father's incubus nature, stirred within her.

"Good morning," was all she could muster up to say.

Suri's eyes widened. "Good morning. It's not the crack of dawn, is it?"

Layla turned and looked out at the bright blue sky. "No. It's late morning."

Suri gazed down at herself in confusion. "What the hell happened?"

"Should I come back?" Maybe she drank too much last night and blacked out. But that wouldn't explain the power emanating from her.

"No. I'm sorry. I must have overslept." Suri stepped aside and waved Layla in.

"Uh, you're going to have to invite me in. Kinda blocked from entering."

Suri shook her head. "Oh, yeah, come on in."

Layla felt the ward melt away. As soon as she stepped over the threshold, she felt it quickly close again. "A little too much to drink last night?"

Suri closed the door but didn't move. Her eyes closed and her head tilted as if she were listening for something. Then her eyes popped open again. "Oh shit! It wasn't a dream. That really happened."

Layla looked at her with concern. "Are you okay?"

Suri nodded distractedly. "If you'll give me a few minutes to get dressed I'll explain everything. You can have a seat in the living room." She pointed toward the room behind her, then hurried toward the stairs lifting the hem of her caftan to keep from tripping as she took them two at a time. "Please don't open any strange doors! I'll be right back down!" she yelled.

Layla entered the living room, feeling a sense of familiarity. When she saw the patio doors, she remembered that she'd been here before through Suri's dream yesterday. She gazed around the room at the warm colors and stylish but comfortable furnishings. Portraits of generations of Suri's family lined the walls. The largest of which hung over the fireplace of a beautiful deep brown-skinned woman dressed in nineteenth century attire, her reddish-brown hair braided and piled atop her head in an intricate twist. As with most paintings during that time, she didn't smile, but there was a hint of humor in her piercing hazel eyes. Eyes like Suri's.

"That's Athena. The first in our family to gain her freedom since we were brought to this land."

Layla had felt the presence of the spirit before she even spoke. She turned, surprised to find a woman who could be Suri's twin if it weren't for her being much older, smiling up at the painting.

"Pearl, I presume?"

Pearl's eyes were kind when they looked at her. "Yes. And you're Layla. I see your mother in you."

"You know of my mother?"

"We've connected just recently. I'm glad you're here. Suri will need all the support that she can get."

"I haven't said if I would help."

Pearl gazed at her knowingly. "I may be old and dead but I'm not a fool. You care too much about this city and its people to watch it fall to the likes of Lilith and Sojourn."

"True, but how do I know I can trust Suri to keep her head about her? From what I could tell, Lilith has already hooked her talons into her."

Pearl shrugged. "That was yesterday. What do you see now?"

"I felt a change within her."

"That change is her coming into her gifts. I'll let her explain. I just wanted to see you for myself before I entrusted you with the well-being of my granddaughter."

"Well?"

Pearl looked her up and down with a smile. "You'll do."

Then, just like that she was gone. Layla stared at the spot Pearl had been standing, then looked up at the sound of Suri coming down the stairs. She still looked as bright and vibrant as she did when she answered the door. It wasn't anything that a normal being would see, but it was obvious to those with supernatural abilities. There was an intensity to her aura that wasn't common. A sharpness to her energy that wasn't there yesterday. Even her appearance had changed. Her hair was now pulled back into an afro puff at the back of her head, and the gold flecks in her hazel eyes were brighter, her sable color skin tone was softer looking, even her movement when she adjusted a necklace that she wore seemed to be more graceful since yesterday. This change was like a siren's song to Layla and she had to tamp down her succubus nature once again.

"Were you talking to someone?"

"Your grandmother was checking me out." The deeper, seductive tone of her voice was evidence that she wasn't doing a good job of keeping it at bay. She cleared her throat. "May I use your bathroom?"

Suri was gazing at her curiously but didn't seem to be affected. "Yes, right down the hall next to the kitchen." She pointed in the direction Layla needed to go.

"Thanks." Layla tore her gaze away from Suri and hurried past her.

By the time she reached the bathroom she could feel her teeth elongating to a pointed sharpness and her wings itched to break free. "Down, girl," she commanded her inner beast.

Suri, not showing any signs that she had been affected by the sexual energy Layla knew she had been giving off, had intrigued her beast further because she loved a challenge. This had never happened before so it took several minutes for her to gain control of herself. When she felt her nature grumble and stalk back into its cave, she put up extra internal barriers to keep it there. She gazed into the mirror, checked her teeth, running her tongue over their now flattened surfaces then flushed the toilet and washed her hands for show before walking back out.

"I'm in the kitchen."

She turned and entered the kitchen.

"Would you like some coffee?"

Layla sat at the same stool she sat at when she visited during Suri's dream. "No, thank you. But if you have milk, I'll take a glass."

"It's almond milk."

"That's fine." Layla just needed the comfort the blandness of milk gave her. Something simple and plain in what was becoming a complicated situation.

Suri went to the refrigerator, took out the carton of milk and a bottle of creamer from the same brand, placed milk and a large glass in front of Layla then poured herself a cup of coffee with a large dollop of the creamer. She also sat beside Layla in the same chair she had occupied in her dream.

"So, what did my grandmother think of you?" Suri sipped her coffee, her eyes twinkling with amusement as she gazed at her over the rim of her mug.

Layla grinned. "She said I'd do."

Suri chuckled. "That sounds like her. Did she tell you anything else?"

"Only that you would tell me about the change I feel in your power."

Suri frowned. "Is it that obvious?"

"Only to another supernatural who may have known you before today."

"That makes sense. Long story short, I had a very enlightening visit with my ancestor Ayomide last night. I accepted my role in this family as well as in stopping what's coming. In exchange, with the blessings of the Seven, she opened my eye to my true power. Then I woke up to you practically knocking down my door." She said the last with a teasing grin.

Layla shrugged and took a sip of her milk. "Just making sure you're okay. I am your bodyguard after all."

Suri rolled her eyes. "Ugh. We are not calling you that. Besides, from what I saw, your role in this goes far beyond bodyguard."

"What you saw?"

Suri gazed guiltily down into her coffee. "I was gifted with a vision. I saw us fighting off demons together. From what my grandmother Phoebe and Ayomide have said, we're going to need to work together to prepare for the battle ahead. Especially since you probably know more about dark magic and demon queens than I do."

Layla was surprised to hear that she knew about Lilith. "Yeah, it seems we both had enlightening visits last night. My father paid me one as well."

Suri sighed. "They all seem to know what's coming, but none of them can be involved with stopping it."

"Yeah, really. What's the use in them having powers untold when they can't use them to help stop the apocalypse?"

Suri chuckled. "Exactly!"

They quietly sipped at their beverages. Layla surreptitiously watching Suri wondering, if they were just regular old humans, would they have met? Maybe gone on a date or something? She had a feeling that under non-apocalyptic circumstances, she would have swiped right on Suri.

"So, what next?" she asked.

Suri gazed into her cup as if searching for the answers there, then looked back at Layla curiously. "Do you know how to fight?"

"Metaphysically or physically?"

"I guess both. I've only used my gifts to help people and I've never gotten into a physical fight a day in my life. I don't even kill bugs in the house. I capture and set them free outside."

"Seriously?"

Suri nodded.

"Wow. Well, I guess we can start with basic self-defense in both forms."

"Okay. Is there a gym or secret supernatural lair we can go to?"

Layla smiled at Suri's joke as she tried to think of where to go that would give them open space and privacy. If they were going to be working on supernatural self-defense, they would need to go someplace secluded. There was only one place she could think of and no one had visited there since Cora Lee passed.

"I may know of a place."

Layla didn't look too thrilled about whatever place she was referring to, and if that was the case, Suri wasn't sure she wanted to go.

"Did you have plans for the rest of the day?"

Suri lifted her hand, ticking points off each finger. "Let's see, yesterday I found out that my family's home was a gateway to other worlds, learned that I was a descendant of an Orisha, that I'm a guardian and priestess, that I may also be the reincarnation of that same Orisha's unborn child and that I've woken up blessed by the Seven with more gifts so that I can battle a voodoo priestess, a demon-possessed cousin and a high-level demoness. At this moment, my only plans for today are to simply make it to dinner without any more mind-blowing revelations."

"Hold up, you're reincarnated from Ayomide's unborn child?"

With everything else that she found out, still finding that revelation hard to believe was crazy. It wasn't until she was getting dressed after Layla's arrival that everything came back to her in a flash of visions that played out like a movie reel in her head. She still didn't remember how she had gotten up to her bedroom, but she did remember the dream she'd had after. It wasn't a dream so much as recalled memories. Ayomide's memories.

Ayomide stood on a high cliff above the ocean watching the sails of another Oyibo ship waving in the distance carrying more of her people. She had managed to protect her village from raids by warring tribes and Oyibos stealing villagers away, but she could no longer continue to just sit by watching it happen to their neighboring villages. Just days ago, Bisi the oldest and most favored daughter of Giwá the Oba from the next village, was visiting her intended Eni, Ayomide's own Oba, when she and her guards were attacked and taken by Oyibo raiders. One of the guards who had been seriously injured and left behind told the search party what happened just before he died from his injuries.

Giwá had been furious when Eni refused to send some of his soldiers to join in the search for the raiding party. Eni had said that since he hadn't taken Bisi as his bride yet, she was not his responsibility. Ayomide had been furious, but there was nothing she could do. Many times, she had bidden Eni to allow her to ask the Orisha for protection for their neighbors, but he had forbidden it, wanting to keep her and her gifts for himself and his people. She had done what she could in secret. Sending prayers for the priest and priestesses in the other villages that had not been blessed with the gifts she had. Visiting and providing blessings when she could to other Obas and their villages that were not as prosperous as her own.

Now, as she watched the ship disappear into the distance she fell to her knees and wept for all those that she could not help. She would do and sacrifice anything to be able to do more. What was the use of having her gifts if she were not allowed to use them to save the people of Yorubaland from slave catchers.

"If you are truly willing to sacrifice to help our children, then wipe your tears and stand tall," a feminine voice commanded her.

Ayomide gazed up to the frightening sight of a wave as high as the cliffs she stood upon moving toward her. She was tempted to turn and run until it stopped before her in a wall of water where a figure began to take shape within its shifting shadows. She watched in awe as the waves parted and a woman, standing twice as tall as her, glided through. Her skin was dark ebony with patches of iridescent sea blue scales along her arms and legs, her eyes were as deep and dark as the ocean she rose from, her hair flowed out and around her head in heavy midnight locs, and atop her head sat a crown made of seashells, pearls, and cowrie shells. The sea flowed around her forming a dress of blue water and white sea foam that undulated over her generous curves.

"Mother Yemaya," Ayomide said reverently before falling to her knees, ignoring the sharp pain of the rocks digging into her flesh, then pressing her forehead to the ground in respect.

She was in the presence of Yemaya, the mother of all living things and goddess of the ocean.

"Rise, child."

Ayomide slowly rose, staring in disbelief at the Orisha before her. "What do I owe this honor, Mother?"

Yemaya's expression was grim. "Your cries have been heard. I too grieve for my children stolen from our land by the Oyibo. I have begged Obatala to intervene, after all, they are his children as well, but he has refused to interfere in such matters of human affairs. He only reminds me that the Orisha are here to maintain harmony of the universe and bless and guide humans on their paths in life as Olodumare sees fit. If Elegua has given my prayers and messages to Olodumare, he has not deemed them worthy of answering. I have even ventured into the depths of the ocean to appeal to Olokun who has been able to stop some of the ships with Oya's help by bringing about angry winds and storms at sea, but neither wish to draw Olodumare's wrath."

Ayomide was surprised enough that Yemaya was speaking to her, but to hear that the goddess of wind and the god of the ocean were tempting the Supreme One's fury by intervening in human lives and going against his edict surprised her further.

Teardrops the size of Ayomide's head flowed down Yemaya's cheeks carving out tracks like water running through divots in the earth. "All I have been able to do is be there for those that are thrown away like the cargo that the Oyibo treat them as. To bless their souls to return home to Olodumare." Her voice was filled with a helplessness and grief that Ayomide recognized as the same feelings she had.

She took a step toward Yemaya, placing her just at the edge of the jutting cliff, then reached toward the goddess imploringly. "Please, Yemaya, tell me what I must do, what I must sacrifice to *be your weapon in this battle. I can no longer bear the burden of my privilege. What is the use of being blessed when I cannot use my gifts to save ALL my people?"*

With a sad smile, Yemaya drew closer to Ayomide. So close that she could see the flicker of iridescent silver as fish darted among the rolling waves of her dress. *"Although I fear we will never save all, especially when there are those who collude with the Oyibo to steal their brothers and sisters. What is needed is someone to guide those that survive the voyage in keeping their faith. They cry and rage against the Orisha for allowing them to be taken from their homeland and family. Some even—"* Yemaya's voice broke with emotion. *"Some even choose to throw themselves to the sea. They would rather their souls be chained to the cold dark depth of the ocean like Olokun than to a life of servitude by the Oyibo."*

Ayomide recognized a mother's grief over losing her child on Yemaya's face. She had seen it too often of late in the villages she had visited that had lost their young men and women to this horrific trade.

"What can I do?"

"I fear what I will ask of you will be too much, but you, a daughter of Oduduwa, the father of Yorubaland, must be the one to do it. It has been your destiny since birth. Just as your grandsire unified the kingdoms of Ife, you are tasked with unifying the stolen children of Ife."

Ayomide gazed at Yemaya in confusion. How was she to unify people who had been taken a world away? It only took her a moment to realize what Yemaya was asking her to do.

"The only way to unify them is to go where they have gone."

"Yes."

"But what of my people here? The ones who are still in danger of being stolen. What of my..." A cold fear made her shiver as she placed a hand over the small mound of her belly.

Yemaya reached forward to touch a fingertip to her hand then closed her eyes. A subtle warmth spread throughout Ayomide's womb. She gazed up at Yemaya and was met with a sad smile.

"Like you, your daughter's soul is destined for something greater for which she too will have to make sacrifices, but not in this lifetime."

Tears blurred her vision as Ayomide shook her head in denial of what she was being told.

"I'm sorry, child, but it is how it should be. You have asked what you can do. Have prayed and made offerings on behalf of your people, and those prayers are being answered now. I know this is difficult, but I also know that you are strong in your faith. Believe me when I tell you that it has not gone unnoticed. Now, you must make the ultimate sacrifice to keep the faith going in a land where the children of Yorubaland are lost and confused. Where their faith, traditions, and memories of their people are being beaten out of them. They need you more than a greedy Oba whose faith is no longer in the Orisha but in power and gold. Are you so blind by your devotion to him that you do not see what he is doing?"

"Eni may not be perfect, but he is a good Oba, nonetheless. He does what he must do to protect his people." Even though she was speaking with one of the seven most powerful Orisha, Ayomide's tone no longer held the respect it had during their talk. She took offense to Yemaya's disparaging remark about her Oba, who also was the father of the child nestled in her womb.

Yemaya shook her head, looking at Ayomide with disappointment. "You do not see what is right in front of your face. It is true that your gifts and prayers have helped to keep your village from the growing raids by the Oyibo, but so has your Oba's dealmaking with them. It is why your neighboring villages have recently been raided while yours remain untouched. Why do you think he did not provide men for his intended's father to go after her? If he turns a blind eye to what is happening and provides the raiders with information about the surrounding villages, then his coffers stay full and his rule grows when he allows you to convince him to take in the people that remain in those raided villages." Yemaya's eyes grew stormy and the water that made up her dress churned angrily.

Ayomide could see past Yemaya that the sea, which had been calm moments before, was also changed by her mood. Had she been so blind by the attention Eni had given her that she did not see the truth of who he truly was? She had known Eni his whole life. Even as a child he had been more concerned about the status of Oba than what he could do for his people as their leader. It was why his father *had made him serve time as a soldier before he would even consider bestowing the title on him. That seemed to humble Eni so when the time came for him to be crowned Oba upon his father's death a year ago, Ayomide had rejoiced with her people. Then, when he came to Ayomide just days after asking for a special blessing from her as the gifted priestess of the village, she had been honored, especially since he had already been blessed by the arabas, the Chief Priest, during his coronation.*

He had come to her often after that. To ask for silly blessings or just to talk. It was always in secret as he said he didn't want to make his wives jealous. She didn't know when her feelings for him turned to affection. If she had to guess she would say it was when he had admitted that he felt as if he could be himself with her. Not the Oba, not the revered son, not the husband duty-bound to create an heir, just Eni the man. She had given herself to him that night and every night he had come to her since. Had that all been a lie to keep her from seeing the truth of what he was doing? Had she been that naïve?

Seeing the anger on Yemaya's face turn to pity told Ayomide that she had been. There would be no reason for the Orisha to lie about Eni's betrayal of his people. She had wasted all this time following his command as if she were one of his wives when all he was doing was using her and her gifts to benefit him. She could have been using the gifts she had been blessed with to help so many other villages. She had learned to tamp down most of her abilities so as not to call attention to herself, but she now knew that had been a mistake.

Yemaya smiled. "There is the warrior I need. Are you willing to sacrifice all to do what must be done?"

Ayomide gazed back down at her hand still resting on her belly. Maybe, if she were careful, she would not have to sacrifice everything. She looked back up at Yemaya. "Yes."

Yemaya nodded then instructed Ayomide on what she needed to do. Afterward, the Orisha placed a large hand over her head to say a blessing of protection over her. Then she watched as she disappeared back into the wall of water before it crashed down onto the shoreline below. Ayomide returned to her village but did not enter the gate. She closed her eyes and listened to the sound of the children at play, the gaggle of voices in the marketplace, the clang of metal against metal as the soldiers trained. This had been the only home she had known, yet there was no one there left to say good-bye to. Her mother had joined the ancestors several years ago. Ayomide had been alone ever since assisting the village priests and using what gifts she felt comfortable revealing to help bless the villagers. Would anyone other than Eni notice she had gone? His betrayal broke her heart but she ignored the pain as best she could, turned and strode away.

Ayomide walked for hours in the direction Yemaya had instructed until she came to a river where she decided to rest and quench her thirst from the midday heat. She knelt along the edge of the bank, cupping water in her hands to drink when the sound of a branch snapping drew her attention. She looked around just as six men on horses, their pale skin ruddy from the heat, looking as if they were about to drop from exhaustion broke through the trees. Shuffling behind them were three women and a man chained together at their wrists. She recognized the print of their wraps from a village she had recently visited. These were the Oyibo that Yemaya said would take her to where she was needed. For a moment, Ayomide considered running back the way she came but there was nothing left there for her. Besides, the men began shouting in a language she didn't recognize as they pointed their weapons at her. One of them walked toward her, snatched her roughly by the arm, and pulled her toward the others. She struggled against his grip but not enough to escape. The others gazed up at her pityingly then back down to the ground. As her wrists were bound and attached to the long chain with the other captives, she could smell the sharp scent of fear mingled with sour body odor coming from the Oyibo and something rose within her that made her clench her fists. Ayomide knew in that moment that she could just as easily use her gifts to free herself and the others, but that was not what she had been tasked with by Yemaya.

After the Oyibo filled their water sacks from the river, they allowed their horses to get water but didn't offer any to their prisoners. Once they were finished, they mounted their horses, then signaled for Ayomide and the others to start moving. They lumbered on for a day before meeting up with another group of Oyibo with more captives. There were a dozen people in that group including two small children clutching onto their mother's dingy and torn wrap. Her face *was swollen and bloody, proof that she had not made her capture as easy as Ayomide's had been. When the Oyibo decided to rest for the night they feasted on roasted game they caught while giving their captives a few sips of water and stale, moldy bread. Ayomide learned where everyone was from through whispered conversation in Yoruba until they were yelled at again to be quiet. Egbe, the man in her group understood their language, which he said was Dutch, because his Oba had traded with the Dutch before they attacked their village.*

Four more days at a punishable pace, with little food and water, that left two from the other group dead on the road ended at the very coastline that Ayomide had been watching ships leave from the day Yemaya had come to her. They were corralled into cages and only then were their chains removed. Ayomide collapsed beside Folani, the mother of the two children who were too weak to do anything but whimper in their mother's arms. She gazed around at the people in her cage as well as the dozens of other cages along the shoreline and knew that Yemaya needed her to see this so that she would understand how important it was for her to make this journey to help her brothers and sisters. She also knew that this was nothing compared to what she would have to endure on the ship. For a people so strong in faith to take their own lives told her more than she needed. She gazed over at the children, now curled against their mother's side sleeping fitfully and she wondered if they would survive the journey.

A sharp pain brought on thoughts of what Yemaya had said about her own child.

"No," Ayomide whispered desperately as another pain had her gripping her belly as if to hold her baby in.

She saw movement out of the corner of her eye but was too focused on clenching her legs together as she felt a trickle of moisture slide down her inner thigh. Arms wrapped around her shoulder and pulled her against the warmth of a woman's body.

"Do not fight it. It will only make it harder," said Folani.

Ayomide relaxed into Folani's embrace, silently weeping as what had been her already beloved child poured from her womb.

❖

Suri had awoken at that moment to Layla's knocking. She now knew why Ayomide had called her daughter. She was Ayomide's lost child reborn. She was the one Yemaya herself had seen when she had placed her hand over Ayomide's belly.

She suddenly felt overwhelmed but pushed it aside as she didn't have time for such feelings. "Yeah, remind me to tell you about it someday. Where is this place you obviously don't want to take me but is the perfect spot to get my Black Girl Magic on?"

Layla chuckled. "It's outside of town."

"Let me just grab a few things and we can be on our way."

Chapter Eight

S uri and Layla had been on the road for over an hour. When Suri and her parents visited over the years, they had never left the city limits. This was her first time venturing into the outer parishes of Louisiana. They stayed on the major highway before stopping in a charming town named Thibodaux where Layla told her that she had to pick up supplies. From there they traveled along a local road for about ten minutes before turning down an unpaved dirt road that Suri would've driven right past without knowing it. It wasn't until they began bumping along a tree-lined road that Layla's midsize SUV barely fit that Suri wondered if she should've told her uncle where she was going. Sure, Gammy, Phoebe, and Ayomide told her that she would need Layla's help, but that didn't mean she should trust her enough to be traveling down an ever-darkening road near the bayou to some remote location where they would probably never find her body.

Suri's eyes widened in fear as the trees began closing in, their long branches reaching toward the car.

"What the fuck?" Instinctively, she began to raise her hand and felt a surge of heat traveling down her arm and her hands began to glow.

The car jolted to a stop. Layla reached over and forcefully lowered Suri's arm.

"Hold up! It's just an illusion!"

As a spindly branch snaked its way up the hood toward her side of the window, Suri shook her head.

"Suri, look at me."

Layla's voice held that same strange tone it did earlier. It was pleasant and commanding but not enough to draw Suri's attention away from the sight of the trees literally moving to block their path. She tried to lift her hands again, but Layla was stronger than her.

"Let me go, Layla. I don't want to hurt you." Her voice reverberated throughout the car in a timbre that she never heard before.

"Dammit, Suri, LOOK AT ME!"

Suri turned her head just enough to be able to peer at Layla but not take complete attention away from the danger outside. Layla's eyes glowed a soft yellow and her skin took on a reddish tinge. Suri finally turned her full attention to her. She'd seen Layla in her full cambion form in the vision Ayomide shared with her, so seeing this subtle change in her appearance didn't surprise her but it did make her hesitate.

"It's an illusion that I created to keep unwanted visitors away from my home. Use your third eye to see the truth."

Suri gazed at her for another moment. She could feel and see Layla's sincerity. She closed her eyes. Took a few breaths and tapped into her powers. She found it much easier to do now than she used to. When she could feel her inner eye blinking open, she opened her own eyes and gazed out the front window. The trees were no longer clawing at the car and the dirt road in front of them was wide enough for at least two cars to come through. There were a few limbs lying in the road, but she could see a Creole-style cottage farther ahead.

She gave Layla a nervous smile. "That's some freaky shit."

Layla's appearance had changed back. "Yeah, sorry about that. Are you okay?"

It wasn't until that moment that Suri realized Layla had practically thrown herself across her. Her right arm was along the back of the seat, her left was holding Suri's arms in her lap, her upper body pressed against Suri's side, and their faces were just inches from each other. Layla's breath was warm and smelled of the chocolate bar she'd eaten a while back. Everything in her pushed Suri to close the distance between them and see if Layla's lips were as soft as they looked. If she'd be as good a kisser as Suri imagined her to be. She resisted, turning her gaze back to the window.

"I-I'm good."

Layla cleared her throat and released her, settling back into her seat to continue toward the house. The two-story cottage was surrounded by a weathered cypress wood picket fence and stood three feet off the ground on a raised brick foundation. The house was built with the same weathered cypress wood as the fence and had a pitched tin roof, a front porch that ran the length of the front of the house, and green shuttered windows. Layla pulled the truck into a carport located just right of the fence.

"You said this is your home? I thought you lived in New Orleans." Suri helped Layla with the bags of groceries she'd bought in Thibodaux.

"I do. The place in New Orleans is one of the places I stay, but this is home. It has been for a long time."

She followed Layla up to the house. On the porch was a porch swing, a café table with two chairs, and a ceiling fan. The French-style front doors opened to a hallway that ran the length of the house to another set of French doors that opened to the back. There was a set of narrow stairs to the right and a wide-open doorway to the left that led to a cozy living room decorated with what looked to be antique furnishings apart from the plush sofa and armchairs. The living room led into a small but modern kitchen, where they carried the groceries, and past the kitchen was a sunroom with a small dining table and four chairs on one side and a worktable and stool with ceiling-high open shelves of bottles flanked by two equally tall apothecary cabinets. The house was bright with windows along every wall to invite in sunshine and fresh air. It took Suri a moment to realize that despite the windows being closed, the house was comfortably cool.

"It's a very beautiful home. Does being back in the woods like this keep it cool?"

"No. I have central air. I turned it on remotely on our way here so that the house wouldn't be a sauna when we arrived. I spent enough of my life toiling in the heat. As soon as air conditioning became a thing, I immediately bought several units as well as added stock to my financial portfolio. I had central air installed in the early seventies."

Suri chuckled. "You've mentioned personally knowing Marie Laveau and now you're saying you were old enough to have been around when air conditioning was invented? What are you, like two hundred years old?"

"Give or take a few years." Layla continued putting the groceries away as if she hadn't just admitted to being two centuries old.

"You're serious."

"Yes. I have no reason to make something like that up. What purpose would it serve? How about I whip us up some lunch then we can get started with your training. If you'd like, you can go upstairs and freshen up. The bathroom is just at the top of the stairs."

Suri stared at Layla in disbelief. Layla didn't look to be much older than her. She was tall, probably around five feet ten inches, with an athletic build. Her slim-fitting jeans molded to her muscular calves and thighs and the denim button-down short-sleeve shirt she wore displayed equally toned arms. Her face was long, angular, and free of blemishes. The only thing that belied her youthful appearance were her eyes. They looked as if they belonged to someone much older and held more secrets and knowledge than someone that looked as young as she, should know. Even her hair was pure black without a single gray in the long cornrows that brushed the top of her perfectly shaped behind.

"I guess I'm not quite done with shocking revelations."

Shaking her head, she turned and left the room. She took her time walking up the stairs to look at a group of small paintings so lifelike that they resembled photographs. The first was of a beautiful, brown-skinned woman dressed in a plain dark skirt and blouse from the sixteenth or seventeenth century with her hair in a wrap standing beside a lake with a large plantation house in the background. She resembled Layla enough for Suri to assume it was her mother. After all, Layla did say she was over two hundred years old so it would make sense that her mother would be around during slavery. The next painting was an older woman with a lighter shade complexion but similar features sitting in a rocking chair with a bible in her lap. Layla's grandmother, maybe? The next was a dark-skinned woman who looked to be about Suri's age whose teasing grin didn't reach the sadness in her eyes. Eyes that had seen the kind of pain that one never really talked about no matter how close they were to you. She stood in a garden beside a cabin that looked like Layla's house but was smaller with no second floor. The last painting was of a very attractive tan complexion man dressed in a dark suit standing along what looked to be Bourbon Street. The dark look in his expression made Suri shiver. It was as if he were looking directly at her from the painting. She could see Layla's eyes and the angular shape of her face in his.

Suri didn't have to guess who this was as she hurried past it. She did wonder who the third woman was. She didn't see a family resemblance to Layla, but the woman was obviously someone special as she didn't notice any other pictures or paintings of anyone else. Maybe she was to Layla what Rachel had been to her. Thinking of Rachel made Suri's heart ache. The violence and supernatural connection between Rachel's, her parents', and Tracey's deaths had bothered her because she never understood why they had happened. Now, thinking back on what Gammy had said about Lilith's interest in her gave her the piece of the puzzle she had been missing. She washed her hands and rushed back downstairs, making sure not to make eye contact with the painting of Layla's father.

As she entered the kitchen, Layla was returning from the sunporch.

"Just in time. I made salads with grilled chicken if that's all right."

"Yeah, that's great. What do you know about the demon Lilith's interest in me?"

Layla smiled in amusement. "Wow, okay. I thought we would ease into that conversation but I guess not. Can we at least eat while we discuss it?"

Suri gazed at the two bowls of salad in Layla's hands and her stomach growled. "Sure. Can I help with anything?"

"If you can grab the salad dressing and that pitcher of tea then we'll be set."

She picked up the bottle of dressing and the pitcher from the counter then followed Layla out onto the porch. It wasn't as cool as the house but comfortable as a ceiling fan circulated the air conditioning drifting out to it. A few feet from the porch was the garden Suri had seen in the painting of the woman on the stairway. There were many plants that she recognized from her own hoodoo work and some that probably only grew in this southern climate. The garden spread out as far as twelve feet to the fence line at the back of the house which bordered the surrounding forest.

"You have a beautiful home."

Layla smiled proudly. "Thank you. It was the first place I came to after I left the plantation I had been raised on."

Hearing what she guessed was true about Layla's past didn't make it any less mind-blowing. "Did you leave after the emancipation?"

Layla looked away with a frown. "No. I didn't know how much chicken you wanted so I put it on the side." She pointed to a bowl of diced chicken set in the center of the table.

As curious as Suri was about Layla's story, it was obvious it wasn't something she wanted to talk about so she decided not to push the subject. She took some time to add chicken and dressing to her salad before taking a few bites to appease her hunger. All the vegetables tasted fresher than she'd had in a long time. She realized it all must have come from Layla's garden.

"In response to your question, I know that Lilith has set her sights on you and has been pushing you toward her path for years now."

"How?"

"The only way she can get to you is if you're alone with a weakened spirit. She's attacked you indirectly to get you to a vulnerable place where that can happen."

Suri balled her fists in anger on the table. "She's the one responsible for my best friend, my parents, and my girlfriend being killed."

"Yes."

That kernel of darkness that Suri thought she'd cleansed away last night throbbed in her chest. She tried thinking of everyone who was depending on her to be strong and do what must be done, but her thoughts kept going back to all that she had lost. How she had spent months wallowing in self-pity and alone because she was afraid to get close to anyone. The lives of those she loved were cut short before their time. Rachel's dream of becoming a mother, her parents' plan to retire and travel, the life together she and Tracey had begun to talk about. All of that gone. The kernel grew until she could feel its roots slinking toward her heart.

"Don't give in," Layla said.

Suri gazed at Layla, expecting to see her transforming like she did in the car, but she was only met with a look of sympathy and concern, which helped to calm her anger. Layla was right. She couldn't give in. Especially since Gammy had told her Lilith wanted her at her full power. Maybe, with whatever training Layla would be giving her today, she could help her get control of the darkness, because there was no way on earth, or in hell, that she was going to let a demon have her soul and body.

❖

Although Layla was concerned by how quickly she felt Lilith's touch spread within Suri, she was also relieved that she just as swiftly regained control.

"In order to know what we need to work on, I need to know what abilities you have."

Suri took a sip of her iced tea, then sat back in her chair with her hands in her lap. She'd barely touched her food. "I'm an empath, a healer, I can channel spirits, use telekinesis, and perform chlorokinesis. I'm assuming those abilities have been enhanced and many more awakened since Ayomide's visit. I can feel the difference."

Layla nodded. "Judging by your reaction when you thought the trees were about to attack, you've gained some defensive abilities. You were able to bring forth various energies to defend yourself."

"Various? I felt the balls of energy building in my hands but that was it."

"You didn't notice it because you were too caught up in the fear the illusion brought, but you had also called forth a wind that whipped through the trees hard enough to bring down a few limbs, the ground shook, and there was a bit of thunder."

Suri's eyes widened in shock. "You're not serious."

"Very much so. If I hadn't stopped you, we would've been caught up in your own personal tornado."

"I'm so sorry! That's why you were laid across me when I came to."

"Yeah. Which means that we're going to have to be careful until we figure out what other abilities you were gifted with. If you're finished, we can start now."

She looked down at her plate. "Yes. It was good. I just lost my appetite."

"Having a demon trying to possess you can do that."

Suri smiled. "Yeah, I guess so. Let me at least help you clean up since you went to all this trouble."

Layla waved dismissively. "It'll only take me a minute or two. Feel free to look around in the garden if you like."

Suri nodded then headed out the door leading to the yard. Layla grabbed a tray from a nearby credenza and placed everything from their lunch on it to carry into the kitchen. After she'd put everything away, she grabbed a couple of bottles of water before heading back out. She stopped to admire Suri's profile as she stood before a sunflower that was almost as tall as her and seemed to be standing even straighter under her touch as she brushed her fingers over the large petals.

"She is beautiful."

"Don't even think about it."

"I wouldn't dare. She belongs to you."

Layla snorted. "We aren't back on the plantation. Nobody belongs to anyone."

"Don't be a brat. You know very well what I mean."

She did but she ignored her father's comment. "How close is Lilith?"

"Fortunately, Suri's ancestor's intervention put a kink in her plan, but I'm sure she's already concocted another."

"If Suri is as powerful as I believe, Lilith has quite a fight on her hands."

"True, but you've seen for yourself the damage that she has already inflicted. Don't let your affection for Suri blind you to that."

"Thank you for the unnecessary advice. Now please leave before she sees you. Your painting already freaked her out, she doesn't need to be scared witless by the real thing."

Isfet chuckled. "Yes, daughter." He placed an affectionate kiss on her cheek then she felt his energy fade as he left.

Layla watched Suri for another moment, fascinated by the sight of the plants and flowers eagerly leaning in for her touch as she strolled down the rows of the garden. If what happened earlier and this were any indication, she was far more powerful than she could imagine.

"You seem to have made some friends."

Suri smiled and her beauty made Layla's heart skip a beat. "They just needed some attention. You don't talk to them, do you?"

Layla snorted. "Uh, no. They're plants."

Suri looked amused. "Plants live and thrive just as you and I do. Like us they deserve a little love, attention, and praise every now and then."

Layla gazed at the sunflower closest to her. If she didn't know any better, she'd think it was looking at her accusingly. "I'll do better." She said to the flower.

Its huge head shifted slightly. That was definitely a nod. She turned to Suri, not wanting to think about her plants listening and responding to her like a human. She had enough to deal with Sebastian.

"There's an open area within a few minutes' walk from here through the trees. It's where I train."

Suri gave her an appreciative glance. "You must train a lot."

Layla had to look away to calm her succubus. "Not much else to do out here in the boonies."

She went ahead of Suri wondering if this was such a good idea. She had never had to fight back her nature like this with anyone. She didn't understand what it was about Suri that brought it out so easily. It wasn't like she hadn't known beautiful women before. When you'd lived for as long as she had and been with as many women as she had, it took a lot more than looks to get a rise out of her. It was obvious there was something in Suri's nature that piqued her attraction so strongly. It could be her power. Like attracting like. Whatever it was, now was not the time to analyze it. Lilith and Sojourn were unpredictable so they needed to be prepared for anything.

After walking for a few minutes, they broke through the trees to an open area that Layla had carved out in the middle of the thick forest of trees that bordered the bayou on the rest of her land. The area was enclosed by a wood post fence in the shape of an octagon to ward off negative spiritual energy. At the far end was a water pump with a pail and a waist-high steel-lined wood storage box. They wouldn't need anything from there for some time. She placed the bottles of water on the box then turned to Suri who gazed at her expectantly.

"I think we should start with simple self-defense moves then, if I feel like you've got that down, we'll move to defensive magic. That sound good to you?"

Suri nodded. "Whatever you think is best. You're the instructor."

"Have you taken a self-defense class before?"

"Not really. I mean I went to a rape prevention class with a few of my co-workers once, but that was years ago. The only things I remember are how to use your car keys as a weapon, how to hit someone in the neck or nose to incapacitate them and, of course, the good old knee to the crotch move."

Layla grimaced. "Take it from me when I say a knee to the crotch can hurt a woman and a demon just as badly as a man."

Suri chuckled. "That's good to know."

"What I want to show you are defensive moves that could be combined with defensive magic to give it more strength. Here let's go to the center for more room. Now, one very effective way to stop someone coming at you, no matter what their size, is a strike to the solar plex or sternum." Layla indicated from the middle of her own chest down to the area just above her abs. "This is effective with or without magic so let's work on without first so that you can get used to the movement. Lift your hand with your palm facing out toward me."

Suri did as she was instructed.

"You're going to strike with the palm and heel of your hand. You aren't slapping someone. You're using the full force of your body to move that person, even if it's just to stop their momentum." She took a few steps back, got into a defensive stance, and demonstrated the palm strike movement for Suri a few times.

"Okay. I think I got it." Suri mirrored Layla's stance and movement perfectly.

"Good. Now I'm going to come at you. Strike as soon as I get within arm's reach."

Layla moved hurriedly toward Suri and received a nice pop in the chest from her palm strike. Because of her supernatural durability, it didn't hurt her, but it would've been effective enough to pause a normal human. "Good. Now, I'm going to put a little more threat behind it. I want you to think about gathering a ball of energy into the center of your palm and pushing it out with your strike."

Suri frowned. "I don't want to hurt you."

Layla grinned. "You won't."

Suri looked skeptical but she took a defensive stance as Layla turned away. When she was back a good distance she turned and saw Suri's lips moving as she intently focused on Layla. She decided not to put too much power behind her speed and just jogged toward Suri to give her enough time to react. They would work on speeding up her reaction time later. As Layla drew close, she saw Suri's eyes brighten just enough to blur her pupils. When she was a few steps away, a ball of energy punched into her chest and took her breath away. She stopped, bending over to rub her chest as she gasped for air.

"Oh my God! Are you okay?"

She saw Suri's feet as she finally caught her breath and felt her rubbing her back. The pleasurable sensation from her touch drew her attention away from her discomfort. She straightened and took a deep breath.

"I'm good. That just surprised me. I wasn't expecting so much power behind it."

"I'm so sorry. It just welled and came out of nowhere."

"What were you chanting?"

"Chanting?"

"Yeah, you were chanting something just before you released the energy."

Suri's brows furrowed. "I don't remember." She closed her eyes and seemed to concentrate for a moment, then opened them with a look of surprise. "I heard a voice in my head chanting something and I think I just repeated it."

Layla didn't like that. "Someone had control of you?"

"No. Nothing like that. It was like they were instructing me what to say. I didn't feel threatened. I actually felt protected."

A thought popped into Layla's head. If what she was thinking was true, then Suri was going to be a formidable foe for anyone coming up against her.

"Let's try something. I want you to go to the other side, turn back to me, but this time don't take a defensive stance. Just react."

"Okay." Suri walked to the far side of the area then turned to face Layla. "Now wh—"

❖

Suri turned just in time to see a blurred Layla heading right for her. She couldn't figure out why she was a blur, but she sensed that she needed to defend herself so she took her stance, recalled the chant and the feel of the energy from moments ago, but this time she put all her strength behind the defensive move, with both of her hands directed at Layla. Her body grew hot as a surge of energy built from her core and flowed through her limbs like molten liquid and shot out from her hands. One moment, Layla was running at her, the next, she was flying backward, slamming through the fence and into a tree with a loud boom that shook the ground.

"Oh shit!"

Suri ran as fast as she could to Layla, now lying prone next to a huge, downed tree, its roots ripped up out of the ground with it. She went into automatic nurse mode, taking Layla's vitals, sighing with relief when she felt her strong pulse. She gazed down at her chest and saw it rising and falling normally, then pulled her phone out of her pocket, turned on the flashlight, and gently began lifting an eyelid with the pad of her thumb to test for light reaction. Suri released the lid when all she saw was a glistening black rimmed with blood red. The distinction between the white, pupil, and iris of Layla's eyes was no longer visible. It took everything she had not to back away in fear. Concern for Layla's well-being was foremost. She continued with her assessment by carefully checking for any head injuries and felt wetness at the back of Layla's head. Layla groaned in reaction to her probing fingers. Suri gazed down to find her grimacing as she blinked her eyes open. They were back to looking normal.

"Lie still. You have a cut on the back of your head, and I need to check to see if you have any other injuries or broken bones."

"Nothing is broken," Layla said wearily as she slowly sat up.

Suri helped her to lean against the downed tree. "Well, you might have a concussion and I need to thoroughly check this wound."

She climbed over the tree trunk and knelt behind Layla. Suri could see the laceration between two braids right at the back of her head. It was long and deep, but there was surprisingly less blood than she would've expected for such a severe wound.

"You're going to need stitches."

"No. I'll be fine in a minute or two."

"You're going to need stitches. Is there a hospital or urgent care nearby?"

"Suri, I'm going to be fine. Really."

Suri sighed with frustration. "I don't know if you know this, but I'm a nurse."

Layla chuckled. "I don't know if you know, but I'm a cambion. I'll heal. Check the wound again if you don't believe me."

Suri gazed back at Layla's head and noticed that the bleeding had completely stopped, and the wound had begun to close. She watched with fascination as the torn flesh slowly knit together and would probably be the size of a paper cut in another minute. She had healed herself and others before but had never seen it happen on its own with a supernatural being. She also didn't know why she hadn't thought to use her gift to heal Layla's injury herself but it didn't matter now. Even the blood that had come away on her hand when she'd touched the wound had dried enough for her to brush the reddish brown flakes off like dust.

"I'm sorry for injuring you. I just reacted." She climbed back over the tree and sat beside Layla.

Layla patted her leg. "It's okay. That's why I came at you that way. I wanted to make sure you could defend yourself against someone with supernatural speed. But, like before, I underestimated your power."

"Obviously, so did I."

Suri gazed at the roots torn up from the ground and the hole where the tree had previously stood. She couldn't believe that she had anything to do with what caused the damage. She also couldn't get the image of Layla flying toward it like a rocket shot from a missile out of her head.

"I have a theory about why you're so much more powerful than you expect."

"What is it?"

"You weren't just gifted with Ayomide's powers but also ones that the Orishas deemed would be most helpful in the coming battle."

The word battle scared Suri, but she knew Sojourn and Lilith weren't coming after her for friendly chats. Hers and her family's future were on the line and there was no way she would just give them up without a fight.

"What powers do you think were given to me?"

Layla looked thoughtful. "From what I'm guessing so far, your mediumship comes from Elegua. The ability to use the force of natural energy, air, and wind from Oya. You're probably also able to use natural electrical currents in the air from Shango. The control over plants from Ossain, and you said you can heal others which is probably from Obaluaye."

Suri frowned. "It seems my cousin Aria and I share a gift from him."

"You're referring to her ability to bring on sickness and illness."

Suri nodded. "Do you think I have that as well?"

"Probably. Could you see yourself bringing illness to an innocent person for your, or someone else's, personal gain?"

"No." Suri didn't even need to think about that. "But I can't say the same for someone trying to hurt those I care for."

"It's good that you're honest enough to admit that. To say otherwise would be naïve, which I don't believe you are."

Layla gazed at her in a way that caused a soft flutter in her belly. Suri shyly averted her eyes down to her hands in her lap. "Well, I guess we should continue training to see what other tricks I've got up my sleeves. If you're up to it."

"I've been worse and kept going. This was nothing." Layla stood and offered Suri a hand, which she accepted. "Maybe after we finish training you can help me cut up the tree. I needed more firewood anyway." She gave Suri a teasing grin.

"Oh, you're funny. Keep it up and I'll give you hives." Suri smiled as she headed back toward the gaping opening in the fence made by Layla crashing through it.

They spent the next few hours working on different physical and magic defensive moves to figure out what powers Suri had. It turned out she could use plants and natural elements for defense or even capturing. At one point, she wrapped Layla in ivy from a nearby tree, sprinkling her with water from a bucket, and then whipping up a mini tornado using the wind and debris from the surrounding forest floor to stop her when she managed to escape. By the time they were finished Layla had bits of ivy, bark, and dirt clinging to her braids and clothes. She was also able to use her own energy combined with air to levitate a few inches off the ground. Layla told her, with enough practice she would be able to move while doing it. By the time they finished Suri was tired but excited.

"This is crazy. I feel like some superhero from a comic. I knew people had gifts, but I had no idea to what extent it was possible to have them."

"That's because unlike those comics or movies, real people with supernatural abilities don't advertise it unless it's for their own selfish gain. You met several of them yesterday."

Suri tried to remember what supernatural humans she met. Other than Layla and her uncle, she couldn't think of anyone.

Layla grinned knowingly. "Phoebe and her little crew of misfits."

Suri should have known. She'd felt strong energies from all of them yesterday, but she was so overwhelmed with all the revelations that she hadn't put too much focus on it.

"I thought you didn't know any of them prior to last night."

"I didn't know them personally, but I knew of them. New Orleans has drawn supernatural beings for centuries. It's a large community so not everyone travels in the same circles, but we all pretty much know of each other."

"You and Kenya don't seem too fond of each other."

Layla snorted in derision. "I'm too lowborn for Kenya to feel anything but disdain for."

"Ookay, well, that's a story I need to hear but, in the meantime, tell me about the others."

Layla did a little shake and all the dirt and debris fell off her without a trace. "Okay. I'll tell you as we're heading back to the city. I want to take you home before it gets too late."

She handed Suri a bottle of water then they headed back toward the house. After Layla packed a few things in an overnight bag, made sure the house was locked up and refreshed her wards, they were back on the road.

"Will you not be coming back tonight?" Suri asked.

Layla sighed. "No. I probably won't be back out here until after all of this is over. I hadn't planned on going into the city for some time, but something pulled me there. I believe that something, or someone in this case, was you.

"Oh." It technically wasn't her fault, but Suri still felt bad. It was obvious Layla preferred the life of a recluse and Suri couldn't blame her. How else could she get away with living here for two hundred years without being noticed.

"So, about Phoebe's coven. Like your grandmother, Phoebe is a very powerful priestess, but unlike Pearl, she practices hoodoo and voodoo. Her shop is the main thoroughfare for anyone in the magical arts and a refuge for supernatural beings of all kinds. Rory is a warlock, hoodoo practitioner, and local celebrity drag queen. He was even offered an opportunity to be on *RuPaul's Drag Race* but turned it down because he didn't want the attention. Cassandra is young but a powerful necromancer. There isn't much known about her other than she was raised in an orphanage in Baton Rouge because they couldn't find a foster home that would keep her or anyone that would adopt her. Rumor has it that when Cassandra was a toddler, her father killed her mother and himself but no one found out until they found Cassandra digging through the neighbor's trash two years later. She had been living in the house with her parents' corpses all that time. The thing was, her father's corpse had all but rotted away, but her mother's looked as if she'd only been dead for a few months despite a gaping hole in her chest from the shot gun he'd killed her with."

"She'd brought her mother back from the dead?"

"That's what they say. She'd pretty much been taken care of by a zombie."

Suri shivered. "No wonder she looks so haunted. What about Leandra?"

Layla grinned. "Other than being your uncle's boo-thang, she's a fairy halfling. Her father was a powerful sorcerer and her mother was an Aziza."

"An African fairy? They really exist?"

"Yep. I don't know the story of how her blond-haired blue-eyed father managed to snag an Aziza, but it must've been true love because she left Africa to come back here with him."

"Wow. Now you have to tell me about Kenya."

Layla frowned. "Do we have to talk about her?"

Suri chuckled. "Yes, even more so now that I know she irks you so much."

Layla sighed. "I haven't had dealings with Kenya directly, but I have dealt with her family in the past. Kenya is from a prominent family of shifters that have lived in this region since before Columbus stole the land."

"A shapeshifter? Like a werewolf?"

"Well, that's one kind. Kenya is a werepanther."

Suri felt as if she'd entered an African fairytale. Orishas, Azizas, and werepanthers. "This is crazy."

Layla chuckled. "You asked."

"Gammy used to tell me stories about tribes in Africa full of mystical beings like Azizas and were-creatures that roamed the forests protecting the land from slave catchers, but I thought they were just fantastical stories told to entertain me."

"I don't know about the stories she told, but that was a common occurrence. There were many raiders sent out to capture people that went missing or were found slaughtered as if torn apart by wild animals. Kenya's family was known to protect runaways escaping Louisiana, Florida, and Georgia plantations before slave catchers caught on and started killing anything that resembled a big cat. So, they found ways to make money from White people and use that money to fund the Underground Railroad. By the time Kenya came along, the Lanes were one of the wealthiest Black families in the area and she wore her privilege like an obnoxious fur coat for everyone to see."

Layla wore the same look of disgust she'd had when speaking to Kenya last night. "You really don't like her."

"I don't know her well enough to say I don't like her. I just know what she's done and the people she's hurt. The Lanes aren't the only tribe of shifters in this area. Like I said, New Orleans, Louisiana, in general, draws supernatural beings like bees to pollen. Werebeasts are very territorial so there was a lot of fighting that went on between the different tribes until a shared disgust of slavery brought them together. A pact was brokered and had managed to stay in place until a certain spoiled little princess managed to get herself caught up in a love triangle that almost brought four centuries' worth of peace to a tragic end."

Suri gazed at Layla just as fascinated with her story as she had been when Gammy used to tell her the folktales that she was realizing might not have all been tales of fancy. "What happened?"

Layla gazed at her with a knowing grin. "You are eating this up, aren't you?"

"Can you blame me? The idea that this could've all been my life if my parents hadn't left New Orleans is mind-blowing."

"Well, the short version is Kenya got into a relationship with Trent Casey, second in command of the local wolf tribe and Bettina Star, daughter of the leader of a neighboring panther tribe. They found out and came to blows, Bettina was seriously injured as a result, and the families were about to go to all-out war until Kenya's father stepped in. He paid for Bettina's medical bills as well as a rumored large monetary settlement, gave up a prime piece of land to the wolves, and sent Kenya off to stay with relatives in Colorado for a year with the threat of cutting her off if she came back any sooner than that. That was ten years ago and she's been a perfect little angel since."

"I take it Bettina is a friend."

Layla nodded. "It took her a long time to recover physically and she still bears internal scars of guilt. To have almost been the cause of a war over a girl she didn't even love has been difficult for her to deal with despite all of us telling her it wasn't her fault."

Layla looked heartbroken on her friend's behalf. Suri placed a comforting hand over the one Layla rested on her arm rest. "I know what it's like to see a friend heartbroken and not be able to do anything about it. I'm sure just knowing you and others that support her is enough and will help her forgive herself in time."

She received a soft grateful smile in return. "Thank you."

Their gazes held for a moment before Layla turned back to look at the road and Suri hesitantly removed her hand and faced forward. Something soft and beautiful passed between them in that look that she felt swell within her heart. Something she hadn't felt since Tracey died. She allowed herself a moment to enjoy it before she pushed it back and tucked it away. There was no time for such feelings, especially for two people so inherently different.

CHAPTER NINE

Layla pulled up in front of Suri's house behind a huge black pickup truck just as the sun was setting.

"That's Uncle Robert's truck," Suri said.

He stepped out onto the porch, arms crossed, looking every bit like the family's protective warrior. "You did tell him where you were, right?"

"Yes, while I was waiting for you in the garden."

"Well, he doesn't look so happy." She hadn't felt a strong power with Robert last night but knowing that his role had been protector for the women in his family, he probably had a lot of defensive magic skills that weren't obvious. She moved to get out of the car with Suri.

"You don't have to come."

"Yes, I do. He's obviously not comfortable with you having gone off with me. It's only right that I try to ease his concern."

Suri gave Layla a curious smile. "Okay."

Layla followed her. Robert met them halfway down the walkway with a mix of annoyance and worry on his face. "Suri, I cannot protect you if you go traipsing off someplace and not tell me until after you're there."

Suri stood on tiptoe to place a kiss on his cheek. "I told you I was safe with Layla and not to worry."

Robert gazed past Suri at Layla suspiciously. "So you say, but how do I know she hadn't forced you to send that text."

Layla simply smiled, understanding his distrust considering what he knew and what had happened to so many of his family members.

Suri looped her arm through his and turned him back toward the house. "Because, as you can see, I'm back home safe and sound. Will you be joining Layla and I for dinner?"

Layla grinned. Guess she was invited to dinner. She followed them as far as the doorway where she felt the magical ward briefly before it opened for her to enter without Suri having to invite her in. She wasn't sure if that was on purpose or there was something wrong. She would have to mention to Suri to refresh her ward just in case. She stepped across the threshold and felt the barrier close again. Robert and Suri had stopped in the hallway.

"I wish I could, but I promised Leandra that we'd go see some new thriller that was just released. I just wanted to make sure you got home safely." He gave Layla a cursory glance.

"Mr. Shields, I know you don't know me other than finding out I had a hand in your daughter's hasty departure from New Orleans, but I have the highest respect for Suri and the position your family is in. I would never cause her harm or knowingly put her in harm's way."

She hoped he could see her sincerity. Unfortunately, when people learned of her being a cambion, whether they were supernatural beings or not, there were always misconceptions about her. With the reputation that many cambions happily lived up to, she understood the confusion, but it didn't make it any easier for her to accept when it happened. It was no different than when Black men were stereotyped as thugs and criminals.

"She also got the thumbs up from Gammy and every other busybody spirit in the house," Suri said with an amused grin. The lights flickered in response.

Robert gazed up at the chandelier hanging above his head then at Layla. "That's all well and good, but I prefer to form my own opinion. I know Phoebe and my mother insist that we should trust you, but I've lost too many people to beings like your people, so you'll have to excuse me if I need more than a vision telling me to do so."

Layla gave him a tight smile. "I understand."

Robert nodded then turned back to Suri. "Promise me that you'll call me before you go anywhere. I trust you, it's beings out there that I don't trust. Human or supernatural."

"I promise. Now go. I'll be fine."

Suri's smile seemed to reassure him. He placed an affectionate kiss on her forehead, directed a warning glare at Layla, then left.

"Sorry about that. Since my parents died, he's been very overprotective. Insisted I call him at least twice a week to make sure I was okay."

"It's understandable. He's been the family's protector for most of his life and now he's been told to trust a stranger to do it because he may not be strong enough to do what may need to be done to continue to keep the family safe."

"And how do you feel about it? You're being thrust into a situation that you had no idea was an issue until yesterday with a group of people you barely know. What's keeping you from walking away?"

Layla took a moment to think about the best way to answer the question. Suri waited patiently for her answer. Her expression was open and her tone curious. She sensed a genuine, kind, and loving nature from Suri that made her bright beauty shine even more. This time Layla's heart, instead of her succubus, reacted with a swell of tenderness. She knew she could trust Suri with secrets she hadn't told anyone before.

"Despite what your uncle may think of me and my people, I'm not completely what I've come from. My father may be a demon, but my mother was a kind, loving, and caring human being who continued to influence the woman I was to become even after she was no longer with us. Her best traits came from my grandmother who raised me and who I still try to emulate to this day. Learning that I was a cambion didn't change the woman she raised. Yes, it still proves to be a challenge at times, but I believe, because of my mother, my grandmother, and my uncle, that despite the demon within me, I'm inherently a good person who refuses to let people like Sojourn and your cousin, or beings like Lilith, destroy the lives of innocent people for their own selfish gain. I will do whatever is necessary to protect you and anyone else that isn't able to defend themselves against their evil in whatever capacity and for however long it takes." She could hear the vehemence in her tone.

"Well, okay then. On that note, I'm in the mood for Thai, what about you?"

Layla smiled with embarrassment. "Sounds good to me."

Suri nodded then took her phone out of her pocket, typed something in, then read off the names of nearby Thai restaurants that delivered. Layla told her which one was the best and Suri placed their order.

"Let's hang in the living room while we wait for the food. If we're going to be working together to save the world we might as well get to know each other."

Layla chuckled. "I don't think we're saving the ENTIRE world but okay."

Suri smiled. "How about the world as we know it."

Layla followed her into the living room. While she sat on the sofa Suri stopped at the bar along the wall.

"Would you like something to drink? Gammy loved to entertain so she always made sure to keep plenty of booze and soft drinks available."

As unpredictable as her physical reaction to Suri had been all day, Layla thought it best not to drink. Technically, it took a lot to get her drunk, but she didn't want to even chance it. "I'll take a ginger ale if you have it."

"Yep. Ice?"

"Yes, please."

While Suri made their drinks, Layla gazed up at the portrait over the fireplace and was a little startled to find Suri's ancestor looking directly at her. She knew it wasn't a play of the light because she distinctly remembered when she was here earlier that the woman's gaze had been focused straight ahead, not looking down toward occupants of the room. Layla gave her a nervous smile. She had been in many haunted houses. Afterall, this was New Orleans. Every building still standing after the Civil War and years of natural disasters had a spirit or two refusing to leave. But Suri's home seemed to be more of a gateway rather than haunted. The spirits here thrived from a force or connection between this world and the spirit world.

"Here you go."

Layla's attention was drawn away from Athena's curious gaze by Suri who offered her a glass, then sat down beside her and took a sip from hers.

Suri held it up. "Seltzer and lime. I think I'm going to refrain from alcohol until I'm more comfortable with my newfound gifts. I don't think it would be too smart to leave myself vulnerable for an attack, physical or spiritual, while drunk."

"Smart thinking. So, tell me about your life in New York."

"Nothing much to tell. After losing my best friend, my parents, and my girlfriend I kept to myself. I went to work and came home. That's it. I stopped taking clients for my side gig as a spirit medium, stopped practicing hoodoo and even lost passion I had for my work as a maternity ward nurse." She grew quiet and gazed down into her glass. "I hate to think what would've happened if I hadn't come here."

Layla not only heard but felt the sadness in her voice. She wanted to reach out, pull Suri into her arms, and comfort her. "I understand some of what you were going through. After the Emancipation I lost touch with what was left of my family as my uncle's wife didn't want to have anything to do with their unholy niece. My uncle wrote when he could, but it was painful not being able to be a part of their lives so I asked him to stop. Then Cora Lee, someone I had known since childhood, came to me for help. Despite knowing who and what I was she ended up staying with me until she died at the age of ninety-five." Layla's heart still clenched with grief when she thought about Cora Lee.

"Is that the woman in one of the paintings at your house?"

"Yes. She would've hated it. Cora Lee never even looked at herself in a mirror."

"She was very pretty."

Layla nodded in agreement. "She felt shame over the things she had been forced to do while she was enslaved and it made her see herself as something ugly and twisted on the inside and out. Despite how she looked in my painting, she would've only seen the ugliness."

Suri's eyes widened in surprise. "You painted those portraits? They look more like photographs than paintings."

"When you've lived for as long as I have you start remembering less and less of the people that are no longer in your life. I painted my family while I could still see them for who they truly were."

"I'm assuming the portrait of the man is your father." Suri frowned and shivered. "Even remembering that one gives me the willies."

"Yeah. Unfortunately, I didn't know painting my father's image would be like giving him a window into my home."

When she had finished painting Isfet's portrait and seen the eyes shift and the mouth curve into his signature cocky grin, Layla almost threw it on the fire but didn't think it would've been fair to have Cora Lee's portrait and not her father's so she kept it. She never had company so it never occurred to her that anyone would see it but her. Besides, he didn't need a portrait to peer into her life, but he did get some amusement using it to communicate with her sometimes and freak out poor Sebastian.

"That can't be fun when you have company."

Layla shrugged. "You're the first person I've brought to the house since Cora Lee died."

"Oh. You must have cared for her deeply."

Layla smiled. "Not at first, but within a few years we had become a comfort to each other. Easing each other's loneliness and pain. I loved her, but I think her pain was too great and kept her from opening herself up to love someone else. I knew she cared for me and gave me everything that she was able to give for as long as she could. In the end I could only hope that I had done enough for her to have been happy even for a little while."

"Did you ever try to reach out to her to find out?"

"No. She was finally at peace and I couldn't bring myself to disturb it."

They sat together quietly for a moment before a notification from Suri's phone broke the silence followed by the doorbell.

"The food is here." Suri set her glass on the coffee table then stood to go answer the door.

Layla suddenly felt a strong sense of foreboding and the presence of a demon. She set her glass on the coffee table and hurried after Suri only to practically crash into her back as she stood just outside the entryway to the living room staring at the door.

"Do you feel that?" she asked.

"Yeah. Are you seeing anything?"

Suri slowly moved toward the door. Through the pane of glass beside the door she saw a young guy dressed in jeans, a T-shirt with the name of the restaurant he was delivering from, and a baseball cap. He peeked in the window, smiled, and waved.

"I have a delivery."

Suri took a step back.

"What do you see, Suri?"

"I can't tell what he is, but he's not human," she whispered.

Layla was also finding it difficult to read the guy. This was some powerful glamour. "You can leave it on the porch. Thanks."

The delivery guy shrugged, set the bag down then walked away.

"When was the last time the wards were strengthened around the house?" Layla asked.

"I don't know. Why?"

"When I came in earlier, I felt a gap in the magic."

"Phoebe was supposed to be keeping the wards up."

Both Layla and Suri jumped and turned around to find Pearl frowning behind them.

"Jeez, Gammy! Are you trying to give me a heart attack?"

"Sorry, Lil' Bit, but there's no time for niceties. You need to strengthen the wards. He's looking for a weak spot and will probably find it soon. There should be cinnamon in the kitchen and some cascarilla powder in the apothecary cabinet in my workroom. You know what to do."

Suri took off at a run for the stairs. Layla gazed back at Pearl. Her image was almost transparent. "They're trying to block you from the other side."

Pearl nodded. "Layla, you need to be here to protect her. If this was just Sojourn and Aria's doing, I wouldn't worry so much, but Lilith is bombarding Suri's connection to our ancestors and Phoebe's magic is no match for her and her minions."

"When you say I need to be here—"

"She means you need to stay here," Suri said as she rushed down the stairs with two small bottles in her hand then headed toward the kitchen.

Layla followed her.

"Gammy and Ayomide think you need to stay here for added protection as you know more about the demon stuff than I do." She set the bottles on the counter, grabbed a small black stone pestle and mortar set and a canister of cinnamon, then set those down as well.

"How do you feel about that?"

"Right now, I'm thinking it might be a good idea but only if you're comfortable with it. We have plenty of space here."

She placed a good amount of the cascarilla powder and cinnamon in the mortar then several dropperfuls of oil from the other bottle she'd brought down. Layla recognized the scent from her own root work.

"Van Van oil to strengthen the powder."

"Yes."

She ground the mixture together with the pestle until it was the consistency of oil paint. Just as she picked up the bowl and went to leave the kitchen there was a loud bang as if someone were trying to crash through a wall of the house.

"Suri!" Pearl called from the hallway.

Layla held out her hand. "Give it to me, I can move faster than you and I know a ward better suited for demons."

Suri didn't hesitate. She handed Layla the bowl and it barely touched her palm before she was off. She ran in search of the four corners of the house, used her finger to draw rune symbols on the wood floors with the mixture, chanting a protective spell over each and was back to Suri within minutes.

"I didn't know the layout of the house so it took me a little longer to find the four corners."

Suri gazed at her in amazement. "You were gone all of two minutes, if that."

There was an angry roar from outside. Suri yelped in fright and Layla wrapped a protective arm around her waist.

"I think it worked." Pearl appeared before them looking more solid. Her brow quirked as she gazed at Layla's protective hold of Suri.

Layla slid her arm from around Suri's waist. "Yeah. I don't feel it outside anymore." She placed the mortar on the counter.

"Neither do I," Suri said.

"Well, if I'm going to be staying here, I'll need to go pick up some things from my place. How do you feel about cats?"

"I've never had one, but I don't mind them. I take it you have one."

"Yes, but he's not your average housecat."

Suri smiled. "As long as he's housebroken, I'm fine."

"Great. The ward is good for a few days so it should keep you safe while I'm gone. I suggest we work together on something stronger and longer lasting tomorrow."

"Okay."

Suri and Pearl walked with her to the door.

"Wait, before you go." Suri opened the drawer of a pedestal table along the wall to remove a keychain with a single key. "You might as well have a key. Gammy always kept a spare around in case anyone lost theirs."

"And it finally came in handy," Pearl said.

Layla accepted the key. "I should be back in about an hour."

Suri nodded then opened the door. "Oh, I forgot about the food."

Layla picked the bag up and sniffed. "It doesn't smell like it might've been tainted, but I'll take it and throw it out just in case then stop and pick up something from one of the other places on the way back."

Suri's smile lit up her face. "Thank you. I'll see you in an hour."

Layla nodded feeling a warm surge of excitement at the prospect of staying with Suri.

❖

Suri watched Layla from the window beside the door allowing herself a moment to admire her long legs and tight behind. She walked with an air of easy confidence that had nothing to do with conceit but of someone who knew and accepted who they were with all the confidence of their two hundred years surviving in this world. That self-assurance was just as sexy as her piercing dark eyes and the way her full lips curved into a lopsided grin when she was amused.

"Are you going to be able to keep your head out of your pants while she's here? If not then I think you should just sleep with her to get it out of your system so that you can both focus on the task ahead," Gammy said from behind her.

Suri grinned as she turned back to her grandmother's spirit. "Was this your plan all along?"

"Of course not. I'm just ensuring that there will be no distractions." The innocent expression on her face didn't hide the gleam Suri saw in her eyes.

"Yeah, okay." Suri went to the kitchen.

"I hate the thought of you shutting yourself and your heart away. We all just want to see you happy."

Suri paused as she reached up in the cabinet for plates. "We?"

"Yes. Your ancestors, your parents, your friends…we're all here for you."

Suri knew Gammy hadn't brought up those she'd lost recently to cause her pain, but it did. Her heart ached, but she shook it off, not wanting the pain to feed the seed of darkness Lilith had managed to plant. She placed two plates on the island.

"I appreciate that, Gammy, but this little alliance between Layla and I is for the sole purpose of dealing with the trouble coming our way. If I manage to survive with my soul intact, my focus will be on fulfilling my duty to the family."

"That doesn't mean you have to do it alone. Who better to share the burden with than a cambion with the heart of an angel?"

Suri gazed at her grandmother with amusement. "Are you seriously trying to play matchmaker right now?"

Gammy grinned. "No. I'm just trying to make sure that my granddaughter doesn't spend her life as an old maid in this house. I don't know how I would've managed without your grandfather. He had gifts of his own."

Suri looked up in surprise. "Gampa was blessed?"

"Not to the extent that our family has been, but he was from a family of powerful Shamanic Magic wielders. He was one himself. It's where Robert gets most of his gifts. The blessed women in our family have always been drawn to partners with similar abilities."

"But, according to the family tree, Athena never married and although it lists her three children it doesn't say who their father was."

"That's because you and Athena have more than a bloodline in common. Her life partner was a Santeria priestess whose brother gladly volunteered to father her children if he didn't have to take care of them. I'm sure you can see why none of that was put in the family history, but if you want to know more, Athena's journal is on the bookshelf in the living room."

Suri gazed at her grandmother in shock. "How had my mother managed to keep all of this to herself?"

Gammy's smile slid into a frown. "As you know, your mother didn't want to have anything to do with the family's blessings and duty. She refused to hear the stories and denied her own gifts so well that I don't even think she remembered she had them, then she moved to New York to get away from all this."

"Mom had gifts?"

"Yes. When she was little, she had a way with animals. Unfortunately, she was teased when other kids noticed her talking to birds and squirrels. It got so bad we had to take her out of the school and enroll her in a private school where no one really knew her. She was ten when she told us that she didn't want her gifts. She wanted to be normal. Wanted the family to be normal. We weren't going to force her to accept what she'd been blessed with so we did our best to keep her shielded from our family's duties and tasks. Robert was sixteen when he decided he was fine with his gifts but he didn't want to have anything to do with responsibilities he would've been charged with when he turned eighteen. It wasn't until the issues with Aria that he took an active role in protecting the family."

Suri shook her head in disbelief. Just when she thought everything that needed to be revealed was revealed and that she could relax, someone threw something else at her.

"Okay. That's enough revelations for the day. I need a break from all this craziness and to just have a normal uneventful evening."

Gammy chuckled. "So, I guess that means no talking to your grandmother's spirit."

Suri smiled. "As much as I love these moments together, yes, that includes no talking to ANY spirits," she said the last loud enough to make sure that any other family spirits that decide they want to make an appearance heard.

"On that note, I'll take my leave." Gammy placed a kiss on Suri's cheek. "Enjoy your evening with Layla." She winked playfully before fading away.

Suri sighed. She could understand why her mother wouldn't have wanted this role. She was beginning to second-guess taking it on herself, but she was already too involved to walk away now. She continued with her task of preparing for dinner with Layla, grabbing silverware and a couple of glasses then placing them next to the plates she had taken from the cabinet. She made a pitcher of sweet tea then double-checked to make sure she had milk for Layla just in case. A hysterical giggle bubbled up at the thought that she was going to be entertaining a cambion as a houseguest in a house full of spirits and doorways connecting their world with the supernatural world of the Orishas. Last month, she was wondering where her life was headed and contemplating very dark thoughts. Then her grandmother's last wishes had been presented to her as if she'd known that Suri would be in a bad way and had planned just for such an occasion. Suri wouldn't put it past Gammy doing that. Despite what had been happening since she'd arrived in New Orleans, Suri was grateful for being brought here and out of the funk she'd been in.

She gazed at the clock on the stove and decided that she had enough time to check the guest rooms for Layla's stay. There were six bedrooms in total including three guest rooms, her room, Gammy's room and Uncle Robert's room. There were also three bathrooms, the main one on the second floor, the private one in Gammy's room and one downstairs. The attic, which ran along the entire length of the house and was once Athena's living quarters before the house was left to her, had been converted into a workroom for whatever magical and non-magical practices each generation of guardians and priestesses needed. Suri figured, if she was staying, she would eventually have to restock and set it up for her own hoodoo work, but for now she couldn't bear the thought of rearranging what had been Gammy's workroom.

Just as she finished placing a small pile of bath linen on the bed in the larger of the guest rooms, she heard the front door open.

"Honey, I'm home!" Layla said in a bad Ricky Ricardo impression.

Suri grinned as a ripple of pleasure ran through her at the briefest thought of them living there not as supernatural allies but as life partners then shook it off.

"Nope. Not happening," she said to herself as she went downstairs.

Layla was kneeling and looking frustratingly into an animal carrying crate. The door stood open but nothing came out.

"C'mon, Sebastian, don't be difficult. You can either stay here with me or deal with a pet sitter for however long this takes, which means you'll have no one to talk to."

"This house doesn't feel right," Suri heard a voice whine in response.

She took a step back as she realized it came from whatever was in the crate. The need to comfort the creature's fear overcame her initial shock. She knelt beside Layla to find a black-and-white cat cowering in the crate with wide nervous eyes. Eyes that were far too human to be an animal. She remembered what Layla had said about her cat not being your average housecat and realized the soul inhabiting the feline had once been human. Obviously one with telepathic abilities that had been carried over into its animal form.

"Hello, Sebastian, I'm Suri and this is my home. I can assure you that there's no need to fear anything in this house."

Sebastian's wide gaze looked from Suri to Layla. *"She can understand me?"*

Suri smiled. "Yes, I can. I'm a medium and as a medium, I can connect to past souls. Since yours is the soul of a former human, I guess I'm able to connect with it."

Sebastian tentatively moved toward the entrance of the crate, sniffed the air around Suri, then stepped fully out, brushing his body along her legs purring softly.

"I like her. She feels like home." Then he trotted off, Suri assumed to investigate the rest of his new surroundings.

She gazed over at Layla's amused expression. "I guess he doesn't need an adjustment period."

Suri smiled. "I think I do. It's going to take a minute for me to get used to hearing a cat's thoughts."

"I didn't think to warn you because it didn't occur to me that you would be able to communicate with him that way."

Suri shrugged. "Considering what's been happening lately, it's not the weirdest thing I've dealt with."

Layla chuckled. "I guess not. Where should I put my things?"

"First room on the right."

"Great. I put the food in the kitchen. I'm starving so I'll just drop my things off and come back down. Thanks again for allowing me to bring Sebastian. He hasn't been on his own in a very long time."

"You're welcome."

Suri was tempted to ask for further details but then changed her mind. The way things had been going, Sebastian was probably some ancient supernatural human reincarnated into a cat. It was going to be strange enough knowing he could "talk" to her. Layla smiled at her knowingly then turned and headed up the stairs. Her first houseguests since arriving and they just happened to be a cambion and a talking cat. Sounded about right.

CHAPTER TEN

Layla lay awake for another hour after they had gone to bed. She and Suri had enjoyed a delicious dinner as they spoke of their very different upbringings. Layla didn't go into detail on why she had left the plantation, but she was sure, with Suri being an empath, that she had read between the lines and knew that it was something too painful for Layla to speak of, even after all these years. She hadn't pushed her just as Layla hadn't pushed Suri to speak of the deaths of her loved ones. Their lives may have begun extremely differently, but they shared a history of manipulation and violence pushing them onto a path neither could have imagined treading.

With a heavy sigh, she flopped onto her side, picked up her phone to turn on a sleep music playlist from her meditation app, then threw a few punches into the pillow to get it bunched just right under her head. She didn't remember falling asleep, but the next time she opened her eyes the house was almost too quiet and the room was bathed in pitch-black darkness. Despite her ability to see clearly in the dark, she couldn't even see her hands in front of her face. The only light came from under the door. She climbed out of the bed and opened the door to find the hallway just as dark as her room and a light coming from under Suri's door.

The only explanation Layla had was that she had somehow been pulled into another one of Suri's dreams, which shouldn't have happened as she had made sure to keep her guard up around Suri since the first time it happened.

She placed her hand on the doorknob but didn't turn it. "Suri."

"Are you going to stand out there all night or come in?"

It sounded like Suri, but her tone of voice had a sensuous quality that piqued Layla's succubus nature. It peeked one eye open with a purr-like growl. Layla closed her eyes, attempting to will it back into the slumber she had managed to keep it in for the past five years but she could feel it unfurling within her.

"Shit."

Layla released the doorknob and attempted to turn away, but her feet seemed rooted to the spot as her succubus stretched throughout her entire body. Suddenly, the door opened and Suri stood before her dressed in a short cotton nightgown that was unbuttoned almost to her waist, barely reached midthigh and was thin enough for the bright light of the room to show the outline of her generous curves beneath. Her auburn curls haloed around her head and there was no mistaking the lustful look in her gaze.

"I've been waiting for you." Her lips curved up to a sexy smile.

Layla barely held her succubus back as she attempted to get a read if this was truly Suri or something else that may have gotten past the ward she had put up around the house.

Suri grinned knowingly. "This is all me. Well, maybe not all me. It's my subconscious. The part of me that happily does the things the conscious me is too afraid to do." She took Layla's hand as she stepped away from the door.

Layla knew that once she crossed the threshold, there was no going back. She tugged her hand to stop Suri. "I will not do anything without Suri's consent."

Suri's laugh was deep and sensual. "Oh, I want this. Believe me. I've been wanting this since we left your house. Why do you think I invited you to dinner?"

Layla still hesitated.

Suri began pulling her into the bedroom. "Besides, this is a dream. What harm could a great sex dream cause?"

A low growl rumbled from Layla's chest. "You don't know what you're asking."

It wasn't until she heard the door close behind her that she realized she had been pulled fully into the bedroom. The bright light hadn't come from lamps but candles surrounding the bed as if it were an altar. Suri released her hand, sauntered toward the bed, her hips swaying seductively with each step, then turned back toward Layla. She reached for the hem of her nightgown, raising it up over her full hips, softly rounded belly, and generous breasts in agonizingly slow movements before tossing it aside. At the sight of Suri's beautiful body and lustful gaze, Layla's battle with her nature was lost. She had gone to bed in a tank top and shorts, which she simply ripped off because she didn't have the patience to remove them properly.

Suri laughed huskily as she climbed onto the bed and beckoned Layla with a finger. As she stalked toward the bed, Layla's incisors lengthened to a point and she ran her tongue over them in anticipation of piercing the delicate skin at Suri's gently sloping neck.

"I will give you one last opportunity to stop this for once it begins…" She let the implication of what she was saying hang in the air.

Suri smiled. "I know what you are and I'm not afraid."

Layla smiled. "You should be."

Suri simply laughed. The erotic sound of it stroked along Layla's skin like fingertips. It had been so long since she'd allowed her nature to have its way. It never felt right taking such liberty of women while they were asleep so she only did it with willing partners, which had been few and far between over the centuries since she did her best not to reveal what she was to humans. There were those that either knew or suspected who allowed fetishism to get the best of them. They volunteered themselves for her succubus pleasure because, despite their curiosity, they would prefer to be ravished in their dreams rather than reality. Although those encounters satisfied her succubus, they left Layla's human side feeling used and guilty so she'd spent the past five years warding herself against herself. It had worked until now. Something about Suri stirred her nature and tore down all the barriers she'd worked so hard to maintain.

As Layla climbed onto the bed, there was none of the fear or hesitation in Suri's eyes that she saw with women she'd been with previously. Suri surprised Layla further by pulling her down into her arms and kissing her hungrily. If Layla didn't know any better, she'd think Suri was part succubus as she aggressively took control. One moment, Layla was on top, the next, she was thrown on her back and Suri was straddling her hips. Their lips hadn't even broke contact during the position change. Their tongues even dueled for position as they kissed and Layla reveled in the power exchange. She sat up, so that Suri was now on her lap and she could have easier access to her body without changing Suri's desire to be on top. Layla broke off the kiss to explore Suri's neck, running the tip of her tongue along the pulsing vein at her neck, having to curb the desire to sink her teeth into them, and continuing her descent to Suri's breast.

Suri's breath came out in quick gasps, her chest heaved with them, making her beautiful breasts tremble. Layla lifted one, finding it full and heavy in her hand. She lowered her head, and suckled Suri's pebble-hard nipple, up to the edge of her smooth brown areola, into her mouth then lengthening her tongue to snake around and tease her nipple. Suri grasped Layla's head, her fingers tangling in her hair, thrust her chest forward as a low moan rose out of her. Suri's whole body was pulsing with a feverish heat that Layla could feel with their bodies pressed together as they were. A heat that her own body began to absorb. In the back of her mind Layla knew the heat was Suri's energy and that if she absorbed too much, she could harm her, but it had been too long since her nature had even a taste of desire, let alone with such a powerful and sensual being as Suri. She couldn't stop even if she wanted to.

She shifted so that she could gift Suri's other breast with the same treatment and received the pleasure of Suri's pelvis grinding against her. With a strength she didn't know Suri had, Layla felt herself being lowered back down against the bed which caused Suri's breast to fall free of her mouth.

"This is my dream, remember?"

Layla saw that Suri's eyes lit with an unnatural glow before she lowered her head and buried her face in Layla's neck. A moment later, Layla sucked in a breath as Suri nipped her then soothed the momentary pain with a slow lick. She did this from Layla's neck, down to her breasts, where she sucked a nipple into her mouth, allowing her teeth to graze her areola before gently biting her nipple.

"FUCK!"

Layla's whole body vibrated and her hips rose off the bed almost bucking Suri off. She gripped the bed sheets as Suri continued her descent in the same manner down the length of her body, leaving trails of pleasure pain as she went. Layla was used to being the one in control. The one seducing and ravishing, not the other way around. It was disconcerting and exciting all at once. She tried to fight it, after all, she was the succubus, but her body grew hot with energy and she discovered it was being absorbed by Suri. But how was that possible? How was any of this possible? Suri had brought her into her dream rather than Layla dream walking into Suri's. Now they were exchanging energy rather than her draining Suri's.

"Let go for me, Layla."

Suri's voice was like a siren song that Layla couldn't resist even if she tried. She relaxed and released her grip on the sheets along with her worry over what should be happening to just let it happen. She was rewarded with the warmth of Suri's lips at the juncture of her thighs, the feel of her teeth grazing her clit, the burning heat of her tongue intimately tracing the outline of her sex before delving deeply inside. Was it the effect of the dream they were in or was Suri's tongue really long enough to stroke Layla's inner walls until they were throbbing with desire? Then she pinched one of Layla's nipples between the fingers of one hand and did the same with her clit with the other, and Layla could feel her vaginal walls contracting around Suri's tongue, trying to pull it deeper and suddenly there was silence. Layla knew she was shouting; she could feel her mouth open and her throat straining, but there was no sound. Just the pleasure and heat surging through and out of her body like lava from an erupting volcano as the bed, or the earth, shifted and shook beneath her. Then the candles around them flared and blurred her vision.

What felt like a lifetime later, the sound of her panting slowly seeped through the haze and the room came into focus. The candles flickered normally, the bed was still and she gazed down to find Suri with a sexy smug grin gazing up at her from between her legs.

"I wonder how many people could say that they sucked a succubus dry."

Layla gazed at her in wonder for a moment then laughed so hard her whole body shook with it. When she was able to catch her breath again, she narrowed her eyes at Suri, crooked a finger at her, then growled, "My turn."

❖

Suri allowed herself to be bold and free. After all, this was just a dream. She probably wouldn't remember it in the morning. At least that's what she had read about sex with a succubus before she had gone to sleep. The victim, well, she wasn't really a victim, usually didn't remember what happened to them after a visit by one. She had also read that they drained energy, but she didn't feel the least bit drained. If anything, she felt more energized. It was probably going to be a different story when she woke up, but nothing a good energy cleansing wouldn't solve. For now, she would enjoy this and not worry about consequences since it was only a dream. She slid up Layla's body, straddling her hips again but Layla flipped them so that she was on top.

"Uh-uh. Like I said, my turn."

Her smile promised that there would be no mercy. Suri was fine with that. It had been too long since she'd given over control. The hook-ups she'd had since Tracey's death had been initiated and controlled by her to ensure that her sexual partners understood that their time together was to satisfy a need, not to start something that wouldn't go anywhere. That had been her goal when she decided to give in to her subconscious self and attempt to seduce Layla. She hadn't really thought it would work, but when it did, she took full advantage of catching her off guard.

Layla lowered her head and brought her lips down onto Suri's for a kiss that left her breathless and wondering as her tongue had brushed along Layla's teeth how she hadn't noticed that Layla's canines had lengthened and become pointed. They hadn't cut her, but now that she wasn't caught up in her own power, she could feel the difference. The thought was lost when Layla took her breast in her mouth as she did earlier. The feel of her long tongue snaking around her nipple and warm mouth practically enveloping the entire tip of her breast had Suri's sex throbbing.

A low growling rumbled up from Layla. "I don't want to hurt you, but your scent of desire is like a drug."

Suri gasped as she felt a delicately pointed tooth graze along her breast. She gazed down toward Layla who looked back up at her with an animalistic hunger that should've frightened Suri but only turned her on more. "I'm not asking you to be gentle."

"What ARE you asking, Suri?"

"For you not to hold back as long as you don't drain me to an empty husk," she said teasingly.

Layla's chuckle was low and deep. Like it had come from the beast Suri could see lurking behind her eyes. Layla allowed the beast to peek out and Suri felt a desire so intense that she almost had an orgasm.

"Be careful what you ask for," Layla said in an overtly seductive tone before lowering her head and taking Suri's other breast into her mouth.

Suri's head fell back onto the pillow and her body felt as if it were on fire. She had felt that same heat while she was seducing Layla. It seemed to be a shared heat between the two of them that grew to a roaring flame that she thought would surely consume them by the time Layla gave in to her pleasure. It was as if Layla's cum was the very essence of pleasure and Suri found herself wanting to lap up every drop.

Layla traveled down Suri's body without leaving a patch of skin untouched by her lips, tongue, and fingers. When her nails grazed along her belly, Suri heard a whimper and was shocked when she realized it had come from her. She had never whimpered. Layla didn't give her time to dwell on it because she took Suri's clit between her lips, slipped her long, tapered fingers into her slit, and matched each stroke of her finger in and out of her with each flick of her tongue over her clit. The rhythm sped up until her finger and thumb were vibrating at a speed that could only be achieved by something battery-operated. Suri's hips had a mind of their own as she squirmed and thrust against Layla's touch, while Layla managed to hold on and keep a steady rhythm. Just as Suri felt that fire again, as if she were about to combust, Layla slowed her manipulations.

Suri whimpered with need. "Please," she begged her.

Layla sat up. "I want to see you cum. I want you to look at the beast you craved."

She offered Suri a hand. Suri accepted it and allowed Layla to pull her up to straddle her lap again.

"You said you know what I am. That you don't want me to hold back. Do you mean that?"

Suri was dizzy with desire. All she could do was nod.

"Remember that you asked for this."

Layla's voice had changed. It was almost hypnotic. Suri knew she could resist but found that she didn't want to. She grasped Suri's hips and tilted her pelvis up. It brought her sex flush against where Layla's clit lay.

"Did you know that succubus are shape shifters when they are in their nature? That they can change to suit the person that they are with?"

"You suit me just fine."

Suri didn't understand what that had to do with anything until she felt a subtle shift between her legs.

"We know what a person desires, even when they don't. Where most succubi use it to take advantage of their victims, I use it to pleasure my partners."

Suri found herself lost in the dark depths of Layla's eyes as she felt something hard and warm slowly penetrating her sex. A thought niggled in the back of her mind. If Layla's hands were on her hips, what was the pulsating fullness settling within the depth of her sex?

"Ride me, Suri."

Suri was still confused but the pleasure was too much to deny. She raised and lowered her hips along the unmistakable length of a penis. Once again, Layla didn't give her time to analyze this surprising change because she lowered her head to take Suri's breast in her mouth and suckled until Suri could focus on nothing but the pleasure she was feeling. She barely noticed when Layla's lips left her breast and pressed against her neck. Without a thought, Suri buried her fingers in Layla's hair, tilted her head to offer her full access to her throat, and felt two pinpricks of pain before pleasure overwhelmed her. Layla's sex stroked and vibrated in and out of Suri's until she could feel the moisture of her arousal coating Layla's thighs. Suri knew that this was it. She was going to combust and literally die from desire, but then her orgasm hit her in waves of pleasure like the sea slamming into the shore during a storm.

"LAYLA!" she heard herself shout, but it sounded so far away, then the heat subsided, as if the waves had distinguished the bonfire in her soul and she sat trembling on Layla's lap.

"Sleep," Layla whispered in her ear.

"Will I remember?" Suri said weakly.

She felt Layla's tongue skim over where she'd felt the pinpricks. "Only if you want to. Do you?"

Suri shifted so that she could look at Layla. It felt like every fiber of her being was bogged down with weight. The tender look Layla gave her made her heart skip a beat.

"I think so."

Layla smiled. "That's not quite an answer, but I guess it will have to do. I'll leave it up to your subconscious to decide." She placed a soft kiss on Suri's lips. "Now, sleep."

Suri felt herself being lifted then laid gently back onto the bed. She was covered with a blanket and another kiss was placed on her temple before she drifted off to sleep.

Suri woke up feeling like she'd been in a prize fight while she slept. Every muscle in her body ached. She gazed up to find the clock on her nightstand showing that it was past nine in the morning. She never slept this late. With a loud groan, she moved as slowly as possible to sit up on the side of the bed but found she couldn't do much more than that. There was a soft knock at her door before it opened and Layla peeked her head in.

"Good morning."

"G'morning," Suri said weakly. All she wanted to do was lie back down and sleep for another day.

"I brought you something to help you get your day started."

Layla was already dressed in a pair of fitted black jeans and a black T-shirt. She offered a large mug she carried to Suri.

Suri took the mug, inhaled the steam rising out of it, then gazed at Layla curiously. "Turmeric, ginger, and green tea?"

Layla nodded as she sat beside Suri on the bed. "I figured you might be sore from our training yesterday. There's also honey. As you know, turmeric and ginger will help with any inflammation and soreness and green tea will give you some energy. I may have also said a healing spell over it for a little boost."

"Thank you." She took a sip of the tea and sighed contentedly. "I've done a two-hour strength class and not felt as sore as I do now."

"I'm assuming you weren't using magic. Yesterday was your first full day with your new abilities. Using magic can drain you no matter how powerful you are."

Since she hadn't had to use her abilities like that before, Suri was going to have to take her word for it, but she felt like she was missing something. She sipped the tea again trying to remember, but her thoughts turned fuzzy. "I'm feeling much better but I think a nice hot shower will help as well."

"Probably. I'll throw something together for breakfast and meet you downstairs."

Suri smiled gratefully. "Okay." She watched Layla leave and found it interesting how quickly she took to having a stranger living with her. Other than college, the only time she had a roommate was Rachel. She and Tracey had been discussing moving in together before…No, she refused to let her thoughts go there. She set the mug on her nightstand then headed out of her bedroom to the bathroom. She really was feeling better after the tea. Not a hundred percent, but at least she could move without wincing in pain.

After Gammy was diagnosed with her heart condition, Uncle Robert replaced the claw-foot tub with a walk-in shower to make it easier for her. She turned the dial to switch from the regular to the rain shower head, got the temperature just right, took off her clothes and stepped directly under the water. She closed her eyes and enjoyed the feel of the water raining down on her. The scent of the fresh eucalyptus and lavender bundle that she had hung in the shower last night mingled with the steam to relax and loosen any sore muscles that the tea hadn't. It also helped to clear her mind as flashes of a dream began to break through the fuzziness from moments ago.

Images of her and Layla doing some very erotic things flashed through her mind in vivid pictures that felt more like actual memories than a dream. As the realization of what she was remembering came to light, Suri sucked in a breath, as well as a mouthful of water, sputtering into a coughing fit as she stepped from under the shower spray, grabbed her robe, slipped and slid her way out of the bathroom, and ran dripping wet down the stairs. She haphazardly knotted the belt of her robe around her waist as she marched angrily into the kitchen yelling, "Layla!" Water from her soaked hair dripped into her eyes and she grabbed a dishtowel from off a shelf to use to wrap her hair with.

She turned to find Layla gazing at her in amusement. "I take it you remembered last night."

Suri went from anger to shock, back to anger at Layla's confirmation of what she suspected happened. "I trusted you! My family trusted you! I allowed you to stay in our home and you dream walk and seduce me on the first night! What the hell!"

Layla held her hands up. "Whoa there! I did no such thing. You initiated it. As a matter of fact, you were the one in control for most of it."

"Impossible! You're the succubus, not me!"

Layla looked offended. "For your information, I haven't dream walked like that in years. You might want to have a little chat with your subconscious because she…YOU…were the one that pulled ME out of my sleep to seduce me. I woke up just as drained as you did. I'm just lucky enough to have self-healing or we both would've been down for the count today."

Suri frowned in confusion as she felt the truth of what she said. "You're serious."

Layla turned back toward the stove, flipping a pancake on the griddle. The wind had blown out of Suri's anger as she felt Layla's words ring true. She sat on a stool at the island in bewildered embarrassment as the memories came to her in greater detail.

"Have you ever displayed signs of a split personality before?" Layla asked.

"No. I mean I've done things that I don't remember doing. Things that I hadn't wanted to deal with but somehow did them anyway. It hasn't happened since just after Tracey's death."

Layla placed a plate filled with perfectly rounded pancakes next to a plate of bacon that Suri hadn't noticed when she'd stormed into the kitchen. "Fortunately, I don't believe it's split personality because you didn't refer to yourself in third person or say *we* when you spoke about yourself. It seems your subconscious takes over to do what you're afraid to do yourself."

Suri didn't want to believe what Layla was saying but it made sense. The first time something similar happened was the morning she found herself standing at Rachel's grave site with a book of dark magic to a spell for raising the dead. Then there were nights that she'd gotten depressed and lonely, gone to a bar or nightclub just to be around people, only to wake up the next morning with a strange woman in her bed and not remembering what happened. She had chalked it up to having gotten too drunk to remember. Other disturbing moments were when she'd found herself standing outside the apartment building of the parking attendant that had caused the death of her parents and not remembering how she'd gotten there, and when she'd woken up lying on the floor in Tracey's apartment just days after her murder with a piece of paper in her hand where she had written the symbols and their translations of the ones that had still been scrolled on the bedroom wall in Tracey's blood.

"Are you okay?"

She wasn't, but Suri nodded anyway then got up to leave. She felt a breeze before Layla was in her path.

"I wish I could say I'm sorry about what happened last night, but I'd be lying. What I can say is that I would've had better control if I'd known that you didn't want it."

Suri gave Layla a nervous smile. "I didn't say I didn't want it to happen. I just hadn't planned on initiating anything, in the dream or real world. Especially with you, no offense, being a succubus. I can't afford to be drained like I was this morning in case we get caught off guard like last night."

Layla grinned. "Well, if it helps, you left me just as drained."

Suri felt her face grow hot with embarrassment. "You said that earlier. How is that possible?"

"I don't know, but it seems that you can absorb another's energy. I don't know if it's just sexual or if you're able to do it as defensive magic as well. We'll have to add that to our training activities. For now, we both need to eat."

Suri gazed down at her robe which was still tied at the waist, but the top had slid open and was revealing way too much for her liking. Although, judging by the heat in Layla's gaze when she looked up, she didn't mind. Suri liked the way she looked at her but closed her robe and stepped to the side to go around her.

"I'll get dressed and be back down shortly."

She hurried past Layla with visions of herself riding Layla's lap as she suckled a mouthful of Suri's breast secretly wishing it hadn't been a dream.

CHAPTER ELEVEN

As Layla watched Suri practically run from the kitchen, she had to force herself not to follow her and make last night's dream a reality. She closed her eyes and pushed her succubus back into its metaphysical cave then went back to finish making their breakfast. She woke up in the early hours feeling as if she'd been the one drained by a succubus. It was a new and fascinating experience for her that she would have to ask Isfet about the next time she saw him. As traumatic as she figured remembering such an intimate experience would be for Suri, Layla secretly hoped that she would remember and maybe even want to repeat it in the real world. But Suri was right. They didn't need the distraction or to place themselves in such a vulnerable position for an attack by anyone, especially Lilith who, judging by last night's close call, was watching their every move.

She set the platter of scrambled eggs on the island with the other food then searched the cabinet for syrup and was happy to find honey, which she preferred on her pancakes. Suddenly, the memory of the moment she had sunk her fangs into Suri's neck and the thick, sticky sweetness of her blood mixed with her energy coating her tongue like honey made Layla shudder with desire. She closed her eyes and listened, easily finding the sound of Suri's heartbeat not because they were the only two in the house but because she could feel its rhythm as if it were her own. Her whole body vibrated with the need to go to her and claim her again. To taste her, fill her, give and take whatever each other needed to reach the pinnacle of satisfaction that they had in that dream.

Layla could sense Suri as she moved around her room, made her way down the stairs, and neared the kitchen. She knew when Suri stood just inside the doorway. Could feel her heart ramp up as she felt Layla's desire permeating the room raising the temperature in the space by several degrees. She could sense when Suri's own desire rose with memories of her dream. Layla's incisors elongated to a point, almost piercing her own lip and a low growl emitted from her throat.

"Layla." She heard her name in a voice whispered with longing and need. There was also a hint of hesitation, which was what probably saved Suri from Layla picking her up, laying her out on the island, and feasting on her as if she were the meal that had been prepared.

"I-I need to run an errand."

Layla's own voice was deeper than she'd ever heard and strained with her own need. She headed for the back door, took a moment to make sure the protective ward that she'd put was still securely in place, then jumped in her car and drove off. To where, she didn't know. It wasn't until she was a few blocks from Suri's house that she was able to control her body's reaction.

"Join me for coffee and beignets." She heard Isfet's voice.

With a weary sigh, Layla redirected and headed toward downtown. She parked at her apartment, a short walk from Café du Monde where she knew her father was waiting for her. He loved pastries and the café had been one of his favorite places to visit since they opened as a coffee stand in 1862. She found him easily as he always sat at one of the outer tables along the wrought iron fence so that he could people watch. She could see the longing in his face for a life he could never have. From the moment Isfet and hundreds of his angelic brethren were sent to earth as the first watchers over mankind, he desired to spend life living as a human. That desire drove him and 199 of his fellow angels to go rogue. Their leader, Samyaza, led them on a rebellion where they turned earth into their own version of spring break. Sleeping with human women, having literally giant babies called Nephilim, and taking it upon themselves to jumpstart the humans they were only supposed to be watching over by teaching them about arts, weaponry, and magic, among other things that God had intended to show them over time, not all at once.

According to many religious texts that talk about the Watchers, most notably the Book of Enoch, the rebel angels fell from God's grace and were sentenced to be chained under earth until judgment day. Isfet told her that might have been the case for some of the fallen angels, but when he and many of his other brethren heard Dad was coming for them, they went to the OG fallen angel, Morningstar, and begged for his mercy. He took them in, saving Isfet and his crew from God's punishment, but he didn't get off scot-free. He still had to spend his days sitting in cafés living vicariously through the humans he had once been a caretaker of. He wasn't even allowed to use his God-given name. Isfet, an Egyptian name meaning injustice, chaos, and violence, was given to him by Morningstar for all the chaos and corruption he'd been a part of during his time as a Watcher. Layla had asked what his true name was when he had told her his story, but he was forbidden to speak it and could not open his mouth to even say it.

She believed he loved her mother so much because, for a little while, she humanized him. She saw past the demon to the angel he had once been and brought that out in him. Layla could see the envy in his gaze, but instead of causing chaos on earth in a fit of jealousy like Lilith, her father lived a pretty quiet life for a top-tier-level demon. That's not to say he didn't torment and terrorize occasionally, just to be a pain in his father's ass like most kids, but he'd grown weary of it in his old age. Layla understood that. While she rarely gave in to her demon side unless it was absolutely necessary, she preferred to stay under the radar and not draw unwanted attention to herself. She and Isfet shared a lot more in common than DNA she thought as she sat in the chair across from him.

He gave her a warm smile. "You look tired. I took the liberty of ordering your café au lait, light on the au lait, and a double order of beignets. I figured you might need to boost your energy."

"Thanks."

His smile turned into a frown. "I'm sorry I wasn't there to assist with your unexpected visitor last night. I knew she was planning something, but my informants have all but disappeared."

"That's not a surprise. She's trying to cut you off so that you can't warn me of anything coming."

Their server set her mug of coffee and a plate piled high with beignets on the table. "More hot chocolate, sir?"

Isfet flashed a broad charming smile. "Yes. Extra whipped cream this time if you please."

The young girl blushed as she nodded and took away his empty mug. Layla smiled. Having been around since biblical times, her father's human form hadn't changed much since she'd first met him in the 1800s. He was the epitome of tall, dark, and handsome, looking to be a distinguished gentleman possibly in his fifties. He still wore his hair long, the silky black locks curling at the end, brushing his shoulders, and a minimal amount of gray outlining his beard. He wore a tailor-cut black suit with a crisp white shirt, the first few buttons undone and patent leather shoes so shiny she could probably see her reflection. He was overdressed for the unusually warm mid-October weather, but he wasn't even breaking a sweat. She saw herself in his angular features and brooding eyes. Sometimes she could even picture the angel he once was and who she also hoped was a part of her.

Their server returned with his refreshed hot chocolate, whip cream piled high, and he rewarded her with another smile which had her giggling. His smile slid into a frown after their server left.

"Unfortunately, this means what little help I could provide is no longer available, but make no mistake, if Lilith moves to hurt you, I will step in."

"No. If you interfere Morningstar will have to rescind his promise of sanctuary and you'll be sentenced to the same fate as most of the other Watchers. I won't be able to live with myself if I'm the reason that happens."

"And I will not be able to live with myself if I have to tell your mother I sat by and did nothing to save our daughter." Isfet reached across the table to place a hand over Layla's. It was a rare display of affection that surprised her. "You are the reason I haven't asked Morningstar to do that very thing and the only good I've done since my early days as a Watcher. No one, not even Father himself will come after you without facing me first."

Layla heard the truth in his words and feared that day would come sooner rather than later and that she'd lose her father. Their relationship was complicated and probably would seem cold to an onlooker for a father and daughter, but they loved each other with a bond that went beyond simple familial attachment. She might be the woman she was because of her mother's and grandmother's influence, but she was the supernatural being that she was because of her father's patient teaching and love. She honestly didn't think she would be alive today if it weren't for his guidance over the centuries.

She flipped her hand and gave a squeeze. "Hopefully, it won't come to that."

Isfet gave her an affectionate smile then pulled his hand back to pick up a pastry. "Now, what has happened that had you calling to me this morning."

Layla frowned with confusion. "I didn't call to you. You're the one that asked me to meet you here."

"Okay, technically you didn't call to me, but I felt an odd disturbance from you last night and this morning. I would've visited you at Suri's house, but you've warded it from demons, which I am."

"Yeah, sorry about that. I couldn't take any chances. I set the ward for any demon outside of myself."

Isfet nodded. "Wise decision. So, what happened? For a brief moment last night, I felt an immense drain in your power, but it quickly surged moments later."

"What you felt was correct and I'm hoping you can explain how it's possible."

With a bit of embarrassment, Layla described what happened between her and Suri. Her father was an incubus so there was no need to be embarrassed about sharing such intimate details with him. She was embarrassed on Suri's behalf because Layla knew she would not be happy to hear that she was telling her father. Isfet listened intently, but his expression remained curious.

"Hmm...Interesting."

"You don't seem surprised."

"It's rare but it's not unheard of for highly sensitive empaths to also be sexual empaths. Particularly if they are sharing physical intimacy with a partner who can reciprocate the emotions brought on by their sexual encounter."

Layla snorted. "Emotions? What happened last night was purely sexual."

"Are you sure? I heard you had a rather possessive reaction to that werepanther threatening Suri the other night."

Layla narrowed her gaze at him. "And where did you hear that?"

Isfet chuckled. "That little necromancer in their group communes with a lesser demon I'm familiar with. She thought to curry my favor to tell me what she'd been told."

Layla was surprised. "Cassandra communes with a succubus?"

Isfet shrugged. "It's difficult for her to maintain relationships considering her abilities and history once they learn who she is."

"I guess that makes sense. I'm sure she has needs like everyone else, but it's kind of sad. The demon gets most of the benefit from that arrangement."

"Not really. From what I've been told, they're both quite happy with it. The necromancer has a partner that doesn't cringe from her touch and Aneth has grown quite attached to her."

Layla gave her father an amused look. "Another demon with a heart?"

Isfet chuckled. "My dear, we all have hearts. Some of us less black than others."

She couldn't fault this Aneth or Cassandra for making whatever they have work. Life was not guaranteed, not even for demons. She believed that if you could find some form of contentment, then take it. That's what her home in the bayou was for her. A vision of Suri standing in her garden came unbidden, bringing on a smile.

"So, you have no affection for her."

She gazed up at her father's knowing grin. Rolling her eyes in exasperation, Layla signaled for their server who hurried over, watching Isfet dreamily. "May I get a box for these?" she indicated the remaining beignets.

It took a moment for the young woman to realize Layla had been speaking to her. "Oh, yes." She hurried away, her face blushing red.

"We so rarely spend time with each other these days," Isfet said wistfully.

Layla accepted the box from the server where she placed the remaining pastries, then stood. Isfet stood as well, towering over her by at least four feet. He held his arms open for her and she stepped into his embrace.

"I promise, after this is all over, we'll spend more time together."

"Maybe you and Suri could even join me for dinner. I'll make my famous etouffee."

Layla stepped on tiptoe to place a kiss on his cheek before stepping out of his arms. "Maybe. I should be getting back."

She didn't want to promise him anything because he would hold her to it and there was no telling where Suri would be after this was all over. Who's to say if she'd want to even stay in New Orleans. Layla attempted to ignore the disappointment of that possibility.

Suri had eaten the breakfast Layla had worked so hard to prepare with Sebastian as company. She tried to listen as he chattered away about his life as a human, but all she could think about was Layla. She could say that she didn't know why she had left so abruptly, but the thrumming in her body would make her a liar. She knew the moment Layla was envisioning last night's dream because her thoughts had pushed their way into Suri's mind. She'd been walking back downstairs and the graphic image of her riding Layla's lap as her teeth sunk into her neck slammed into her mind like a physical blow that almost knocked her down the steps. She'd gripped the railing to keep from falling, but her steps didn't slow. She continued to be pulled down the stairs, to the kitchen and to Layla as if they were magnets. When she arrived at the kitchen, she gripped the doorway so tightly her knuckles ached from the strain of resisting the need to go to Layla and offer herself up to make the dream a reality. Then Layla had turned to her with a hunger in her eyes that made Suri moan. The next thing she knew, Layla was running out the back door and she was left with an intense hunger of her own that none of the delicious looking food that had been prepared could appease.

Suri also knew when Layla left the vicinity of the house as the desire slowly and achingly faded. She tried distracting herself by eating since she needed it to build up her energy and didn't want so much of it to go to waste, but knowing that the light and airy pancakes, the perfectly crisp bacon, and the fluffy eggs were all prepared by Layla just made her think of Layla's hands which also brought on visions of them all over Suri's body. So, she ate until her physical hunger was satisfied, put the food away, then decided that an inventory of Gammy's workroom was long overdue. She made her way to the attic with Sebastian following along. He found a spot on one of two plush high-back chairs tucked in a corner of the room with a small table between them. It was the perfect reading nook. She and Gammy used to spend hours up here when she was little reading to each other or with Suri cuddled in her lap as she told her fanciful stories of magical beings. She wondered, knowing what she knew now of her family's connection to the supernatural, if the stories were more truth than fantasy. Sebastian curled up into a ball and fell promptly to sleep, snoring as if he were still human.

Suri found a notebook in a drawer of the worktable and began cataloging bottles of liquid and powders, plastic baggies of crushed plants and herbs and packets of seedlings that took up the shelves and apothecary drawers of the room. It was just distracting enough to shed the last vestiges of the sexual tension she'd felt but not enough to stop the worry of how they were going to be able to share a living space for a currently undetermined amount of time.

Suri placed a jar of black mustard seed back on a shelf. "Gammy, I can feel your eyes on me." She continued with her work without turning around.

"I wasn't trying to make my presence a secret. I just didn't want to mess up your count."

"I don't know if Layla and I staying here together is going to work."

"From what I hear, sounds like it's working fine." There was a tone of humor in her voice.

Suri shook her head. "Is there no privacy in this house?"

"Not if you don't shield your private space. Your grandfather and I learned the hard way that spirits don't respect your privacy."

She turned and gave Gammy a pointed look. "Yes, I see."

Gammy held her hands up. "Don't look at me that way. I didn't see anything. I'm just going by the tittering going on around here."

Suri turned back to take count of a shelf full of small dropper bottles filled with oils. "I don't plan on it happening again so there's no need for a privacy shield."

"Would it be so bad if it did? In your dreams or real life? You've shut yourself away too long. Some companionship might do you some good."

"I'm not looking for companionship and even if I was, it wouldn't be with someone like Layla. She's a two-hundred-year-old cambion who doesn't look a day past thirty and just as much of a loner as I am."

"You weren't always a loner. Layla's situation was brought on by necessity. Yours was out of fear. There is no reason for you to fear getting close to anyone now. Especially someone like Layla who can handle herself in the face of evil much better than any human companion you could end up with, won't be fearful of your gifts, and won't force you to hold back on using them because of that fear. It's the reason women in our family always end up with companions with gifts of their own."

"You know she's right," said that little voice in Suri's head.

"Shut up, you've gotten me into enough trouble as it is," she said quietly.

"Excuse me?" Gammy said.

Suri set her notepad down with a sigh. "Sorry, I wasn't talking to you." She wasn't going to be able to focus on her task now. She turned and sat on the stool at Gammy's worktable.

Gammy nodded in understanding. "Sometimes when we suppress parts of ourselves for too long, they find a way to break through. I'm assuming that's what you're experiencing."

"Yes."

"You know what you need to do to stop it."

She knew, she just didn't want to do it. To allow herself to fully give in to whatever emotion she pushed back into her subconscious to avoid feeling, scared her. Sadness and despair turned to anger which brought on the darkness that gave Lilith a gateway into taking her soul. Loneliness sent her looking for meaningless physical connection that just made her more depressed. Unfortunately, those seemed to be the only feelings she had when she wasn't doing her best to feel nothing at all. Except for last night. It might have been a dream, but Suri felt more passion and joy during that encounter than she'd had in a very long time.

"You know I'm right."

Suri gave her a mock frown. "You're always right. That doesn't mean I have to like it."

Gammy chuckled, then placed her hand on Suri's cheek. "You know I love you, Lil' Bit."

Suri leaned her head into the featherlight touch. "I love you too."

"Your roommate is home. I'll see if I can get you two some privacy to talk."

"Thanks."

Gammy gave her cheek a pat then faded away. A moment later, Suri felt a shift in the ward around the house then the beep from the alarm sensor on the door sounded.

"Suri!" Layla called.

"Up in the attic!"

There was a nervous flutter in her stomach as she heard Layla's footsteps coming up the stairs. She busied herself with reorganizing the worktable, despite it not needing it.

"Hey."

Suri gazed up with a nervous smile. "Hey. I left you some breakfast just in case you didn't eat. You left in such a hurry."

Layla gave her a sheepish grin. "Yeah, about that...I think we need to talk."

Suri nodded. "I agree."

"Excuse me, sir," she said as she scooped Sebastian up and then set him back on her lap as she sat down. Without missing a beat, he curled up and fell back to sleep.

Layla gazed at the cat in exasperation as she sat in the other chair. "Don't get used to this."

"I'm assuming you left because of the sexual energy that was about to burn the house down." Suri figured there was no need to sugarcoat it.

Layla chuckled. "Yeah. So, I wasn't the only one."

"No. I hadn't even made it all the way downstairs when I was hit with it along with some very clear memories from my...our... dream." Suri's face heated with embarrassment.

"If we're going to continue staying under the same roof, we need to figure out how to deal with this."

"Seems to be more of a me issue since I'm the one that pulled you into my dream, which I still don't understand how that happened."

"I can answer that. I hope you don't get upset, but I spoke to my father about it as he has far more knowledge as an incubus than me."

Suri was a little embarrassed by the thought, but since there was a slim chance of her meeting Layla's father, she could deal with it. "Under normal circumstances I'd probably be upset that you told your father about such intimate details, but I can make an exception for this."

"From what I told him, he believes that you're a sexual empath. Have you heard of that?"

"Yes, but I've read very little on it. I began showing empathic abilities when I was very young, but they grew stronger as I got older. My friend Rachel and I researched the different types of empaths, and when that one came up, we were too embarrassed to read up further on the subject."

"I'll save you some research time. Sexual empaths' abilities intensify during sexual encounters. They absorb the energy their sexual partners give off during intimacy, so if the energy is toxic or angry, then you absorb those emotions. If it's happy and loving then you absorb those emotions."

Suri thought back on the meaningless hook-ups she'd had after Tracey's death to try to appease the loneliness and grief, but they rarely made her feel better. There were the few that left her feeling as if she'd taken a shot of adrenaline and left her practically euphoric for a week, but most left her feeling more depressed, lonely, and even angrier than she did before the encounter. Learning that she may be a sexual empath explained so much.

"Is it common for someone with such abilities to drain the person they are intimate with the way you said I drained you? And without having actual sex?"

Layla grinned with amusement. "It is when your sexual partner is a succubus combined with you also being a telepath."

Suri's face flushed hotly. "I see. What was your father's recommendation to solve the issue?"

"He didn't have one, but I think I do. We have two options. The first is to just let things happen—"

Suri vigorously shook her head. "Nope, next."

"I don't know if I should be amused or offended," Layla said with a mock frown. "The other is for you to have a conversation with your subconscious since that's who initiated the encounter in the first place. If you genuinely don't want a repeat of last night, I can control my succubus as I don't share such intimacy with someone who doesn't want it."

The problem was that Suri had wanted it but didn't want to mix business with pleasure, that's why her subconscious had taken control of the situation.

"That sounds like a reasonable plan."

One Suri hoped would work. It was a relief to know what was going on and why she was not only missing bits and pieces of time but also why she'd grown darker and more depressed with each sexual encounter over the past few months. Obviously, her partners had probably been doing the same thing she was. Trying to fill a hole of loneliness.

"Now that we've gotten that settled. Is there anything you would like to work on today?" Layla asked.

"There is something I'd like to do. I haven't investigated the basement other than when I visited with Ayomide. It's probably good if you know what's down there as well since you'll be staying here for some time. I'm also a little scared to go back down there and investigate alone," Suri said with a smirk.

"Are you sure? That's obviously been a family secret for longer than I've probably been alive. I wouldn't want to piss off any ancestors by stepping on sacred ground."

"Gammy and Ayomide both insisted you stay here. I can't imagine they wouldn't want you to know what you're getting into by doing so."

"Okay, great. Let's go explore a magical basement, but first I really do need to eat some actual food. I had a couple of beignets, but I don't want to chance encountering any supernatural forces with my energy not at its peak."

"There's a refrigerator full of leftovers from this delicious breakfast that was made," Suri said teasingly.

"I'll have to check it out."

"How about I meet you down there after I have a little discussion with myself."

Layla grinned. "I wish I could be a fly on that wall. Sebastian, let's leave Suri to her task."

The cat stretched in Suri's lap then jumped down to follow Layla. *"Since you two insist on interrupting my nap I guess I'll join you,"* he said wordlessly.

Suri chuckled, still amazed by being able to telepathically communicate with a cat. Once she was alone, she opened one of four drawers she had discovered during her inventory that contained more stones and crystals than she could name. Each one lay in its own divided slot to avoid intermingling. She chose amethyst, clear quartz, moonstone, and obsidian. The combination of the stones and crystals helped to open and align the subconscious mind with the conscious mind. If she could get the two on the same wavelength then maybe she could avoid the mess that the two not working together had made of her life so far. She took the stones down to her room, collected her selenite bowl that she had used for her cleansing, and placed them in there. Then she lay on her bed, placing the bowl just above her head on her pillow to tap in to her third eye, closed her eyes, and performed a meditative breathing exercise.

Suri knew her third eye had awakened when a bright light flared behind her lids. As it slowly faded, she was sitting rather than lying down on the bed with a mirror image of herself sitting across from her. She raised her hand to see if her image would also raise it and got a chuckle in return.

"I am not your mirrored reflection."

"No, but you're becoming a pain in my butt."

Her subconscious laughed again. "You can't say I don't make our life exciting."

"Maybe a little too exciting. I think we need to get on the same page from this point on. There's too much at stake for us to continue the way we have."

Subconscious Suri sighed in resignation. "You're right. I just hated seeing us so miserable."

Suri gave her an understanding smile. "I know. Maybe, if we get through this with our mind and body right, we can work on how to remedy that together. No going rogue."

"Okay, but just so you know, once I got Layla into the bedroom, the rest was all you." Her subconscious smirked.

Suri's face heated with a blush. "Yeah, well, she shouldn't have been pulled into my dream in the first place. Are we good?"

"We're great and in sync from now on." Her image smiled brightly. Suri couldn't remember the last time she had smiled so happily.

"Thank you."

Her subconscious waved as the vision faded into bright light once more and Suri blinked her eyes open to find herself lying alone on her bed. She was surprised at how easily she'd been able to connect to herself and come out of it. It must be an effect of her strengthened abilities. She placed the stones on her nightstand. She would cleanse and take them back up to the workroom before she went to bed. Before leaving her room, she took a moment to do a mental check and found that she felt more connected to herself than she had before. As if she were solid and whole again. She left the room with a happy little bounce in her step.

CHAPTER TWELVE

Layla had just finished cleaning up from her late breakfast when Suri entered the kitchen looking like she'd just come back from a day at the spa. She seemed more relaxed, her aura was a soft, swirling combination of blue, purple, and white, and an easy smile brightened her face.

"How'd your chat go?"

"Very well. We're now on the same page so there should be no more incidents like last night. Are those beignets from Café du Monde?" She indicated the bag Layla had left on the counter when she returned.

"Yes. That's where I met my father this morning. You're welcome to them."

Suri's smile broadened. "I haven't had these in so long. Gammy used to take me for hot chocolate and beignets for Christmas. I could never bring myself to go there when we would visit after she died. It was like our special place."

"My father and I often meet there. It's his favorite place to sit and people watch."

"Your father doesn't sound like your stereotypical demon."

Suri took one of the powdery confections from the bag, bit into it, and moaned with pleasure. The sound brought back memories of last night and Layla had to turn away before she broke her promise to keep her succubus under control.

"No, he's definitely not that."

"Oh, my gawd, that is so good. You need to hide these or I'll eat the whole bag."

Suri appeared next to her at the sink to wash her hands. The seductively sweet scent of her energy washed over Layla temptingly, making her want to bury her nose in Suri's warm neck. Suri turned just as Layla was drawing close and her eyes widened in surprise.

"L-Layla." Suri sounded nervous.

"Hmm," Layla growled.

Suri took a noticeable step back, which was like a cold slap for Layla. She took a step back as well.

"Shit! I'm sorry."

Suri's breath was coming out in pants and her hands were balled into tight fists at her side. "No, I'm sorry, I should probably keep my distance. I was drawn to you suddenly and used needing to wash my hands as an excuse to be near you."

"What were you feeling before that happened?"

Suri's brow furrowed. "Eating the beignet brought back memories of happier times and I felt joy. Then suddenly I was overwhelmed by the scent of chocolate and the need to be near you."

Could her father have been right? Did Layla feel something more than a physical attraction to Suri? She thought it was the seductive sound of Suri's moan that had drawn her beast forward, but it was more than likely the joy Suri was feeling. They were connected emotionally and Layla didn't know what to do about it. She sure wasn't going to tell Suri. She was dealing with enough right now without hearing that after only knowing her for a few days, Layla was somehow developing an emotional attachment to her. She tried not to smile at the thought that her energy had the scent of chocolate for Suri just as Suri's had the scent of honey for her. It gave the term being sweet on somebody a new meaning.

"I think we can handle this. It doesn't seem to be as bad as earlier. We just need to have better control of keeping our distance when it happens." Layla didn't know if she was trying to convince Suri or herself.

Suri didn't look convinced but she smiled. "Maybe a good distraction will help. Let's head downstairs."

She hurriedly turned to leave the kitchen. It only took Layla several strides of her long legs to catch up with her, but she kept an arm's length of distance between them as she followed Suri into the living room where she moved a wall tapestry aside to reveal a door. Judging by the immense power she felt emanating from the door, the source of it must be very old.

"How long did you say your family has had this house?"

"Since 1830, but Athena had been living here for sixteen years before she inherited it."

"So, no one in your family lived on this land prior to that?"

"No, why?"

"Just curious."

That's over two hundred years of having a family of supernaturals under this roof, but the source of the power felt much older than that, almost ancient in comparison. Suri unlocked and grasped the doorknob and Layla felt her power connect with the ward that had been placed on the door before it fell aside like a curtain being drawn. She opened and stepped through, holding it open for Layla, who hesitantly followed, expecting to be rebuffed by the ward, but she felt nothing but a sense of welcome. It was as if they were expecting her. Suri turned on a light switch just inside the doorway and the flickering glow of faux torches along the wall lit their way down the staircase.

As Layla placed her hand on the railing, she could feel that the wood of the railing and stairs were made from a very old magical tree. The murals along the ceiling and walls were done with spelled paint which gave it its lifelike appearance. She could almost smell the greenery surrounding them, hear the birds chirping in the trees, and see the clouds shifting in the sky. Her skin tingled with the power surrounding them as she stepped off the stairs into the main corridor.

"The first room here is where Ayomide's altar is located. The other doors I haven't ventured into yet. They kind of freak me out." Suri gave a slight shiver.

"I'm not surprised. I don't how it's possible, but the source of your family's magic is so deeply embedded in these walls that I can't believe they haven't been here since Ayomide's time."

Layla gazed at the first door just past Ayomide's. Carved into the wood was the image of a woman standing at a crossroad before a set of oversized disembodied hands offering the woman two pathways. She turned to the first door on the other side with the carved image of a goddess-like figure floating above a body of water. She didn't need to see the others to know what these doors led to. She turned to Suri in disbelief.

"These doors are gateways to the Seven."

"Yeah, altar rooms where we make offerings and prayers for direct contact with those Orisha like Ayomide's room."

"No, Suri, they're direct gateways to the most powerful of the Orishas."

Suri gazed at her in confusion then her eyes widened in realization. "You're telling me that if I open this door," she pointed to the one with the goddess floating above the water. "that I'll be face-to-face with Yemaya, the goddess of motherhood and the sea, not an altar room?"

"Well, she wouldn't be standing there waiting to greet you as soon as you opened the door, but you would enter a representation of her world where you would make offerings and speak directly to her rather than praying to an altar and waiting for your prayers to be answered.

Suri turned in a circle, her eyes flicking nervously over each door. "So, I have a basement full of gods and goddesses. No wonder Sojourn was using Aria to get to the family."

"It's also why your family's power is so strong. You literally are guardians to Orisha gateways."

Suri shook her head in disbelief. "I thought it just meant we had rooms of altars where our family's gifts would give us a stronger connection to hearing prayers that we deliver for ourselves and others that we assist."

"It's still kind of the same except, instead of laying the prayers at an altar you're laying them directly at the Orisha's feet." Layla tried easing Suri's shock with an encouraging smile, but it didn't seem to work as she began pacing the hallway anxiously rubbing her hands together and mumbling.

"What the hell was Gammy thinking pulling me into this craziness. What the hell was I thinking coming here. This can't be real. Then again, I spent an hour sitting in a room chatting with my long dead ancestor, who also just happens to be a minor Orisha, as if we were enjoying afternoon tea. Now I'm supposed to guard actual magical entrances leading directly to the most powerful Orishas in the universe like it's just an everyday chore to manage. Nope, not happening."

Suri headed for the stairs but was stopped when Pearl appeared before her with her arms crossed looking very obstinate.

"Suri Pearl Daniels, get yourself together. I've coddled you for far too long. This family has a responsibility that has been handed down from generation to generation of Lansford women. It's an honor and responsibility that is not passed along lightly. Only the strongest of us are privileged enough to be given this task. Your ancestors and the Orisha themselves have deemed you worthy and you're about to walk out on us?"

"Gammy, this is too much."

Pearl gazed at her with understanding. She took Suri's face in her hands. "Lil' Bit, you don't think this scared the living daylights out of any of us? You heard Ayomide's story. Imagine how she must've felt after accepting Yemaya's task. This is nothing compared to what she sacrificed and endured. You are more than strong enough to bear this burden."

Layla could feel the fear of disappointing her family rolling off Suri in waves. She stepped up beside her, then grasped her hand.

"You won't be bearing it alone."

Pearl released Suri and she turned to face Layla.

"You've got me, your uncle, and Phoebe's crew. We're all here for you."

"Do you remember why I called you my Lil' Bit?" Pearl asked.

Suri gazed at her. "Because I was a little bitty you."

Pearl smiled, her eyes sparkling with tears. "I was wrong. You are so much more than that. You're stronger and more blessed than I ever was. We're each given the gifts we have for a reason. Yours were given to you so that you could accomplish so much more than I could've imagined. Don't let fear of disappointing us or of the unknown keep you from your full potential. There's no doubt that you're going to make mistakes, but at least you have an army of gifted"—she reached for both Suri's and Layla's hands. Her hold was light but solid—"and found family to hold your hand through it all."

Suri gazed at her again and Layla's heart filled with a possessiveness like she'd never known. She knew in that moment that she would battle Morningstar himself to keep her safe. She gave her an encouraging smile and a gentle squeeze of her hand.

"We got this."

Suri looked at her curiously. "Are you sure you want to get mixed up in this? I can only imagine how daunting this is," she waved her hand around to indicate the doors. "Let alone dealing with Sojourn, Aria, and Lilith. I wouldn't blame you one bit if you just left and retreated to your house in the bayou until it all passed."

"Maybe if it were just Sojourn and her merry band of worshippers, but anything involving Lilith will have far more reaching affects than your family or even New Orleans. I've lived a mostly peaceful and quiet life these past two hundred years, and I'd like to keep it that way for however many years I have left. If that means partnering with an Orisha-blessed, gateway-guarding, hoodoo priestess, I'm all in."

Suri felt calm and safe gazing into Layla's eyes. She hadn't felt either of those since her parents' deaths. She looked over at Gammy and smiled. "I think I'm fine now, but you can't blame me for freaking out. This is a lot to take in in such a short time."

Gammy nodded. "I know and I'm so sorry it had to be this way."

"Someone just tripped the ward. No one dangerous but you do have a visitor," Layla said.

The doorbell rang a moment later.

"I'll see you soon," Gammy said then was gone.

The doorbell rang again.

Suri sighed. "I guess we better see who it is. They seem insistent and I'm in no rush to investigate down here any further today."

Layla chuckled. "Honestly, neither am I. I don't know how an Orisha will feel about a demon spawn crossing into their domain."

Suri didn't know how she felt about crossing into an Orisha's domain, but she was going to have to do it at some point. She assumed, as the guardian, they would want to meet her. She could imagine how that would go.

"Excuse me, Obatala, the father of mankind, I just wanted to introduce myself. I'm Suri, I'll be taking over from my grandmother

who, just in case you didn't know, died thirty years ago, which more than likely means nothing to you as the concept of time is probably meaningless in your universe."

She giggled.

"Something amusing?" Layla asked.

"This whole situation borders on ridiculous."

Layla nodded. "I don't know a lot of people who would be taking this as well as you have. As a matter of fact, when faced with so much supernatural in such a short time, many have been driven to madness."

She had said it so matter-of-factly that Suri thought she was joking, but the serious expression on her face told her otherwise. "Well, that's comforting," she said sarcastically then jogged ahead of Layla up the stairs.

When she got to the door, she peeked out the window first to be safe and was surprised to see Phoebe, who smiled and waved cheerily, and Kenya who gazed around warily.

"This is a surprise," she said in greeting.

"We have some news to share and thought it would be best to do it in person," Phoebe said as she entered. Her eyes widened in surprise at seeing Layla. "Well, hello."

"Good morning, Phoebe. Can I get you anything?"

"A cup of coffee would be great if you have it."

Kenya looked annoyed. "I told her we could have just asked you to come to the shop, but she insisted on coming here." She gave Layla a cursory glance but didn't acknowledge her.

Suri was trying not to be offended by the way Kenya's nose wrinkled with distaste as she looked around the foyer.

"Phoebe, why don't you and Kenya get settled in the living room while Layla and I get the coffee."

Phoebe nodded then headed toward the living room with Kenya following. Suri followed Layla into the kitchen.

"It's starting to feel like Grand Central Station for the supernatural around here."

Layla chuckled. "I have a feeling it's not going to change anytime soon."

Suri sighed. "Seems that way. I'll get the coffee together if you don't mind sharing what's left of your beignets. Gammy would not be happy to have guests in the house and not offer them food."

"We are in the south," Layla said.

They worked in companionable silence as Suri got the coffee brewed in an electric pot then placed the pot with cups, sugar, and creamers on a tray, then offered Layla a tray for the beignets, plates, and napkins. Suri found it oddly comforting how well they managed to work around in the kitchen without getting in each other's way. She missed this type of companionship in her life.

"Ready?"

"Yep but let me carry the heavier tray and you take this one." Layla slid the tray with the pastries toward Suri.

Suri followed behind her, shaking her head in wonder. Not that she had any experience with interacting with cambions, but she found it very difficult to believe that Layla was the child of a demon. Suri was undoubtedly doing what most people probably do which was unfairly stereotyping her. Just like there were good and bad humans, there were probably good and bad cambions. Afterall, they were half human. She and Layla set the trays on the coffee table. Suri served Phoebe and Kenya their cups, allowing them to decide what they would add to it, then made Layla's just the way she liked it, heavy on the milk and sugar, without even thinking. It wasn't until she was handing it over to her and saw her grin that she noticed what she had done. She quickly turned away, poured a cup for herself, and sat down beside Layla. Phoebe grinned knowingly. Kenya looked annoyed.

Suri chose not to acknowledge it. "So, what was so important that you had to come across town to tell us."

Phoebe took a sip of her coffee before responding. "Pearl's prophecy regarding Sojourn has begun. Kenya can tell you more."

Suri gazed over at Kenya whose expression was still one of distaste. "I realize this is more modest for your taste, but it's still my home and I'd appreciate you wiping that look of disgust off your face."

Kenya blinked a few times before her expression turned confused then regretful. "My apologies. This is a beautiful home. I always loved coming here when Pearl was alive because she always welcomed me so warmly. I sense a shift in energy that seems heavier. You don't feel that Phoebe?"

"Of course, I do. I'm sure it probably has to do with not only Layla being here, but also the fact that Suri has fully come into her abilities."

Suri looked at Phoebe in surprise. "How did you know?"

Phoebe shrugged. "I sensed it as soon as I saw you."

Kenya nodded. "There's something else. A darker ward than the one that previously surrounded the house."

"We had a visitor last night that the previous ward wasn't guarded against, so we had to strengthen it against demons," Layla explained.

Kenya quirked a brow. "Marking your territory?"

Layla started to speak but Suri interrupted her. "Can we please stick with the task at hand. You two are welcome to head out into the backyard for your pissing contest after. What's going on with Sojourn?"

Kenya briefly bared her teeth at Layla then turned a smile on Suri. "We've been watching her since she arrived in Mississippi. She hasn't made a move to come back here until yesterday. It seems she's had your house watched which is how she found out you were in town. My sources tell me that she and a select few of her followers have been in touch with ones still located in New Orleans planning for her return."

Suri turned to Layla. "Do you think last night's demon was one of hers?"

Layla frowned. "My father confirmed that it was one of Lilith's demons." Her frowned turned into a scowl. "Unless she's joined forces with Lilith."

Suri's stomach dropped. "Is that possible? How would they even know about each other?"

"Lilith wants you, so she'll know about anything and anyone getting in her way," Layla said.

"She could use Sojourn and Aria to distract and weaken you enough to make her move without barely lifting a finger," Phoebe said worriedly.

Layla stood and began pacing, then stopped in front of the tapestry hiding the basement door. "Suri, I know you weren't ready for this, but we may have to pay visits to some Orishas." She turned back giving Suri an encouraging smile.

Suri shook her head. The thought of crossing the threshold of any of those doors down there, apart from her family's ancestor room, scared her to death. "No, there has to be another way."

"I agree with Layla," Phoebe said. "We need advice from a being on equal footing as Lilith."

"Which were you thinking?" Kenya asked.

Phoebe seemed to think about it. "Ogun or Oya."

Kenya nodded. "Maybe both."

Suri was not thrilled to have them discussing her crossing into the world of the Orisha as if she had no say in the matter. "Excuse me. I'm still in the room."

Layla sat back down beside her. "This is ultimately your decision. No one can force you to do anything you're not ready for."

She knew they were right. She didn't know anything about Sojourn or Aria for that matter, but they were both only human, despite the demon inhabiting her cousin. She didn't think it would be difficult to stop them, especially with Layla's and Phoebe's coven-like group on her side. Lilith, on the other hand, was something she couldn't imagine contending with. It was obvious before she came to New Orleans that Lilith was doing a damn good job at achieving her possession of Suri. If she continued allowing her self-doubt in her abilities and what she had to do to continue, it would be like handing herself over to the demon on a silver platter. Ayomide might have been the emissary of the Orisha blessings Suri had received, but she still needed guidance for the upcoming supernatural battle ahead and who better to advise her than the god of justice and protection and the fiercest warrior goddess?

Suri sighed in resignation. "Fine, but not today. I need one day, just one day of normalcy."

"But you're not normal," Kenya unnecessarily pointed out with an exasperated expression.

Phoebe patted Kenya's leg. "I think we can afford to give Suri a day. She's had a lot thrown at her in a short period of time and has managed it remarkably well under the circumstances." She stood, giving Kenya a look that brooked no argument, then turned back to

Suri. "I would suggest having Robert here with you as they're familiar with him. If they see that he trusts Layla to protect you then there's a pretty good chance that they won't smite her on the spot." She gave Layla a wink.

Suri walked them to the door. Phoebe pulled her into her arms for a brief hug then grasped Suri's hands. "You're stronger than you think. Just believe in yourself and it will all fall into place."

Suri smiled. "Thank you."

Kenya gave her a soft smile then frowned at Layla who stood beside Suri. "Don't fuck things up for her demon spawn."

Layla gave her a smirk. "You know, curiosity isn't the only thing that can kill a cat."

Kenya responded with a sharp hiss.

Layla emitted a low growl.

"Children!" Phoebe reprimanded. Kenya grinned then followed her out.

Suri closed the door, turned her back on it and leaned against it as if she were barring anyone else from entering. She'd only been in town for three days, yet it felt like much longer with everything that had occurred so far.

"I think you need a day out of the house."

"That would be great. What did you have in mind?"

Layla grinned. "Leave it up to me."

CHAPTER THIRTEEN

Layla could feel Suri's anxiety while everyone had been talking about what she should do so she could understand her need for a little normalcy. She had the perfect distraction.

"When was the last time you were here just as a tourist?"

"As a tourist? Never. Before my grandmother passed, I was too young to really do much sightseeing. After that, we only came down for the holidays."

"Well, put your walking shoes on for a day of normal, non-supernatural relaxation."

"Really?" The childlike excitement on Suri's face warmed Layla's heart.

"Yes. There will be no speaking to spirits, then again, we're in New Orleans, so at least no spirits connected to you. And no thinking about Orishas and demons."

"Sounds like the perfect day already. I can be ready to go in ten minutes," Suri said as she hurried toward the stairs.

Once Suri had disappeared out of sight, Layla went to the living room to clean up the coffee service. Using her preternatural strength, she carried the coffee service tray in one hand and the tray of untouched beignets in the other for quicker clean-up. Knowing Suri enjoyed the beignets, she placed them in an airtight plastic container to keep them fresh. She felt Suri's presence as she got ready for their day out. She was vibrating with excitement and Layla loved that she had a hand in causing it. She knew there had been very little cause for happiness in Suri's life this past year, then add the overwhelming events of the past forty-eight hours, and Layla couldn't blame her for being so excited about a simple day out.

She was just leaving the kitchen as Suri bounced down the stairs announcing, "Ready!"

She had changed from the sweatpants and T-shirt she had been wearing into a charcoal gray, long-sleeve cowl neck fitted top with a white tank top underneath that dipped low enough for a generous view of cleavage, black jeans that hugged her shapely hips and emphasized her lush behind, and black sneakers. She had pulled her hair back into a full, curly afro puff and wore no makeup. Despite the casual attire, Layla thought she looked just as desirable fully clothed as she did naked in her dream. Ironically, her succubus wasn't the one to respond. Her heart filled with a softness of emotion that she almost didn't recognize because it had been so long since she held such affection toward anyone. Knowing Suri was an empath, she tucked the feelings neatly away in the figurative treasure chest where she stored all unnecessary emotions.

"Great." She passed Suri hoping her smile gave nothing away except the friendliness she wished to extend.

Suri followed her to the door but hesitated to step out onto the porch. Layla could feel her anxiety creeping back. She was afraid to leave the safety of her home. Layla grasped both her hands with an encouraging smile.

"You're safe with me. I will do anything within my power to keep you from harm," she said softly as a warmth of magic spread from her hands to Suri's.

Suri gazed down at their clasped hands in surprise then up at Layla again. "Did you just make a magical oath?"

"Yes."

"What happens if you break it?"

Layla shrugged. "I don't intend to."

"Layla—"

Layla shook her head. "If you're going to ask me again why I'm doing this, don't."

Suri gave her a warm smile. "Okay."

"Good. Now, let's officially get your non-magical day started."

After Suri locked up the house, they headed out the front yard, but instead of going to her car, Layla passed it. Suri hesitated for a moment before following alongside her.

"We're not going to walk all the way into town, are we?"

"Nope."

Suri gazed at her curiously, waiting for more, but Layla just smiled. They didn't have far to go before reaching their destination, a stop for the St. Charles Avenue streetcar line.

Suri's grin was wide. "I haven't been on the streetcar in years."

"The best way to see New Orleans. Sometimes, when I want to escape and feel a little more human, I spend the day going around town on the streetcar people watching and sightseeing just like a regular tourist."

Suri chuckled. "Little do your fellow tourists know that they have a supernatural being sitting right beside them."

"You'd be surprised how many of us supernatural beings do something similar."

"Seriously? There are others that do that?"

"Yep. I'm sure you'll sense them if they come on board during our ride. Just don't make it obvious if you do. Like I said, they just want to feel human."

As if to prove her point, just as they reached their stop at Audubon Park, a dapperly dressed elderly gentleman stepped aside to let them off.

He tipped his hat at them in greeting. "Have a wonderful day, ladies." Then boarded the streetcar.

As the doors closed behind him, Layla saw Suri's gaze narrow at the retreating vehicle. "I don't know what he was but that man wasn't human."

"You're right. He's a jinni in human form."

Suri looked at her as if she were waiting for Layla to deliver the punchline of a joke. "You're serious." She gazed after the streetcar, now too far in the distance to see anyone on it.

"When I was little, Gammy tried to convince me that she and Phoebe had met a jinni once while they were on a trip to Africa when they were just out of college. He supposedly told her this fantastic tale about his granddaughter having been cursed to a lamp and that he was searching for her. Of course, I believed her because I was only four years old, but as I got older, I knew, like all the other stories she'd told me, that it had to be just that, a story. Now I'm beginning to believe that her stories were in fact true."

Layla knew who she was referring to. Isfet had spoken of that very jinni once. He had been one of the most feared Black Jinn ever known during the battles of angels and jinn, then had changed his ways and created an island for other jinn like him. "I'm familiar with the jinni she told you about. My father has had dealings with him, but that's a story for another time when we're not trying to be normal humans with no special abilities."

Suri looked at her with disbelief then shook herself. "Yeah, okay. So, why Audubon Park?"

"I thought fresh air and nature would be a great way to kick things off. A walk through here always helps to clear my head or simply gives me some time to just be in the moment."

Suri nodded. "I could see that. I used to love going to the botanical gardens in New York. Being amongst all the plants, flowers, and trees. It's what I imagine the afterlife would be like for me."

Something about the way she said that concerned Layla. "Do you think about the afterlife often?"

Suri didn't immediately respond and Layla wouldn't push her to do so. She gave her the space to decide if she wanted to share or not. They strolled a path that snaked alongside a small body of water called Olmstead Lake for a few moments before Suri sighed.

"After Tracey's death I was inconsolable. Her family was so kind to me when they could have just lost my number after the funeral, and even Uncle Robert came to be with me during that time, but nothing could ease the pain and guilt that I felt over being the one responsible for her death. After Gammy warned me during my parents' funeral about the darkness after me I should've just stayed to myself, but I selfishly allowed Tracey into my life and she paid the ultimate price for it." She took a shuddering breath before continuing.

"Then suddenly the babies that I helped to deliver developed complications or illnesses shortly after birth. As if my very touch brought on sickness. They all appeared to be normal complications that could occur, but it was too much of a coincidence for me to believe that. I started to believe that the darkness chasing me, growing in me, was being transferred to those innocent babies. I took time off from work, which probably wasn't the best idea because it gave me more time to wallow in guilt, depression, and loneliness. More time to think about the only way I could see out of the darkness and not bring any more death to anyone else around me."

She stopped walking to peer out at a small island, known as bird island, in the middle of the lake. Layla hated the pain those memories brought Suri. She stood quietly beside her, reaching over to grasp her hand to give what comfort she could.

"I don't know if Gammy foresaw this or it was pure coincidence, but I honestly don't know if I would be here if she hadn't instructed me to come to New Orleans. Whatever the reason was, it saved my life."

"I can't tell you not to feel guilty for the loss of your family and friends or those babies, because I understand why you feel that way. What I will say is that none of it was your fault. That lies solely with Lilith. I'll also say that I'm glad you chose the option to come here rather than the other."

Suri gave Layla's hand a gentle squeeze. "Thank you. Despite the unbelievable events of the past two days, so am I."

They stood that way for several minutes, holding hands, gazing out toward the bird refuge where a multitude of egrets and herons dotted the shoreline and trees. Then Suri turned toward Layla. "So, what's on the agenda for the rest of the day? As much as I love the quiet beauty of nature to clear my head, I would much rather be distracted from my thoughts with something livelier."

"Got it. Then you'll love our next stop."

Layla didn't release Suri's hand as she turned to head back the way they came. A short time later, they were back on a streetcar. She could see Suri surreptitiously gazing around and knew that she had picked up on supernatural energies from other riders. Layla recognized a few regulars that rode through town like her. The others looked to be tourists. They all sent a subtle smile or nod her way when their gazes happened to catch. As they rode along, Layla gave Suri a rundown of historical sites along their route until they reached their destination. Stop number twenty-four on the St. Charles line, Superior Seafood & Oyster Bar. Suri wanted lively and she would get it at the popular restaurant that was always filled with locals and tourists looking for affordable Creole seafood cuisine. They were seated at a table with a view of St. Charles Avenue.

"I'm going to assume you enjoy oysters."

"I could probably eat the whole order of a dozen of the chargrilled ones by myself."

Layla chuckled. "Okay, so we'll start with two dozen oysters. One for you and one for me. Anything else appeal to you or will the oysters be enough?"

Suri snorted. "I'm going to give you fair warning, I love food. You couldn't tell that by how little I ate the other day, but this," she pointed to the menu, "I can eat all day. If I didn't work out as often as I do, I'd probably be big as a house."

"I like a woman with a little meat on her bones and who isn't afraid to eat."

Suri grinned. "Well, prepare to fall in love."

Too late, Layla thought to herself but laughed out loud. When their server arrived, Suri ordered her dozen oysters along with an order of the cast-iron cornbread and a cup of crawfish and crab bisque to start, shrimp and grits for her entrée and pre-ordered the bread pudding for her dessert. Layla liked a woman who wasn't afraid to eat because she enjoyed eating as well. She ordered crawfish beignets, chicken and andouille gumbo, and a catfish sandwich. As a cambion, her metabolism ran a little different than Suri's but she knew she would still need to get a good run in the morning to make up for this lunch. Layla didn't know if it was her admission while they were at the park or the food, but Suri's spirit seemed lighter. Layla asked her about living in New York and she chatted away about her life there during happier times. Layla spoke of her travels through the two centuries of her life.

"Wow. To have seen the world change over all that time must have been fascinating."

"It was interesting, frightening, and heartbreaking. I witnessed six wars, emancipation, Jim Crow, the Civil Rights movement. I lived through decades of our people being abused and slaughtered then treated like second-class citizens after they put their lives on the line for their abusers in every one of those wars. It was also lonely since getting close to someone was almost impossible. I've made human friends through the years, but it makes it difficult when you age as slowly as I do and outlive all of them."

Suri frowned. "My apologies. That was very naïve of me not to think of all that."

Layla waved dismissively. "No need to apologize. It's a common assumption that I take no offense to."

"I've been meaning to ask you since our training yesterday after you healed yourself, are you immortal?"

"No. Because I keep my human and demonic sides balanced, I age at a much slower rate than humans. If I tapped more into my demonic side my aging would eventually pause and I would become immortal like any other demon."

"Are you ever tempted to do that? Be more demonic?"

Layla hesitated to respond as memories of those times in her long life still filled her with a rage that she didn't want Suri to witness or even feel with her empathic abilities.

"If it makes you uncomfortable to discuss, you don't have to talk about it."

Her gaze was so full of warmth and understanding that Layla felt compelled to tell her. As if talking to Suri about it would help soothe the rage.

"There were moments in my life when I almost succumbed to the demon in me. The first was the reason I left the plantation where I was enslaved."

Layla told Suri about her rape and what followed. There was no judgment in her eyes when she admitted to almost killing Jonas. She looked furious on Layla's behalf. She didn't know if that would change when she told Suri about the slave catchers that had come after her.

"You're stronger than me. I honestly think I would've gone through with it."

"I don't think you would. The guilt you've felt all this time over deaths you had no hand in shows that you have a good heart."

"So do you. I sense the kindness and concern in your heart and see it in the way you've been helping me."

"Well, I certainly didn't have it then. Jonas sent a slave patrol out for me and joined them. They tracked me to the cabin. If my father hadn't been there to warn me, they probably would've captured me, but he gave me the power to defend myself. I placed a ward around the cabin to keep them from approaching, but it didn't stop the bullet from one of their pistols from tearing into my shoulder. My pain and anger fed the power my father had joined with mine and all I saw was a red haze."

The memory of that day came to her as clear as if it just happened.

❖

"Massa Jonas, please, just leave me be. I don't wanna hurt nobody."

Layla could feel the same surge of power she'd felt when she'd almost taken Master Jonas's life growing with what her father had given her. She really didn't want to hurt anyone. She just wanted to be left alone to be the good person her mother saw in her.

Master Jonas sneered. "I don't give a damn what you want, nigga. What I want is to string you up and whip the hide off your back until you're begging me to end your miserable life. Shoot her but don't kill her."

The command had barely left his lips before a shot rang out and pain seared through her right shoulder. It was quickly overtaken by a rage so strong her vision was coated in a red haze.

"Shall I destroy them all?" her father said wordlessly. She could feel his presence beside her but he kept himself from being seen.

"No, they mine to punish."

She didn't recognize the dark fury in her voice as her own. She didn't know what the men were seeing, but she could smell the fear rolling off them and gloried in it. She took control of their minds then made them all dismount, draw their guns, and sent their horses and the dogs away. She kept Master Jonas out of harm's way but not to protect him. She wanted him to watch and know how powerful she was. The patrolmen whimpered and begged as she forced them to turn their guns on each other, aim straight at their hearts, and pull their triggers as one. Then she released Master Jonas from her hold and watched as it took him a moment to realize he could move on his own.

"You're a demon," he whispered fearfully before turning and running into the woods.

"Yous best remember that if you come at me again!" she yelled after his retreating figure.

Layla approached the men lying on the blood-soaked ground. One still lived. A boy not much older than her, his eyes wide with fear and regret, blood gurgling from his mouth as he tried to speak. She heard his thoughts of his mother having to care for his three siblings alone. Layla felt no sympathy for him because he had held no sympathy for her when he pulled the trigger of the gun that put the bullet in her shoulder. She knelt beside him, staring into his eyes to show him the hell that awaited him. He silently begged God for forgiveness, but as she felt her father reappear beside her in all his demon glory, she knew when the boy recognized that there would be no forgiveness for him.

Layla had been gazing off into the memory as she told Suri what happened so she was surprised when she gazed back at her to see sympathy and understanding instead of horror.

"This was the first moment where you embraced your demonic side."

"Yes. It took me weeks of battling with myself and having my father and my mother's spirit there to keep me from totally turning over to the dark side. My mother had begged for my father to help. He put a ward on the cabin not only to keep people out but to keep me in until they could help me see reason through my madness. I didn't want anything more than to go back to the plantation and burn it all to the ground. I didn't think about what that would do to my family and the innocent people still there. I just wanted Jonas to pay for what he'd done to me."

Layla wondered at the lack of the remnant darkness she always felt thinking about that moment. Then she noticed that Suri's hand was covering hers on the table. She had used her empathic abilities to help Layla.

Suri shrugged at her questioning gaze. "I felt your anger and pain and I wanted to ease it. Tell me about the other time you almost gave in. Let me soothe that pain as well," she said gently.

Layla realized that she felt a heaviness lifted from her spirit. She had been carrying the anger from that day around for so long she didn't know any other way to feel. Was she ready to let go of the rest? Something told her that was what she needed to do to be able to help Suri with what was coming. She turned her hand over and intertwined her fingers with Suri's, receiving a sweet smile in return. She talked about the darkest and longest period that she had given over a little more control to her demonic side from the early 1900s to the civil rights era. Just because she mostly kept to her little house in the bayou didn't mean that she wasn't aware of what was happening with Black people out in the world. She spent a good amount of that time as an avenging angel for any beaten, raped, and lynched Black person south of the Mississippi. Because she believed death was too kind for the men committing the injustices, her punishments were more terrifying than death.

Layla would dream walk with the purpose of filling their thoughts with visions of them being the victim of the horrific crimes they had committed. Night after night, they would be bombarded with images so real that they would wake up screaming and begging for their lives. Many would go mad and either need to be committed to an asylum or choose a more permanent solution to ending the agony. It was whispered throughout the Black communities that Mami Danto, a powerful mother figure in the voodoo tradition, had been brought to life to avenge her children. Layla didn't bother correcting them as long as her people knew that someone was out to protect and avenge them when she couldn't save them. It was the only time her parents disagreed when it came to guiding her. Her father saw nothing wrong with what she was doing since she wasn't directly taking anyone's life. Her mother's spirit understood but feared for Layla's soul. Her mother's concerns were valid since Layla found herself taking sadistic pleasure from what she was doing and began feeling an internal slowing signaling that she was tapping too far into her demonic side. Becoming a full-on demon or immortal wasn't appealing to her so as much as she despised allowing the violence to continue without repercussion, Layla had to force herself to stop. It was like trying to kick a drug habit cold turkey and wasn't the least bit pleasant. But she had no regrets for what she had done. When she finished telling Suri her story, she felt even lighter. She gazed at her curiously, meeting Suri's content smile.

"I had no idea I was carrying such heaviness."

"I've found, when I've helped others with easing feelings they couldn't shed, that you don't have to feel bad for something you may have done for it to take a heavy toll on your spirit."

"You've helped others this way?"

"It's rare but there are times after a medium session that the person I've done the reading for is still carrying some grief or sadness after the session that they didn't realize and end up coming back to me for a cleansing. Sometimes all it takes is what we just did, them talking it through while I empathically take the heaviness away. Others I'll have to do a complete spiritual cleanse involving candles, sage, the works."

"Taking on others' grief, guilt and anger doesn't get to you?"

Suri shrugged. "It used to but I've learned how to store it away until I can cleanse myself, which I used to do regularly before Tracey's death. I also stopped performing readings, practicing hoodoo, and using my gifts. I figured why bother since whatever darkness was taking everyone away was finding me anyway."

Layla gave her hand a gentle squeeze. "I'm sorry."

Suri's smile in return was soft. "No need for you to apologize. It wasn't your fault. Besides, all of that brought me here to my family's home, this dangerously delicious food and new friends."

Their gazes held and Layla found herself wanting to just spend the rest of the day lost in Suri's bright eyes. The sound of someone clearing their throat drew her attention. She looked up to find their server looking guilty for having interrupted.

"Would you like your dessert now?"

"Impeccable timing." Suri slipped her hand from Layla's, smirking as she took a drink of water.

Layla chuckled. "Yes, please."

"What's next?"

"Are you ready for strolling and shopping in the French Quarter to work off all this food?"

"You had me at shopping."

CHAPTER FOURTEEN

When Suri arrived in New Orleans just a few days ago, she had chosen to stay at a hotel in the French Quarter rather than her uncle's house. She had wanted time to just be alone before facing her uncle and what her grandmother was requesting of her. If she had known then of their family's legacy, she probably wouldn't have gotten on a plane to come here. She had stayed in her room, ordered room service, and refused to venture out until she needed to go see Phoebe for the keys to the house. It had been months since she had used her medium gifts, stuffing them deep down in a mental well that she hadn't planned on dipping in ever again. She hadn't been prepared for the spiritual energy that slammed into her upon arriving in the city. Energy so old and powerful that her weak attempt at tamping down her gifts was shattered like a ball thrown through a window. Her head had buzzed with all the voices wanting to be heard. Then, when she arrived in the Quarter she had to practically wade through a thick pool of seen and unseen spirits clamoring for her attention. She tried not to make eye contact with any of them, but they knew what she was. She had to ward her room against them just to get some peace.

Now, as she and Layla got off the streetcar, she could feel that same energy but, instead of incessant buzzing that gave her a headache, it was like a quiet hum that gave her comfort. She was home. This town was where she was supposed to be. She saw spirits, but knowing what she had experienced when she arrived, she had made sure to put her own guards up to let them know not to approach her unless she allowed. They had barely gone a block before a scowling female spirit wearing a ragged dress from over a century ago kept popping up in Suri's path. She ignored her and kept walking.

"Not today," she said gently.

The spirit ignored her and even attempted to gather energy to block Suri's path.

"You heard her," Layla growled without even looking the spirit's way.

The woman looked at Layla in surprise then fear and disappeared.

"Thank you. Most respect my guards, but she seemed pretty determined. Maybe I can come by here before we head back to see what she needed."

"Nope. I told you this is a day of normalcy. Talking to ghosts isn't normal." Layla grinned.

Suri chuckled. "Considering my life, that is normal."

"Hadn't thought of that. Okay, so this will be a day of abnormalcy for you."

They smiled at each other, then Layla offered her hand. "Are you ready to walk off some calories?"

Suri placed her hand in Layla's warm grasp. "Yes."

They strolled through the French Quarter window shopping and people watching until they reached the open-air shopping of the French Market District where Suri decided to splurge a little on some of the handcrafted jewelry and clothing offered by various vendors. Other than food and essentials, she hadn't shopped for herself in quite some time. Before the tragedies in her life, her wardrobe had been her favorite color of pink as well as other bright and vibrant colors in an eclectic mix of bohemian contemporary pieces, unique handcrafted jewelry and accessories, and fashionable footwear. The toll of each loss in her life showed in her appearance. Her mass of curls that she gloried in displaying in various styles was pulled back into a bun or afro puff no matter the occasion. Her attire outside of work was made up of muted colors, jeans, sweat suits, and stretch pants. Makeup and jewelry were an afterthought. She no longer cared about her appearance since there was no one in her life to look good for. Other than the bright caftan she'd worn when calling to her ancestor Ayomide, she hadn't brought anything else with much personality. Now, as she passed shops with colorful dresses and tops, hand-dyed headwraps and scarves, and bold chunky jewelry, she craved her old style again. By the time they left the marketplace she was carrying one of two shopping bags filled with pieces that she could mix and match with what she brought with her, Layla carried the second.

Their next stops were various galleries located throughout the quarter. Layla had kept her promise to make it as non-supernatural of a day as possible apart from the spirits and energy of other supernatural beings mingling in the crowded streets, which of course she had no control of. Suri was having a wonderful time and did her best not to think of it as a date, although it felt very much like one as they continued holding hands. She found that it grounded her at times when the energy could have overwhelmed her without having Layla there as a distraction. She wondered at how quickly she was developing feelings for her and wished that she could blame the sex dream, but she had felt a connection to her the moment she had seen her standing on her balcony. She had been drawn to her until she recognized the darkness that represented Layla's demon. Now that she was getting to know her and sensing that Layla may be feeling the same way, Suri's attachment to her grew. It was as if Layla were the part of her that she hadn't realized was missing. She decided to enjoy this moment because there was no telling how long they had before all hell broke loose.

"I may have worn some pretty good walking shoes, but I think even they need a break right now."

"Oh, of course. Why don't we grab a quick drink. I know the perfect spot and it's just up the street."

"Okay."

Layla's pace slowed as they strolled along Bourbon Street. They stopped at the corner of Bourbon and St. Phillip where the infamous Lafitte's Blacksmith Shop Bar was located. It was late afternoon so the evening revelers weren't out yet, but there was still a good crowd. Layla managed to find them a table in the corner.

"You get comfortable, and I'll get us a couple of drinks," Layla said.

"I haven't even told you what I want."

"No need. You can't come to Lafitte's for the first time without having their signature drink."

"Uh-oh, should I be worried?"

"Not at all." Layla gave her a mischievous smile and wink.

Suri watched her, admiring her confident stride as she navigated her way to the bar. She also noticed various other admiring glances, including the bartender who gave her a flirtatious smile as she took her order. Suri ignored the twinge of jealousy as she looked away and around the room. A couple seated in front of a fireplace seemed to be in a quietly heated argument. Just past them, Suri noticed a figure in the shadows. She knew it was a spirit and could just make out the outline of a wide brim hat, dark attire, and the glint of a pistol handle and sword at its waist. The figure stepped a little further into the light, tipped his hat at her with a mischievous grin, then disappeared back into the darkness. A moment later, a brass candle stick holder flew off the mantle toward the couple's table, knocking the guy's glass of beer over into his lap. He jumped out of his chair with a curse then looked down at the candle holder in confusion. The woman's surprised gaze was on the shadow Suri had seen the spirit step out of. He was no longer there, but she was pretty sure he'd briefly shown himself to the woman as he was tossing the holder. Her boyfriend, Suri assumed since she didn't see rings on their fingers, angrily tossed the holder back toward the fireplace, then drew the woman's attention before he turned to storm out of the bar. The woman hurriedly followed but kept gazing back at the fireplace with a grin.

"What was that all about?" Layla asked.

"I believe Monsieur Lafitte doesn't like to see people fighting in his bar."

Layla gazed over at the table where the couple had been sitting and a server was now cleaning the spilled beer.

"Ah, I see. Your drink, madam." She set two large glasses with a purple frozen beverage on the table.

"What in the world?"

"It's officially called the Voodoo Daquiri, but the locals like to call it the purple drank. Sip it slow and don't ask for another unless you want me carrying you home."

Suri looked at the drink skeptically then took a sip. The taste reminded her of the purple slushies she used to get as a kid. By the third sip she realized why she was warned to take it slow. Despite all the food she had for lunch, she began to feel the euphoric effects of the alcohol.

"I can see where it gets its name from. This stuff is dangerous because it's one of those drinks that sneaks up on you."

Layla chuckled. "Yeah, there should be a warning label on this and hurricane cocktails sold all over the place. Folks end up in drunken stupors before they even start barhopping in the evening."

"Well, you don't have to worry about that with me. I was never a fan of drunken stupor, even in college. Speaking of evening, what is the plan for the rest of the day?"

Layla shrugged. "I hadn't thought past this afternoon. What would you like to do? We can have dinner here in town."

"I'm still stuffed from lunch, but maybe something light followed by dancing?"

In recent months, a night out dancing for Suri was a means to find someone to temporarily fill her bed and the huge hole in her heart. Now she just wanted to dance simply for the enjoyment of it.

"Okay. There are a few places I think you'd like, but we'd have to come back down this way since most places with dancing probably won't really get jumping for several more hours."

Suri frowned. "Duh, I don't know why I didn't think of that. Maybe another night then."

"The other alternative is that we could hang out at my place."

"If it won't be an inconvenience, that would be great. I could change also," she said, indicating her shopping bags. "Although I don't have any appropriate shoes."

"We can stop and pick up some dancing shoes on the way. Unless you broke the bank shopping at the market," Layla teased her.

Suri smiled. "I think I can afford one last purchase."

She took a few more sips of her drink then pushed it away. She was already looking forward to the night out and didn't want to put it off. To her surprise, they left Lafitte's to go half a block to Layla's apartment. Suri had been so distracted when she had first walked past here two days ago that she hadn't recognized the neighborhood.

"Well, wasn't this convenient for your suggestion to hang at your place until we went back out."

Layla's face darkened a bit with a blush. "I hadn't planned this."

Suri took pity on her. "I know. I couldn't pass up teasing you."

It was a three-story building with a wrought iron gated courtyard on one side and parking on the other. Since Layla's car was at Suri's house the only other vehicle looked to be a motorcycle covered with a tarp. There was a keypad above the doorknob, two doorbell buttons, and two locked mailboxes. Suri briefly glanced at the door of the first-floor apartment then followed Layla up the stairs to the second. There didn't seem to be outside access to the third floor.

"So, it's just you and your downstairs neighbor?"

"Yes. When I bought the building, it had been a one-family, but I didn't need all that space and figured it would be of better use as a rental property so I converted it to a two-family. I live upstairs. I use the downstairs apartment as an Airbnb rental."

"It's a prime location so I'm sure you get a lot of renters."

"Yeah. So many that it's booked all the way to Mardi Gras."

"Wow. Do you stay here when you have renters?"

"I try not to. As you can tell by where my main home is located, I like having my privacy."

Suri nodded. "I can understand that."

As if on cue, she heard the beep of the keypad lock then the front door opening followed by the sound of female laughter. As she waited for Layla to unlock her apartment door, she glanced back to see four young women with layers of beads around their necks laughing and talking excitedly as they swiped the card key lock on the apartment door downstairs. They didn't even notice Suri and Layla at the top of the well-lit stairway.

"How did they not even see us?"

"The hallway past their door is glamoured. All they see when they look up is an empty stairway."

"Okay, now that's taking privacy to a whole new level. They don't wonder about the mysterious homeowner they hear above them?"

"I'm sure they do but as long as they have a nice place and no issues during their stay, they don't question it. Besides, most Airbnb renters don't meet the homeowners."

"I've never used the service. It always seemed kinda creepy to vacation in a stranger's home."

Layla chuckled. "I could understand that when people rent out their actual home or rooms within their homes. This is technically like renting a short-term apartment. Speaking of which, welcome to mine."

Layla stepped into her apartment then aside to allow Suri to enter a foyer that opened to a large living space designed in neoclassical style. It was elegant with Greek columns, high ceilings, large windows that let in lots of light, and spacious. The furniture was spread out throughout the space with thoughtful purpose toward comfort and style. There were two fireplaces, one in the first sitting area with a large screen television above it and another in the second sitting area flanked by two bookcases and two high-back chairs. Between the living and kitchen space was a staircase leading to the third floor. The apartment appeared to be what it was, a temporary place for Layla to lay her head for a few nights when she was in town, unlike the cozy, lived-in warmth of her house near the bayou.

"It's nice," Suri said.

Layla looked amused. "Just nice?"

Suri smiled. "It's very nice. I just prefer the house. It feels more like you."

"Ah, I see. You're right. This place serves its purposes when needed, but it's definitely not the comfort of home. We can get you set up in the guestroom to get ready."

"Okay."

The rest of the apartment was done in the same minimalist comfort style. Even the hoodoo workroom Layla showed her looked more like a lab than a place to practice root work.

"It serves its purpose," Layla had commented with a shrug in response to Suri's questioning gaze.

Their last stop on the tour was the guestroom. "Is an hour enough time for you to get ready? We can go to dinner and have drinks before hitting the club."

"That's plenty of time."

"Great. I'm just across the hall if you need anything."

"Thanks."

Layla gazed at her for a moment before turning and walking out of the room, closing the door behind her. Suri could tell that she had been attempting to hide the longing that was behind that look, but she had felt it anyway. She sat on the end of the bed staring at the door, wanting so much for Layla to come back and make last night's dream a reality. But she couldn't allow that to happen because once they crossed that line, there would be no turning back. As much as she had been trying to deny the impossibility that with each passing moment that they spent together, she and Layla were developing feelings that went beyond the physical intimacy she saw possible in her dream. Feelings that would need to go unrequited because Suri didn't know if her heart could take investing in another relationship and losing that person if this whole situation went to hell in a handbasket. Because Layla wasn't immortal and despite her self-healing abilities, she could still be mortally wounded. Suri instinctively knew that Layla would also be devastated by her loss, but unlike Suri, Layla's heartbreak and grief would turn her into something dark and deadly and Suri didn't want to carry that burden into the afterlife as she would never get any peace.

She would continue to enjoy what Layla was trying to do for her today, but tomorrow she was going to need to set some limits to ensure that their partnership would stay within the boundaries of what they had been brought together to do. There wasn't room beyond that for anything else.

Layla stood in her closet staring at her clothes, but her focus was on the turmoil of emotions coming from across the hall. She respected Suri enough not to delve into her mind to find out what exactly those emotions were, but she could still feel the heaviness in her energy enough to know that they were there. It was one thing when her attraction was purely physical, but now she was too emotionally attuned to Suri and didn't know how to handle it. As much as she had cared for Cora Lee, it was minute compared to her feelings for Suri. Then she had foolishly bound them together with that damn magical oath to protect her. She didn't know what she was thinking, but therein lay the problem. When she was with Suri, her heart overrode her mind. She had seen the fear in her eyes and wanted nothing more than to ease it. Spending the entire afternoon doing and saying whatever it took to keep Suri distracted, to see her bright smile and hear her joyous laugh.

Layla knew it had probably been a long time since Suri had felt relaxed enough to freely do either and she wanted to be the only one to give that to her. To bring joy and hope back into her life. To keep the darkness and despair that she had been wallowing in all these months at bay. She, a child of darkness and light, wanted to be the light in Suri's life, and the potential of that scared the shit out of her. After Cora Lee, she'd spent a century avoiding anything that resembled what she was feeling for Suri because she couldn't bear the thought of watching them fade away due to aging, sickness, or both. Although the thought of losing Suri to the danger ahead or worse, to Lilith's control, was more unbearable.

"Take it one day at a time, child. There's no sense in fighting fate." Layla heard her mother's voice in her mind.

"Fate can kiss my ass," she said with disgust.

Was it fate for her father to seduce her mother? Was it fate for her mother to die birthing her? Was it fate for Jonas to violently steal her innocence? Was it fate for Suri to lose practically everyone she loved? If so, Orunmila, Fa, Enekpe, Klotho, whoever Fate truly was seemed to be a cruel bitch who delighted in other people's misery. With a sigh of resignation, she decided not to dwell on anything but continuing to give Suri the relaxing day she promised. She'd worry about what fate had in store for them tomorrow.

An hour later, Layla gazed at her reflection in the mirror and almost didn't recognize herself. Since she didn't have much need to dress up for a night out, most of her wardrobe consisted of jeans, button-down shirts, T-shirts, and various styles of casual shoes, all which would have been fine for a light dinner and dancing, but she found that she wanted to put a little more effort into her appearance as it was a special night for Suri. She was able to piece together an outfit that was still comfortable but less casual which included a white button-down open collar shirt with the sleeves rolled to her forearm, a charcoal gray twill double-breasted, three-pocket fitted vest, black raw denim jeans with the cuff rolled up and black lace-up oxford boots. She had even taken her braids out to leave her waist-length hair hanging freely in curly waves, did a subtle smokey eye, and tinted lip gloss to give her natural lip color a shine. It had been years since she had worn her hair in any style other than cornrows or plaited twists or took the time to put on makeup. She had to admit, she liked it. She finished the look off with a pair of large diamond stud earrings then crossed the hall to collect Suri.

Before she even lifted her hand to knock, the door opened and the vision before her left Layla speechless. If she didn't know any better, she would swear that an Orisha goddess stood before her. Suri wore an ankle length, black, African wax print fabric, mono shoulder sundress with vibrant, multicolor Ankara patterns, a fitted waist, and a slit that ended just above her mid-thigh. Her hair had been freed from its poof, parted on the side, and framed her face in a halo of natural auburn curls. She had a smoky eye like Layla's, but her lips looked far more tempting with the lush blood red lipstick she wore. Her accessories included cowrie shell dangle earrings, a cowrie beaded choker necklace, and matching wrist cuff.

"Is it too much?" Suri asked worriedly.

"Uh...no...it's perfect. You look amazing."

"Thanks. I don't know what made me buy this dress but I'm glad I did."

Layla gave her an appreciative glance. "So am I. I'm going to have Oshun herself on my arm tonight."

Suri chuckled. "Now you're exaggerating. You look quite amazing yourself." She reached up to smooth away a lock of hair from Layla's face, letting her fingers trail through the long locks. "Your hair is soft," she said wistfully then seemed to shake herself from a trance. "Give me just a sec to put my shoes on and I'll be ready to go." She held the shoes up that Layla hadn't even noticed she was holding then sat down to put them on. Layla followed then held her hands out for the shoes.

"Allow me."

Their gazes held for a moment before Suri handed her the shoes with a shy smile. They were a pair of flat open toe strappy sandals that laced up her calf. Layla knelt before her, then gently lifted a foot to slide the first shoe on. She heard Suri's quiet intake of breath as her fingers brushed along her calf to wrap and tie the string. By the time Layla did the same with the other shoe she could feel Suri's desire tickling along their connection. She gazed up from where she was kneeling to find Suri watching her with passion glazed eyes. Layla knew that all she had to do was ask and Suri would be ready to continue their night in bed rather than a nightclub, but she wouldn't do that. Her heart and her succubus had been waging war with one another since yesterday and it seemed her heart had claimed victory because she wanted more than one night of passion from Suri.

"Ready?"

Suri nodded, then Layla stood and offered her hand. Suri placed hers in it and allowed Layla to lead her from the bedroom. A shuddering sigh escaped when they crossed the threshold, as if she had been holding her breath waiting for Layla to decide whether to stay or go.

"You know, it's funny but I didn't think I'd be hungry after our huge lunch but suddenly I'm famished," Suri said as they left the apartment.

Layla grinned. "Me too." She knew it was probably from the brief exchange of sexual energy that had passed between them. "The restaurant is about a fifteen-minute walk from here. We could take my bike if you aren't up for walking."

"So that is your motorcycle. I don't mind walking. Maybe you can take me for a ride someday soon."

"I'd like that."

Suri grasped her hand as soon as they exited the building giving Layla a warm feeling of contentment. There was no need for conversation as they strolled along Bourbon Street, the crowds of people growing as they neared the heart of the French Quarter. Dinner was enjoyed at Galatoire's "33" Steakhouse where they continued sharing more about their lives over oysters Rockefeller, turtle soup, and petite filet mignon. Then moved to the restaurant's bar for post dinner cocktails. Layla couldn't remember having such a wonderful time. Not even during the roaring twenties when she used to run the streets of Harlem with her father being charmed by some of the era's most beautiful women did she enjoy herself as much as she was with Suri. This outgoing, fun-loving, smiling woman she was today must have been who she was before Lilith brought so much tragedy into her life.

She didn't want the night to end and was delighted when Suri still wanted to go dancing after dinner and drinks so they left the restaurant headed for Oz, a popular gay nightspot in the French Quarter. There was already a line of people waiting to get in.

Suri began swaying her hips as they waited. "I hope we can get in soon."

"I could get us in."

"Nope. No magic, hoodoo, or any other supernatural tricks today, remember? We're just a couple of regular folks standing in line like all the other regular folks."

Layla chuckled. "Okay."

The line moved slowly and Layla worried that by the time they got to the door they wouldn't be able to get in.

"Layla?"

She gazed up to see a tall, lanky woman with an ebony complexion, a buzz cut, long angular features, a bull ring in her nose, earrings along both ear lobes, dressed in a black leather vest with no shirt, denim and leather pants, and biker boots loping toward them.

"Bettina! I heard you were up north." Layla stepped out of the line to embrace one of her oldest and very few friends.

"Yeah, I was in Toronto for my brother's wedding. I'm surprised to see you out and about. You usually avoid the city like a plague this time of year."

Layla gave Suri, who watched them curiously, a quick glance then stepped aside. "A friend needed cheering up. Bettina, this is Suri. Suri, this is my friend Bettina."

"Suri, it means Red Rose, correct? What a beautiful name for a beautiful woman."

Layla ignored the spike of jealousy over Bettina's appreciative glance.

It didn't seem Suri was falling for her wolf friend's easy charm. She gave her a friendly smile as she shook her hand. "Yes, it does. It's a pleasure to meet you."

"So, what are you doing out here tonight?" Layla asked.

"I'm meeting some of the pack here for a night of debauchery. Why don't you and Suri join us. We've got our own section with bottle service. And you won't have to stand in line."

"That's up to Suri. It's her night."

Suri nodded enthusiastically. "You won't have to ask me twice."

Layla was a little annoyed that she wouldn't have Suri to herself, but seeing her excited smile was worth it. They followed Bettina to the door where she simply gave the doorman a nod and he stepped aside to allow them to enter.

"I'm impressed," Suri said.

Layla smiled. "Bettina's family is very well connected."

Bettina led them up toward an alcove left of a stage where she was greeted by half a dozen similarly dressed women. They lovingly greeted Layla as well and all seemed to have the same reaction to Suri as Bettina did.

"What is she?" Bettina whispered loudly in Layla's ear to be heard over the music.

She wasn't surprised that Bettina could feel but not recognize Suri's energy which contained some very ancient and powerful magic that hadn't been felt around here in centuries.

"I'll explain later. Too many ears."

Bettina nodded then offered Layla and Suri glasses of champagne.

"What are we celebrating?" Suri asked.

Bettina grinned. "My promotion to a pack leader."

"Congratulations!" Layla raised her glass.

"Thanks. I guess I've been forgiven for the Kenya debacle."

"It wasn't your fault in the first place."

"I should've known better. Lesson learned. Now let's party! Suri, do you dance?"

Suri's face beamed. "Does the sun rise every day?"

"Do you mind?" Bettina asked Layla.

"Totally up to her."

Bettina smirked knowingly. "Just one dance then she's all yours."

Suri took Bettina's offered hand then gazed back at Layla as she was lead to the dance floor mouthing, "You're next."

Suri may not be all hers like Bettina said, but watching her move with such wild abandon to the base pumping from the speakers Layla knew, without a question, that she was all Suri's. All she had to do was ask.

CHAPTER FIFTEEN

Suri couldn't remember when she had felt this relaxed and free as she allowed the music to carry her away. With her loping gait and lankiness, Suri hadn't expected Bettina to be such a good dancer, but she moved as gracefully and lightly on her feet as she would have expected a werepanther to do. A couple of songs later, Layla tapped Bettina on the shoulder. Bettina nodded, gave Suri a wink, and danced away.

Layla leaned in to be heard. "I hope you don't mind me stepping in?"

"Not at all."

The DJ transitioned from traditional house to tribal and Suri's hips seem to have a mind of their own as they moved in sync with the Afrocentric beat. Layla pulled her close and Suri saw something primal in her eyes that called to her soul the way the music called to her body. Their bodies moved together in a rhythm that felt as natural as breathing. In that moment, Suri felt as if they were the only two on the dance floor. She and Layla were so caught up in their dance that it took some time for them to realize that everyone else on the floor seemed to be caught up in the music, swaying and gyrating with each other in a trancelike state. That's when Suri felt the heavy sexual energy surrounding them.

She breathed heavily, as if she'd just done a run. "Are we causing this?"

Layla gazed around them. "I'm going to assume we are. We should probably sit down."

She sounded as breathless as Suri as she took her hand to lead them weaving through the hot, sweaty bodies on the dance floor. When they reached Bettina's table, half a dozen pairs of eyes glowed a bright gold as they gazed at Suri and Layla.

"What the fuck was that?" one of the women asked.

Suri gazed back toward the dance floor to see everyone looked around in confusion. Even the DJ seemed to be thrown off as he awkwardly switched into R&B classics. Some people shrugged off whatever happened and continued dancing while others gazed at their partners with embarrassment as they left the floor.

"I think y'all might want to get some fresh air before we have a situation." Bettina eyed Suri and Layla hungrily as she ran her tongue over sharp elongated canines that weren't there before.

Suri noticed the rest of the group had also been affected in the same way.

"It was good seeing you again, Bett. I'll reach out to you soon," Layla said nervously.

"Yeah, you do that," Bettina said with a low growl.

Suri had just enough time to smile and nod before Layla hurriedly pulled her toward the entrance of the club. When they got outside, she breathed a sigh of relief.

"That was interesting," Layla said.

Suri shivered at the raw desire in Bettina and her pack members' eyes. "And a little frightening."

Layla continued holding her hand as they began walking. "We were fortunate that Bettina is a strong leader. Her control kept the rest of her pack from shifting right then and there."

"What happened?"

"Us. Our energy spilled over to affect everyone around us."

"But all we were doing was dancing."

Layla grinned. "Is that all?"

Suri couldn't deny the pull of the music and Layla's energy. The combination of the two was what she imagined taking ecstasy would be like. The feeling still thrummed through her body. Even the simple contact of Layla's hand in hers felt like an intimate touch bringing her nerve endings to life. Suri wanted her and she was tired of fighting it.

"Let's go back to your place."

Layla gazed at her knowingly. "Are you sure?" Her voice was husky with desire.

"Yes."

Layla looked around then frantically flagged down a taxi coming up the street. Suri almost laughed as she tapped her foot impatiently while the taxi slowly inched its way toward them due to all the foot and vehicle traffic in the street.

Suri gave her hand a gentle squeeze. "There's no rush. It's not like I'm going to disappear or something," she said.

Layla leaned in toward Suri, their lips barely touching. "I just don't want what happened in the club to happen out in the open on a busy street."

She closed the distance to deliver a soft, lingering kiss that left Suri tingling all over. When the taxi finally pulled up, she couldn't get in fast enough. She was surprised at how much she wanted to continue their kiss once they were in the vehicle, but she didn't want to take a chance that their energy would affect their driver so she attempted to breathe through the heat and desire rising within her. She could feel Layla trying to hold back as well. Both focused their attention on the scenery outside the car windows while their hands were tightly clinging together as if they needed to maintain some type of physical contact. It seemed to take the driver even longer to find his way out of the slow-moving traffic.

When they finally pulled up to Layla's apartment, she paid their driver double the fare she owed and had her house keys out before she even climbed out of the car. They barely stepped into the entryway before she had Suri against the wall kissing her the way she had been craving the entire car ride. She moaned loudly as Layla tore her lips from Suri's to kiss a heated trail to her neck, grazing her teeth along the sensitive flesh.

"We're not going to make it upstairs at this rate," Suri said breathlessly.

Layla lifted her head and rested her forehead against Suri's. "Have you ever teleported?"

Suri couldn't speak so she simply shook her head.

"Okay, then this would not be a good time to experience it for the first time."

She gave Suri another quick kiss, unlocked and opened the second door, and wrapped her arm around her waist as they went upstairs. The door hadn't even closed before Suri was shrugging out of her dress, pushing Layla against the wall, and pouring all the desire she'd been holding back into a kiss that noticeably raised the temperature of the apartment despite the cool air from the air conditioner. She broke the kiss to fumble with the buttons on Layla's vest, managing to get them undone with a little frustration. Not wanting to struggle with the buttons of her shirt as well, Suri hurriedly pulled it out of the waistband of Layla's pants and just ripped it open. Buttons popped and flew everywhere.

"Sorry."

"No problem."

Suri slid her hands into the open shirt and pressed her lips to Layla's again. Her desire and need grew the longer their kiss continued. She wanted to be in a bed with her body pressed against Layla's, but that required them to stop kissing, which she didn't want to do. Especially as Layla's hot hands smoothed along her waist, up her back to unhook her bra and toss it aside. The next thing she knew, she was the one up against the wall as she felt Layla's lips leave hers, travel along her chin, down the column of her throat where she bared her teeth to graze along Suri's heated flesh. Suri moaned at the sharp scraping that added just enough pressure to bring a pleasurable pain but not enough to break the skin as she continued her descent between her breasts, not breaking contact as she knelt before Suri, grasped the waistband of her panties, and slid them down her hips. She began to nip at her belly, once again not breaking flesh, snaking her tongue around her navel, working her way down until she was at the juncture of Suri's thighs. She stopped and Suri whimpered in disappointment.

"Lift your foot."

She frowned down at the knowing smirk on Layla's face but did as she asked so that Layla could remove her panties from one foot then the other, tossing them with the rest of her clothes nearby. Suri felt vulnerable as she stood naked except for her sandals, but she didn't mind as it felt like Layla was caressing every inch of her with her hungry gaze. She placed a soft kiss on the mound of Suri's sex before standing, placing Suri's arms around her neck, then set her hands under Suri's thighs to lift her legs up and around her waist. Suri held tightly as Layla carried her as if she weighed nothing up the stairs, to her bedroom then gently lay her on the bed before stepping back to undress.

Suri watched until she was standing naked and beautiful before her. There didn't seem to be an ounce of fat or loose skin on Layla's hard muscled body. It was as if she'd been sculpted by Obatala himself. Her golden skin was smooth and unmarred, which wasn't surprising considering she had the ability to self-heal. Suri sat mesmerized as Layla stalked toward her, dark eyes glistening like the night sky filled with stars, long dark hair framing her face and torso, with the look of a lioness hunting her prey. Only Suri didn't want to run away, she was more than happy to be devoured by her huntress. When Layla stopped before her, she grasped Suri's face, and lowered hers for a kiss that began slow and passionate before quickly turning to hungry desire. It was as if they couldn't get enough of each other, but somehow Suri's desire to explore Layla's body overrode their all-consuming kiss.

She tore her lips from Layla's to move fully onto the bed. Layla joined her, but before she could take control again, Suri pressed her onto her back, then straddled her hips.

"You are so beautiful," Suri said in awe.

Layla ran her hands over Suri's hips and waist. "So are you. It's as if Oshun herself fashioned you as the model for the grace, elegance, and beauty of womanhood."

Her words were like an added caress of her touch. Suri's body flushed with desire in response. She lowered her head for a passionate but brief kiss then continued her exploration of Layla's body, kissing, caressing, massaging every hardened plane from her neck down to her toes.

"Turn over."

Layla did as she asked. Suri swept her mass of hair aside and was given quite the shock to find an intricate and very realistic tattoo of two huge, folded bat-like wings covering Layla's back from between her collar bones, across her shoulders, and brushing along the top of her behind. Suri remembered seeing Layla with similar wings in the vision Ayomide shared with her. Had they been a dreamscape symbol of the tattoo? There were no signs of actual wings in Layla's back.

She tentatively brushed her fingers along the upper joint of the wing. Layla moaned and Suri snatched her hand back as the tattoo seemed to shiver along her back.

"They're real?" Suri asked in a combination of awe and fear.

"Yes. Since I can't very well walk around with wings protruding from my back, this is how they appear unless I shift into my demonic side. They're also extremely sensitive to touch."

Suri traced her fingers along the joint once more, now fascinated by how the tattoo, and Layla, reacted to her touch. She continued tracing along the spindly bones, brushing her palm over the flaps of skin between the bones. Layla squirmed and moaned beneath her, gripping the pillow so tight her knuckles strained against the skin of her hand.

"Suri," she said breathlessly. "If you continue, I'll have no control over them breaking free which would not be good with you sitting so close to them."

As if on cue, Suri could feel the skin beneath a long talon at the tip of the wing above Layla's behind begin to rise. She snatched her hand away and the skin slowly flattened out.

"I'm sorry," she panted, desire coursing through her.

Layla gazed at her over her shoulder with eyes shining even brighter. "Don't be."

She shifted to sit up which left Suri on her lap in the same position she had been in the dream, except real life felt so much better. She buried her face in Suri's neck.

"Suri, I have never met any woman like you. You do things to me and make me feel ways I never thought possible." She grazed her teeth along Suri's neck and collarbone.

"Layla," Suri moaned as she arched her back to give Layla free rein to whatever she wanted as she tangled her fingers in Layla's thick hair, grinding her hips against Layla's pelvis, her desire reaching fever pitch.

"Now you turn around," Layla said.

Suri did as she was told, feeling as if she'd do anything Layla asked her if she could feel the euphoria her touch brought. She now sat between Layla's legs with her back pressed against her chest. Layla reached around Suri to take a breast in her hand then reached the other around Suri's hips, dipping her long slender fingers between her thighs. As she pinched and teased Suri's nipple and sunk her fingers into her heated sex, Suri pressed back against Layla as if she would merge with her. Layla played along Suri's neck with her lips and teeth and Suri bared her throat for what she knew Layla wanted. Layla's fingers played Suri like an instrument, plucking at her strings of desire until she couldn't hold back any longer before her sharp canines pierced the sensitive area between her neck and collarbone. Suri felt as if she were exploding into tiny pieces of light that would take a lifetime to put back together.

Moments later, she could feel herself knitting together, piece by piece. As Layla peppered the side of her face with kisses, Suri could feel something soft and leathery wrap around her. She blinked her eyes open then jerked in surprise to find herself in the embrace of Layla's wings.

They started to recede. "Sorry. They suddenly have a mind of their own."

Suri gently grasped the edge of one and gazed back at Layla with a smile. "No, it's okay. I was just surprised."

Layla gave her a nervous smile in return and brought her wings partially back around them. Suri brushed her fingers along the pitch-black skin that felt like the softest leather, along the bony arm that looked so fragile but felt as hard as steel toward the pointed talon at the tip of the wing wondering if it were as sharp as it looked. Layla shivered under her touch.

"I thought they would be much bigger."

Layla's chuckle was low and husky. "I didn't even know you knew that I had wings."

Suri reminded her about the vision Ayomide had shown her. "They stood a good six feet away from you and almost the length of your body."

Layla was quiet for a moment. "That makes sense if I was in my full battle form."

"It was a frightening and awe-inspiring sight to behold." Suri turned back to face Layla, wrapping her arms around her neck, and stroking her fingers along the arm of her wing. "You're awe-inspiring in any form you're in."

Layla moaned, wrapping her arms around Suri's waist. "If we are going to continue this, I need to put them away or someone may get hurt."

Suri watched with fascination as the wings spread then folded in on themselves until they disappeared behind Layla and melded back into a tattoo. Then Layla flipped them so that Suri was on her back.

"You had a chance to do some exploring, now it's my turn."

Layla did just that. Exploring every inch of Suri's body down to removing the sandals she still wore and sucking and nibbling on each toe of her feet then she proceeded to make slow, torturous love to Suri, bringing her to the height of pleasure then pulling back until she was begging for release. Only then did she have Suri straddle her face and brought her to another splintering orgasm. But it wasn't enough, Suri needed more. She worked her way down Layla's body to finish what she'd begun before she was distracted by the wings and devoured Layla as eagerly as she had been devoured. Pulling and drawing her orgasm out until Layla was begging her for mercy. Only then did Suri feel satiated as she curled up along Layla's side, both breathing heavily.

"There is no way we are getting up out of this bed to go back to the house until morning," Layla said weakly.

Suri kissed her once more, loving the taste of their essences mingled on her tongue. "Fine with me. Big spoon or little spoon?"

Layla gazed at her in confusion.

Suri grinned. "Do you prefer to be the big spoon or little spoon?"

Layla chuckled as she smoothed her hand down Suri's back and grasped her behind. "Definitely big spoon."

Suri laughed then turned so that her back was to Layla who pulled up a quilt folded at the foot of the bed to cover them then pulled Suri into her arms. She'd never felt as safe with anyone as she did in that moment wrapped protectively in the cocoon of Layla's embrace.

Layla slept peacefully entangled with Suri when she felt other presences in her home. She awakened to find Suri also stirring awake then gazing at her worriedly.

"Do you feel it too?"

Layla sighed. "It's my parents. Stay here."

"No, she should also hear what must be said," her father communicated wordlessly.

"It seems they want to see us both." Layla went to her armoire, opened a drawer, and pulled out two pairs of night shorts and shirts.

Suri looked at her in confusion. "Your parents want to see me?"

She tossed one pair on the bed for Suri. "Yes. If we don't go out there, they'll probably come in here. They usually have no respect for my privacy."

That got Suri moving. She grabbed the clothes and hurriedly dressed. She was curvier than Layla so the shorts barely covered her behind and the shirt strained against her breast. She looked sexy as hell and Layla hoped her parents' visit would be a short one because all she would be able to think about was getting Suri back in bed. Suri attempted to adjust the tight-fit clothing so Layla took mercy on her, offering a robe, which was small as well but covered her enough that she wouldn't be self-conscious about what she wore. Layla took her hand as they left the bedroom and made their way downstairs. Her father lounged in his favorite spot on the sofa and her mother stood with her back to them gazing out the window. Her parents rarely visited her at the same time.

"To what do I owe this pleasure at this ungodly hour of the morning?"

Layla's father stood. Layla could feel Suri's fear as she stepped partially behind her. Her father must have felt it as well because he gave Suri a sympathetic smile.

"I'm aware that you've been warned to stay away from creatures like me, but I wouldn't harm you, child."

Suri kept her position behind Layla but she loosened the death grip she'd had on Layla's hand. "Old habits die hard."

He nodded. "That's understandable considering what you've been through." He gazed at their clasped hands. "It's good that you've done the deed. It will strengthen your bond."

Layla rolled her eyes. "Way to make an awkward situation even more so."

"Isfet, don't embarrass them," Layla's mother reprimanded her as she turned from the window and stood beside him.

He gave Ruth an amused grin. "What? I only speak the truth. There's no better way to seal a bond between a fated couple than with sex."

"Father! Really?" Layla gazed back at Suri apologetically and was met with a grin.

"Glad to know my parents weren't the only ones capable of embarrassing me in front of people I dated."

Layla grinned. "Oh, is that what we're doing?"

Suri playfully punched her in the arm then looked shyly away.

Layla gazed back at her parents who watched them with interest. "I'm sure you two didn't come here to talk about our sex life."

"No, but as your father said, consummating your relationship will give you an advantage for what's coming," Ruth said, then looked at Isfet to continue.

"Lilith is planning her attack for the night of All Hallow's Day," Isfet said.

Layla snorted. "Halloween? Really? A little too on the nose, isn't it?"

Isfet shrugged. "Lilith was always one for the dramatics. What better night for a powerful demon to claim an avatar on earth than the one night where the gates between earth and hell is most vulnerable and she and her minions can do the most damage."

Layla sighed with frustration. "And Morningstar still isn't willing to step in to stop her?"

"He's the one that gave me this information since she managed to cut off my sources. Her attack won't be outright. She'll be utilizing a distraction."

"Sojourn," Layla said.

"Yes."

"What about my cousin Aria?" Suri had moved to stand beside Layla again.

"There isn't much I can tell you about her other than she is with Sojourn, but Lilith has paid her little attention. Sojourn is the one that she's given the power to get you to where she wants you."

Layla gave Suri's hand a gentle squeeze. "I won't let anything happen to you. I swear it on my life."

"I know." Suri gave her a sweet smile that made her heart skip a beat.

"Suri, are you willing to swear the same for Layla?" Ruth asked.

Layla gazed at her mother curiously. "Will there be a need for her to?"

Ruth smiled sadly as she came forward to place a hand on her cheek. Her touch felt more solid than it ever had. Layla chalked it up to it being so close to Halloween.

"The fight ahead of you both will have moments of darkness. You will need to be each other's light to guide you out of it. I will no longer be here to keep the darkness at bay." She placed her other hand on Suri's cheek. "Suri will be your light now."

Layla didn't like the look on her mother's face. "What are you saying?"

She lowered her hands and stepped back. "We didn't just come here to warn you of what's coming. I'm also here to say good-bye. I've done all I can. Now it's time for me to move on."

Layla's heart clinched the way it had when she witnessed her mother dying after bringing her into the world. She knew this day would come eventually, but it didn't make it any easier to accept.

She released Suri's hand and stepped toward her mother. "When?" She could hear the pain in her voice.

Ruth grasped her hands. "Soon. I've been given a little time to say good-bye to you and your father." That explained why she appeared more solid. "He's taking me to Paris one last time." She gave Isfet a quick glance that held more love than Layla thought he deserved considering his original intentions for Ruth.

Layla wouldn't let a chance like this go by without doing something she had never been able to do with her mother. She pulled her into her arms and just held her for a long moment. Soaking up and committing to memory the feel of a mother's loving embrace.

"I love you, Mama. It scares me to think where I would be without your light to guide me all these years. I hope you'll finally be at peace." She didn't hold back the tears that spilled down her cheeks.

Ruth's embrace tightened. "I love you too, my beautiful baby girl. You are and always have been my heartbeat." She placed a soft kiss on Layla's cheek then released her to go to Suri.

"Your grandmother said you were blessed, Suri, and I can clearly see what she meant. There's a light in you that can brighten the darkest soul. You're also surrounded by so much love. Embrace it, let it fill you and don't be afraid of sharing it with those deserving it." Ruth turned slightly, reaching for Layla.

Layla took her hand and she placed it into Suri's looking between the two of them. "Fate brought you together. Only you can decide if you want to stay that way."

"We must go, my love," Isfet said gently.

Ruth nodded then placed a soft kiss on both Layla's and Suri's cheeks. "I may no longer walk among you, but I will always be with you in spirit." She turned to accept Isfet's offered hand.

"I will do whatever I can to help you defeat Lilith," he said to Layla.

"Don't jeopardize your standing with Morningstar for a fight that's not yours," Layla said.

"I'll worry about Morningstar. You focus on strengthening that bond." He gave them a mischievous smile and wink before guiding Ruth to disappear into the shadows.

"I can honestly say that was the most interesting first meeting of the parents I've ever had," Suri said.

"Yeah, I bet."

Layla gazed sadly at the empty spot where her parents had just been standing. The realization that it would be the last time they were all together, the last time she would have her mother keeping her from giving in to her dark side hit her like a ton of bricks. She folded into herself; her stomach tied into knots as fear of what her future held without her mother's spirit meant. She didn't even notice that she'd fallen to her knees on the floor until she saw Suri kneel beside her.

"Would you like me to take the pain away?"

Layla shook her head, unable to speak past the lump in her throat. She wanted to feel this loss. To remember how much it hurt to lose someone and know that she could survive it. Her mother had done more than enough to keep Layla on the right path. She deserved the peace she would be receiving because of it. It was up to her now to continue with all that her mother's spirit had taught and given her to stay on that path. Suri didn't try to ease her pain, but she did stay by her side as Layla quietly wept which was a comfort as well. She gave her grief a short time to run its course then tucked it away. They had a situation to deal with and she had no time to wallow in her feelings. She wiped her tears away, stood, and offered Suri a hand as she stood as well.

"Are you okay?"

"No, but I will be eventually. We've got a little less than a week to get ready for a confrontation of epic proportions."

Suri gazed at her skeptically for a moment then seemed to accept what she said. "That gives me time for my meet and greet with the Seven. I'll text Uncle Robert to meet us at the house in an hour."

"You do realize that it's the crack of dawn."

"I don't think we can afford to waste a minute of time."

Layla nodded in agreement. "The streetcar isn't running this early and getting a car service at this hour will probably take more time than if we took my bike back to the house."

Suri's face lit up. "Okay. But what about the stuff I bought today?"

"Gather it all together, I'll teleport it to the house, pop back in here, and we'll be on our way."

"Why can't we just teleport there?"

"Because I would prefer not end the night that we just had with you throwing up all over me."

Suri grinned. "I guess there's no worry about bags of clothes and accessories throwing up all over you."

"Very true. I also think we need to eat before we go. I don't know about you, but our activities last night were draining."

Suri grinned. "Yeah, I guess that's a good idea, especially if we're going to be road tripping in and out of Orisha kingdoms."

Layla whipped them up omelets, toast, and coffee, which they hungrily ate. After a quick clean-up, Suri collected her clothes that had been left by the doorway. As they headed upstairs to get dressed Layla noticed her gazing down at them with amusement. She was probably wondering if her parents had noticed the dress and undergarments tossed aside in the middle of the floor.

"They didn't need to see the clothes to know what happened. My father could easily read our energy."

"Could you imagine if they'd popped in during?"

Layla chuckled. "I don't think that would have happened. My father may not respect privacy, but he has a sense of these things and would have known not to interrupt. And before you ask, no, I don't make it a habit of bringing ladies up here. You're the first."

Suri's lips trembled as she seemed to be trying not to smile. "I wasn't going to ask but that's good to know."

While Suri was in the shower, Layla teleported into the house to drop her bags off and feed a very cranky Sebastian who was none too happy about being left alone all night without warning. Fortunately, his anger was somewhat mollified by Layla bringing the rest of the salmon she'd had at the apartment with her. She teleported back home just in time for her to have a quick shower then they were on their way. Having Suri on her bike was also a first for Layla. Even when she was out riding with Bettina and her crew, she never had anyone on the bike with her. She couldn't imagine it being anyone but Suri from now on. She enjoyed the way her arms wrapped around her waist. Not too tight because she was trying to be brave but tight enough to let Layla know that she was still a little nervous. The streets were clear and quiet, which was when she normally liked to open it up to let the speed and adrenaline take over, but she chose to keep it at a cruising speed so as not to frighten Suri. When they arrived at the house Suri opened the garage so that Layla could store her bike until she could take it back home. Robert was sitting on the porch waiting. He stood and pulled Suri into a hug then gave Layla a small smile.

"Nice bike," he said in greeting.

"Thanks."

He nodded and walked into the house with Suri. Layla took that as a sign that he was warming up to her, which would hopefully go a long way when it came to their introductions to the Seven. She seriously didn't want to be smote down by an angry god taking offense to Robert bringing a halfling with one foot in hell and the other on earth in their presence and introducing her as their newest guardian's protector. That would suck.

CHAPTER SIXTEEN

They spent an hour gathering items for offerings to each of the Seven, placing them on individual trays, and having Layla teleport to and from the basement to place them outside each door. Then Suri performed a cleansing for all of them, changed into the robe she'd worn to greet Ayomide while her uncle also changed into a tunic and pants in the family's color. Suri and her uncle gazed wide-eyed at Layla when she joined them wearing something like what Robert wore but in purple.

Layla shrugged. "It was on the bed. I thought one of you might have left it."

Suri and Robert shook their heads, then Robert circled looking her up and down.

"You'll do."

Layla looked amused. "Uh, thanks, I think."

They headed down to the basement where the enormity of what was about to happen hit Suri head-on. Not to mention that her mind was racing in too many directions. Thoughts of last night with Layla, her parents' unexpected visit, all that they had revealed, the short time they had to prepare for Lilith's arrival, and the prospect of meeting actual gods and goddesses all swirled around her head like a tornado. Her uncle took her hands in his. They stood before the doorway to Elegua's domain. He was the first of the Orisha created, the messenger between the human world and the divine, and guardian of the crossroads of life. He embodied a dual nature, chaos, and harmony. He was often compared to the Greek god Loki. You wanted to stay on his good side, which was why they were visiting him before the others so as not to offend him.

"Suri, look at me."

She did as he asked, focusing her gaze on his deep brown eyes.

"This is your legacy. You were born to do this and have already been blessed by our ancestors and the Seven. This is just a formality."

"It feels more like having the job interviews after I've already started the job."

Robert smiled. "I can see how it would appear that way, but it's more like meeting your clients after you've taken the job."

Suri smiled also then took a calming breath, letting her uncle ease her anxiety.

"Better?"

She nodded.

"Good. Layla, would you mind carrying the offering. Since you'll be her protector it's best if you present it."

Layla nodded then picked up the tray. Suri noticed that she looked just as nervous as her. Robert placed the key in the door and the pictures and symbols glowed brightly. Once they dimmed, he turned the key and opened the door. He stepped through first followed by Suri then Layla. Suri almost stumbled as she looked around to find that they were in a huge freaking forest beneath her house. They stood on a well tread path that led to three other paths. Elegua's crossroads. Robert knelt at the center crossroad and Suri and Layla did the same. In his clear deep voice, he repeated the prayer to summon Elegua.

"I invoke the guardian spirit of the roads, Elegua. Blessed Orisha, owner of the keys of destiny. Tireless messenger who watches over the sacrifices made by the living and the dead. You know everyone and everything that exists between Heaven and Earth. Pleading before you, I call you to help me in all my vicissitudes. Your name I cry three times so that your mercy may be the talisman that leads me to success. Elegua blessed, come to my call. Elegua blessed, listen to my request. *Ashe*."

They knelt there for what seemed like forever but was probably only a few minutes before a figure appeared on the road ahead walking toward them. He was tall, taller than her uncle, very muscular, with dark ebony skin that glistened as if oiled. He wore a red-and-black garment gathered at his waist that came to his knees, cuffs on his biceps made of hammered silver and cowrie shells, red headwrap, and carried a red-and-black club with a hooked end. His image wavered between a little boy, a man in his prime, and an elderly man. It felt as if Suri's heart slammed against her chest and beat so loud that everyone had to hear it. She had to avert her eyes or she would surely go mad if she continued staring. When he finally stopped before them, she could see his feet but wouldn't dare look up past that. Her uncle must have signaled Layla because she felt a shift beside her as Layla stepped forward to set the tray of offerings before him. A yo-yo and candy bar for his childlike self, a cigar and rum for his prime self, and hard candy and smoked salmon for his elder self.

"It's been some time since I've had visitors at this gateway." His voice was surprisingly soft.

"Forgive us, Elegua, we lost our last guardian many years ago before she had time to train Suri, our new guardian."

"Yes, the loss of Pearl was a great tragedy. She was a truly devoted guardian. I assume you are the one who has regularly left offerings in her absence without staying to at least speak with me?"

Suri could hear the annoyance in his tone and felt her uncle tense. If they ended up offending Elegua none of the other gods would even think about seeing them. Robert lowered himself further, prostrating at his bare feet.

"I can only ask your forgiveness, Elegua Blessed. I did not think I was worthy of sitting within your presence without our guardian with me."

Elegua sighed. "Yes, well, true as that may be, if you are bringing offerings, a bit of conversation would not go unwanted. Now, present this new guardian to me and tell me why you've also brought this other impure being with you."

This time Suri felt Layla tense in response to his insult. She had to bite her tongue to keep from defending her.

"I present to you Suri, blessed by Ayomide to inherit the role of priestess and guardian of New Orleans." Robert waved her forward. "I also humbly present to you Layla, a cambion of extraordinary power to act as Suri's protector in my stead." He waved Layla forward.

Suri peeked up at Elegua to find him gazing down at Layla curiously. "I sense a greatness in you as long as you continue to walk in the light. Will that be a problem for you, cambion?"

He hadn't said cambion in a disrespectful tone, but Suri still saw the tick in Layla's jaw before she responded.

"No. That will not be a problem, blessed one. As long as I am duty bound to protect Priestess Suri I will always walk in the light."

"And once that duty has ended?"

Layla paused a moment before answering. "I sincerely cannot say."

Elegua chuckled. "Your honesty is refreshing. I approve, but it's not my blessing that you will need for your duty as protector. Ogun will be the one you must impress, but I will put in a good word for you." He gave her a wink.

When he turned his gaze on Suri, she quickly pointed hers back toward his feet. "Raise your head, Priestess Suri. Let me get a good look at you."

Suri's heart hammered in her chest once again as he lifted his club, placing the curved end under her chin to raise her gaze up to his. He had transformed into the elder he sometimes presented as he studied her intently. Suri fought the fear clawing its way through her body and the urge to tear her eyes from his, which seemed to garner some respect as he smiled with satisfaction.

"I accept you as a fellow guardian, Suri. I hope, unlike your neglectful uncle, you will do more than simply drop offerings off as if you're one of those food delivery services you earthbound beings are so fond of." He quirked a brow at Robert who looked away with embarrassment. "I so looked forward to your grandmother's visits. Our talks were a highlight of my endless days," he said wistfully.

"I will do my best," Suri said.

He removed the club from beneath her chin. "See that you do. You may go. The others anxiously await your visit."

He turned back toward the path, once again transforming from one persona to the next. The final one was a little boy skipping down the path playing with the yo-yo before fading from view. They all breathed a collective sigh of relief followed by Layla's nervous chuckle.

"One down, six more to go."

Suri wiped her hand down her face. "I don't know if I can do this six more times. My nerves are fried."

Robert gave her arm a quick squeeze. "You'll be fine. This was the hard part. If Elegua has already communicated his thoughts to the others then the rest is just formality."

Suri found that difficult to believe. "If you say so."

Layla collected the empty tray and they exited the forest back into the basement hallway.

"Yemaya is next since she is the one that led Ayomide to this path," Robert said.

Suri thought her introduction to Elegua was nerve wracking, the thought of facing Yemaya, her family's goddess mother was even more daunting.

Layla reached over to grasp her hand. "You got this."

That one simple touch and phrase was enough to calm Suri's nervousness. "Thank you."

Layla nodded then picked up the tray outside Yemaya's doorway. As with Elegua's when Robert placed the key in the lock, the images on the door glowed brightly for a moment then dimmed. What greeted them on the other side of the door made Suri gasp in awe. They stepped onto a white sandy beach just a few steps away from an endless sea of clear turquoise waters below a bright blue horizon. She had to look back at the open doorway to believe that she was still in the house. When she turned back Robert was kneeling in the sand and she and Layla followed suit.

"Goddess who is Mother of All, Queen of the Deep Sea, Protectress of women. Allow your presence to be known throughout this sacred space. We who call upon you as Yemaya, Our Mother, Our Womb of Creation, ask that your love rolls and washes over us as the waves of the ocean, as the rivers from your breasts. Yemaya, Mother Whose Children are Fish, You who are comfort, inspiration, and forgiveness, We call you forth to enter our hearts. *Ashe*."

Before Robert even finished the prayer the waters churned and the waves crashed against the shore spraying them with warm ocean water. Then the waters began to recede, gathering further out into a huge wave.

"Don't move," Robert warned her.

Suri sort of knew what to expect after the vision Ayomide had shared with her, but it didn't make it any less frightening to witness in person.

"Layla, quickly place the tray at the water's edge," he instructed.

Layla hurried to place the tray of cowrie shells, white roses from the garden, and slices of watermelon at the water's edge before the wave came crashing in on her, then she rejoined them. The tray was pulled out as the huge wave came rushing toward them then suddenly stopped at the shoreline towering a good twelve feet. A figure stepped forward out of the waves dressed in the same attire as Ayomide's vision, but instead of floating in the wave she stepped onto the sandy beach.

"Rise, my children, and embrace your mother," she said in a softly commanding tone.

Suri rose and was awestruck by the goddess's dark beauty. Her ocean-blue-tinged skin and smattering of aquamarine scales gave her an ethereal glow. She stood a full head taller than Robert who walked into her embrace without hesitation. Then she took his face in her hands and smiled affectionately down at him.

"I was saddened to hear of your loss. Priestess Pearl was a wonderful guardian but she was just as wonderful as a mother."

"Yes, she was."

Yemaya placed a kiss on Robert's forehead. "Be blessed, my son, and tell me why you've summoned me after all this time."

Robert stepped aside so that Suri could be seen. "I present to you Suri, the family's new priestess and guardian, blessed by Ayomide."

Yemaya held her arms open with a smile. "Step forward, child."

Suri took a hesitant step forward. Yemaya's arms wrapped around her and stole her breath as water flowed around and through her. Pouring into her nose and mouth, making her feel as if she were going to drown. Instinct told her to fight, but something else told her to just let it envelop her. She closed her eyes and took it all, then opened them to find herself floating weightlessly in the sea. She wasn't afraid because she knew that Yemaya was there to protect her, then she began floating to the surface, taking a lungful of air as Yemaya gently released her, then took her face in her hands as she did Robert.

"You are all that your mother Ayomide hoped for and more than worthy to carry on her legacy. May your children be blessed with your wisdom and strength to do the same." She placed a kiss upon Suri's brow.

Suri was filled with pride. "Thank you, Mother Yemaya."

Yemaya turned to face Layla. "And you, protector. You are your mother's child, but I fear what you've inherited from your father could be your downfall, but that is for Ogun to judge."

"So, I've heard," Layla mumbled.

Suri looked from her to Yemaya, waiting for the goddess to smite Layla on the spot but she simply smiled. "You'll do well to keep that attitude in check when meeting Ogun, protector. I would hate for Suri to lose you so soon after finding you."

"You have my blessing, Priestess Suri." Yemaya turned back toward the wall of water that she had emerged from and disappeared within its shadowy depths once again.

The water crashed upon the shoreline, leaving the tray their offerings had been on, which were gone and replaced by a beautiful freshwater pearl bracelet and pendant necklace set on a silver chain. Layla collected the tray offering the jewelry to Suri.

"This is a very good sign," Robert said as he helped Suri put the necklace on. "This will prove to the others that Yemaya has approved of you. Between this and Elegua's good word, we shouldn't have any issues."

Suri simply nodded. She wouldn't feel comfortable enough to let her guard down until they exited the final gateway still in one piece.

❖

By the time they stood outside the final gateway, which was Ogun's, one of the oldest and most revered Orisha known as the god of energy, creativity, war, and hunting, Layla's ego had taken a serious beating. Many supernatural halflings were looked down upon by both beings they were created from, but cambions were considered the lowest of the low because of their demon connection. If Layla had embraced her demon side there would be no question as to her acceptance by those dark beings. If she had embraced her human side then there would be no question of her being human. But she had learned to balance both, which put her in the position of being able to pass into either world if needed but with obvious signs that she was neither fully one nor the other. Gods, no matter what religion, were not known for their humility so to have a lowly halfling brought before them to be accepted as a protector for someone so important to them was a slap in the face.

Except for Yemaya, she had been sneered at, insulted, demeaned, and sometimes outright ignored by the other five of the seven they met. Now, standing before Ogun's door with a bruised and battered ego, knowing that his acceptance would be the one to make or break whether Layla would continue as Suri's protector was almost too much.

"Wait, I need a minute," Layla said as Robert began to place the key in the lock.

She set the offering tray back on the floor, turned toward the stairs, then sat dejectedly on a step with her face in her hands. She sensed Suri before she even sat down beside her.

"I'm so sorry you've had to go through this and would completely understand if you wanted to walk away. We've been at this all day; I don't know how you've managed to keep your composure this long."

Layla gave her a sad smile. "Sixteen years living as a slave on a southern plantation along with two hundred more years of living between worlds as a half breed not truly being accepted in either one gives you thick skin. Yeah, the insults and name calling irk me, but not as much as the fact that they don't believe a lowly cambion is worthy of protecting their precious guardian." She didn't mean for that to sound as bitter as it did. "Sorry."

Suri's gaze was filled with understanding. "You don't need to apologize. It doesn't matter what any of them think. If I'm going to do this, it will be on my terms and one of those terms is that you will be my protector. I'll fight tooth and nail to make sure that happens. I trust you with my life. Besides, you swore an oath. I wouldn't want you cursed with boils or some weird disfigurement if you forfeit it." She reached up to run a finger along Layla's jawline. "I kinda like the way you look."

It amazed Layla how that simple touch relieved all her frustration and anxiety. She leaned forward to place a soft kiss on Suri's lips. "Thank you."

Suri smiled and stood, offering Layla her hand. "Let's do this."

They made their way back to Robert who smiled tiredly. "It's been a long day, are we good?"

"Yes," they answered in unison.

Robert nodded. "Layla, I'm sure you figured out by now that this introduction is mostly for your benefit. I and every other protector before me had to go through this same introduction you are about to experience. Ogun is not one for sarcasm, jokes, or unnecessary speech. He's direct and prefers responses to his questions to be direct and honest. Despite what you might think the other Orisha believe you are, you've proven your worth by withstanding their treatment with quiet respect. I'm sure Ogun has seen that."

Layla was surprised to hear the admiration in Robert's tone. That honestly meant more to her than anything Ogun could say or do as Robert's shoes were the ones she would be filling and he was the closest family Suri had.

"Thank you."

Layla picked up the offering tray, which was the heaviest and had the most items as they were representing offerings from Robert and Layla. Several iron nails, slices of beef steak, plantains, pomegranate, cigar, rum, and a necklace of black and green beads. They crossed the threshold through a wall of heat into a smithy where a forge burned brightly and the sound of metal upon metal rang in their ears. Standing at the forge was a man not much taller than Robert but was twice as broad in the shoulders, chest, and arms. His harshly planed face and muscular torso were covered in black tribal markings and glistened with sweat from the heat of the forge where he was slamming a massive hammer down on a piece of metal. He wore a skirt made of blue fabric and leather strips, leather sandals, metal bands on his wrists and biceps and a strip of leather holding his locs, which were laced with cowrie shells and black and green beads, away from his face.

Layla could withstand a lot. She was, after all, the child of a demon, but being in this enclosed space so close to the heat of the forge was almost unbearable. She glanced over to see sweat pouring from Suri's and Robert's faces, but they seemed to be withstanding it as well. They all knelt, and despite Ogun standing before them, Robert still recited the summoning prayer, then had Layla bring the offering tray forward reciting her own greeting.

"By the hammer and the anvil, I greet you, Ogun. Forge my will as you forge iron."

"What makes you worthy of being our guardian's protector, child of Isfet and Ruth?" Ogun asked without looking away from his task as he set the metal he'd been hammering back into the fire. His voice was deep and gruff like someone who spoke little and spent a lot of time around smoke.

Layla was caught off guard by him acknowledging her parents rather than what she was as the other Orisha had done. "I am strong of mind, body, and abilities. I have worked very hard to stay on the path of light and have dedicated my life to using my abilities to help our people in their times of need. I promise to devote that same dedication in protecting our guardian."

Ogun lifted the metal out of the fire and turned to place it in a vat of water. Steam hissed and the dry heat in the room turned to a thick humidity that made Suri gasp and begin to hyperventilate. Without looking away from Ogun, Layla reached a hand back toward her and felt the tight grip of Suri's hand in return.

"Breathe slow steady breaths," she told her wordlessly.

As the steam cleared and Suri's breathing slowed, she gave Layla's hand a squeeze to let her know she was fine and released her.

"Strength and ability are all well and good, but that is not what makes one worthy of protecting our guardian. To be a protector one must be ready to sacrifice one's life for our guardian. Maybe you need a moment to rethink your answer."

He pulled the metal piece he'd been working on out of the water, placed it in a vise, and brought out carving and sharpening tools. As he worked Layla racked her brain for the answer he could be looking for. She knew the longer it took the more Suri and Robert would have to suffer the heat of the forge. She had begun to care too deeply for Suri to make her suffer for her failing whatever tests she had endured up until this point and frustration was wearing on her nerves. She understood what the role of being Suri's protector called for and she couldn't think of a better protector in this situation than one that could traverse between planes like she could and knew what to expect from the evil coming at Suri. What more did these high and mighty beings want from her? She gazed up at Ogun in annoyance as he continued to ignore them as he hammered, chiseled, and sharpened whatever he was creating. He held it up for inspection and Layla could see that it was a wicked looking spearhead the length of her forearm to her fingertip with a serrated edge on one side and a sharpened flat edge on the other. Satisfied with his work, he picked up a long wooden spear handle, adhered the blade to it, placed it in the fire once more then in the vat of water again. Once he was finished, he finally turned to face them, his dark eyes piercing Layla's.

"Robert, what makes a guardian's protector worthy of their role?" Although the question was directed at Robert, he held Layla's gaze.

"Dedication and love for the guardian we are duty bound to protect at all costs. We must be willing to lay down our lives to keep our guardian safe from those out to do evil or harm."

"I ask you once again, Layla, what makes you worthy of being Suri's protector?"

Layla finally realized from what Robert said and the softening tone of Ogun's voice, as well as his using her and Suri's name, the answer he was looking for. She gazed back at Suri who still managed to give her a patient and encouraging smile despite the sweat pouring down her face and drenching her robe and remembered their day yesterday, the bond they strengthened even before their intimate night together. Their connection the moment they met. The pain Layla had carried with her for so long that Suri had willingly eased without a thought. The comfort she was able to bring Suri just by giving her a day to be "normal." Then last night that became more than just a transference of energy. Layla had given a vital piece of herself. She turned back to Ogun and spoke from her soul.

"My guardian and I share a bond that goes beyond simple devotion and dedication. As long as there is breath in my body so there shall be in my guardian's. If the day comes when I must lay down my life in defense of my guardian, I will do so without hesitation for my guardian's life far outweighs mine. My heart and soul belong to my guardian and so shall be used in whatever capacity my guardian requires."

Ogun smiled for the first time since they entered the smithy. "The fates have chosen well with this one. Rise and stand before me, Protector Layla."

Layla hadn't realized she'd been holding her breath until it came out in a whoosh of air as she stood then stepped forward.

"Layla, daughter of fallen archangel Isfet and guardian angel Ruth, protector and benefactor of Olodumare's children, I accept thee as the one and only true protector of Guardian Priestess Suri until the day one or both of you shall leave this plane to join Olodumare's kingdom. Do you promise to fulfill your duty without doubt, malice, or deceit in your heart?"

Layla's heart filled with pride. This was what all her struggling to remain on the path of light had come to. There was no longer the dreaded prospect of living another lifetime alone without a purpose that didn't push her closer to the dark side, which was what carrying the constant threats her people endured almost daily was doing to her. She could help them by helping Suri. She didn't have to worship Orisha to do what she was being tasked to do. She just had to believe in the importance of what Suri and her family were doing and her role in it.

"Yes, I promise to fulfill my duty as protector with an open and pure heart and mind."

Ogun nodded, gripped the spear in both hands, slammed it on the ground seven times before it glowed a burning orange in his hands as if for a final forge where words and symbols were burned into the wooden handle and on the blade. Once the glowing symbols dimmed, he offered the spear to Layla, which she accepted reverently.

"As long as you remain pure of heart, this weapon, forged by my hands, will help you defeat all enemies that stand in your path. Robert, step forward."

Robert stepped up to stand beside Layla.

Ogun placed a fatherly hand on Robert's shoulder. "You have served us well. What happened with Guardian Pearl was no fault of yours and is not a burden you should carry. Ease yourself of this guilt as your role as protector is not quite done. There is another who will need your guidance soon enough. For now, it is time to pass the legacy on as it was passed on to you from your father."

Robert bowed his head. "Thank you, Mighty Ogun, for your many blessings." He partially turned toward Layla. "Speak the following prayer so that Ogun may pass final judgment of your pure and open heart and mind."

He seemed to pause, as if to give her a moment to change her mind. In that pause something moved in the shadows near the forge. Layla forced herself to remain completely still as a dark shape moved toward them forming into a slender, medium-sized dog with ash black fur, a long muzzle, pointed ears, and eyes that were filled with an ancient wisdom watching her curiously as it sat obediently beside Ogun. Layla recognized it as the Africanis, a breed indigenous to Africa since ancient Egypt and known for its intelligence, loyalty, and hunting prowess. Dogs were also Ogun's animal symbol so she assumed this dog was an extension of its master. What that would mean if Layla failed this last part, she didn't want to know so she did her best to take the time they were giving her to clear her mind of any doubts about what she was being tasked to do.

Robert recited the prayer for her to repeat. Layla took a calming breath, bowed her head toward Ogun while avoiding the dog's wizened gaze, and repeated the prayer putting all her belief not of a greater power or religious figure but of her devotion to Suri into her recitation.

"Ogun, bless me with protection, of your shield, sword, and divine light so all enemies retreat in fear, Ogun, bless me with refuge inside your light, by your powers, I am removed from my enemies' sight. *Ashe*."

There was a tense moment of silence when the dog stood, moved to Layla, sniffed made a little *whuff* sound, then sat beside Ogun once again.

"It is done. May Olodumare rain blessings upon you all."

The fire in the forge flared bright enough to blind them then the air popped and everything was quiet and cool. They stood in an empty and dark smithy with no sign of Ogun or his dog. Layla gazed at Robert then Suri who had been covered in sweat seconds ago and now looked as fresh as they did when they first entered through the gateway.

"Let's not do that again," Suri said as she turned and headed for the door. Layla was right behind her, but Robert hesitated. Standing and gazing at the quiet forge.

"Uncle Robert?" Suri said in concern.

"After Aria left with Sojourn, I threw myself into learning about our family's legacy, finding out what gifts I had, and how I fit into it all in the hopes of finding a way to get her back. Mama knew when you were a baby that you would be next in line for guardian and had Pop train me to eventually become your protector. Then he passed and I became Mama's protector. Thirty-five years preparing for a role I'll never step into because I failed my child by denying our legacy and her gifts. Mama never told anyone, but despite Aria being born so gifted she was never going to be the next guardian. A strong and gifted priestess, yes, but not the guardian. It was always you because you were the unborn child of Ayomide that Yemaya saw in her vision. But my fear of accepting the truth denied my child the opportunity of the greatness that she was bound for. My denial of our legacy set her on the wrong path and has brought us here to this point today. Being removed from my role as protector is a just punishment for my lack of faith and I accept it willingly." He turned and gave them a sad smile. "It's probably for the best. My heart truly wasn't in it after Mama passed because I felt like I failed her also. Once again, she was hurt because of my failing Aria."

Suri took Robert's hand. "You haven't failed anyone. Look how you stepped up to help me when my parents refused to see me and my gifts. Gammy's spirit wasn't my only guide. Our phone calls, your letters and gifts, our long talks when we visited here or when you came to New York all had a hand in helping me embrace my gifts. You've been my teacher and protector all these years and I don't know what I would have done if you hadn't been here for me. Aria was young and vulnerable and Sojourn took advantage of that to try to gain something she had no right to. She is the only one at fault for what happened to Aria and Gammy, not you."

Layla could see that he wanted to believe Suri, but his guilt ran far too deep for him to accept it. She understood that. She carried the guilt of her grandmother's death with her daily. No one could prove it at the time, but Layla knew the fire that burned down her cabin was set by Jonas. He'd admitted it when she visited him like a wraith in the night while he lay on his deathbed old, alone, and destitute on his family's abandoned plantation. He'd locked her in the cabin while she slept, lit the fire at the only door of the cabin, and hid in the trees watching it burn while Layla's grandmother had screamed in terror as her uncle and some of the other male slaves attempted to save her by trying to use an axe to chop through a cabin wall, but the flames had pretty much engulfed the building by the time they had been aware of the fire. All they could do was helplessly stand by as her grandmother suffered a slow horrible death. She had been tempted to finish what a life of drinking and misery had done to Jonas, but instead, she saw that he suffered in another way. He was forever bound in purgatory to that miserable land with no opportunity to redeem his soul to set it free. There was no redemption for evil like him. Despite the justice she was able to get, Layla would forever blame herself for letting her anger get the best of her when she cursed Jonas's manhood. She had taken something of great importance from him, his pride and legacy, and he had retaliated by taking someone of great importance to her. So, yes, Layla understood Robert's guilt and that no comfort Suri could provide would ease it until he was ready to release it.

Robert pulled Suri into a hug then pressed a kiss on her forehead. "I don't know about you but I've had enough of Orishas, legacy, and plane tripping for the day." He took her hand to lead her out of Ogun's smithy back into their world then shut and locked the door with a relieved sigh. "It's all yours now." He handed the ring of keys to her. "Ladies, please try holding off any dramatic events until at least after noon tomorrow."

Suri grinned. "We'll do our best."

Robert gazed at Layla. "I'm not just entrusting you with the life of our guardian, but the most important person in my life. If anything happens to her under your watch you will see what a true protector's wrath is like. Good night." He turned and left without a backward glance.

"Okay then," Suri said.

"You know, I think I would rather face Ogun's dog than your angry uncle."

Suri began collecting the empty trays outside the doorways. "Well, right now all I want to face is a pizza, a glass of wine, then bed."

Layla took the stack from her. "Why don't you go up and order something and I'll finish up down here."

"Okay. I'm not even going to argue."

Layla watched Suri trudge tiredly up the stairs. Once she was out of sight, she set the trays down to collect the spear Ogun had presented her. An inscription was etched into the handle in what she assumed was Yoruba, which she didn't understand. She would have to ask Suri. The well-honed and deadly sharp iron blade also had etchings. These she recognized as the Adinkra symbols for strength, courage, and wisdom. She also felt a powerful magic imbued in the weapon. She hefted it above her shoulder and was surprised by how light it was as well as the natural feel of it in her hand considering she'd never used a spear before. She preferred her daggers or her double-bladed katana, both a gift from her father, on the few occasions she'd had to use an actual weapon to defend herself against any creature foolish enough to incur her father's wrath by attacking her. Despite her having had those weapons for over a century, the spear felt more hers than those did.

Suddenly, everything they had just gone through sunk in and she gazed at the spear then Ogun's door in awe. She'd met and dealt with all manner of supernatural beings in her life and travels except a god or goddess. Let alone seven in one day and to have one of the most powerful and revered gods of them all create a custom weapon just for her was mind-blowing. Layla Jeffries, former slave, and demon halfling was now a blessed protector of a powerful Orisha priestess and guardian wielding a weapon fashioned by Ogun himself to defend her charge against the mother of demons. If someone had told her a week ago that this was where she would be she would've laughed in their face. Now it took everything in her not to begin laughing in hysterical disbelief.

❖

Suri sat upstairs at the kitchen counter in her own shock and disbelief. She didn't know how long she'd been sitting there staring at the floor. She remembered ordering food but had no idea where or what she ordered. They had just spent the past twelve hours in the presence of seven Orisha gods and goddesses and she felt like her brain was fried after being blown so many times throughout the day. There were moments where she had to pinch herself to make sure she wasn't dreaming as she entered through a door in her basement to end up standing in a whole other world and environment speaking face-to-face with a religious deity. Even if her parents had embraced her gifts and her grandmother had survived to train her for this role, she didn't think a lifetime of training would have prepared her for what she'd just experienced.

"You look just as shell-shocked as I am."

She practically fell off the stool and squeaked in fright to find Layla standing beside her. "Are you trying to give me the heart attack I'm surprised that I haven't had already?"

"Sorry. I called your name from the other room but I guess you didn't hear me. Are you okay?" She set the stack of trays on the counter looking very much the mighty protector holding her spear from Ogun.

"I honestly don't know. It's probably delayed shock." Her phone dinged with a message. She gazed at it with a tired sigh. "The food is here. I have no idea what I ordered."

"I'll get it." Layla propped the spear against the island and left the kitchen.

Suri watched, ready to back her up if the delivery guy turned out to be another of Lilith's lackies. Layla collected a bag and pizza box without incident and headed back to the kitchen.

"Let's see what we've got here," she said as she set the food on the island.

There was a large plain cheese pizza in the box and the bag contained an order of garlic knots, fried ravioli, and containers of garlic sauce and marinara. Her stomach growled at the sight of the food. They hadn't eaten all day.

"Couldn't find a vegetable on the menu?" Layla said with amusement.

Suri's face heated with a blush. "Sorry. That's my go-to stress eating order. Let me throw together a salad to go with it."

"I think marinara counts as a vegetable."

Suri chuckled as she got up to grab plates. They loaded up on what they wanted then sat beside each other at the island and hungrily dove into their food.

"I was wondering if you could take a look at the inscription on the handle of the spear and tell me what it says," Layla said between bites.

Suri licked sauce off her fingers then reached for the spear and was dealt quite a shock. She drew her hand back with a hiss of pain. "What the hell?"

Layla quickly grasped her hand. There was a lightning-shaped scorch mark in her palm.

"Is it bad?" Layla asked worriedly.

"No. It looks worse than it feels. It just stings a little. Can you hold the spear up so I can see the inscription?"

Layla did as she asked. Suri read the inscription which had been written in Yoruba.

"That explains it. Ogun bound the weapon to you. Only you can use it."

She placed the spear back down then reached for Suri's hand to gaze curiously at the already fading mark. "So, no one can even touch it?"

"I guess not without something like this, or worse, happening."

"Interesting." Layla placed a soft kiss on the palm of Suri's hand then gently released it to continue eating.

If Suri weren't so worn out from the late night and crazy day that they shared she would allow the shiver of pleasure Layla's kiss brought to encourage more kisses, but she'd probably fall asleep as soon as her head hit the pillow. As it was, she didn't think she could sit there much longer eating before she fell face-first onto her plate. She managed to finish her pizza but had no energy for anything else. Including the wine that she said she wanted before she came upstairs. She pushed her plate away.

"Well, I'm done."

"Me too." Layla pushed hers away as well.

Suri stood. "Clean up and call it a night?"

"Sounds like a plan."

Together they made quick work of putting the leftover food away, checking that all the doors and windows were locked and turning out the lights before Suri turned on the house alarm. They headed upstairs where Sebastian stood watching them from the top step looking annoyed.

"That makes two days you have left me to fend for myself all day. Also, whatever you all were doing down there gave me the creeps so I just stayed up here," he said to them wordlessly.

Suri stooped down to give him a head scratch. "I'm sorry, Sebastian. Will a bit of catnip with your breakfast in the morning make up for our indiscretion?"

He purred as he pushed his head against her hand. *"It depends on what's being served for breakfast."*

Layla laughed. "You're spoiling him."

Suri gave one final scratch then stood as he bounded down the stairs. "I'm treating him as I would any houseguest." She found Sebastian quite fascinating.

They stopped in the hallway between their rooms. Suri wasn't sure how to act after last night especially since they hadn't had a chance to talk about it or their newfound relationship.

"Any thoughts on the gameplan for tomorrow?" Layla asked.

"Gathering the troops, maybe later in the day to give us and Uncle Robert time to recover from today."

"Okay."

There was an awkward moment of silence that Suri couldn't stand after they'd become so comfortable with each other.

"I know we're both tired, but I don't want there to be any awkwardness between us after last night," Suri said.

Layla looked relieved. "Neither do I."

"Good."

Suri stepped toward Layla just as Layla was moving toward her. They took each other in their arms for a slow burning kiss then both grinned.

"Your room or mine?" Layla asked.

Suri took her hand to lead Layla to her bedroom.

"I hope you won't be too disappointed if we just sleep. I don't think I have the energy to do anything else."

Layla grinned. "Believe it or not, I was going to ask the same thing. Big spoon or little spoon?"

Suri smiled. "Little."

They undressed, climbed into bed, and Suri sighed with contentment as she was once again protectively wrapped in Layla's arms.

CHAPTER SEVENTEEN

Suri awakened to find herself standing outside a new door in the basement located at the very end of the hall with no memory of how she got there. In her hands were the keys to the gateways, a bottle of honey, and a bottle of spicy rum. On the door before her etched in the same style as the other doors, was the image of a woman and man facing each other in a forest with a river flowing at the woman's feet and sparks of fire at the man's. She didn't recall seeing a ninth door, let alone one with two Orishas represented. She gazed down at the bottles in her hand and back at the door again and her heart sped up with disbelief. There were only two Orishas that she could think of requiring an offering of honey and spiced rum. Oshun, the goddess of love who rules over everything in life that flows, and Ogun, the god of iron and war and the forging of civilization. It was said that the two together bring a balance to the world.

The question was, where did this door come from and why was Suri there? She had visited both Orishas earlier today. Or was it yesterday? Either way, she had paid her respects to them and didn't know if she could handle two Orishas together. She attempted to turn around, but her feet were rooted to the floor. Unless she wanted to break her own ankles, she wasn't going anywhere but forward. With a sigh of exasperation, she placed both bottles in one hand, holding them by the necks to search for the key she needed. Of course, there was an extra key that hadn't been there before. She stuck the key in the lock, watched the images glow and dim, then turned the doorknob. Her feet had no problem moving now. She was tempted to turn around and run but had a feeling she would only fall flat on her face.

ANNE SHADE

She stepped through the doorway into a forest temple with a life-size statue of a kneeling Olodumare as an altar. Before the altar with their back to her knelt a beautiful young woman with honey-toned skin dressed in bright shimmering robes, headdress, and cowrie and gold jewelry like what she'd worn when Suri met her earlier and Ogun, his torso still covered in black tribal markings and hips encased in a fawn-colored skirt. Not knowing what else to do, Suri knelt, placed the honey and rum a distance in front of her, then prostrate herself to properly greet them both.

"Praise to Oshun, goddess of love and understanding, and praise to Mighty Warrior Ogun, god of strength and protection, for allowing me to be within your presence. How may I serve thee?"

"You may rise, Priestess." Oshun's voice was soft and soothing.

Suri rose and was surprised to find them both standing just a few feet from her. Oshun smiled sweetly at her while she twirled a string of cowries around her fingers and Ogun took a swig of the rum before tucking the bottle in a sack at his waist then crossing his arms over his expansive chest to regard Suri curiously. Suri fought the urge to rock nervously from one foot to the other under their intense regard.

"Step forward, Suri. We have one last blessing to gift you," Ogun announced.

Suri closed the distance leaving about a foot's worth of space between her and the intimidating figures.

"Do you know why we chose Layla to be your protector?" Ogun asked.

"Because of her promise to devote her life to protect me?"

"Imagine it in the way of the Yin and Yang symbol. You are the light to Layla's dark. You balance each other," Oshun explained.

"Do you know of the story of Oshun's dance?" Ogun asked.

Suri smiled. "Yes, it was one of Gammy's favorite bedtime stories."

The story tells of a time when the world teetered on the edge, and despite their immense powers, the male Orishas couldn't bring balance to the world. Chaos reigned and Oshun, who was the embodiment of grace and beauty, stepped up to save the day. She performed a dance so powerful and mesmerizing that even Ogun, the most reclusive of the gods was drawn to her. He emerged from the depths of a dense

• 250 •

forest and found himself drawn in by Oshun's dance. Together, their energies intertwined, harmonizing the world, and reminding all of the strength inherent in grace, elegance, and unity. Ogun and Oshun gazed tenderly at each other as if remembering that moment. Although Oshun was known to be the mate of Shango, god of thunder, she and Ogun had a special bond. Then Oshun turned to Suri and reached for her. Suri placed her hands in hers.

"You and Layla were brought together because you are the embodiment of what Ogun and I were creating that day. Your world is imbalanced and it is up to you and Layla to bring harmony and unity to it before darkness overwhelms it. Where Ogun and I kept the world from teetering over the edge, you must keep the light burning and the darkness at bay."

Suri shook her head. "Isn't it enough to do what my grandmother and all the others before me did? Help guide our people in the faith and keep the gateways safe? Why do I need to become some savior to the world?"

"Foolish child. It's not the world, it is your people that need saving. Your task is not that different from what Yemaya asked of your mother Ayomide. Be a light in the darkness. Bring hope where there is doubt and fear," Ogun said.

Oshun gave her hands a gentle squeeze. "Show love, and fury if needed, to help your people survive the ills this world showers upon them."

"If Layla and I are the embodiment of you, why isn't she here also? Why does this always seem to land on me?"

Suri knew she sounded like a petulant child, but it hadn't even been a week since she arrived in New Orleans and her whole life had been turned upside down into a fantasy novel she couldn't escape from. It was a wonder she hadn't completely lost her mind by now.

"Because you are a descendant of Oduduwa, the first Oba made on earth, the creator of the people of Ife. You must set the path to continue his work and lead where others must follow. Yorubaland lives on in you, Suri," Ogun said in a reprimanding tone as if Suri should have known better than to ask that.

Oshun gazed up at him with annoyance then gave Suri a gentle smile. "We know you did not ask for this and that you have sacrificed much for a faith that seemed to have abandoned you, but you have not been abandoned, Suri. You stand before us now, having survived when most would have given in to the darkness, because of the strength your ancestors blessed you with. I don't speak of just physical but the strength to love when it isn't deserved, the strength to heal when you're also in pain, the strength to uplift when all you wish to do is turn your back. Ayomide sacrificed you, her unborn child, to be her people's light in the dark so that you could be reborn to continue being that light. Like Ayomide, you are being given a choice. Will you continue the path she and Oduduwa before her paved?"

Suri sighed. "I don't feel like I have a choice."

Ogun's big hand landed surprisingly gently on her shoulder. Suri gazed up at him to find his expression as stern as always, but there was compassion in his gaze. "War and conflict are not easy, even for a god of war. I sought refuge in the forest for solitude to heal and quiet my soul and would have stayed there, hiding from the chaos the world had fallen into had it not been for Oshun's dance. She alone attempted to do what others mightier than her could not. Her power and strength called to me, healed me, and I had no choice but to join her or watch the world fall to ruin."

Suri looked more intently at Ogun and noticed that the markings on his body weren't just for design, they covered scars. Ogun wasn't only known as the god of war. He has also been known as the symbol of resistance in the African and African American culture, the warrior who fights against injustice and oppression. His scars weren't only from great battles with armies but from the smaller battles Suri and her people had fought daily throughout history. He understood what it meant to sacrifice and dedicate his immortal life not only as a warrior but a protector. He was not asking Suri to do anything he or her ancestors hadn't already done. What he would continue to do many times over. She wasn't an Orisha with an unending lifetime, but she could make the life she lived something worthy of her ancestors' sacrifices and respect.

Ogun nodded as if he knew Suri had finally accepted her fate. He kept his hand on her shoulder as Oshun released Suri's hands and placed hers on her other shoulder.

Suri bowed her head and the words came unbidden. "Oshun, goddess of rivers and love, Ogun, protector and master of iron, balance tenderness with might, harmony with conflict. I seek your united strength, Oshun, let healing waters cleanse my wounds, Ogun, fortify me against life's challenges. In your dual embrace, grant me safety and renewal, Bless me with protection and healing, always. *Ashe*."

"Suri, Priestess and Guardian, receive your blessing," Oshun said.

Suri felt a warmth flow from Ogun's hand throughout her body growing so warm she could barely stand it until something cool and comforting flowed through her like water through a stream and eased the warmth.

She gazed back up to find the Orishas eyes filled with pride. "Thank you."

They nodded, turned, and disappeared into the forest together. Suri stood before the temple of Olodumare with tears in her eyes. She didn't understand why she, instead of Aria or any of Aunt Ruby's daughters or granddaughters was chosen for this role, but she would do her best to honor Olodumare and her ancestors. She bowed her head again.

"Mighty Olodumare, the Ultimate Essence and Ruler of all! I humbly approach you, seeking your divine embrace and blessings. Shield me on this earthly journey and guide my steps in alignment with your divine plan. As I voice my plea to the vast expanse, may the spirit of Ori Inu keep your divine presence ever vibrant within me, guiding my actions toward the path set by the Highest Power. *Ashe*."

She took a deep breath and for the first time felt none of the doubt, anger, and darkness that had driven her these past months.

Layla awakened to find herself alone in Suri's bed. She lay there smiling, remembering the feeling of falling asleep with Suri in her arms for the second night in a row. She had never minded the prospect of spending her life alone until now. In just days, Suri had managed to secure a place in a vision of Layla's future that she would have never thought possible. She frowned as she realized that as wonderful as it felt, it also scared her because if anything happened to Suri, Layla didn't know if she could survive it without the dark feelings of pain and loneliness or even revenge depending on what happened to Suri overwhelming her. She needed to put a stop to what was happening between them before it was too late. She could be Suri's protector without also being her lover. She couldn't imagine there being a rule saying that a guardian and protector had to be romantically involved. Afterall, Robert was his mother's protector after his father passed. Which proved love and devotion to the guardian wasn't inclusive of intimacy.

Layla got out of bed determined to tell Suri that they could not cross this line again. If this was to work, they had to keep their relationship out of the bedroom. She could feel Suri nearby but not in the house, which meant she was probably in the garden so she took her time showering and getting dressed then made her way downstairs. Suri had already made coffee so Layla poured herself a cup, went to the back door, and gazed out to see Suri standing in the garden dressed in a white headwrap, a white peasant top, white capri pants, pink Crocs with little animal charms, and a green garden apron. Layla chuckled. Only Suri could wear all white while gardening and not care. Movement at Suri's feet drew Layla's gaze to Sebastian who chased a butterfly flitting around the plants. She gazed back up and her heart skipped a beat at the radiant smile on Suri's face as she spoke to a rose bush. The large white flowers bloomed as if she were the very sun for which they drew life. She suddenly wished she were that flower and realized that there was yet another shift in Suri's energy.

After a moment, it hit her. There was a balance and an acceptance that wasn't there before. Up until that moment, Layla could sense Suri's insecurity and doubt about the role she was stepping into. That was all gone and replaced by a calm and self-assuredness that had her practically glowing. Even Sebastian was drawn in by it as he followed her around the garden like a lovesick fool. Layla felt its pull as well but fought to ignore it. She came down here with a plan and she was determined to follow through with it. She took one last sip of coffee for fortification, set it on the counter, and practically marched out the door.

"Good morning." Suri turned that smile on Layla. She almost caved, but she shook herself out of its hypnotic trance and refocused.

"Good morning. I think we need to talk."

Suri cocked her head to the side as she gazed at Layla curiously. "It's too beautiful a morning to look so serious. Is everything okay?" She placed a flower clipping in a basket hanging off her arm.

Layla cleared her throat, finding it difficult to speak the words she wanted because she didn't mean them. "I think we should keep our relationship strictly platonic. We don't want to blur the lines when it comes to how best to protect you."

Although it stayed in place, she hated to see Suri's smile dim and the telltale sign of hurt in her eyes. "I understand."

She turned back to snip another flower off the vine then headed back toward the house without a backward glance.

"If you want my opinion—"

"I don't," Layla said to Sebastian then followed Suri into the house.

She was arranging the flowers she'd picked in a glass vase.

"So, are we still meeting with everyone today?" Layla asked in a lame attempt to get them back on a good note.

"That's the plan. I called Phoebe already. She'll reach out to everyone else to tell them to meet here at six. I'll text Uncle Robert later this morning."

She finished her arrangement and carried it into the living room to place it on the mantel beneath Athena's portrait. Layla could swear the woman was looking down at her with disappointment. She looked away and strode over to a nearby bookshelf.

"Would you be comfortable if I included Bettina and her pack from last night? It wouldn't hurt to have a little extra help. Especially since we'll be down a person as it might be best to have Phoebe stay behind and protect the fort."

"Do you trust Bettina to be okay around Kenya?" Suri stood beside her.

Layla had to fight the urge to reach over and touch her. "I trust that they can both put aside their baggage for a greater purpose. Besides, after what they witnessed between us at the club, she's going to want an explanation."

They stood quietly together. Layla could sense that Suri wanted to say something and she ached to take back her words, but it was for the best.

Suri must have thought so also. "Okay. I'm going to make breakfast." was all she said then left the room.

Layla watched her go then went back over to the fireplace. She hadn't been imagining things. If possible, Athena's visage looked even more disappointed than she had before.

"It's better this way for everyone involved." A snort of derision sounded in her head.

Breakfast was a quiet affair during which Suri read from something that looked like a journal as she ate. Just as they finished their meal, she slammed the book shut.

"I have an idea. According to Athena's journal, she and her protector would use Ogun's gateway to practice their defensive skills. Back then they couldn't just drive a couple of hours outside of town to practice in a secluded wooded area. Ogun offered them a kind of supernatural training facility. What do you say we try it?"

Layla gazed at her in surprise. "After yesterday you want to go traipsing back through a gateway?"

"It will be different this time. Ogun knows us. He's the protector's spiritual guide. I can't imagine he wouldn't welcome the opportunity to train with you."

Layla laughed. "You mean kick my ass. Suri, he's the god of war."

"He's a warrior first." She looked as if she knew something Layla didn't. "It will just be until our meeting with the others. I can't sit around here all day doing nothing."

She seemed genuinely excited and Layla felt guilty over breaking off their affair so she'd be willing to try it if it made Suri smile again. "Okay, but I'm not training in a room heated like the furnace of hell."

Suri grinned in amusement. "You won't. According to Athena, all we need to do is take a few cigars with us, knock on the door seven times, then ask Ogun for his wisdom and guidance in battle and the gateway should be prepared for what we need."

"Okay," Layla agreed hesitantly.

After changing into workout attire, Suri and Layla stood outside Ogun's gateway. It seemed Pearl and Robert stockpiled cigars in a mini humidor Layla hadn't noticed in the attic workroom. Suri held a whole unopened box as she knocked on the door seven times and requested the wisdom and guidance of the great warrior Ogun. Then she placed the key in the lock, took a deep breath, and opened the door. They stepped into a Zulu style warrior training hut with a huge arena attached. Standing in the middle of the arena was Ogun.

"Protector, I knew you would be a warrior worthy of my guidance," he said to Layla slapping his club in and out of the palm of his hand.

Layla gazed over at Suri. "Remember, this was your idea."

Suri gazed at her worriedly. "Maybe this wasn't such a good idea."

"Well, I can't imagine that he'll kill me since he is the one that made me your protector."

Layla tried to give her a smile of reassurance that she wasn't really feeling. She had been trained by Isfet. She couldn't imagine him not being a worthy opponent for Ogun so she stepped into the arena with her spear in hand and her throwing knives and katanas secured in the cross-body harness she wore.

"Guardian, Oya will assist you with your training in the hut," Ogun said to Suri.

Layla gazed over at her as she hesitantly went into the hut where the goddess of wind, storm, and lightning awaited her. She wondered what it meant that they were personally being trained by two of the Seven themselves and not been assigned to train with minor Orishas. Several hours later, as Layla lay sprawled on the sofa barely able to lift the cup of healing tea Suri had made, she only half listened to Suri's apologies. She wouldn't tell Isfet, but Layla had learned more from Ogun in the short time training with him than she had in two lifetimes of training with her father. It didn't hurt that the spear he had created for her acted as if it were an extension of her own arm. She was sore as hell, bruised from head to toe, and had nicks and cuts that would be fatal on another person but she also felt more alive than she had since her years as a dark avenger for her people. What she would be doing would also be for her people as she was protecting the key to their faith. Her body would fully heal within an hour or two but the feeling she had would last for as long as she remained by Suri's side.

❖

"Will you stop apologizing. I'm fine," Layla said after another of Suri's apologies.

There were no physical signs of Layla's ass kicking by Ogun, but that didn't make Suri feel any less guilty for unwittingly setting her up for it. Her training with Oya, on the other hand, was pretty damn awesome. The goddess taught Suri how to control the elemental abilities that she discovered she had while training at Layla's house. By the end of the session, she felt like Storm from the X-Men as she wielded and manipulated air, wind, and rain like she'd been born to it. She didn't know what any of that would do when she faced Lilith, but at least she'd be able to handle anything Sojourn brought with her.

"I just can't get the image of you flying through the wall of the training hut and skidding to a stop on your back at Oya's and my feet." Suri shivered at the memory of the shredded T-shirt and skin on Layla's back as she sat up.

Layla grinned. "He got a lucky shot in."

Suri shook her head in exasperation. "Whatever. I think I'll keep our training schedules separate. I was so worried Ogun was trying to kill you that I could barely focus after that."

She knew Ogun probably had been tough on Layla because of what she would be coming up against. If she could keep up with a fearsome warrior like him, then she could take anything Lilith could send their way. They had decided to continue training until the day of their standoff with Lilith which, according to Isfet was happening in just a few days on Halloween. Layla would continue training with Ogun and Suri would train with a different Orisha depending on what skill they believed she needed to master in that time. As always, it went through her mind how unbelievable her life had become in such a short time. She honestly believed that if she didn't have the foundation of her gifts, her grandmother's spirit guiding her through the years, and the Book of Blessings she would have completely lost her mind in those first few days. Every guardian before her had the advantage of knowing what they were getting into early in life and were guided into it by the guardian before them. While she'd had her grandmother with her in a way, she had conveniently left all of this out. The doorbell interrupted her thoughts.

Layla stood. "I'll get it."

"Thanks."

Suri watched her walking away, admiring the way her Adidas track pants molded to her firm backside, the shift of her back muscles under the fitted tank and her long, tapered fingers swinging at her side. Her fingers itched to trace the outline of the wings tattooed along her back, her hands ached to cup and mold her ass as she thrust her hips, and her body craved the sensual touch of her fingers. Layla stumbled at the archway, gripping the wall for support. It groaned under the pressure of her grip. Suri realized she hadn't blocked her thoughts and Layla was reading them loud and clear. The temperature in the room noticeably changed and she threw up a mental wall, stood and hurried over to open the doors leading out to the courtyard to let some fresh air in. She had her back to Layla but could hear her trying to breathe through what was going on. The doorbell rang again.

"Coming!" Layla yelled.

A moment later, Suri heard voices in the foyer that grew louder as they neared the living room. She pasted on a smile then turned to greet their guests. Phoebe and Kenya entered first followed by Rory, Leandra, and Cassandra. After the greetings were done everyone claimed their seats, with Phoebe, Kenya and Leandra taking the sofa across from Layla and Suri, Rory taking the window seat which allowed him to lounge like he had on the chaise at Phoebe's, and Cassandra sat on the floor in a corner between the window seat and fireplace looking like a pale willowy ghost girl sitting in the shadows with her chin resting on her knees. Suri offered everyone refreshments from the coffee and tea service with crumb cake she had made again while they waited for her uncle.

"Don't you look like a cozy domesticated pair," Kenya said as Layla helped Suri serve.

"I'm surprised you're familiar with the concept," Layla said sarcastically.

Kenya started to respond but Phoebe beat her to it.

"If I didn't know any better, I'd swear you two goading each other was a sign of affection."

Layla and Kenya both frowned at her but said nothing further. Suri gazed everywhere but at Layla as the others grinned in amusement. For the briefest of moments, even the edge of Cassandra's permanent frown twitched upward until she noticed Suri looking at her, then she directed her gaze down to her combat boots. Just as Suri was about to text her uncle, the doorbell rang again.

"Did he forget his key?" Layla asked as she stood to answer the door.

Suri shrugged. She heard the low rumble of a conversation but it didn't sound like Robert's deep baritone. Layla came back followed by Bettina dressed in her biker denim and leather holding her helmet in her hand and looking very uncomfortable.

"Bettina, it's good to see you again. Welcome to my home."

Bettina gave a slight bow at the waist. "Thank you for having me, Priestess."

Suri's face heated with embarrassment at being greeted so formally after they'd spent quite some time on the dance floor the other night. "Please, Suri is fine. Come in." Layla did the introductions to everyone but Kenya who wouldn't even look up to meet Bettina's gaze.

"Kenya," Bettina said.

"Bettina. I'm surprised to see you here."

"I asked her to come seeing as she was just promoted to a pack leader. It wouldn't hurt to have more allies in the area," Layla said.

Kenya nodded. "That makes sense. I'd heard about your promotion. Congratulations."

Bettina smiled. "Thanks."

To Suri's relief, that was the extent of their interaction before Bettina took a seat in one of the side chairs. A half hour later, her uncle still hadn't shown up.

"Leandra, have you spoken to him today?"

"Yes, earlier this afternoon. He told me he'd meet us here. He seemed fine. Sounded a little tired but that's to be expected after your day yesterday."

"This isn't like him. He hasn't even answered my texts. I'm going over there." Suri stood.

"I'll go with you," Layla said, following her.

Just as they entered the foyer, the door opened and her uncle entered looking as if he'd seen a ghost. Which, considering he grew up in this house, shouldn't be that shocking. He closed the door and leaned against it looking dazed.

Suri grew nervous over the strange energy coming off him. "Uncle Robert? What's wrong?"

She heard footsteps as the others joined them.

"Bobby?" Leandra hurried to him, taking his hand in concern.

"Aria came to see me."

There was a collective gasp. Suri took his hand, trying to get a read to see if he'd been injured. He gave her hand a squeeze and smiled sadly.

"She didn't hurt me. She came to warn me…warn us…about Sojourn."

"A little late for that," Kenya said.

"She was actually sent to deliver a message from Sojourn asking to meet. She provided a time and place."

"Let me guess, Halloween night."

Robert nodded. "Probably not the way you were expecting to spend your birthday."

"Your birthday is Halloween?" Layla said.

Suri shrugged. "Yep. Ironic, isn't it."

Robert continued. "She wants to meet at ten at an abandoned warehouse just across the border in Metairie. It seems she's claimed it as her temple."

"There's more, isn't there?" Suri asked.

"Aria said it's a trap. That Sojourn is being used to lure Suri out in the open for Lilith. Lilith has promised Sojourn that with Suri under her control she'll place Aria as Guardian so that she could control the gateways through her."

"It's obvious that Sojourn has no idea how the guardian is chosen or that her placement needs to be blessed by the Seven," Phoebe said.

"This doesn't sound right to me. No offense, Robert, but why would Aria be foolish enough to tell you all of this?" Kenya said.

"I found it suspicious also. Like she was trying to use my feelings for her as her father to lull me into a false sense of security so that I would let my guard down to weaken the group."

"That sounds reasonable considering the demon possessing her could be manipulating the situation on Sojourn's behalf, but you don't think that's it?" Layla said.

Robert shook his head. "When she first arrived, I could tell it wasn't Aria speaking, but as soon as the message was delivered—" his voice broke on a sob. "Aria came through."

"It could have been the demon still manipulating her," Layla said softly.

"No! I know my little girl's energy better than my own," he said vehemently.

"Bobby, why don't we go sit down," Leandra encouraged him with a tug of her hand.

He gazed down at her with an affectionate smile and nodded. Suri had his other hand as they led him into the living room toward the sofa she and Layla had been sitting on. She could feel the pain and heartbreak seeing Aria had caused him, but he blocked her from easing it. She and Leandra sat on either side of him while everyone else found seats nearby.

"What did Aria have to say?" Suri asked softly.

"She said she and the demon were tired of being under Sojourn's control. It seems she knew what the demon was when she thought she was tricking Sojourn into using Aria's body. Aria was beginning to see Sojourn's true nature and that she'd been manipulated to leave us. She told Sojourn that she was leaving and coming back here so Sojourn used the demon's offer to get what she wanted. She tricked the demon, found out its true name, then bound it to Aria for her to control. She now had the power she sought as well as control of Aria's. They want to be released but can't raise a hand to Sojourn to free themselves."

"They're hoping by revealing all this to you that we can find a way to defeat Sojourn and free them," Phoebe said.

Robert nodded. "There's one other thing. Lilith has given Sojourn control of a demon army posing as worshipers in the hopes that we won't put innocent lives in danger when she decides to attack."

"That's not surprising," Layla said.

Somehow, through all the unbelievable situations Suri had been through these past days she never once truly considered the danger she was walking herself and her family and friends into by confronting Lilith until this moment. Sojourn was willing to sacrifice other human lives to get what she wanted. Was Suri willing to do the same to keep what she had? She gazed around the room not feeling right about asking them to help her.

"Are you okay?" Layla asked.

"No. I can't ask any of you to put your lives on the line this way. This is my family's battle, not yours."

"Well, it's a good thing you didn't ask us. We all knew what we were getting into when we made our oaths to your grandmother," Phoebe said.

Suri was shocked. "You made an oath to Gammy?"

"Technically, it's an oath to our priestess and guardian, which, in this case now falls to you. We are duty bound to help our priestess spread the faith and ensure our guardian's standing within the community," Kenya said.

"You can of course break the oath, but it won't change our willingness to be by your side to help defend your legacy," Rory said.

"Personally, I'm here because the thought of having a demon and a crazed voodoo priestess running around New Orleans doesn't sound as appealing as one might think," Bettina said with a grin.

Suri gazed at their determined faces in disbelief. She went from living a life of loneliness and despair to being surrounded by all these wonderful and dedicated people. Her heart felt full.

"Now that we've got that settled, we need to make a plan," Kenya said.

As Suri had barely had a fist fight in her life, she sat by as Layla, Kenya, Bettina, and her uncle brainstormed their battle plan. Phoebe wasn't too happy about the decision to leave her behind at the house, but she saw the reasoning in it. Sojourn had no idea Suri had her own mini army so she probably wouldn't be expecting anyone but her and Robert to show up. They decided that they would arrive as a united front hoping it would intimidate Sojourn to back down but Layla had a feeling that having Lilith's support would give the voodoo priestess more confidence than she normally had.

"No matter what Sojourn thinks she can throw at us, the most important thing is to keep Suri clear of Lilith," Layla said.

They all nodded in agreement. Once they felt they had a good plan, everyone except Robert left. He promised Leandra that he'd meet her back at his house. Once he was alone with Suri and Layla, he let the despair that he'd obviously been hiding take over as he dropped his head in his hands and wept. Suri stayed beside him, to lend whatever support he needed.

"Suri, I need you to promise me something."

"Anything, Uncle Robert."

"No matter what happens to me, please promise me you'll free Aria. Even if it means…" He couldn't finish but Suri knew what he meant.

"I promise I'll do whatever is in my power to help her." She refused to promise to take her own cousin's life, no matter what she'd done.

That seemed to be enough for him. "Thank you." He stood looking older than she'd ever seen him and left.

CHAPTER EIGHTEEN

Layla knelt gulping water from a nearby stream. She'd just finished training with Ogun and wanted to take a minute for herself before leaving his plane. She splashed water on her face then sat upon a boulder wondering if this would be her last night in this fantastical house that she didn't even know existed until a week ago. The last night she would share a dinner with the most amazing woman she had ever known. A woman that she was more than willing to lay her life on the line for and not regret it for a moment. Despite too many moments to count when she could feel Suri's sensual thoughts and emotions, Layla had kept her promise to herself to not let their relationship slip into an intimacy that could cloud either of their judgments at a critical moment.

"Such heavy thoughts in the midst of such peacefulness," Ogun said as he sat beside her and dipped a drinking gourd into the stream.

"Are you aware of what we face tomorrow?"

"Yes, we all are. It is why we've worked so hard to prepare both you and Suri."

"I know that you can't interfere in the lives of humans, but is there anything I can do to ensure Suri's safety in her confrontation with Lilith?"

Ogun sipped at the water in his gourd. "You are an excellent and brave warrior, Layla, but even you cannot fight this battle for Suri. She must face this enemy on her own."

Layla gazed at him worriedly. "Will she survive?"

"That will wholly be up to her. If she has the will to fight, then she can survive anything."

Layla sighed with exasperation.

Ogun chuckled. "I take it that answer did not satisfy you."

"No, but it was honest. That's the least I can ask for." She stood and collected her weapons then gave a slight bow toward Ogun. "Thank you for your guidance and wisdom."

"May it be a blessing to you in battle."

When Layla straightened, she was alone. Where Ogun had been sitting a green and black beaded necklace with a single cowrie shell hanging it from it sat in his place. She picked up the necklace, placed it around her neck, then left drawing strength from the gift.

After a quiet dinner together, Suri decided that an evening of watching comedies was called for to take their mind off tomorrow. It was nice to sit with her acting as if they weren't about to tread into a battle for their lives and Suri's soul. But as soon as she was lying alone in her bed her mind kept wandering over the possible scenarios where their plan could go awry. A knock at her door interrupted her racing thoughts.

"Come in."

Suri opened the door and poked her head in. "I hope I didn't wake you."

Layla sat up in bed. "Not at all."

"Good, do you mind if I stay with you tonight? Strictly platonic, of course. I just can't bear to sleep alone drowning in my own thoughts."

Despite the temptation it would be, Layla couldn't tell her no. She slid over then lifted the covers as an invitation for Suri to join her. Suri hurried into the room and climbed into bed facing Layla.

"Thank you."

"You're welcome."

They lay quietly contemplating each other before Suri spoke. "I have another favor to ask."

"Okay."

She hesitated before continuing. "If Lilith succeeds in making me her avatar, I want you to end it. For good."

Layla's heart skipped a beat. "Are you asking me to kill you?"

"Yes. I don't want to be used as a weapon or her plaything to control."

"Suri, please don't ask that of me. Besides, we won't let it come to that."

"Layla," Suri said, her eyes sparkling with tears.

"All right. *If* it comes to that, I promise to do what must be done." That was all she could promise. To say the words would make her biggest fear a reality.

"Thank you." Suri pressed a soft kiss to Layla's lips then turned her back and snuggled close.

Layla wrapped her arms around Suri wishing that they could just stay that way and that tomorrow would never come. But tomorrow did come and with it came the forecast of one of the coldest Halloweens on record in New Orleans, according to the weather report. Suri had laughed noting that mid-fifties was downright balmy this time of year up north then announced that she would be spending a good part of the morning in her ancestor altar room and performing a spiritual cleanse to prepare for the night. Layla prepared in her own way by checking her weapons, ensuring her blades, as well as her talons on her wings were sharp. She also decided it wouldn't hurt to perform her own hoodoo spiritual cleansing. The tension in the house throughout the day was as heavy as the incense Suri had lit throughout. Sebastian sneezed and complained for a good twenty minutes before Layla let him out into the yard for fresh air.

To distract herself further, Layla went out to the garage to check on her bike. She noticed a wall of tools that must have belonged to Suri's grandfather and decided to do some quick repairs that she had been putting off. It was the perfect activity to keep her busy for hours until the alarm she'd set on her phone reminded her that they were making dinner for everyone. When she went back into the house, she could smell the spicy scent of gumbo.

"You started without me," she said to Suri who stood stirring the contents of a large pot dressed in a white tunic and palazzo pants with gold embroidered collar. Her hair was pulled up into her signature afro puff. She looked loose and relaxed.

"You looked pretty involved with your bike, so I didn't want to interrupt you. I left you the cornbread to make." She gave Layla a playful wink.

They worked in companionable silence. Layla mixed the cornbread using her grandmother's recipe which she still remembered as clear as day. Then Suri threw together a salad and they worked as a team to set the table in the formal dining room, adding two center leaves to extend it and adding the additional chairs that sat along the perimeter. The table had obviously been made for large family gatherings which was handy since they would be having a full house with everyone that had been there earlier as well as the six shifters from Bettina's pack.

Layla could see many nights like this one with the two of them preparing dinner together, sharing a life of quiet domesticity. A life not worrying about selfish demons and voodoo priestesses out for revenge. Would that be possible if they survived the night?

"Layla, what has you thinking so hard that I can practically hear your mind whirring?"

"Tomorrow."

Suri sighed. "Tomorrow seems so far away."

"According to Annie it's only a day away," Layla said with a grin.

Suri laughed and the sound filled Layla's heart with joy. She was determined that they would survive this night and when they did, she would tell Suri she'd made a mistake about putting a stop to their budding romance. Life was a gift and she'd be damned if she would spend it denying her own happiness.

Suri had done her best to keep her heart and mind free of negativity, to cleanse herself of any doubt that Lilith could grab on to and use against her. Even made offerings to the blessed ancestors she'd learned about reading Athena's journal just for extra measure. Now, sitting on the back of Layla's bike as they rode toward their meeting with Sojourn, made it all seem like a distraction to keep her from thinking about what was really happening. They could all be racing toward their death. Sojourn wasn't the real threat, Lilith was. This was all a game to her, and they were the pieces for her to manipulate with the ultimate prize being Suri. How were they going to defeat a demon queen without the intervention of a higher power? What were the chances that any of the Orisha would defy Oludumare's command to not interfere in the lives of humans the way Yemaya, Oya, and Olukun had interfered with the slave trade during Ayomide's time?

Suri pressed herself against Layla's back wanting so much to tell her to turn around. For everyone that was following them to do the same. But that would just put off the inevitable. Lilith would eventually do what she'd been doing for the past year, taking everyone that she loved from her. Suri couldn't bear that happening to the people now surrounding her, especially Robert and Layla. A little voice in the back of her mind pointed out, but isn't that what was going to happen tonight? Instead of them being taken out one by one, Suri was leading them directly to their deaths all in one sweep. She squeezed her eyes shut willing the voice away. It was that same voice that kept her alone and depressed back in New York.

"Breathe, Lil' Bit." Her grandmother's voice whispered on the wind rushing past them as they rode.

Suri took a deep breath then felt Layla reach down to give her thigh a quick squeeze as if to punctuate her grandmother's words, so she took another deep breath. The internal voice quieted and although there was still a niggling of fear, it wasn't the crippling despair that had tried to push its way back in. Layla slowed as they pulled off the road into the parking lot of a small warehouse. The only vehicle in the lot was a minivan with Mississippi license plates. Bettina and her crew pulled up on their bikes, Robert pulled up in his pickup truck with Leandra, Rory and Cassandra and Kenya roared in last in her overpriced sports car.

"This doesn't look creepy at all," Kenya said as they gathered in the lot.

"I sense one untainted and thirteen tainted souls inside," Cassandra said, her voice raspy from disuse.

Layla nodded. "It's Sojourn, Aria, and the worshippers she told Robert about."

"Fifteen against fourteen, easy peezy," one of Bettina's pack said, rubbing her hands gleefully.

"Don't get too cocky. There's no telling what Lilith has up her sleeve. Just because we don't sense anything or anyone else doesn't mean they're not out there."

"Layla is right. Be ready for anything," Bettina said.

"And stick to the plan. No one attacks unless they make a move first," Layla said.

They all nodded.

"How safe are shifters with Aria's ability with animals?" Kenya asked Robert.

"She promised not to participate in any fighting," he answered.

"Can we trust her word seeing as she's being controlled by Sojourn?" Kenya asked.

"Yes. She and the demon may be bound to Sojourn, but the demon is the only one who is also controlled by her. Aria may not have control of her body when the demon has been commanded to do something, but she still has control over when and how she can use her gifts," Robert said.

"I don't think Sojourn will sacrifice losing Aria in a battle especially if she believes she's the key to accessing the gateways," Layla pointed out.

"I agree," Suri said.

She may not know a thing about planning battle strategy, but she did know human behavior. Sojourn's goal was to get access to the Seven and her belief that Aria is the only way to do that is what may ultimately save her cousin's life.

Layla turned to her and took her hands. "Are you ready for this?"

"No. I don't think I ever will be so let's just do it."

Layla smiled then lifted her hands to place a kiss on her knuckles. "I've got your back no matter what."

Suri saw the tenderness in Layla's gaze and her heart soared. "Just as I have yours."

She did her best to silently communicate with Layla that she felt the same way. Layla nodded then released her to collect her weapons from Robert's truck. Dressed in a black fitted T-shirt, black jeans, and black combat boots with her hair in long braids down her back, her katanas strapped in a body harness, her knives in hilts at her waist and the spear from Ogun in her hands she looked every bit the warrior protector. Suri also realized that the vision Ayomide had shared of her and Layla fighting together would happen that night. But did that moment show their victory or the moment before their destruction? She didn't know nor could she focus on it. She had to keep her head in the moment so that she wouldn't put anyone in more danger than they already were. She reached for her uncle's hand, he gave hers a gentle squeeze as they walked toward the building with Layla on her other side and the others following close behind.

As they neared the entrance the door opened, and a young woman dressed in a plain white sack dress and white headwrap stepped out.

"Our priestess only expected the priestess and her uncle," the young woman said.

"Just as your priestess has worshippers, so do I," Suri said more confidently than she felt.

The woman looked over the group, her eyes landing on Layla and her weapons nervously.

"Just think of me as security for our priestess," Layla responded with a smirk.

The woman shrugged then turned her back to them as she turned back into the building assuming they would follow, which they did in a line with Layla taking the lead ahead of Robert then Suri and the others. They went down a short hallway with a few offices on either side then into the open warehouse area where there were rows of pallets with mattresses on both sides of the room, people kneeling on cushions in a semi-circle in the center, and at the far end was a plain looking woman probably in her sixties with a salt-and-pepper afro, ruddy mocha skin, dressed in bright colorful garish robes and chunky beaded jewelry sitting on a high-back chair as if she were a queen ruling over her court. Next to her, on a low stool sat someone Suri assumed was her cousin Aria. She had the same thick curly auburn hair Suri had inherited from their grandmother. Her soft delicate features and willowy frame must have come from her mother, but her height and dark intense eyes were definitely Uncle Robert's. She wore a white sleeveless maxi dress and orange headwrap. Was the orange a sign of her loyalty to her family rather than Sojourn? Layla got her answer when Aria's eyes met hers and she gave a slight nod.

The young woman that had escorted them in whispered something in Sojourn's ear, causing her to frown, then knelt on an empty cushion in the circle.

Sojourn pasted a smile back on and waved them forward. "I'm impressed, Priestess, that you managed to gain followers in such a short time."

Suri stepped forward just to the middle of the semi-circle. Everyone with her formed a similar semi-circle around her. "You have followers, I have family, there's a difference."

"Family is fickle." She gazed from her to Aria and back. "Followers are devoted."

Suri gazed around at the people kneeling on the pillows. They all seemed to be in some hypnotic trance. "How devoted are your followers, Sojourn? Are they willing to die for your selfish cause?"

"Are you willing to die for yours?" Sojourn asked.

Suri didn't hesitate to answer. "Yes. I'm willing to sacrifice all for my faith, my legacy, and my family." She made sure to look at Aria as she said that.

Although her expression remained impassive, her cousin's fists balled in her lap, her only show of emotion. Suri gazed back at Sojourn. "You didn't bring me out here to discuss who is more devoted to their cause. What do you want?"

Sojourn stood from her throne-like seat to stand just outside of the circle of worshippers. "I want what is due to me for showing Aria her greatness when her family failed to do so. I want to place her in her rightful role as guardian." She turned, looked back at Aria, and nodded. Aria moved to stand beside her.

"So, you're doing this for Aria," Suri said doubtfully.

"It's always been for Aria. Since she walked into my office as a sad, gifted child whose parents refused to accept her for who she was, I knew that I had to be the one to save her. That it was Bondye's will for me to help her."

"You mean to manipulate and kidnap her. It's people like you that have turned voodoo into the negative image people see it as today. Bondye doesn't speak directly to followers. His messages are delivered through the loa, and he would never command anyone to kidnap a child from their family." Suri's grandmother made sure she was just as knowledgeable in the voudon religion as she was with the Orisha as the two tended to overlap. Just because she didn't practice it didn't mean she wasn't aware of the culture.

Sojourn frowned. "You come into my temple and insult me?"

Sojourn's worshippers slowly stood; their focus no longer dazed but directed at Suri's group.

Suri raised her hands in surrender. "Sojourn, I did not come here to fight you or to get anyone hurt. You asked for this meeting. Unfortunately, I cannot give what isn't mine. To Aria or anyone."

"But you can step down as guardian to allow Aria to step in."

Suri shook her head. "It doesn't work that way. The role was not just given to me. There is a whole ritual. I had to be accepted by our ancestor and the Seven. They could have easily deemed me unworthy."

Sojourn frowned. "You're lying."

"What would be the point in me doing that?"

"So that we'd be discouraged from helping Aria achieve her rightful place."

Suri knew she wasn't going to get through to Sojourn, so she turned to Aria. "Is this what you want, Aria? If so, if the Seven say that you are worthy, I'll step aside. All I want is for our family, our legacy, to thrive to help our community. I'm willing to make any sacrifice if it's what's needed to do that."

"Don't speak to her! She doesn't know what's good for her. I'm the one that's been here, I'm the one that's raised her into the powerful woman she's become. I've been the only parent in her life that accepted and loved her for who she was." She stroked Aria's hair like she was a dog.

Robert stepped forward. "You didn't accept her for who she was. You used her for what you thought she could get you. You made her a weapon of destruction when she was just a child. You wouldn't know how to be a parent if the instruction manual hit you in the head," he said angrily.

Sojourn sneered at Robert. "I guess you want to do this hard way. Fine."

She grabbed Aria's arm and stepped back. Her worshippers closed the circle around Suri and her group. Layla eased Suri into the middle of their inner circle and spun her spear in the air threateningly. Her uncle Robert called a wicked blade and shield to himself out of thin air. Kenya, Bettina, and the other werepanthers partially shifted, their hands turning to deadly claws as they snarled. Cassandra murmured something as she removed an amulet from around her neck and a dark mist rose from the ground and swirled around her. Rory slipped off the trench coat he'd been wearing and now stood in a cat suit and combat boots pulling two machetes from a harness like Layla's as he stood in a defensive stance. Even Leandra stood in a defensive stance, her hands lit with a bright unearthly glow from fairy fire. They were ready to defend her and possibly kill these innocent people in the process.

"Sojourn, please, it doesn't have to be this way," Suri pleaded.

"It does if I can't have what I want." She nodded and the worshippers moved in.

"Remember, these are humans possessed by demons. They don't know what they're doing. Injure, maim, but don't kill them," Layla said.

"She couldn't have picked an open field for this little tête-à-tête? This space is too confining for a real fight," Kenya said with a growl.

Within a matter of seconds, it seemed all hell broke loose as the worshippers came at them at once. Suri could see that her group tried not to deal fatal blows, but they would just get back up and keep coming. Eventually, the injuries and wounds they were being dealt would kill them if they weren't killed outright. Suddenly, the mist that had been swirling around Cassandra spread outward and around the worshippers who all fell limply to the floor as the mist gathered and flew into the amulet she held. A moment later, the bodies twitched as black ooze poured from their mouths into small puddles that began taking human form.

"I've separated the souls from the bodies so there's nothing for the demons to latch on to," Cassandra said.

"Does that mean we can kill these little shits coming at us?" Bettina yelled.

"Yes!" Layla said.

"Nooo!" Sojourn yelled angrily. She grabbed Aria and ran toward a back door.

No one even waited for the demons to form before they ran up and slashed, stabbed, and sliced them to pieces that turned to ash and disappeared.

"Was that it? That's all she had?" Rory said.

"I doubt it," Layla said.

Suri stared down at the lifeless body of the young woman who had let them in then turned to Cassandra. "Can you put their souls back?"

"Yes."

She chanted over the amulet and strolled around placing the souls back into the bodies. The ones that weren't too injured to move gazed around in confusion. The others with serious wounds lay groaning and crying in pain. Suri did what she could to heal them without draining herself as she didn't know what was coming next. Rory retrieved a few vials from the inside pocket of his trench coat, walking around having the worshippers drink from them. Within moments, they were unconscious.

"They should be out for at least an hour. Hopefully enough time for us to finish this and get them some medical help," he said.

"We have to go after Sojourn," Suri said.

They followed her out of the door she'd seen Sojourn and Aria leave through. It led out to the back of the warehouse to the edge of a forest. Suri placed her hand on a tree and focused. She heard the whispering of the trees telling her which way to go.

"This way." She ran in the direction she was being led.

"Suri, wait!" Layla called from behind before she popped up in Suri's path.

"What are you doing?" Suri cried as Layla attempted to block her.

"We can't just run headlong into what could be a trap."

"What if she has more innocent people out there?"

"We will deal with them, but you getting yourself caught won't help."

Suri knew she was right, but it scared her that they had almost taken innocent lives. She directed Layla in the path the trees were telling her and they came to a clearing where Sojourn stood in the middle of a pentagram chanting.

"Looks like she's calling in the big guns," Bettina said warily.

"She's in the protection of the pentagram so we can't physically stop her," Layla said.

Suri walked up to the edge of the star. "Sojourn, please, don't do this. Whatever Lilith promised you is a lie."

Sojourn continued chanting. The ground began to tremble, and the trees whispered warnings to Suri. She stepped back away from the pentagram as it glowed then lit with a fire that scorched the marking into the earth. Sojourn stepped out of the star laughing maniacally.

"She promised to get you out of the way. That's all I need," she said.

The ground split and dozens of dark figures clawed their way out of the dirt growling and hissing.

"Shit," Bettina said just before Suri watched her contort with the sound of bones cracking and popping as she and her pack shifted to their werepanther form.

"Dammit, I just bought this outfit," Kenya said just before her pink designer track suit ripped to shreds as she shifted as well.

The panthers were on the demons as soon as they escaped the hole, claws and teeth ripping their charred leathery skin to what looked like beef jerky. Rory and Robert slashed and chopped their way through a group, black blood splattering them as they went along. Leandra was small and able to teleport so she wove in and out attacking with her fairy light, disintegrating any demon in her path to nothing but ash and smoke. Cassandra somehow managed to get the ones coming at her to turn around and attack each other and Layla seemed to attract the bulk of them as more poured from the crevice. She whirled her spear around and through demon bodies so fast it was just a blur in her hands. Suri joined her using her ability to manipulate air to slash through anything coming her way or to toss them toward one of her other friends to destroy. She heard a whoosh of air at her back and turned just in time to see Layla transform into her demon form. This was her vision, but Suri had a feeling that this was also only the beginning. Just as in her vision, she fought back-to-back with Layla using everything she had learned during her training to fight back the demons. Suddenly, there were no more pouring out of the crack. Everyone gazed at it warily waiting for something, but all was quiet. Even Sojourn watched expectantly.

Layla grasped Suri's hand. "Are you okay? Any injuries?"

Suri shook her head in disbelief. "I'm fine. You?"

"I'm good."

"Did that really just happen?"

"Yes, but I don't trust it."

"The quiet before the storm?"

"Exactly."

"Did you really think I would make it that easy for you?"

A feminine voice reverberated around the clearing then the ground shook once more. Steam then fire shot up from the hole sending everyone scurrying for cover. Suri was standing on the ground one minute and flying the next as Layla snatched her up to move farther away from the flames. They joined the rest of their group gathered at the edge of the clearing. Suri watched as a feminine figure rose out of the flames then landed just outside the crack. She was tall, shapely with a smooth ivory complexion and flaming red hair wearing a sheer gauzy long white dress and her feet were bare.

"Lilith, I presume," Suri said nervously.

"Suri, I've waited so long for this moment. Come, let me look at you?"

"No, I'm good right here."

Lilith laughed. It would be seductive if it weren't laced with evil. "There's no sense in fighting this any longer. Come willingly and I'll spare your people."

"No." Suri hoped she sounded more confident than she felt.

"Your choice."

Lilith raised her arms and more demons crawled up out of the flames. They may have had the same blackish leathery skin, but they weren't the scrawny screeching ones that they had just battled. If there was a gym in hell, these looked like they had spent some time in it.

"You've got to be kidding me," she said.

Layla turned to her. "I need you to stay here. Do not move from this spot no matter what happens. I can't fight the way I need to if I'm worried about also trying to protect you."

"But I can help."

"No, please, Suri. This is what I'm here for."

She turned to Cassandra. "Stay here and protect her. I know you can manipulate the demons so you're the best person to keep them away from her."

Cassandra nodded.

"Be careful," Suri said.

Layla pressed a kiss to her forehead. "I'll be back in a flash." Then she teleported into the fray.

CHAPTER NINETEEN

Layla teleported in and out trying to use the element of surprise to strike when she could. She mostly used the spear, but when it happened to still be stuck in a demon before she could retrieve it, she used her katana blades to decapitate and slice her way through. Suddenly, it was quiet again except for the sound of heavy breathing from her and the others. She grabbed her spear out of the muck of what was left of a demon on her way to join them.

"I don't know how much more of this we can take," Robert said.

The werepanthers' sides heaved in and out with their breath. Some limped from injured paws, blood matted in the fur of others from open wounds as they joined them. Blood trickled from a cut on Robert's cheek. Rory's eye was turning a purplish black as he stood there. Leandra was pale and leaning into Robert weakly. Layla wished she could tell them that was the worst of it, but she knew what Lilith was trying to do. Weaken them enough to leave Suri defenseless.

"What if we attack Lilith directly before she has a chance to call any more of her hell boys. She won't expect that and maybe we can catch her off guard," Rory suggested.

"We can have Suri distract her. Make her think she's giving up then strike," Robert said.

Kenya gave a growl in response. She was for that idea.

Layla teleported to Suri and quickly explained what the others came up with. Suri gazed over at them.

"I agree, they can't take anymore. Another wave could break them," she said. "But do you really think she'll fall for it?"

"Honestly, no, but it's worth a try. I'll be right there if things go awry."

Suri nodded.

"I could do this all night," Lilith said, as if she'd read their minds.

"No, please, no more," Suri pleaded, hoping it was convincing.

"Aaaw, have your little friends had enough?" Lilith said.

"No, but I have." She walked hesitantly toward Lilith. "Why me?"

Lilith met her halfway. "Because you piqued my interest. I knew you would be powerful and who would be more worthy of being my avatar than one descended from a deity."

"You took everyone I loved from me and expect me to come to you willingly?"

"No, but it made you more susceptible of being convinced to do so. You think you're powerful now, how powerful do you think you would be as my avatar? You wouldn't need to be at the beck and call of gods who are too frightened to interfere with the lives of humans. You could have the ability to visit planes of existence you never thought possible. You could help your people with the power to destroy your enemies at the snap of a finger. I could give you the gift of immortal life so you could spend it with the one you love and never fear losing her."

Layla tensed as Lilith directed her evil gaze at her.

"Is that what you think I want? To no longer have the gift of faith. To have the ability to destroy others at my will. To not experience the gift of life as it was meant to be lived. All these years of watching and wanting and you don't know me at all. If you're going to promise a life of eternal damnation, at least make it worth my while."

That caught Lilith off guard as she gazed at Suri in surprise, which Layla took advantage of. "NOW!"

She teleported planning to reappear behind Lilith and putting her spear in her back. To throw her off even further and give the others a chance to attack, but that's not what happened. Layla teleported, heard Suri scream her name and reappeared to find herself dangling by her neck in Lilith's grasp.

"You're as foolishly brave as your father. I can't imagine why they chose a demon urchin like you as Suri's protector. She has more power in her little finger than the two of you put together and deserves much more than to be an errand girl for a bunch of gods whose own worshippers have turned their backs on them. It's only a matter of time before the Orisha will be long forgotten. Their stories are only told in folktales to entertain children." As Lilith spoke, she continued squeezing. Layla dropped her spear to claw at her fingers as she gasped for air.

"Please, let her go," Suri cried desperately.

Layla could see the others frozen in shock as they watched Lilith squeezing the life out of her. She gazed at Suri, tears running down her cheeks, love in her eyes. Well, at least she wouldn't go without knowing if it were possible for them to have shared something deeper. Her vision flashed in and out, she felt her esophagus being crushed, and knew that it would be a matter of seconds before she found out who would be coming to collect her soul. Her mother or her father.

"I'll do it!"

"SURI…NO…" Layla screamed in her head.

Lilith stopped squeezing just enough to let a sip of air slip through. Layla gasped at it. She turned back to Suri. "What was that?"

"I'll be your avatar! Just please let her go."

Lilith flicked her wrist and Layla found herself soaring through the air before slamming into a tree. She heard the sickening snap of her spine before everything went numb. She landed with her head angled in a way that she could see Suri running toward her, screaming her name, then being pulled back by an invisible force to stand before Lilith once again. Lilith held Suri by the arm then raised her other arm as a signal for what would probably be the final attack before she and Suri disappeared.

More demons, these with bat-like wings, long talon claws for hands and feet and razor-sharp teeth in wide, gaping mouths came screeching out of the opening. All Layla could do was lie there and watch as everyone scrambled to fight or take cover. She could feel her body trying to knit itself back together, but it wouldn't be fast enough for her to help her friends or to get Suri back. She closed her eyes and begged for death to take her.

"It is not your time yet, daughter."

She opened her eyes to find Isfet kneeling before her in all his dark, angelic and demon glory, black feathered wings spread wide and black battle armor shining bright.

"Father?" she said in disbelief. Maybe she had died.

"You are not dead yet."

He laid his hand on her belly and she was flooded with a warmth that spread outward filling her limbs and spine. When it faded, she could move and feel her fingers and toes.

Isfet stood and offered her a hand. She took it and allowed him to pull her up. "Come, daughter. It's been a century since we fought side by side."

He jogged out into the fray where Layla noticed other demon lords in battle armor fighting as well. She had so many questions, but now obviously wasn't the time for them. She took her katanas in hand and joined the fight.

Suri's head was pounding, and she didn't know why. She kept her eyes closed until it subsided then slowly blinked them open to find herself lying on the floor of the warehouse where they'd met Sojourn but the followers that they'd left behind were gone. Confused, she sat up, looked around and saw Lilith sitting in Sojourn's chair.

"Ah, Sleeping Beauty awakens," Lilith said.

"Where are my people?"

Lilith waved dismissively. "Occupied at the moment. I thought we could use this time alone."

"Why? I said I would be your avatar. What more do you want?"

Lilith steepled her hands beneath her chin. "Here's the thing. I find myself in a quandary as I've developed an affection for you. You have a fire and determination that I admire, and I feel like making you my avatar would dim that."

Suri gazed at her in confusion. "So, what are you saying? You're going to let me go?"

"Not necessarily. I want you to become my concubine." Lilith smiled. Once again it would be seductive if it wasn't attached to so much evil.

"Excuse me?"

"My concubine, my companion."

Suri couldn't believe what she was hearing. "If I had originally refused to be your avatar, why would I want to be your concubine?"

"Because you'll get to stay here but every so often, you'll come to my domain to spend time with me." She looked at Suri as if that made perfect sense and couldn't figure out why she wasn't getting it.

"No."

Lilith sighed as she strode toward Suri, standing before her with her hands clasped in front of her and a pretty pout on her face. "Why must you be so difficult. Must I remind you of what I'm capable of?"

She grasped Suri's hand and suddenly Suri was thrust into a memory that wasn't her own. She stood hidden in the shadows watching Rachel enter the ladies' room. Then, just as Rachel left the stall, what looked like Suri's hand came up and put a cloth over her face until she was unconscious. The next memory was of her dumping Rachel's mutilated body in the bushes.

"Please, stop," Suri begged her, trying to snatch her hand away.

"No, I think you need a little more convincing."

The next memory was of her parents' deaths from the viewpoint of the garage attendant driving the car. The next was Tracey's horrific death from the viewpoint of her killer, who was never found.

"You know what all of those deaths have in common?" Lilith asked.

"You, you sadistic bitch." Suri was finally able to wrench her hand away.

"No, Suri, you. They were all people you loved. People who were in the way. Just like all those people you brought with you tonight. Because you chose to come to New Orleans, to once again let people into your lives, you put them in danger. As long as you keep fighting me, you will be the reason another one of them suffers. Their deaths will be on your conscious."

"No," Suri whispered.

All the guilt, despair, and darkness she felt when she realized that anyone close to her was in danger returned. At least when she agreed to become Lilith's avatar to save Layla, she wouldn't have been aware of anything going on, but as her companion, she would be a willing and active participant in whatever dark pleasure Lilith enjoyed. She couldn't bear the thought of that, but she also couldn't bear the thought of being the cause of more loved ones' deaths. Lilith's offer seemed the lesser of two evils. At least she would be able to live a life when she wasn't with the demon, but what kind of life would it be? She wouldn't have her family, the legacy, Layla... her own soul.

Lilith reached up to stroke her cheek. "That's it, Suri, give in to the darkness. What has the light given you but more people to lose."

Was she right? Had she accepted a life of light only to put it and those she loved in danger again?

"Suri, wherever you are, hear me. I'm fine, we're all fine, don't give in to Lilith's lies."

"Layla?" Suri whispered.

"No," Lilith said. She grasped her hand again and the image of Layla slamming into the tree and lying broken on the ground, then Uncle Robert being gutted by some flying demon with talons as long as her arm, the house up in flames with Phoebe trapped inside. She released Suri's hand. "That is what you have to look forward to if you refuse my offer."

Suri knelt on the floor, her head in her hands wailing in despair. Then the horrific visions were replaced by one of Layla surrounded by a light so bright Suri almost covered her eyes.

"Suri, I'm here. I feel your pain and the lies Lilith is filling your head with. Fight it, Suri. For you, for us, for your family."

"Lil' Bit, open your eyes. See the truth. Remember who you are. Remember who you came from."

Suri released her head, opened her eyes, and saw Lilith for what she truly was. Not the pale beauty she portrayed herself to be but the ugly darkness she had allowed herself to become in her anger and bitterness for how she was treated after her banishment from the Garden of Eden. She stood and faced Lilith.

"I refuse your offer."

"Then you will suffer until you do."

She reached for Suri, but Suri escaped her grasp then raised her hands where a ball of light gathered and threw it at Lilith who stared in shock as the light flamed and spread over her body. She attempted to beat the white flame off, a horrific scream rising and echoing out of her. Suddenly, there was a flash and they were back in the forest with everyone staring toward them in shock.

"Suri?"

She turned to find Layla running toward her. At the same time, she saw out of her peripheral Lilith in her full demonic form flying at her with claws bared. Layla teleported but Lilith dodged her katana and descended on Suri. She noticed Layla's spear lying on the ground, reached her hand toward it, then felt it slap against her palm. Ignoring the searing pain that followed, she shoved it upward just as Lilith reached her. The spear pierced her dark leathery skin with a thunderous crack straight into her chest. Lilith gazed down in shock at the handle protruding from her chest then at Suri who still held it despite her palms being on fire.

She smiled, black blood pooling out the corner of her mouth. "I chose better than I thought," she said before turning to a cloud of ash and flowing back down into the crack in the ground.

"Suri!" Layla ran to her, looking her over. "Are you all right? Did she hurt you?"

"No, but your spear did." She released the hilt to let it drop and found angry red welts on the palms of her hands.

"Allow me."

Suri gazed up to find Isfet standing beside Layla dressed in full armor covered with charred chunks. She hesitantly offered him her hands. He placed them in his and she felt her palms grow warm. A moment later, he released her and she looked down to find her hands completely healed.

"Thank you."

"It's the least I could do for the sacrifice you made to save my daughter." He turned to Layla. "I must go. Morningstar may have a few choice words for me after this."

"Thank you for coming. I hope he isn't too hard on you."

Isfet smiled and gently laid a hand on Layla's cheek. "Whatever punishment he has will be nothing to the pain of losing you."

He turned and stepped over the edge of the crevice followed by several other men clad in dark armor. The ground sealed up and the pentagram faded as if nothing ever happened. Suri gazed around the area and saw that everyone else had gathered over where Sojourn and Aria had been when the battle began.

"It seems the demons weren't told that Sojourn was on their side and attacked her and Aria. Sojourn was killed, her body carried off and Aria was injured trying to help us in the fight," Layla explained as they made their way over to the group.

Suri found her uncle holding Aria in his lap. She had a chest wound that gushed blood. Suri knew from her nursing training that her heart had been punctured. She was surprised that she wasn't dead already. Her body must be trying to self-heal. Suri placed her hand over the wound to try to help, but it wouldn't knit together.

"It's the demon within her," Cassandra said. "His presence is keeping the wound from healing."

"He wasn't expelled when Sojourn was killed?"

"That's...not...how...it...works," Aria said weakly.

"Sojourn would need to break the bond herself or Aria would need to die."

Robert moaned.

Suri had an idea. "Cassandra, can you do what you did in the warehouse for the worshippers? Will that release the demon?"

"It should but I don't know the extent of the bond Sojourn placed on them."

"Could you at least try?" Robert asked.

Cassandra gave him a sad smile then nodded. She lifted her amulet from beneath her shirt, murmured the same chant she had earlier before Aria took a gasping breath then went still. A grayish mist left her body and went into the amulet. Everyone waited with bated breath for something to happen, but there was nothing.

"I'm sorry," Cassandra said.

Robert wept openly, holding Aria's body tighter. Suddenly, her body convulsed in his arms. He loosened his grip then her head fell back, and a thick black fluid rose out of her open mouth, gathering into a puddle nearby. The sound of metal scraping followed as everyone with a weapon readied to destroy whatever came out of the goo. A human form took shape that resembled Aria.

"I won't hurt you. Thank you for freeing us. I never meant to cause her any harm. She's a good person that got caught up with an evil woman." It looked wistfully at Aria then melted into the earth.

Cassandra already had her amulet out to place Aria's soul back into her body. Suri pressed her hand to the wound to start the healing process as soon as she was animate. The mist swirled from the amulet back into Aria, who took a gasping breath a moment later. Suri could feel the wound knitting back together and sighed with relief. Aria sat up, looking at her with tears in her eyes.

"After everything I've done, you still saved me."

Suri wiped the blood off her hand on her tunic. Covered in demon blood and bits of leathery flesh, she would be burning it as soon as she got home. "What you did was no fault of your own. You were manipulated. You did what you had to do to survive."

She lowered her head in shame. "That doesn't make me any less guilty."

"No but the fact that you feel guilty shows that you're a good person."

She gave Suri a tentative smile.

"Okay, now that the family reunion is complete can we go get dressed now?" Kenya said.

Suri gazed up and looked quickly back down as she hadn't even realized all the werepanthers had shifted back to their human form and were completely naked. She assumed they all brought extra clothes because she couldn't imagine them riding home that way. At least Kenya was in a car, the others were on motorcycles.

"What about the people in the warehouse? Shouldn't we call for emergency services?" Suri asked.

Layla grinned. "Isfet and his crew took care of them. Healed them, wiped their memories, and sent them back to Mississippi in the minivan thinking they had come to New Orleans and gotten lost."

Suri shook her head in amazement. That was probably why the warehouse was empty when Lilith took them there. "I guess that saves us having to figure out how to explain all of this."

A short time later, after making sure nothing was left behind for humans to find and the shifters were fully dressed again, they made their way back to the house. They were greeted by a relieved Phoebe who had gathered a supply of bandages, ointments, and healing tea to help with the injuries of those that weren't self-healing. Suri knew she would be sore and weak tomorrow after using so much of her power, but at least she was alive to feel anything at all. After everyone left, she and Layla had a chance to shower. While the house was quiet, Suri sat on the sofa gazing at the fire Layla had lit in the fireplace wondering where they went from here.

"Happy birthday to you…happy birthday to you…"

Layla came in carrying a slice of the left-over crumb cake with a single candle in it. Suri smiled as she continued singing happy birthday wonderfully off key then blew out the candle when she was finished.

"I guess better late than never."

"Hey, it's not quite midnight yet. You've got a full two minutes. What did you wish for?"

Suri closed her eyes, felt the presence of her ancestors all around, opened them to gaze at the woman she loved, took Layla's face in her hands, and kissed her slowly to make sure there was no mistaking what she wanted.

"Nothing. Everything I could ever want, or need, is right here."

Layla brushed a stray curl away from her face with a soft smile. "I never imagined that I could ever be as happy as I am at this moment. I love you, Suri."

Suri didn't bother to hold back tears of joy. For the first time in what felt like forever, she wasn't afraid to love someone and to wholeheartedly accept their love in return.

"I love you too, Layla. For however long we have together and beyond."

They kissed again. It communicated all the love that they had just confessed, and Suri's heart felt as light as if it had sprouted wings and taken flight. She slowly broke off their kiss, took Layla's hand, and led her upstairs. Their lovemaking that night was slow, tender, and peppered with more whispered words of affection before they fell peacefully asleep in each other's arms.

❖

Suri awoke in the basement again. This time she stood outside the doorway to her ancestors' altar room. Was this a dream or had she been brought down here like the last time when Shango and Ogun had summoned her? She gazed down at herself and noticed that she was dressed in an orange sundress and leather sandals. In her hand was the ring holding the keys to all the doorways. She didn't question what had brought her down here or try to leave like she did the first time this happened. She simply unlocked the door, but instead of the small altar room, she entered a large grass meeting lodge where a circle of women sat before a welcoming fire glowing in the center.

Suri gazed at all their faces, recognizing her grandmother and Ayomide and some of her other ancestors that she had either seen as spirits in the house when she used to visit or in the family photo album her grandmother had kept. They were all dressed in varying attire of white with accessories in the family's color of deep orange such as hats, headwraps, sashes, or beaded jewelry. One woman whose spirit Suri had never seen, whose face graced the portrait over the fireplace, and who Suri had become most curious about since she had begun reading her journal walked toward her. Athena wore a simple white dress from her era and orange headwrap with a large onyx-and-silver broach pinned to the front.

"Welcome, Suri." Athena wrapped her arms around her and squeezed gently.

"Am I dreaming?"

She pulled away just enough to give Suri an amused smile. "Does it feel like you're dreaming?"

Suri felt the heat from the fire, smelled the earth beneath her feet, felt the breeze blowing in the entrance, heard the trickling of water from a nearby river as clearly as the experiences she had through the other gateways and they were very real.

"No."

Athena nodded. "We'll have a little chat later." She led Suri to a seat beside her grandmother before taking one on the other side of her.

Gammy grinned. "Hey, Lil' Bit."

Suri grasped her hand. "Hey, Gammy."

Ayomide, who sat beside Athena, rose. She gazed around at all of them with a proud smile. "We are gathered here today to welcome my beloved daughter Suri as a Blessed One." Ayomide's gaze landed on Suri and her eyes glittered with unshed tears. "She has more than proven that she is worthy of carrying on our line and preparing our future Blessed for their journeys."

Suri's heart swelled with pride and her own eyes filled with tears. She stood to join Ayomide then knelt and prostrate herself on the ground.

"I have kept the path that my destiny has indicated to me. I have the duty to always follow the path that destiny marks for me. I am a faithful follower of the wise advice of my ancestors. Today I pray that the love of my ancestors covers me and protects me from all my detractors, that my enemies and their evil deeds cannot harm me. Therefore, I praise the ancestors and the elders listen to my prayers. *Ashe.*"

"*Ashe.*" She heard many voices respond in unison.

"Rise, Suri, and accept the blessings of your ancestors," Ayomide said.

Suri stood to find that she was now surrounded by all the blessed. Ayomide, Athena and her grandmother all placed a hand atop Suri's head then everyone around them placed a hand upon each other's shoulders until they were all connected to the three women touching her.

"Suri Daniels, descendant of Oduduwa, daughter of Ayomide, guardian of the Orisha, priestess of our people, we are one, we are many, we are strong, we are love, we are like the wind that can create good, we are also like the storm that can destroy that which is bad. We are all together, we are family, we fear nothing. We bless you with our love, wisdom, and strength for all that you have done and that you will do. *Ashe.*" Ayomide's voice was loud and clear.

The others responded with an *Ashe* that reverberated throughout the lodge. Suri was filled with the light of their blessing. She felt it mend the shattered pieces of her broken heart and soothe the grief that she'd been carrying for so long. She felt whole once again. When she opened her eyes, she stood alone with Ayomide, Athena and her grandmother. Ayomide took her face in her hands.

"I could not be prouder of you than if you had been born from my womb."

Suri felt her face heat with a blush. "I'm honored."

Ayomide placed a kiss on both Suri's cheeks then turned and left the lodge. Her grandmother was next, pulling her into a tight hug. It was the first time since she'd died that Suri felt the embrace and not just the impression of one. She squeezed Gammy tightly in return, tears making her vision blur.

"You've done well, Lil' Bit." She released Suri and placed a kiss on her forehead. "I'll always be near if you need me."

Suri was too emotional to do anything but nod. Gammy smiled knowingly and stepped out of her arms. She took a few steps before Suri ran up and hugged her from behind.

"I love you, Gammy."

"I love you too, Suri."

Suri hesitantly let her go and watched her leave the lodge with tears streaming down her face. She turned to find herself alone with Athena who offered her a hand. Suri wiped her tears away and placed her hand in Athena's. They left the lodge and to Suri's surprise, stepped into the courtyard of the house. Athena led them to a cement bench beside the water fountain. She gazed up at the sky where the moon shone full and bright and the few constellations not blocked by light pollution sparkled like diamonds against the dark velvet night.

"Isabel used to love coming out here and just sitting for hours staring up at the sky. It was like she could see past what was visible to the human eye. As if the heavens revealed their secrets to her," Athena said wistfully.

Suri gazed up, following the outline of Orion's belt. "I remember reading in your journal that she had second sight."

Athena nodded. "With all gifts, it was a blessing and a burden. Isabel believed that it was possible to change the outcome of a vision if you chose a different path. She never understood when she would receive a bad vision, warn the person involved, then watch as they still made the choices that would lead them down the path that she warned them against. Ironically, she ended up doing the same thing when she had a vision of her own death."

Suri looked at her in surprise. "She saw her own death and didn't try to change the course?"

Athena smiled sadly. "No, because changing it would've put me in harm's way. There were many who were jealous of her power and her position as a protector. One was a local planter, Silas Belford, who got his wealth through dark magic and sacrificing slaves. As soon as he found out my employer Miss Trudy was sick, he tried to get me to be his mistress. He knew who I really was and what I was to become and he wanted to position himself as my protector in the same way Sojourn had tried to do to Aria. But I saw him for the evil he was and told him so. Then I met Isabelle, and as much as I fought being drawn to her not just spiritually but physically, the Orisha would not be denied their protector for their guardian."

She smiled at Suri. Suri knew how pointless it was to try to fight what fate and the Orisha wanted.

"We did our best to appear as two spinster friends living a quiet life together to the human public, but our supernatural community knew and most accepted the truth of our relationship. The ones that didn't accept it kept to themselves and we did the same. But Silas took offense that I would want a woman with nothing to offer but herself over him and his wealth. He tried many times to use dark magic to drive Isabel away, but it wasn't strong enough to break through the protective magic around us. Each time he tried, he would have a bout of bad luck, which we had nothing to do with, but he blamed us anyway. Then rumors started spreading that he was involved in several prominent folks' deaths, but before the law could get ahold of him, he disappeared. We thought we were rid of him and after many years with no word of his whereabouts, we let our guard down."

A soft magnolia scented breeze blew through the courtyard and Athena closed her eyes as it rustled the tendrils of curls that had escaped her headwrap and settled around her face.

"Isabel planted that magnolia tree as a gift to me right before it all happened." A tear dripped from her lashes. "Like Sojourn, Silas bided his time until he believed everything had died down. He came back, darker, and more powerful than before. As you know from my journal, Isabel and I ran a small shop like the one Phoebe has now. Isabel had been up all night at a prayer vigil, so I offered to close, but she insisted on doing it herself. She wouldn't even let me stay to help.

Not long after I left, some intuition told me to go back, that Isabel was in danger. I had nowhere to turn the buggy around so I just jumped off and started running back toward the shop. She had locked the door but hadn't drawn the curtain over it so I could see her standing behind the counter with her back to the door just standing and looking toward the storeroom. I had almost breathed a sigh of relief when I was suddenly filled with dread and saw a large dark figure approaching her from the storeroom. I banged on the door, screaming her name, but she didn't move so I ran around to the back of the shop and found that door locked as well."

Athena's eyes were haunted, as if she were reliving that moment. "Then she was beside me and I knew it was too late because it was her spirit. She told me about the vision she saw and that the only way to stop Silas and keep me and our children safe was to let it happen. Silas had used astral projection to get into the shop with the intention of killing her and using magic to draw me to him. He believed killing Isabel would leave me vulnerable for the taking. He underestimated Isabel who counteracted his spell with one of her own that left his soul trapped on the plane if she died."

Suri reached over to grasp Athena's hand. "I can understand why she did it. I was willing to sacrifice myself to Lilith to save the ones I love."

"I understand as well. I just wish she had told me before she decided to do it on her own. Maybe, together, we could have found another way." Athena wiped her tears away with a sigh and gave Suri's hand a squeeze. "I told you this because Layla will also face a choice that could change the course of her life even further."

Suri's heart skipped a beat. Before she could ask the question that she didn't want to ask, Athena shook her head and gave her a comforting smile.

"Her decision won't be that life-changing. As protector she will tap less and less into her demon side, becoming more human. She'll still be able to use many of her supernatural abilities, but that dark part of her that kept her connected to her father will fade over time, if she chooses to continue as your protector."

"Why wasn't she told this by Ogun when she swore herself to be protector?"

"Your situation is one that we or the Orisha have never faced before. We've had all kinds of supernatural humans as protectors but never a cambion. Her future hadn't been foreseen until after she had accepted her duty. She must be told so that her choice was made knowing all that it demanded."

Suri frowned. "I have to be the one to tell her."

Athena nodded. "As the protector has promised to give her life to protect you, so you must promise not to intentionally put her life in danger. Her not knowing the truth could do that."

Suri sat quietly thinking about what Athena was saying and the possibility of Layla choosing to walk away so as not to lose such an important part of who she was. Her cambion side saved her from a life of continuous abuse at the hands of her master. Her cambion side saved her from being killed time and again. Her cambion side saved and avenged people in their community for over two centuries. It was her biological and spiritual connection to her father. Would she want to give such a vital part of herself up if she were in Layla's position? Knowing how she felt about her, Suri would have no problem doing it but she wasn't Layla.

"Her love for you is the same love Isabel had for me. Trust in that if nothing else."

"If Layla chooses not to remain as my protector, will Uncle Robert be required to step back into the role."

"No, there is another. The shifter in your group."

With the addition of Bettina, there were two shifters in their group, but Suri immediately knew who Athena was referring to. "Kenya."

Athena nodded. "Pearl was like a second mother to her and she would do anything to protect her and this family. She had hoped that she would become the next protector once Pearl had prepared you to step into the role. Then Pearl passed and Phoebe told Kenya about the last vision Pearl had before joining the ancestors that spoke of Layla's involvement. Kenya's dream of being a part of something bigger, something important was snatched away just like that. Because of what happened with Bettina and her other lover, Kenya has been trying to prove herself and had hoped, as protector, that she would have the opportunity to do so. I believe she still harbors hope that maybe Layla will fail and she'll be able to step in."

Suri tried to imagine spending her life with Kenya as her protector instead of Layla and found that just the thought of it felt wrong. Layla was the one meant to be by her side. She didn't have, nor could she see herself having, the connection they shared with anyone else. She would tell Layla what Athena said about her connection to her demon side, but she wouldn't force her to stay if that was too much of a sacrifice. If she had to live with another protector, then so be it. Her duty as guardian far outweighed what she wanted.

"The Orishas have chosen well," Athena said with a look of approval. "It's time for me to go but know that I and all those before you will always be here if you need us."

Suri smiled at Athena with tears in her eyes. "Thank you."

Athena pulled her into a tight embrace before taking her face in her hands, placing a tender kiss on her forehead then whispering against it, "You are blessed." Suri felt the warmth of the blessing spread throughout her body before her vision went dark.

EPILOGUE

Layla stood gazing out the kitchen window at all the activity in her yard at the house in the bayou. This wasn't the first time she and Suri had invited people over, but she still found it weird to have guests after having spent so long being alone here. It had been over two years since Suri came into her life and turned her world upside down, and Layla had no regrets. If she were given a choice to do it all again, she wouldn't hesitate or change a thing. She'd found love and friends and gained a purpose in her life that helped to make a difference in so many others' lives.

Not even Suri waking her in the early morning hours after their battle with Sojourn and Lilith to tell her about her talk with Athena made her regret the decision she made. Layla had been surprised to hear that she could completely lose her connection to her demon side in her role as protector. While telling her, Suri had offered Layla the opportunity to walk away and that Kenya would step into her place. Layla had no doubt that Kenya would make an excellent protector, but it felt wrong. She was Suri's—mind, body, and soul—because of that, there was no one, not even Robert, who could truly protect her the way she needed. Layla understood the sacrifice Athena's partner Isabel had made and wouldn't hesitate to do the same if she were put in the same position. Sacrificing such a major part of herself, basically the other half of herself, was worth it to love and protect Suri. She told Suri that very thing and the look of relief on her face had told her how difficult it had been for Suri not only to tell Layla the truth but to also give her a way out.

Layla had spoken to her father the next day about it. Worried that with the loss of the one thing that connected them and her mother now having moved on, she would lose him as well. Isfet swore to her that no matter what Morningstar or their father commanded, their connection would always be there because he was her father first and foremost. She had felt the magic in his oath and had been comforted by it. It took several months after that for signs of her demon gifts fading to show. It began with a burning pain across her back waking her in the middle of the night. Suri had hurriedly lifted Layla's shirt to find her tattoo flaring an ugly red. Layla had tried to open them but nothing happened. She didn't feel the shift of muscle and bone that occurred when she spread her wings, just the constant burning for what felt like forever but had only been several minutes before it faded to a dull ache. Although she had rarely used them, she felt like she understood what an amputee felt at the loss of a limb. That was the only time she wondered if what she was doing was worth it. Then she had seen the love and concern on Suri's face and knew that it was. Suri was her life now and she vowed that she would face whatever may come with that life without any further doubt or regret. She also realized that she wouldn't have to worry about watching Suri grow old while she continued to slowly age. They would grow old together and Layla wouldn't have to live another lifetime heartbroken over losing her.

Layla proposed to Suri on her birthday the following year which was followed by a small wedding with just their close family and friends a month later at the bayou house. Shortly after their marriage came the discussion of having a baby and searching for a donor through a fertility clinic that was known in their community to specialize in supernatural conception. They had been overjoyed when Rory volunteered to be their donor which had been a relief to both her and Suri since they were hesitant about utilizing a donor they didn't know. They were thoroughly surprised when they found out they were having twins who were born looking like mini versions of Layla and Suri despite Suri's eggs being the only ones used since Layla, as a cambion, couldn't conceive without utilizing her succubus nature which had gone the way of her other demon gifts.

Their son, Nathanial, somehow inherited Layla's golden skin and dark features. Their daughter, Pearl, inherited Suri's rich brown coloring and ginger hair. Isfet had determined that they had exchanged energy so often that it must have affected the babies. Even in the womb they had formed an attachment unusual for fraternal twins. As they developed, despite them being in their individual placentas, ultrasound video showed them with their foreheads and hands pressed against each other's through the thin membranes between them. As if they were trying to stay connected through the physical wall separating them. At the time of their delivery, three weeks earlier than their expected due date and through cesarean, Nathaniel came out first unusually quiet and alert until Pearl was delivered with a hearty wail and she was placed beside her brother. Like a magnet, they folded into each other, limbs tangling together. Suri had said it was the first sense of peace that she'd felt from them since they'd been discovered trying to connect in the womb.

The doctors had to carefully disentangle them to get their vitals, weight, and measurements, which had sent waves of anxiety from them to both Layla and Suri. Layla had hovered nearby, always the protector, making sure they were okay and she could swear she saw relief in Nathanial's dark eyes so like her own as he watched her in return. Their doctor, a strong warlock, was just as amazed by the babies' alertness as they were. When they finally finished poking and prodding them, then swaddled them tightly in their little blankets, they had handed both to Layla, who balanced them expertly as if she had held two babies all the time as she took them to meet their Mama Suri.

During their time at the hospital, Nathanial and Pearl were not content unless the nurses put them in the same bassinet cart. That continued after Layla and Suri got them home. They had been gifted with a twin bassinet, but it wasn't enough. Layla had to cut out the mesh screen separating them to keep them from fussing. Nathanial refused to eat unless Pearl ate first, he didn't go to sleep unless his sister fell asleep first, and as soon as he woke up, he would look for her. If she happened to not be there because Suri was feeding her, Layla would have to pick him up and show him where Pearl was or she and Suri would be overwhelmed with his anxiety. They quickly realized that Nathanial had intuitively taken on the role of Pearl's protector. A sure sign that Pearl would be carrying on her family's legacy of being a blessed one. That was confirmed within their first year when Pearl began to show early signs of having gifts.

If there was a toy that she wanted but it wasn't nearby, it would move across the room to her, plants perked up when she was nearby, Sebastian interacted with her as if he understood her baby babble, and when Nathanial cut his finger while they were playing he had turned to Pearl, said "Boo Boo," then she had kissed it the way Suri would do when they got boo boos and it had healed. They had been shocked by that last one because if her healing gift was that powerful already what would it be like when she was older. Suri had turned to advice from her ancestors who suggested that she speak with Orisha Ibeji, twin sibling gods. In the Yoruba religion twins are a divine blessing as they offer blessings, guidance, and protection. They're considered protectors of the family unit, preserving the sanctity of their homes and the peace, stability, and happiness of their family's environment. Ibeji twins were also known to exhibit wisdom beyond their years, having outwitted Elegua once when he attempted to trick them as they journeyed through Yorubaland.

Suri had been able to confirm that Nathaniel and Pearl were in fact living embodiments of Ibeji, which would explain why they appeared to be so advanced for their age. They had barely begun to crawl before they were toddling around the house driving Layla and Suri crazy trying to keep them out of trouble. By their first birthday, not only were they able to talk well enough to be understood, but they seemed to have their own language. She and Suri also suspected that they communicated telepathically with each other as well. Suri regularly spoke Yoruba and French to them which they had quickly begun to pick up and use as well.

As Layla gazed out the window at their family and friends gathered for the twins' first birthday, she felt as if she would burst with happiness. She couldn't help but chuckle as Isfet marched around the yard with a twin on each shoulder as they squealed with delight. That had been another surprise. Her father had happily taken on his role as grandfather as if he'd been waiting his whole life to do it. He would even babysit for them to give Layla and Suri a break from the madness parenting two precocious twins had become. He spent more time earthbound and seemed quite content. Her life was fuller than she could have ever possibly imagined and it was because of Suri.

Layla gazed over at her wife talking and laughing with Robert and their other guests, Phoebe, Leandra, Cassandra, with an actual smile on her face, Rory and Kenya, the latter of which were the twins' godparents. Layla hadn't been too keen on Suri's suggestion of making Kenya a godparent, but she reminded her of what Athena said about Kenya needing to feel as if she had a purpose, and protecting the twins was the perfect way to give that. Layla had softened to Kenya when she saw how touched she had been by the offer. Then there was Aria who had completely turned her life around after being saved from Sojourn's manipulations. Robert had taken her in without hesitation and helped her get her life back on track. He'd paid for her to go to nursing school then doula training. She was content living a quiet life, healing and helping to bring life into the world with both her training and her gifts. She still suffered bouts of guilt over the things she had done while she was with Sojourn, but she had come to accept that it hadn't been all her doing.

Suri turned and smiled at her, then made her way toward the house. When she entered the kitchen, she wrapped an arm around Layla's waist, and placed a kiss on her cheek. "Is the cake ready to go out?"

Layla gazed down at the three-layer cake that she had taken out of the refrigerator moments ago, frosted half in the protector's color purple for Nathaniel and the other half in the family's orange for Pearl.

"Yep, just have to put the topper and candle on it."

Layla picked up the cake topper, a rainbow with a cloud on each end with the twins' names and placed it on the cake then a number one candle in front of the rainbow.

"Perfect," Suri said.

Layla turned and pulled Suri into her arms. "Just like our family."

Suri smiled happily. "In spite of all my gifts, I wasn't truly blessed until you came into my life."

Layla's heart swelled with love. "I'm the one that's blessed. Despite my long life, I wasn't truly living until you came into mine."

She pressed her lips to Suri's and opened herself up to share everything she felt for this miraculous woman, all that she'd brought into her life and received, and all the love that Suri felt in return. Yes, she was the one that had been blessed beyond measure and knew that she would continue to be blessed in this life and the next with this woman at her side.

The End...?

Author's Note

I hope you enjoyed *The Blessed*. The city of New Orleans has always fascinated me. There's so much rich cultural, religious, and paranormal history that if a city could talk, New Orleans's dark whispers would have multiple lifetimes of stories to tell. If there were any city that would be filled with supernatural residents, have homes with gateways to ancestors and African gods, New Orleans would be it, so what better location for *The Blessed* to take place than there.

This story allowed me to not only stretch my paranormal fiction chops but also indulge in my love of researching African American history and culture. As a matter of fact, I enjoyed it so much that I almost lost myself in the research and had to frequently remind myself that I was writing a book! In writing *The Blessed*, I only scratched the surface of the Orisha, Voudon, and Hoodoo religions and practices. If I've piqued your interest in any of those topics, here are some sources that I used to tell Suri and Layla's story.

Belard, Angelie. *Hoodoo for Life: The Complete Guide to Rootwork and Conjure with 125 Authentic Hoodoo Magic Spells.* Independently Published. 2022.

Hill, Sylvia. *African Spiritual Practices: A Comprehensive Guide to Yoruba, Santeria, Voodoo, Hoodoo, and the Orishas.* Joelan AB. 2023.

Lumpkin, Joseph B. *The Books of Enoch: The Angels, The Watchers and The Nephilim.* Fifth Estate. 2015.

Siedlak. *Monique Joiner.* Oshun Publications, LLC. 2021.

Silva, Mari. *Orishas.* Independently Published. 2021.

About the Author

Anne Shade loves sharing stories about women who love women featuring strong, beautiful BIPOC characters. Anne's works include, *Femme Tales*, queered retellings of three classic fairytales and is short-listed for a 2021 Lambda Literary Award; *Masquerade*, a roaring 20s romance; *Love and Lotus Blossoms*, a coming of age, and coming out story listed as a Publishers Weekly Best Books of 2021; *Her Heart's Desire*, a sweet, coming out romance; *Securing Ava*, a romantic intrigue; and *Three Wishes*, a paranormal fantasy romance. Anne has also collaborated with editor Victoria Villasenor for the Bold Strokes Books anthology, *In Our Words: Queer Stories from Black, Indigenous and People of Color* and has a novella in the *My Secret Valentine* collection with authors Julie Cannon and Erin Dutton. When Anne isn't writing, she dreams of the day when she can welcome readers and authors alike for a stay at her future bed and breakfast.

Books Available from Bold Strokes Books

Close to Home by Allisa Bahney. Eli Thomas has to decide if avoiding her hometown forever is worth losing the people who used to mean the most to her, especially Aracely Hernandez, the girl who got away. (978-1-63679-661-1)

Golden Girl by Julie Tizard. In 1993, "Don't ask, don't tell" forces everyone to lie, but Air Force nurse Lt. Sofia Sanchez and injured instructor pilot Lt. Gillian Guthman have to risk telling each other the truth in order to fly and survive. (978-1-63679-751-9)

Innis Harbor by Patricia Evans. When Amir Farzaneh meets and falls in love with Loch, a dark secret lurking in her past reappears, threatening the happiness she'd just started to believe could be hers. (978-1-63679-781-6)

The Blessed by Anne Shade. Layla and Suri are brought together by fate to defeat the darkness threatening to tear their world apart. What they don't expect to discover is a love that might set them free. (978-1-63679-715-1)

The Guardians by Sheri Lewis Wohl. Dogs, devotion, and determination are all that stand between darkness and light. (978-1-63679-681-9)

The Mogul Meets Her Match by Julia Underwood. When CEO Claire Beauchamp goes undercover as a customer of Abby Pita's café to help seal a deal that will solidify her career, she doesn't expect to be so drawn to her. When the truth is revealed, will she break Abby's heart? (978-1-63679-784-7)

Trial Run by Carsen Taite. When Reggie Knoll and Brooke Dawson wind up serving on a jury together, their one task—reaching a unanimous verdict—is derailed by the fiery clash of their personalities, the intensity of their attraction, and a secret that could threaten Brooke's life. (978-1-63555-865-4)

Waterlogged by Nance Sparks. When conservation warden Jordan Pearce discovers a body floating in the flowage, the serenity of the Northwoods is rocked. (978-1-63679-699-4)

Accidentally in Love by Kimberly Cooper Griffin. Nic and Lee have good reasons for keeping their distance. So why does their growing attraction seem more like a love-hate relationship? (978-1-63679-759-5)

Fatal Foul Play by David S. Pederson. After eight friends are stranded in an old lodge by a blinding snowstorm, a brutal murder leaves Mark Maddox to solve the crime as he discovers deadly secrets about people he thought he knew. (978-1-63679-794-6)

Frosted by the Girl Next Door by Aurora Rey and Jaime Clevenger. When heartbroken Casey Stevens opens a sex shop next door to uptight cupcake baker Tara McCoy, things get a little frosty. (978-1-63679-723-6)

Ghost of the Heart by Catherine Friend. Being possessed by a ghost was not on Gwen's bucket list, but she must admit that ghosts might be real, and one is obviously trying to send her a message. (978-1-63555-112-9)

Hot Honey Love by Nan Campbell. When chef Stef Lombardozzi puts her cooking career into the hands of filmmaker Mallory Radowski— the pickiest eater alive—she doesn't anticipate how hard she falls for her. (978-1-63679-743-4)

London by Patricia Evans. Jaq's and Bronwyn's lives become entwined as dangerous secrets emerge and Bronwyn's seemingly perfect life starts to unravel. (978-1-63679-778-6)

This Christmas by Georgia Beers. When Sam's grandmother rigs the Christmas parade to make Sam and Keegan queen and queen, sparks fly, but they can't forget the Big Embarrassing Thing that makes romance a total nope. (978-1-63679-729-8)

Unwrapped by D. Jackson Leigh. Asia du Muir is not going to let some party girl actress ruin her best chance to get noticed by a Broadway critic. Everyone knows you should never mix business and pleasure. (978-1-63679-667-3)

Language Lessons by Sage Donnell. Grace and Lenka never expected to fall in love. Is home really where the heart is if it means giving up your dreams? (978-1-63679-725-0)

New Horizons by Shia Woods. When Quinn Collins meets Alex Anders, Horizon Theater's enigmatic managing director, a passionate connection ignites, but amidst the complex backdrop of theater politics, their budding romance faces a formidable challenge. (978-1-63679-683-3)

Scrambled: A Tuesday Night Book Club Mystery by Jaime Maddox. Avery Hutchins makes a discovery about her father's death that will force her to face an impossible choice between doing what is right and finally finding a way to regain a part of herself she had lost. (978-1-63679-703-8)

Stolen Hearts by Michele Castleman. Finding the thief who stole a precious heirloom will become Ella's first move in a dangerous game of wits that exposes family secrets and could lead to her family's financial ruin. (978-1-63679-733-5)

Synchronicity by J.J. Hale. Dance, destiny, and undeniable passion collide at a summer camp as Haley and Cal navigate a love story that intertwines past scars with present desires. (978-1-63679-677-2)

The First Kiss by Patricia Evans. As the intrigue surrounding her latest case spins dangerously out of control, military police detective Parker Haven must choose between her career and the woman she's falling in love with. (978-1-63679-775-5)

Wild Fire by Radclyffe & Julie Cannon. When Olivia returns to the Red Sky Ranch, Riley's carefully crafted safe world goes up in flames. Can they take a risk and cross the fire line to find love? (978-1-63679-727-4)

Writ of Love by Cassidy Crane. Kelly and Jillian struggle to navigate the ruthless battleground of Big Law, grappling with desire, ambition, and the thin line between success and surrender. (978-1-63679-738-0)

Back to Belfast by Emma L. McGeown. Two colleagues are asked to trade jobs. Claire moves to Vancouver and Stacie moves to Belfast, and though they've never met in person, they can't seem to escape a growing attraction from afar. (978-1-63679-731-1)

Exposure by Nicole Disney and Kimberly Cooper Griffin. For photographer Jax Bailey and delivery driver Trace Logan, keeping it casual is a matter of perspective. (978-1-63679-697-0)

Hunt of Her Own by Elena Abbott. Finding forever won't be easy, but together Danaan's and Ashly's paths lead back to the supernatural sanctuary of Terabend. (978-1-63679-685-7)

Perfect by Kris Bryant. They say opposites attract, but Alix and Marianna have totally different dreams. No Hollywood love story is perfect, right? (978-1-63679-601-7)

Royal Expectations by Jenny Frame. When childhood sweethearts Princess Teddy Buckingham and Summer Fisher reunite, their feelings resurface and so does the public scrutiny that tore them apart. (978-1-63679-591-1)

Shadow Rider by Gina L. Dartt. In the Shadows, one can easily find death, but can Shay and Keagan find love as they fight to save the Five Nations? (978-1-63679-691-8)

The Breakdown by Ronica Black. Vaughn and Natalie have chemistry, but the outside world keeps knocking at the door, threatening more trouble, making the love and the life they want together impossible. (978-1-63679-675-8)

Tribute by L.M. Rose. To save her people, Fiona will be the tribute in a treaty marriage to the Tipruii princess, Simaala, and spend the rest of her days on the other side of the wall between their races. (978-1-63679-693-2)

Wild Wales by Patricia Evans. When Finn and Aisling fall in love, they must decide whether to return to the safety of the lives they had, or take a chance on wild love in windswept Wales. (978-1-63679-771-7)